The Wewelsburg Covenant

The Wewelsburg Covenant

John Braun

BRAUN PUBLISHING

First published in 2011 by Braun Publishing

ISBN 978-0-62050-734-9
e-ISBN 978-0-62050-735-6

© 2011 John Braun and Tom West

All rights reserved. This publication may not be reproduced or transmitted in any form without the prior written permission of the copyright holders.

This book is a work of fiction. Any resemblance to actual persons is purely coincidental.

Visit www.wewelsburgcovenant.blogspot.com for free extras and to connect with John Braun.

For my family, with love.

Author's Note

Wewelsburg is a seventeenth-century castle in Germany that lords over the picturesque farmlands of the Alme Valley in the Paderborn district. With a colossal circular north tower, joined to two smaller south towers by heavily fortified walls, Wewelsburg is the only triangular-shaped castle in Europe.

On 3 November 1933, *Reichsführer* Heinrich Himmler, the leader of the *Schutzstaffel* (SS) – the 'state within a state' and the most fearsome cog in the Nazi death machine – visited the castle for the first time. Himmler had been searching for a spiritual home for the SS which he thought of as a knightly order, a reincarnation of the Teutonic Knights.

In 9 AD, an alliance of Germanic tribes led by Arminius had ambushed and shattered three Roman legions and their auxiliaries led by Publius Quinctilius Varus in the Battle of the Teutoburg Forest near Wewelsburg Castle. The Roman advance in the region was halted, and it was a defining moment for German unification. An ancient Westphalian legend foretold of a future battle at Wewelsburg, known as the Battle of the Birch, at which an eastern army would be crushed by a western army, which Himmler identified with the forces of Germany's Third Reich.

Wewelsburg was therefore historically and prophetically significant to Himmler, who decided on the same night of his first visit that it would be the spiritual centre of the Reich, his very own 'Camelot'.

In 1934, Himmler signed a hundred-year lease for the castle from the Paderborn district, for one hundred marks, and in August of the same year, reconstruction work began at the castle to transform it into a Nazi 'Mecca'. A concentration camp was set up – Niederhagen – which would claim more than 1 200 lives during the castle's reconstruction.

Initially, the castle was to be a *Reichsführerschule SS*, an SS school at which SS officers would be trained in pre- and early Aryan history, archaeology, astronomy and ideology. It would be the centrepiece of a fortified complex of buildings including SS barracks, a residential suburb and farmlands for high-ranking SS members. Himmler's knights would rule over the region, and the world, from this Aryan heartland.

On the upper floors of the north tower, Himmler refurbished the *Obergruppenführersaal*, a meeting room where the *Reichsführer*'s highest knights, the twelve leaders of the SS, would receive instructions from their grand messiah. Beneath the *Obergruppenführersaal*, a crypt was developed, a cavernous dome-shaped vault, with twelve low, seat-like pedestals crowding around a circular indent. Built with special acoustics and ambient lights, this was Himmler's 'Realm of the Dead'. It is thought that the ashes of the fallen SS generals were placed in urns on the twelve pedestals, and the dead were commemorated in special occult (and some believe satanic) rituals designed to unleash Nordic occult powers.

Himmler's knights were fashioned on the Arthurian concept of the knights of the grail. The Holy Grail (German *de Heilige Gral*) was thought by Himmler to be a Nordic object of vast occult power which would help the Nazis win the war if he managed to find it. Wewelsburg Castle was to be the home of the grail.

But the Aryan dream was deferred as Europe collapsed in a heap of ruins before the Nazis' eyes in the first half of 1945. The Nazis made plans to escape, forging fake identification documents to slip through the Allies' net. As many as 20 000 Nazis escaped to Argentina in the months following the war.

A network of former Nazi *kameraden* known as ODESSA (*Organisation der Ehemaligen SS-Angehörigen*, the Organisation of Former SS Members) was established to assist the Nazis to escape via 'rat lines' in Europe, and to resettle in South America, primarily in President Juan Perón's pro-fascist Argentina. Billions of dollars' worth of Nazi war loot was smuggled out of Germany to help the escapees to establish themselves, and to realise their dream of setting up the Fourth Reich. (It is also little-known that before and during the War, a number of high-ranking British individuals sympathised with the Nazis.)

Only one official meeting took place in the *Obergruppenführersaal* at Wewelsburg Castle, in March 1941, when the leaders of the SS were briefed on the plans for Operation Barbarossa (the German invasion of Russia that would backfire and eventually lead to the Third Reich's downfall).

But another meeting reportedly took place in December 1944. The Reich was tilting towards ruin. Little, if anything, is known of the contents of this meeting ...

Part I

1
Wolfschanze
Location Unknown
October 2012

Swells of water rose, gathered in the gloom and rushed in, column after column, smashing the basalt walls of the island and sending curtains of foam erupting and vanishing as quickly before the gritted eyes of three 'fishermen' who crawled along a ledge. The path they were on twirled around the island to a conical tip where the towers and battlements of a fifteenth-century castle poked through the mist like a row of jagged teeth.

They crawled one behind the other. The man in front was their leader. His blue eyes mirrored the brightness of the storm. He led his team into the protection of an overhang as a faint hum sounded from the skies that the other two hadn't made out yet.

The men huddled together, glad for a buffer against the wind. The hum became an echo that banged off the cliffs above and below them: the whir of an approaching helicopter. The leader pushed his right index and middle fingers to his ear and spoke in German.

As he sat on his haunches, his coat flaps opened to reveal the butt of a machine gun, several grenades and a handgun clipped to his belt.

'*Wolfschanze* Command, this is D-Patrol Squadron Leader, come in.'
'Command here. State your position, over.'
'We have an approaching bird from east-southeast heading on *Wolfschanze*. Confirm status, over.'

The other two pressed their fingers against their ears to make out the woman's voice: 'Approaching bird is friendly. The Eagle comes in to nest, over.'

'Status received, over and out.'

The men crawled back out onto the ledge. The helicopter swooped down, a black speck against the navy sky, banked and then came in to roost behind the Gothic spires of the castle known as *Wolfschanze*, residential headquarters of the leaders of the Fourth Reich.

In the northeast tower, an old man cradled in his deathbed listened the helicopter descend and touch down on the cobblestones of the courtyard.

A tall man with broad shoulders and dark hair, in a long coat and red scarf, climbed out of the helicopter.

James Trevellian made his way into the castle, ascending flights of stairs in the northeast tower and entering the room his dying father lay in. The flames licking off the bed of pink-orange coals were a comforting sight.

He appraised his father. Franz Wagener seemed peaceful. The opera *Der Ring des Nibelungen* played in the background, an epic by Hitler's favourite composer Richard Wagner.

Franz was blind, and his body riddled with cancer. It had begun in his prostate, but had spread quickly to the rest of his body. It stretched the membranes along the insides of the old man's bones like stone scratching against glass and the pain induced delirium. In the past few months, Franz had believed at various times that Hitler had triumphed, the world was a conglomeration of Nazi-ruled colonies, that Russia had obliterated America with nuclear weapons. But miraculously, the disease also seemed to have the opposite effect when Franz was almost clairvoyant.

James leaned closer to look at his father. Sunken hollow sockets shot open and stared back at him. Along the side of his face, a long scar was carved like a deep river across his cheek. A disembodied voice spoke.

'I sense you are troubled.'

James was silent.

'You mustn't be troubled on my behalf. My death will set me free. I will join the *Einherjar*, the Nordic warrior souls of a thousand generations.'

It was the clairvoyant voice today, thought James, always mixed up with grand Nordic mythology.

'I can see the promised city,' Franz continued, 'there are the golden leaves of the divine tree Glasir, glittering in the celestial light. In the halls of Valhalla are German kings and warriors. Bismarck, Hitler and Himmler, with Odin at the head of the table on a mighty throne. They are drinking mead brought to them by *valkyrie*. The hall's ceiling glows with the golden shields of fallen Teutonic

Knights. The blessed stag eats the leaves of Glasir and rivers flow to earth from its horns.'

Thunder coughed and the sea brawled. Rain began to pelt sharply against the windows as the old man continued.

'One thing keeps me clinging to this mortal coil, James. It is the realisation of the Aryan destiny. You will be faced with a choice. I can foresee it now. Do not be misled by fools, or those weaker than you. Do not forsake your Aryan heritage. Never forget who you are.'

Thunder cracked as a maddening light searched the room. In the flash, James saw his father's eyes light up. Franz drew in a sharp breath and then exhaled: 'How are the plans?'

'Things are going well, father. Ingredients will be secured from Russia. The submarines are almost all ready. Our troops are primed for battle. Dissent in the Middle East also plays in our favour.'

'What about the stone?'

'Our source in Nepal is on the brink of solving a final clue. We will have it, in time.'

Franz tried to lean forward, but he stopped short, grimacing, and began to cough. James knew better than to try to help, there wasn't much he could do. When the coughs had subsided, Franz forced his words out, rasping: 'Push on, *Führer*, push on. Never let up until Himmler's dream is realised. Always remember who you were brought up to be.' Fervour possessed him as he began to shake. His voice rose in pitch and his eyes glowed. 'Go now, bring back the stone! Stoke the fires of war, turn the cogs of death and unfurl the final victory banner. March over the continents and crush the Jews and their sympathisers beneath the feet of the greatest war machine ever built!'

Franz drifted back to his palace in the sky.

2
Helambu
Nepal

An old monk followed a track that carved through a valley. It twisted beside a river, ran up over and around foothills that were terraced with rice fields, and finally climbed to a hilltop where a phone booth was located, inside of which was the only landline phone for miles around. Distant bronze-capped peaks studded the Himalaya in the late-afternoon sun.

He walked brusquely, the material of his deep-maroon robes crinkling as he leaned into the wind. Passing several porters leading yak trains in the opposite direction, he reached the hilltop and entered the booth, rummaged through his satchel and clipped a voice distorter to the mouthpiece. He inserted a few coins, called a number with an Israeli dialling code and heard the familiar voice on the other end of the line: 'Hello?'

The monk delivered a code that would allow the man to identify him: 'Nine, eight, ten, six, twelve.'

There was a pause, and then the man had answered, 'Go ahead, Badger.'

The monk, Badger, held the receiver tight, cupping his hands around it and his mouth. He didn't speak any widespread language. Instead, he spoke code. Numbers and letters. Each character corresponded to a syllable in Hebrew. The syllable in turn corresponded to more numbers and then those to another set of syllables from which the message would be made out. It was a code language called NAKA, used by Mossad.

The man on the other end recorded the message on his notepad. The words he furiously scratched down were as follows:

'Have solved final clue to stone. Expecting visit from T's men. Can't say if will survive this time round. Last time brutal. Source confirmed T travelling to Russia, Moscow. Then monastery on Anzer Island, White Sea. Looking key to unlock stone. Coordinates and time follow …'

After rattling the details off, Badger clicked the phone down and admired the auburn glow on the mountain peaks.

3
Mossad HQ
Tel Aviv

Two suits huddled around an aluminium table in a room known as 'the Grinder', more like a tin can than an office, seven floors up in the sky. The room was typical for Mossad headquarters: bare aside from a silver table, two steel chairs, a strip of carpet, a steel filing cabinet, and a window.

Between the men on the table was a packet of cigarettes, a lighter and an ashtray in which a neglected cigarette lay, a long tail of ash curling from its tip.

One of the suits was middle-aged. He wore a 24-carat gold band on his ring finger. He was of medium build, with a paunch pushing out over his belt. His face was not unhandsome, but his lips stretched thinly, and his voice was empty as if the joy had been sucked from it by personal troubles. His name was Steven. At least, that was the name by which he was known at the place where he worked.

The other suit sat staring out of the window, his tie loose around his neck. Tanned, ruggedly handsome and of a higher rank than his colleague, Ben had what some thought was a brilliant strategist mind and had been promoted to Director of Operations.

The suits sat with a riddle, a snippet of new information that had come from the phone call. Steven spoke in Hebrew.

'I had them run the tests.'

Ben was quiet. His mind raced, jumping between words and clues, wondering how to treat the new information. Steven's voice was annoying, grating on his nerves.

'We couldn't trace his location, as usual, but he used the code that he always does. Recent electronic whispers out of Moscow also link a few phone calls between Trevellian and an FSB agent, who has been known to sell plutonium to just about anyone with enough money. Trevellian is about to travel to Moscow.'

Steven assessed his intellectual and hierarchical superior's face. His eyebrows slanted inwards, as if he were in deep thought, but otherwise it gave away little. Steven picked up his cigarette and pulled on it deeply.

'Conditions are ripe to strike against Trevellian, Ben. The only problem is: how to organise a sting operation in such a short time?'

Usually months of planning were required for Mossad operations. Safe houses and letter boxes had to be set up, and as many as eight case officers, known as *katsas*, were used to carry out meticulously rehearsed operations that had been timed and practised down to the last second. In this case, the agents used would have been known as 'jumpers' – *katsas* who worked foreign countries.

'It seems our previous attempts at blocking Trevellian from obtaining nuclear materials are paying off,' Steven continued. 'He's getting increasingly frustrated. And that means rash decisions and mistakes.'

Ben was passive, and Steven's tone became more and more desperate. 'Let's send in our best, Ben. Let's send in Agent Fox, from *kidon*. He's the most ruthless killer we have.'

Kidon was a unit that carried out the agency's dirty work; its agents were trained assassins, some of the best in the world. Steven watched Ben shift in his chair as his cigarette burned to the butt. Ben reached for the packet and pulled out another. Clutching it between his lips, he fired up a lighter and inhaled deeply. Slowly, he began to speak, his eyes narrowing as the cigarette danced on his lips.

'I've reviewed the tapes myself. We have no reason to believe that it was not Badger. The code number and use of NAKA confirms that. There was something in the rhythm of his code when he was speaking to me … it was … *him*.'

Ben tipped his cigarette in the ashtray. 'What you are proposing, however, is not going to solve our problems. Trevellian is a good leader, by all accounts, yes, but the body will simply grow a new head. What you forget, is that Trevellian may have important information on the other Nazis. How deep does their organisation go? Or how high up in certain governments? Also … Trevellian could lead us to the base.'

Steven made as if to answer, but Ben continued. 'He's more useful to us alive than dead. If they are securing plutonium, it confirms our suspicion that they are building warheads, while our attention has been fixed on Iran all this time … What you also forget …' a column of smoke escaped his mouth and circled in the air above '… is that there are other ways to get information besides capture and torture.'

Steven shook his head. 'What other way could possibly work on someone so …' he searched for, reached far for the word: '… *brainwashed*?'

'Need I remind you how many agents, including our own, have fallen for the charms of a honey pot?'

Steven looked doubtful. 'Who, Ben?' He looked at him pleadingly. 'We've set up prostitutes for him in the past. He never takes the bait.'

'Trevellian will fly in a few days, giving us next to no time to prepare an assault. We have no one good enough in Russia at present who could pull this off, even though we have a network of *sayans* and jumpers. But none of them are well-trained or experienced enough. These guys all need two years to prepare a cover. So ... send twenty of your best *katsas* and some *neviot* from Listening Department, and try and get close to Trevellian within a single day. What do you think will happen?'

Steven didn't answer, still looked puzzled.

'They will rush in like fools.' Ben took another pull on his cigarette and looked out over the city. 'Rather, send in our finest assassin, home-trained and home-based. The man you mentioned, codename Fox, from *kidon*; the one who lost his family to that Hamas suicide bombing in Tel Aviv. A man who, *surely*, has hatred for any group, such as Trevellian Enterprises, that supplies Hamas with arms. Instead of having Fox kill Trevellian, let Fox capture him. Then send in the honey pot. Agent A, also from *kidon*. Let her follow Fox, so that she can "rescue" Trevellian and pretend that she wants to work for him. She speaks German and Russian fluently. Have you seen how beautiful that woman is?' Ben whistled softly and shook his head, smiling. 'She's gorgeous. Trevellian won't resist this one. He'll take the bait all right. She should've been in television, or modelling. In any case, this way, we can also trace Trevellian's father, Franz, the bastard who escaped Germany to South America without a trace after the war, and we can make a bit of a public scandal out of his arrest and trial, like we did with Eichmann in 1960. We'll get to the bottom of this secret base, and who knows where it will lead us?'

'But both agents have no cover?'

'Let them blend as they go. We know how effective they both are, based on their final tests before becoming full agents of *kidon*. Their provisional cover will be as agents of Trevellian Enterprises' competitors in the arms industry – corporate espionage agents working for BEA or Lockheed Martin, looking to glean secrets on Trevellian's arms business. Agent A is of Russian descent. Both she and Fox speak the language, although Fox not as well. Remember, Agent A did a reconnaissance mission in Moscow a few months ago. She discovered some pretty big Russian military secrets. She knows the lie of the land.'

Ben finished his cigarette, stubbed it out and stood up.

'Let's keep it tight. I will be happy to brief them.'

'What if Badger is wrong? What if the Eagle isn't about to travel to Russia?'

Ben answered: 'He will.'

'What makes you so sure?'

'He is hunting for something else.'

'What is he after?'

Ben had already left.

4
Wolfschanze

James made his way further up the tower to a study room. What had his father meant when he said that James would be faced with a decision? The way he had said it almost implied that it would be some kind of test, a test of character perhaps. But how could the old man know? Had the cancer finally got the better of his mind, even to shade out his so-called 'lucid' moments?

Questions swirled and remained undiluted. But they seemed to fill him with conviction, determination to see his father's dream through to its conclusion.

James entered the room and paused in thought in the doorway. Frieda sat rigidly behind her desk. A framed portrait of James hung on the wall behind her. It faced a set of steel-framed windows looking out onto the sea. There was something about those windows, James thought, and the woman behind the desk that seemed to match. Perhaps it was her steel-framed glasses with the Coke-bottle bottoms. Though she reminded him of a librarian, he knew she was more than she let on. A ruthlessly efficient organiser, James's secretary could easily run some of the best companies in the world better than many of the CEOs that James knew personally.

'*Mein Führer*,' Frieda said, noticing his frown but choosing not to comment. 'Just in time … there's a call for you.'

He walked over to the desk, and picked up the receiver. He cupped it and asked, 'Who is it?'

'*Herr* Parcival, *mein Führer.*'
'Line secure?'
'Yes.'
James nodded curtly.
'*Ja?*' he spoke into the phone.
'*Aben, mein Führer. Herr* Parcival here.'
'*Herr* Parcival, news?'
'The same you have been waiting for. A turning point in the history of the Aryan race. After years of living among the Sherpa monks in Nepal, Badger has solved the final clue.'

James smiled. 'Good to hear, *herr* Parcival. I want him interrogated. Use force if you have to. Listen, he's been useful to us, and I hate to have to say this, but he knows …'

'Too much? Say no more, I understand. He is due some leave, I think, is what you are trying to say, *mein Führer*. A very long holiday.'

'I will debrief you myself. And if anything goes wrong this time, *herr* Parcival, we may look into a little vacation for you too …'

'*Jahwol, mein Führer*, I understand.'

The line went quiet as Parcival hesitated. James smiled to himself at his own twisted joke. He wouldn't have carried out the threat to Parcival in any case, but Parcival, like most others in the chain of command, took threats such as this seriously. Their unquestioned respect for leadership, James noted, was at the same time their biggest strength and greatest weakness, and it was James's job to let on to those in the chain that he was ruthless, whereas those closest to him knew differently.

'Is there anything else?'

'The …' Parcival hesitated again, '… the *dietrich*. The key. Said to be needed to unlock the stone.'

'Where?'

'Russia. I will transmit the location in an encrypted message. I know that your men will travel there soon. I thought it prudent to suggest, if I may, *mein Führer*, that you travel with them, to help them secure the materials, but then to travel on to the monastery where the *dietrich* is kept.'

'I'll consider it, soldier. Do not disappoint me.'

'The next time we speak, I will have more good news for you. *Sieg heil!*'

5
Mossad HQ
Tel Aviv

Ben Hariri sat on a hard plastic chair and spoke into a phone.

'The word is that Trevellian is travelling to Russia himself. His men have failed several times to secure plutonium. Their deals have always gone wrong at the last minute, when our own agents intervene. We seem to be the only agency doing anything about these bloody Nazis. Anyhow, close calls, all of them, but successful so far.'

Ben pictured Agent A, Anna Leonova, wrapped in a towel, her body still steaming from the shower, perhaps painting her toenails or dabbing her hair dry as she spoke into the phone.

That would be a sufficient contrast, thought Ben, mirroring who she was. A gorgeous woman, too beautiful to be involved in this kind of work, talking trade with her 'controller', in this case the Director of Operations himself.

'And where else to turn but Russia,' Anna answered, 'the McDonalds of the world's plutonium supply. Is it that FSB man again?' she asked.

'Vladimir. Yes, he's the seller.'

'Scumbag that one. What's the brief?'

'You're going in after him.'

'You expect me to go in without a credible cover, at such short notice? What am I to do? Is this an assassination?'

'No, it's a kidnap operation. There's nothing we can do about the lack of time. This is an urgent op, and you *will* have a cover.'

'What – an agent begging to be killed by Nazis?'

'Don't get smart,' Ben snapped. 'Your cover is Sandra Greer. You work as a corporate espionage agent for Lockheed Martin, a rival arms company …'

'With all due respect, sir, I know what Lockheed Martin is. Will there at least be a safe house, some helpers, *sayans*, other *katsas*?'

'I'm afraid not, Anna. This is too urgent. Listen,' Ben leaned forward and picked up a packet of cigarettes, shook one out and lit it, placing the pack and lighter back on the table. 'You're the best we have. Here's what's going to happen. All I can say is that someone is going to kidnap Trevellian in Russia. In Moscow. We have all the details. It's your job as Sandra to rescue him. It must look like you're trying to prove yourself to him, as if you want to become a Nazi yourself, and then hopefully he'll take the bait and recruit you. If he does, we'll have someone on the inside.'

'Listen, this is the most bizarre operation I've ever heard of.'

'Yes, I know. It's risky, but ...'

'Who's the kidnapper?'

'I can't tell you.'

'You can't tell me? Listen, Ben, I've put my life on the line for you countless times. I respect you and your decisions. For years I've undertaken missions for you that were insanely dangerous. But not once have I even heard of such a thinly planned operation.'

'I know, I know. Listen, Anna, an ordinary *katsa* would not be able to pull this off. That's why I'm giving this to you. As a member of *kidon*, and the finest we have, you're my only hope. I have no idea what's going to happen out there in Russia, but I trust you to deal with anything. I've got a full set of equipment for you – including tracking devices, fake IDs, and passports.'

'What if, on the other side, I need transport?'

'We'll enlist the help of *sayans*. If you need help, contact us; there are thousands, no, *millions* of Jewish *sayans* in Moscow, thousands of places to hide, and hundreds of different covers to take. Trevellian's meeting is on the fringes of downtown Moscow, at a place called the Shamrock Bar, so you'll be able to go on foot, or use public transport. It will be safer. You can make your way around less surreptitiously.'

'*Great*. Will I at least have a piece?'

'No.'

'What the hell do you expect me to do in a tight spot?'

'Talk your way out of it. You're the best goddamn actor the Institute has ever seen. I know you can do it. Shape-shift as you go. Borrow identities. Blend in ...'

'I don't know, Ben. I need to think about this.'

'Sleep on it. I'll call you in the morning.' Ben stood, about to hang up.

'One more thing,' Anna said. 'This person doing the kidnapping.'

'Yes?'

'Do I know him or her?'

'I can't disclose that right now. Just trust me. Look, he'll kidnap

Trevellian in Moscow, take him to a pre-planned location, and you will break in and rescue him.'

'So it's a "he" then?'

Anna smiled. She'd called his mistake.

'Can I expect resistance from this mystery kidnapper?'

'You may, and you may not.'

'Say I'm successful. How am I supposed to get close to Trevellian? I mean *really* close; close enough to learn some real secrets – like the location of the base? These aren't things they just hand out to new employees like brochures.'

'I'm sure you'll find a way, soldier.'

'Why don't you just be blunt with me and tell me that I'm a *honey pot*, that I need to sleep with him like some cheap whore? Has this even been approved by the higher powers?'

'Get some rest. We'll talk tomorrow.'

'Right. Maybe I'll dream of the afterlife. Or … what's the point? I'll be there soon enough.'

'I'll call you in the morning.'

Ben hung up, sighed, and dialled Agent Fox, hopeful that the second agent would go easier on him than the first.

'It's Ben … Yes, thank you, and you. Listen, the mission we spoke about this morning. Your cover documents – passports, the works – are coming to you with a *bodel* … The target is to be captured alive, Fox. Under *no* circumstances should he be killed … When you have him at the location, someone is going to rescue him. You must put up a fight, but let that person win … Good, glad you understand. Speak to you tomorrow.' Before Ben hung up he added, 'You know, I really like how you *don't* ask questions, soldier.'

Then he stood, pensive, scratching his beard, not knowing that a much longer race than he was anticipating was about to unfold in Russia.

6
Moscow
Two days later

An icy wind whipped the shivering avenues of the city. It flicked up the corners of the *führer*'s coat as he walked towards an entrance to a Metro station, the National State Library to his right and a block of grey buildings on the left. To the south, a ruby-red star glowed at the top of the Kremlin's Troitska Tower. James eyed his flanks to check that no one was following him. It was an important meeting, and nothing should be left to chance.

James's thoughts turned to the man he was about to meet. Vladimir was an employee of the Russian secret service, the FSB, with connections to scientists close to Russia's decommissioned nuclear weapons programme, a process ongoing since the fall of the Berlin Wall.

He'd been warned by Vladimir to come alone. But two ghosts drifted like vapours off the streets, no more than leaves fluttering behind corners, shadows dancing out of sight. Crammed into a small 1980s Russian-built Lada Vas-2105, cruising behind James at a safe following distance was Roger, his personal bodyguard. Another of his men, Patrick, followed on foot.

James walked through the Metro entrance and stopped near the door to assess any potential traps. He scanned the platform: brilliant chandeliers, bright and sparkling, dangled from the mosaic ceiling; murals hung on the walls, and an old woman sat, surrounded by a cloud of bags, cradling herself against the wind that nipped in through the entrance.

A train whooshed in and eased to a stop. It was the last northbound train for the night. James boarded, sat down and the train moved forward. A hooded man sat a few rows down, swaying from side to side as if drunk, singing an old Russian war song and clutching a pole.

The train eased west before snaking north. It glided into a station and stopped. James got off and found the nearest exit. He looked across a grimy street splayed with the Irish-green reflection of a neon sign: 'The Shamrock Bar, Since 1991', as young as so-called freedom in 'Mother Russia', mused James. The outline of the Lada was visible some way down the street. Patrick would be around too, thought James as he crossed the road and entered the bar. Bells chimed as the door swung shut behind him.

There was a lone patron at the counter, propped up on a bar stool. In front of him were several empty glasses and an ashtray heaped with cigarette butts. He wore a leather jacket – standard Russian civil servant issue – with his collar turned up. It was Vladimir, enveloped by a cloud of smoke. James sidled up to the bar. A groggy-looking barmaid sauntered over and stared at him blankly.

'Beautiful night for a White Russian, don't you think?' James said, looking over the barmaid's shoulder and into the mirror, straight into Vladimir's sharp eyes. The barmaid sighed – *Bloody tourist*, she thought – before throwing a sloppy White Russian together. Vladimir nodded. 'Indeed, a beautiful night, even for a white German.'

Suddenly Vladimir's face broke into a glorious smile. He turned to face James and slapped him on the back.

'I have been looking forward to meet you, Jamies! Come, have drink.'

Vladimir slipped a half jack of vodka out of a coat pocket and shouted: 'Bitch, bring glasses!'

The barmaid came over sheepishly, slipping James his White Russian before handing two glasses to Vladimir.

'What? No ice?' he boomed. 'Pour me some ice from your cold heart.'

Ice was dispensed. Vladimir laughed as he poured out the vodka. '*Vodka*. You know is meaning "little water"?' He handed a glass to James. '*Nazdarovye*.'

'Cheers. *Prosit.*' James replied.

Their glasses clinked together. The men settled back in their seats and drank. James looked at the framed picture of the barmaid that hung above the shelves of booze. Its caption read 'Employee of the Year'. He motioned to the picture and asked, 'How many people work here?'

'One.'

Vladimir winked at the barmaid who looked at him scornfully, shaking her head. 'I understand English, you pigs!' she spat and stalked off into the kitchen. Vladimir snorted.

'She need more crack to make her quiet. I see dealer here two times tonight already.'

He produced two cigars, nipped them, gave one to James and held out a Zippo.

'Money train.' Vladimir lit his cigar and held it up to scrutinise it. 'Mark of new successful Russia. More bling in streets now than ever before in my country. Seen how women in Moscow streets dress? Like whores!' He grinned, flashing a gold tooth. 'What better way to celebrate than with cigar?'

'Vlad – can I call you Vlad …?'

Vladimir shrugged, picking up one of the *zakuski* on the bar – Russian hors d'œuvres eaten with vodka to absorb the alcohol – and swallowed it whole. This particular *zakuska* was a boiled egg stuffed with caviar. He reached for another, motioning for James to continue.

'I hear you can get me ingredients.'

Vladimir nodded. 'My friend, you heard right,' he said, chewing. 'I can get what you need.' He swallowed a big gulp of vodka and smacked his lips together. 'But I must warn you, many people want to bakes cakes these days. Price has gone up since 9/11 and Middle East uprisings in 2011.'

'Money is not an issue,' said James quietly. 'What we aim to do will be of more worth than any sum on earth.'

'Huh,' grunted Vladimir, 'What you want do? You want blackmail Bummer? You want burn world to ashes?' Vladimir laughed, shook his head and added, 'Ah, these *extremists*, they are *all* same.'

'Forty-eight kilos. Put a price on that.'

Vladimir's smile disappeared. 'Ten million. In euros.' He swirled the ice around in his glass and swallowed what was left of the liquor, crunching ice and staring ahead. 'Twelve cans for twelve cakes.'

'Done,' said James.

'You will be sent the location to make collection later by encrypted message.' He paused. 'I trust you, Jamies, *for now* …'

'Good, then, I think we have a deal.'

Vladimir raised his empty glass in salute and James reached out to shake Vladimir's hand. What happened next happened fast. A shadow slunk out of a dark corner, as if peeling away from the wall paint, a shady-looking man with a hood. The man withdrew a pistol and raised it. Acting on instinct, James pushed Vladimir down and dived towards the exit. He rolled, was up on his feet and midway through the pub's door when three shots rang out.

James drew his Walther PPK 9 mm with silencer and fired a return volley, but missed. Crouching on the kerb outside the pub, he saw that Vladimir had fallen to the floor.

The Lada's engine fired up from down the street and screeched to the entrance of Shamrock Bar within seconds. As James jumped into the passenger's seat, he saw Patrick, dressed as a hobo, emerge from beside a dumpster. James signalled to him with two short jabs of his fingers: *Follow him.*

The Lada sped off into the night.

James banged his clenched fist on the dashboard and swore. Roger's eyes were peeled to the road, his hands clutching the wheel at either side.

'Who was that, *mein Führer?*'

'How the *hell* should I know? You and Patrick were meant to stake out the location before I got there. Was that never part of your secret service training, or have you gotten slack?' James looked out the window. The sidewalks of Novy Arbat Ulitsa were heaped with snow. Roger kept quiet and gunned the car through the street that ran parallel to Arbat Ulitsa, one of Moscow's oldest roads with its wide vistas teeming with tourists by day.

'I'm sorry, *mein Führer*, there is no excuse,' Roger finally said, veering into a side street.

'Okay,' James was calming himself down. 'Okay, let's think it through in the office. We need to know who that was and what they were really trying to do. More importantly, how they knew about the meeting.'

The pull of the turning car made James clutch at the handle on the inside of the door. As they drove on in silence, James recalled how the hooded man had appeared. The echo of the three whips of the assassin's silencer played over in his mind, and Vladimir falling to the floor, clutching his chest. James wondered if he was still alive.

Roger checked the rear-view mirror compulsively. He slipped the car into an alley and stopped outside a door that looked like the dark mouth of a snake. The body wriggled up four storeys, the shiny bricks forming a scaly skin. Two steps led up to the door, beside which a light flickered.

James got out and scanned left and right. All was quiet. He walked quickly to the door, pressed the buzzer and waited. Beside the button was a logo engraved on a metal plate. It belonged to a multinational arms manufacturing company known as Trevellian Enterprises that produced some of the most advanced weaponry and military technologies in the world. It was a plain red square, with a white circle in the middle, inside which was a black iron eagle, its head in profile, looking left. Its wings were stretched out widely, and it clutched an oak wreath in its talons. Within the wreath were embossed gold letters: 'TE'. The eagle's eye glinted deep red as it caught the reflection of the dim light of the alley.

'Yes?' Frieda answered.

'*Adler,*' James replied.

There was a buzzing sound, and a click. James pulled the door open and stalked up two flights of stairs. On entering the office, he took his coat off and threw it onto the rack. He paced across the polished wooden floor to a mahogany desk, sat in the chair behind it and steepled his fingers. Now everything was going to hell, he thought.

There was nothing in his surroundings to ease his anxiety. The sort of grandeur to be expected of a top Forbes company was conspicuously lacking in the office. It was Spartan, with only the desk, two chairs, a bookshelf, and a brown bear rug splayed out beneath a window that eyed the alley. It was an *unofficial* office, one from which dirty work was carried out, and one that might be packed up and deserted easily. The books on the shelf were a mixture of mass-market thrillers, biographies of prominent spies and a few 1930s academic titles on racial superiority and eugenics theories, and a well-worn copy of *Mein Kampf.* On the desk was a pile of the day's papers from around the world.

On the wall behind the desk was an enlarged photograph of a young boy, a black and white. The boy's chin was tilted upwards condescendingly. His gaze peered through the lens. The eyes had an unsettling, disquieting arrogance. Something gnawed at his soul. His arms were folded across his chest defensively. One had to be familiar with the picture to know that the young boy was Adolf Hitler. Only then did his eyes glint and the long gap between the nose and the top lip seem to colour itself in with a characteristic strip.

Through a communicating archway to the only other room on the floor came the faint sound of keyboards clacking and the slow regular hum of a machine that never slept. Behind the computers, speaking on the phones and pointing at the television screens flashing international news headlines, were four bright MIT graduates specialising in information and communications. Each had been hand picked by James to see to the day-to-day running of Trevellian Enterprise's more nefarious business in Russia. The young men were known within the organisation as Membranes, Mems for short. They controlled what information came in and what went out, but also provided useful intelligence analysis.

Roger stood in front of the desk. His feet were planted slightly apart and he looked on. Sourced from the German secret service, BDN, Roger was now a BEAD man, an agent in Trevellian Enterprise's own secret service, known euphemistically as the Business Environment Analysis Division, and funded by the company's deep coffers. Roger was entrusted with the personal protection and transportation of James, CEO of Trevellian Enterprises. He'd worked his way through the ranks by carving out a name for himself as a hand-to-hand combat extraordinaire with unbelievable strength and superb driving skills. As James stared at him, Frieda walked in and stood smartly to attention beside Roger.

'*Aben, mein Führer,*' she said, clicking her heels together.

'*Aben,*' James replied. 'Bourbon please, Frieda.'

Frieda walked over to a cabinet beneath the picture of Hitler. James placed a hand over his eyes and reached into his pocket. He brought out a cigar, nipped it, lit it and swirled the smoke with a puff through his lips.

'Who do you think it was, *herr* Roger? In the bar ...'

Frieda made her way to James and handed him a drink. He took it and sipped.

Roger tried, '*Mein Führer ...*' but he was cut short by the buzzing of the cell phone in James's pocket.

'*Ja?*' James answered.

'It's Vladimir.' The words were spoken harshly, in a wounded voice that took James off guard.

'Vladimir?'

'I am still here, but I talk quick. Deal is still on.'

James couldn't help smiling.

'But Santa is not well.' Vladimir coughed. 'He must ask two of his elves to deliver gifts. In exchange, Santa asks ten cold, hard blue frogs. I will send time and location.' He ended with an unholy volley of coughing.

'Did you see the man who tried to ruin Christmas?' James heard a lighter grate, the rustling sound of tobacco being burned deeply and an inhale of breath before Vladimir answered. 'All I see is nine mil with silencer. This Grinch wore hood over his head. He could even be drug dealer, bloody depressed maniac, who knows?'

The line went cold.

7
Moscow

The man lay on a rooftop near Shamrock Bar. He'd crawled, spider-like, up a fire escape in a dark alley behind the pub, and waited for his pursuer to chase his ghost through the dimly-lit streets. As part of *kidon*, Fox had memorised the street plans of every major city in the world, Moscow included. It was worth it now. He knew exactly how to throw a shadow off. His satellite phone buzzed in his pocket. He answered, pressing it close to his ear to catch every word, spoken by the voice that was muffled by a voice distorter.

'One, five, eight, six, three.'

Badger always prefaced his messages with a string of digits, the sum of which totalled a double-digit figure whose numbers were sequential, in this case, twenty-three: two, three.

'The Russian is still alive. He will sell the Eagle ingredients at a place near the Ural Mountains. If you want him, this is your chance.'

'Where and when?' asked Fox. He usually didn't speak back, but things were pressing.

'Coordinates and time follow ...'

Fox listened, memorising each number and letter. He'd stopped wondering how Badger had access to this information. Word at the Office was that he had a source within Trevellian's outfit.

Fox hung up and checked the location on his phone. 'Shit,' he whispered. 'One thousand two hundred bloody kilometres away, how the hell am I going to get there in time?' He sent an encoded email to Ben: 'Eagle got away, received info from Badger, meeting still happening, southern Urals, 1 200 kilometres from current location, need transport … here are coordinates and time.'

As he waited for the reply, his eyes glazed over and the seconds turned into minutes, the lights faded and nostalgia crept up on him like a shadow.

13 January 1990. Gordon Beach, Tel Aviv. We sat at a table on the kerb at a roadside café overlooking the calm seas on a perfectly clear day, beneath the bluest sky. The sea was beautiful, it glittered and danced in the sunlight. There were yachts and boats out in the bay. How I wished to have a boat of my own!

Father was in a good mood, he and Mother had been playing a naughty game all day as we walked in and out of the shops. Father got paid extra so we were buying a lot of stuff. Father bought Mother a beautiful red dress with pretty lace frills. Each time she wasn't looking, he tapped her on her bum and she would laugh and try to do the same to him. Each time I would laugh as well, and baby sister would join in. We were going to Gordon Beach next after ice-creams.

A man walked in. He was carrying a guitar case. I asked him as he passed our table if he was going to play songs. He didn't smile and walked on. I think he was scared. Rivers of white yumminess trickled and oozed over my knuckles and I tried to play the game of gobbling them up before they reached my pinkie.

That's when the world went black.

I couldn't hear anything. There was dust everywhere and father's head was lying on a pile of rubbish. It was like sister's dolls' heads – the ones that popped off – because it had just been torn away from his body and was shredded, oozing. His eyes were no more seeing, just hard and cold like marbles, staring at me, at nothing. His arm was next to Mother, who was buried under bricks and rubble. Her legs were twisted and her foot was next to her face. She was smiling; her eyes were open, and she looked like an angel.

There was broken glass and I cut my hands. I was crying. I couldn't hear anything. Only a screaming voice in my ears that was full of hurt like demons screeching in a nightmare. I was calling for Mother but she couldn't hear me, crying.

Then sound came back suddenly, and there were sirens wailing and people shouting for help, and in the middle of all this there was this lady. She was just sitting there, on her knees, praying to God. But she wasn't asking for anything, she was giving thanks to God for the beauty of the world. Sister was red and full of blood too. I vomited on the floor, staring at all the broken puppets.

Later, I was told that their strings had been cut by a group of people called 'Hamas'.

Fox's glazed eyes gradually came back into focus. He was staring at the concrete floor, struggling to overcome the rage that the memory never failed to induce, breathing hard and fast. He'd memorised the account that he'd told to police, that had been tape-recorded, years before, of the day his family had been murdered. It was a noose that had grown legs and followed him from orphanage to orphanage, family to broken family as he stumbled like a clumsy reject through his childhood.

Now, here's a chance, he thought. Trevellian ... so big and important, within his sights. Ben said 'capture'. Fox had ideas of his own.

His phone was buzzing. He blinked, swallowed, and answered. A woman's voice this time, in comforting Hebrew: 'This is the Office. Regarding your request, you are to meet Anne Boleyn in a cave at "Dmitri's Place". Here are the coordinates ...'

Fox committed them to memory, said thank you and the line went dead. He punched the digits into his satellite phone and saw a small black pin on a map about four kilometres northwest of his position.

'Anne Boleyn.' A codename for Agent A. What was Anna doing in Moscow?

8
Mossad HQ
Tel Aviv

Ben picked up his phone and read the coded message from Fox. 'Shit,' he whispered to himself and, closing the message, dialled a number and waited, staring at a code sheet for the phrases he would need to use.

'This is the Office. They didn't accept the deal and walked out of the meeting. A new meeting has been scheduled, business associate F is to attend; you are to shadow. Travel by train. The one you looked into last time. Help F onto the train but he is not to know that you are also in on the meeting. It may jeopardise the deal. Meet him at Dmitri's Place. Here's where.'

Ben hung up and typed a message on his phone and pressed 'send'.

9
Moscow

Agent A, sitting on the edge of a hotel-room bed, received the coordinates and whispered softly to herself. 'Business associate F? What is Fox doing in Russia?'

'Travel by train?' What did that mean? 'Surely they don't expect me to take the Metro 2!' Anna shivered. The Metro 2 was Russia's secret ghost express, a metro running beneath Russia, connecting its strategic military bases. The reference to Dmitri's Place confirmed her suspicions. It was a dingy little hellhole of a cave beneath the city, where she had undertaken a mission a few months back – the entrance to the secret train lines. 'How am I supposed to follow without him knowing?' Anna swore and drew in a long, nervous breath.

James put the phone down and took a sip of bourbon. Things were looking up. Ice clinked against his teeth as he took in a deep satisfying gulp that burned the back of his throat. 'The deal is still on.' Roger and Frieda blinked and nodded, wide-eyed and obedient. His phone beeped.

'And here …' he said, '… are the GPS coordinates, and a time. Easy as clockwork. Look them up, would you?' he tossed the phone to Roger.

'On it,' Roger said, hurrying out of the room. James turned to Frieda and said, 'Wake the captain up. Tell him to get the Learjet ready.'

Frieda lingered. She took in James's handsome face. Although forty-eight, James seemed to get handsomer every year. She imagined running her fingers through the thick brown hair with attractive greying tufts at the temples; cupping his face with her hand as she stared into his eyes. Her romantic ideas, yes, she had to admit, sometimes seemed to her to be from the 1950s, but James fitted that bill. The eyes ... the eyes were the colour of a stormy sea, she thought. Smooth jaw line, thick eyebrows, almost too perfect, like a movie star. But he seemed strangely unconscious of his looks. Instead of vanity, there was, Frieda thought, an unsettling air about him, of a wounded animal, like a creature caught in a trap ...

'Frieda?'

She snapped to. 'Yes, consider it done, *mein Führer*,' and turned on her heels and walked out of the room.

James turned and stared out of the window, his mind racing at the prospect of securing such a large quantity of plutonium. Finally, things were coming together, he thought, now, if only he could get his hands on the *dietrich* ...

Roger barged in, grounding his fledgling reverie.

'The location for the deal. Eight kilometres north of Mount Yamantaw, in the southern Ural Mountains. We've checked it out on satellite maps and placed it at a medium-sized pond, almost as big as a lake, in the wilderness. Very remote. It's close to the secret underground Russian military base, Mount Yamantaw. I presume you are familiar with ...'

'Yes,' said James. 'A facility half the size of Washington DC, where all the Russians run if there's ever a nuclear war. The base is connected to other important locations by the Metro 2 ...'

'Yes,' said Roger, 'And near to some of the plutonium facilities. Beloreck Airport is thirty-five kilometres away from Yamantaw.'

Roger paused for a brief moment, took a deep breath and then continued. 'Patrick phoned, *mein Führer*. The man he was shadowing must be damn good. He managed to throw Patrick off. You know, the only man who could possibly have given Patrick the slip like that is ...'

'Agent Fox, yes. You're right, *herr* Roger. I have to give it to him. That agent is bloody good at shadowing. How far is Yamantaw from Moscow?'

'One thousand two hundred kilometres east.'

'Then Frieda and I will fly. You'll take the SLS. You leave immediately. Get Frieda to clear our landing at the airport. Keep it hush, as usual.'

'Of course.' Roger turned to leave, but James stopped him.

'There's one more thing, *herr* Roger. Prepare a few bags, with ten million in hard currency ... euros.'

10
Moscow

Following the map on his phone, Fox jumped over a roadside railing and jogged carefully down an embankment that led from a main road down to the banks of the Moskva River. The wail of a far-off muezzin called the faithful to prayer as the first light of day hugged the horizon. He connected with a rough path that ran down beneath a bridge from the main road to the other side of the Moskva, and slowed up beneath its arch as the pin that represented him on the map drew up with his destination. It must be here somewhere, Fox thought, looking around. There was an entrance to a dimly-lit cave to his right. The smell was appalling – a mixture of urine, faeces and smoke. 'HQ always chooses the best meeting places,' Fox muttered to himself.

As he came nearer to the cave's entrance, which looked like a hole blasted into the wall by cannon, two beggars carried a TV into the cave, placed it down and began to quarrel. A stray dog hovered like a leaf over some scraps, sniffing; deciding that they weren't edible and then blew off into the grey-blue shadows after some promising scent of food.

Fox walked with a limp, and with a hood over his head, his eyes shone beneath it like two metallic glints. All at once, a group of beggars huddling closely together at a brazier stopped talking to look up at him. He smiled as he passed them and greeted: '*Dobroe utro, Dobroe utro, Dobroe utro*! Good morning, good morning, good morning!' Staring into each of their eyes in turn, like a madman or a drunkard, he began to sing in a garish voice. Fox was glad for the Russian lessons Mossad had given him at the Mossad Academy. They'd gone to the fine detail of teaching the agents old war songs, but Fox couldn't remember which one was which, so he settled for the first one that came to mind. It was 'Comrades let's bravely march', which he sang in an exaggerated, deep soldier's voice:

'Comrades let's bravely march, Our resolve gets stronger in the struggle, We will fight our way, Towards liberty ...'

To Fox's surprise, the beggars lauded him and some joined in. Their voices faded as he left them, entering the cave.

Debris lay about, the props of broken dreams; tables with linoleum tops, chipped chairs, cracked porcelain lamps and patchy teddy bears with the stuffing coming out.

Finding a chair stripped of upholstery, Fox sat down and scanned the walls around him. All that he'd been given by HQ was a set of coordinates and two words: 'Dmitri's Place'. What could it mean?

An old man stirred beneath a rag and some newspapers, looked up. His weathered face was carved with hardship, like furrows on leather. His mouth, twisted by many bitter years and cold winters, was slightly open, revealing a line of jagged rotten teeth. Fox looked from the man to the wall. Above a hole of crumbling bricks was the inscription: 'DMITRI'S PLACE'.

He was about to rise, but the beggar's croak settled him down: 'Dmitri still lives there, you know, even though they killed him. Killed him because he knew secrets. Found something down there. We don't talk about that, oh no!' The man burst out laughing. 'Oh no, I wouldn't go in, if I were you. They'll kill you.' His smile was twisted and he began laughing, the putrid smell of stale breath mixed with alcohol rose like a cloud.

Fox shook off his misgivings and made his way over, crouched and climbed through. Inside, it was dank, water dripped from the roof. He avoided the puddles of water and cast his torchlight all over the walls. It was a long, thin tunnel, with the remains of an incomplete Metro platform, a long slab of concrete that pushed up to one side. It still had some of the signage and the cracked tiles and bricks. From beside the platform near Fox's feet, rusted train tracks ran to a dead-end wall on the far side. The ceiling was arched in a semi-circle. Behind the raised, crumbling platform was a wall of white-painted bricks. Fox was about to turn back, standing in front of the wall, when the light danced over a red brick, half way up the wall, that seemed out of place amongst the sea of white ones.

Shining his torch along the face of the wall, Fox noticed that the grouting between the bricks was missing, forming a jagged dark line that ran down from the red brick. Then, to the left of the red one, the same thing: a line of missing grouting that led horizontally across for about a metre.

Fox walked up to the wall and ran his finger along the line. Is it a door? The red brick also seemed offset from the surface, as if it were a massive button. He decided to take a chance.

He reached up and pressed the brick in. A grating sound set his teeth on edge as the wall seemed to crease inwards. Fox threw his shoulder against the wall and heaved. It groaned and crunched as it opened further, as if it were on hinges. A third push produced a crack wide enough for Fox to slip through.

On the other side was a dark, close chamber. Fox swung the flashlight around to see a hole in the floor, with the top of a steel ladder poking through. Climbing down the ladder, his foot finally struck air. He shone the torch downwards; beneath him, about two metres below, was the floor of another cave. He slipped off the ladder and landed smoothly. The flashlight came out and he searched the walls. This was the place: '666' and 'Dmitri's Place' were spray painted all over the walls in red. The torch began to falter, and finally, the light died.

With nothing to do but wait for Anna, Fox pulled a massive hunting knife out of its sheath, which was clipped to his belt beneath his coat, and a long flat stone, which he pushed out of a material holder. Pushing the blade against the edge of the stone and his finger, he felt for the angle he wanted, nice and sharp, and began to grind the blade against the stone.

11
Gorky Park
Moscow

Anna's eyes combed the street outside Gorky Park. No guards were around. She hadn't slept well and had watched the dim purple haze of dawn crest the skyscrapers and melt slowly into the weak yellow light of mid-morning. Anna checked her watch: ten thirty. She'd kept Fox waiting, but it couldn't be helped. She had to source appropriate clothing for the mission: a yellow overcoat, red hardhat with a headlamp and gumboots, from the hotel's maintenance room. The task hadn't been quick or easy.

She jumped up and clutched the top of the Park's outer wall, pulled up and jumped over it, landing softly on the grass on the other side.

Her mission according to Ben was to lead Agent Fox underground to the Metro 2, the secret train line built by Stalin that connected all of Russia's strategic military command posts; shadow him, undetected, to the southern Urals and capture Trevellian. Well, put that way, she thought, it sounded simple. She had keyed the coordinates sent to her by Ben into her phone, and was shocked to see the blinking dot 1 200 kilometres east of Moscow. Now that she knew she was shadowing Fox, her purpose had changed. She obviously knew Fox a lot better than Ben did, Anna reflected. There was no way Fox would not jump at the opportunity to kill Trevellian. Whether HQ knew it or not, it was her job to stop him.

Frozen footpaths crossed the lawns. The lamplights beside the path were like strange orange moons beside the naked trees that raised their skeleton limbs to the sky. Anna made her way towards the Park's centre, nimble and sleek as she cut through the shadows.

She crossed the bridge that led over the Moskva to the other side of the Park, passing frozen ponds on which children skated like whirling figurines. The path traced the river. On either side of it, rollercoaster rides curled up, metallic spaghetti structures twisting into the sky beside a Ferris wheel. Anna crossed the main thoroughfare, making her way closer to the fountain at the centre. Beside it, she found what she was looking for: a grid that concealed an air vent. Sliding the grid aside, she lowered herself in and pulled the grid closed. Crouching, she followed the air vent that kinked right before opening to a ladder. The flaky rungs peeled beneath her palms and the scent of sulphur and sewerage drifted on the air.

Anna entered a brick-lined canal, ankle deep in the Neglinka River, the river that had first been diverted underground by Catherine the Great, and to her right, a short tunnel crumbled to reveal a cave. Inefficient engineering practices of the early days of the construction of Moscow's Metro had resulted in extra tunnels and hollows beneath the city, where the city's scum now dwelled. She found a ladder that led to an opening and slipped through the hole into another short tunnel. She slipped through a hatchway and dropped to the ground, square in the middle of a cave. She didn't need to see the man crouched in shadow to know that he was there.

'I thought you would never come,' a steely voice whispered.

12
40 000 feet
Russia

James flicked over another page of *Mein Kampf*, and read distractedly. They would land in an hour. The Learjet's cabin was cool and spacious. Trevellian Enterprises had been the first and most important of Bombadier's clients to receive the Learjet 85 ahead of its official release in 2013. James preferred the plane to some of the other more expensive options on the market. It was compact, fast and well-finished, worth the investment of seventeen million dollars. They had spent some small change on finer details, including a custom paint job of matte black offset by the red and white Trevellian Enterprises logo on the tail.

James reached for a copy of *Der Spiegel* and read the lead story.

Protests bring Tehran to a standstill

Downtown Tehran was rocked early Thursday morning by widespread protests carried out by Iran's Green Movement, the country's only opposition to spiritual-leader-turned-dictator, Ayatollah Ali Khameini.

More than half a million protestors took to the streets with banners denouncing Khameini, wearing gasmasks, brandishing batons and makeshift weapons, and carrying riot shields. Khameini's spokesperson later declared at a press conference that there was a 'third hand' behind the riots.

The protestors declared support for the embattled leader of the Iranian Revolutionary Guard Corps, General Mubarak Husseini, who was accused earlier in the week by the Ayatollah of betraying the Islamic revolution. Pictures of Husseini meeting with unsuccessful presidential candidate for Iran's 2009 election, Mir-Hossein Mousavi, surfaced on the Internet last week, prompting an outburst by Khameini last Friday denouncing the IRGC's leader.

In a press release issued later on Thursday, Khameini's spokesperson said that the protests were 'the work of that Satan, America, and also that cowardly group of Jews, Mossad, who seek to destabilise our nuclear programme. It is also the work of General Husseini, who seeks power for himself.'

Meanwhile, violence has spread across the border to Baghdad, carried out by supporters of a Shi'ite cleric Mahmood Bazargan, who has risen to prominence following his fiery weekly religious sermons at some of the most important mosques across Iraq. The unrest comes in the wake of the complete withdrawal of US forces from Iraq and the violence that rocked the entire region in early 2011.

Khameini's spokesperson was quoted as saying that the protests provide further reason for Iran to withdraw its signature of the Nuclear Non-Proliferation Treaty. Article 4 of the treaty allows countries to pursue nuclear development for civilian usage, which Khameini argued, is the sole purpose of Iran's nuclear programme. It is not clear how Thursday's riots are related.

Security analysts estimate Iran to be able to produce nuclear weapons by 2015 ...

James put the paper down and stared at the white and brown patchwork of countryside. The plan was coming together. Israel would fall like a house of cards.

Forty thousand feet below, Roger was heading east across Russia towards the Urals at terrible speed. He chuckled as he flicked the transmission pedal on the steering wheel to gear down and overtake a BMW 323 idling along the M-7.

It was a different universe behind the wheel of his custom-built SLS AMG compared to the Lada-Vas he had been forced to drive in Moscow. Its V10 engine purred at his finger- and toe-tips. The gears changed easily with a specially-fitted nine-gear Tronic transmission. The car had voice-activated Internet browsing and specially designed software that allowed up-to-the-minute contact with HQ, satellite offices or agents on the ground. Its paint job had also been customised: a special graphite finish, matte black with the Trevellian Enterprises logo on the crest of the bonnet.

As the M-7 stretched eastwards, the road was lined with copses of pine trees, their branches like shelves, or arms, thought Roger, holding up bundles of snow. The sun sank, and the horizon glowed purple. The fog lights of the SLS came on as a mist sank lower over the road. Snow-covered wooden farm houses dotted the landscape as the SLS purred through the small towns of Kirzhach and Pokrov, the domes and tiers of orthodox churches poking through the mist, as lazy tractors rolled by. Next were the city of Vladimir and then the patchy farmlands around Suzdal.

As Roger neared the intersection with the M-5 which would snake towards Mount Yamantaw, he commanded: 'Transmit TE Eagle 85', and waited for the fold-down screen on the passenger's side of the windscreen to bring up a picture of Frieda seated in the Learjet.

'*Ja?*'

'It's Roger,' he said as he looked into the rear-view mirror, where the car's webcam was located.

'I know?' Her patience wore thin with him sometimes.

'I'm making good progress. I'll be at the destination in time.'

'I will inform the *Führer*.'

'Transmit out.'

Frieda disappeared from view.

'Audio on,' Roger commanded as he clicked three gears down and gunned the car towards the southern Urals to the thick motifs of Wagner's 'Under the Double Eagle'.

James was jolted to attention by his captain's voice.

'We have begun our descent. We've made good time.' James sat upright and called for Frieda to come over to the back of the plane.

'Have you checked in with Parcival?'
'*Jahwol, mein Führer.*'
'Has he reached Badger yet?'
'He will be checking in with him any time now. Roger called to say that he's on track.'
'Good. Report back to me once you've heard from Parcival.'

13
Helambu
Nepal

A thousand prayer flags fluttered in the wind. Green, blue, dark red, yellow and white pieces of cloth, each representing a Buddhist element, were tied onto a line that was stretched between the bronzed tip of a stupa and a crevice in the side of the mountain. Prayers were pressed in ink onto the pieces of cloth, which were tied onto a line and hung out so that the Buddhist wind horse, *lungta*, would carry the prayers on its wings in the four sacred directions. The stupa was a tiny building with an angular Chinese-style roof, built high up in the mountains for monks to meditate and pray in. In it, the old monk Badger was seated, lotus-style, absorbed in chant.

He visualised two Nazi agents tracking through the mist of the valley below. Tall, blond Westerners in windbreakers, with large packs slung over their shoulders like tourists. Badger knew that they were no sightseers. They were BEAD agents, working for Trevellian. They followed a path that twisted through the valley beside a river gorge, through thick rhododendron forest, up the mountainside towards the hilltop Sherpa village. They didn't carry guns, but Badger knew that their semi-automatics would be hidden in their bags, or beneath their windbreakers. The path exited the thick undergrowth of forest and broke open to a dimming amethyst view of the village in the distance.

A group of children in bright robes surrounded the Nazis as they reached the outer crumbling walls of the village. The children thought that the Nazis were tourists, the lifeblood of Nepal. A child reached out to touch them.

Parcival swung out with a cane and connected with the outstretched hand of the Sherpa boy, smacking it with a crack of wood against bone. The children's smiles vanished in an instant, and they disappeared into the mist to warn their parents about the approaching danger.

By the time the Nazis had reached the protected, cobbled streets, the residents of the stone cottages, with bright light-blue window-sills and orange doors, prayer lines trembling between the gompas and houses, stood outside their homes and held their children close.

Parcival shouted: '*Wo bist du*, Badger?'

The leader of the village, an ancient monk, shuffled forward, pressing on a cane, and smiled at them. It wasn't that he didn't know who they were – he knew exactly, and why they were here – but he had already forgiven them for what they were about to do. He poked his cane up the hill towards the stupa, nodded and said, 'Ba-jer.'

Parcival pushed the old man aside and withdrew a gun. The two Nazis scrambled up the path towards the stupa.

14
Moscow

Anna didn't reply to the whisper. A faint blue light washed in from an adjoining tunnel, barely sketching the outline of a man seated on the cave's floor. He was on his feet in a split second and closed the space between them. He swept Anna up, her legs folded in response around his waist and she bit his lip, more in surprise than out of passion, as he pushed her against the wall and kissed her.

She placed a teasing finger on his lips. 'We have work to do, Fox,' she purred into his ear. Fox placed her down.

'How do you think you would have made it to the southern Urals in time?'

He didn't reply.

'Courtesy of Russia's ghost express.'

'You did a recon mission a few months ago in Moscow.'

'I did, and you won't believe what I uncovered. Until now, no other agents aside from me know about this, you're the first. Only those at director level and higher ...'

'I missed you.'

Images of the evening they had spent together around a fire, sharing bottles of wine and memories on a beach in Tel Aviv, suddenly came tumbling back into her mind ... The night had ended at Fox's apartment, and Anna had woken up to regret, whereas Fox awoke to a sense of possession of the intimacy of the night before. It was risky. They both knew that they could lose their jobs over it, if anyone were to find out.

She had been drawn to him, had been lulled by his story of how he had lost his family. As an orphan child herself, his story struck a chord with who she was, and why she was working for Mossad.

That night he had been different. He opened up to Anna a side that she hadn't known existed, a tender side that showed that deep down he did hurt the way others did, the way she did. But the morning after, she saw the glaze return to his eyes like film that blotted out colour; the glaze of a killer who had stopped feeling a long time ago. He was too far in, mired too deep in hatred.

Fox had made her realise that she wasn't perfect either. She thought that she could fix the world, the Mossad psychologist had told her, but she needed to fix herself first.

Anna dug in her backpack to produce a headlamp and handed it to Fox. He pulled it on and stood in the darkness, trying to search out her features. He didn't need to see her to know how gorgeous she was. He imagined the wispy brown hair touching the front of her shoulders when she was naked, the long brown legs that folded neatly into the abrupt curves of her perfect ... there was no other way to say it, he told himself ... her *perfect* ass, perfect in size, shape ... completed by her handle-grip hips, and then leading upwards, her pert breasts and wide hazel eyes that flitted everywhere.

'You know the way from here?' Fox asked. Anna wondered if there was a hint of tenderness lingering in his voice; she couldn't tell.

'Follow me.'

She slung the backpack on and took off. They entered a concrete tunnel that opened to another, lower square-shaped tunnel. The walls vibrated strangely.

'Cars,' said Anna, answering Fox's unasked question.

The tunnel snaked right and cascaded down several steps. Bricks lay strewn about in the water, thin gas pipes lined the roof. The passageway broke open into a massive hole about thirty metres wide, an elevator at the edge of it disappearing to a bottomless pit. Climbing down a ladder that lined the wall of the elevator's shaft, they slipped quickly down several levels, and at the bottom they slid off the ladder and through a door into a wider tunnel. Small red and blue lights on the walls cast a peculiar glow, as if they'd entered a futuristic *Bladerunner* world, Anna thought. Passing a turbine on their left, they came to a big iron door and Anna produced a key, unlocked it and gave it a push. It slid open with a creak and they slipped through.

'Turn off your headlamp,' Anna whispered. 'Russian soldiers nearby …'

Fox squeezed her arm in recognition and turned off the light. They had entered an underground nuclear hideout bunker, 'designed to house four thousand of Moscow's top people in the event of nuclear attack,' Anna whispered as they slid quietly along the edge, Anna feeling her way with her hand until she felt a kink in the wall: another door. She produced a key and turned it in the lock.

'Got the keys from Vadim Mikhailov, a Moscow underground explorer. Didn't come cheap either. He's been looking for Ivan the Terrible's secret library for years.'

'Did he ever find it?'

'No, but I think I found something arguably more interesting.'

'What?'

'A military secret. You'll see.'

A yellow wedge of light grew as the door creaked open. They slipped through, Anna closed the door and locked it. The square tunnel beyond was well lit, with thick pipes running overhead, sloping downwards towards an elevator at the far end. As they glided along the tunnel, voices boomed from down the passage.

'Soldiers!' Anna grabbed Fox by the arm and pulled him into a room leading off the corridor, dark, and filled with metal shelves containing all sorts of tools with barrels on the floor. The voices grew louder.

Fox and Anna crouched in a corner, waiting in silence. The lights suddenly came on, and Fox peered through a gap between the wooden crates behind which they hid, to make out two soldiers in military uniform.

'What do we do?' Fox whispered.

'Wait.'

One of the soldiers began to laugh at a joke the other had made. He leaned down to pick up some threads of wire and a soldering gun. There was a hissing sound. He clutched at his neck, blood spilling from a dart that stuck into it. He looked at his friend in bewilderment and horror then his eyes turned upwards as he slumped to the floor. Another hiss followed, and the other soldier crumpled to the floor.

Anna lowered a dart shooter and put it back into her inside coat pocket. Discreet and handy, like her Beretta, it was one of Anna's favourite weapons. She stood up, moved across the floor to where the men lay, and flipped the light switch. Fox followed her. She began to undress one of the men.

'That was some plan,' Fox said.

Anna shrugged. 'Should keep them quiet for a few hours, at least. Better than killing.'

She removed an identification card from the man's top pocket and angled it to catch the light of the adjoining tunnel before handing it to Fox. It said 'Sergey Baranov'.

'Here. Replace the ID picture.'

Fox worked quickly on the ID card with his knife. It opened easily. He placed his own ID-sized photo over Sergey's, produced a small tube of glue and stuck the card together again, then dressed quickly in Sergey's clothes.

Anna searched around the room for a hiding place for the comatose soldiers. She found a cupboard door to one side and opened it to reveal a set of shelves, at least a metre deep to the wall and mostly empty. Together, they heaved and dragged the two men across the floor, manoeuvring them into the space before closing the door and sliding three barrels in front of it.

'Now, at the other end of that corridor is an elevator. Take it down to minus seven. There's a train platform down there. The train will take you to Yamantaw. Go east, of course, not west. It only runs in two directions down there, and there's scant signage. Not exactly commuter-friendly. You'll have to find your way to the surface from there, but look out for an emergency exit sign on the platform at the other end.'

'Is the train what I think it is?' Fox stared at her.

'Yes, the Metro 2.'

Fox's eyebrows creased. 'I thought that was folklore in military circles? And "crazy" circles?'

'Think again.'

'Thanks for the help ...'

Fox leaned in and kissed Anna, stroked her cheek, then turned and walked towards the tunnel.

15
Beloreck Airport
Southern Urals

The Learjet took a graceful final turn and touched down smoothly. Its matte black coat was shimmering, and the cabin windows glowed amber, catching the last rays of the sun as it turned and made straight for the control tower. It made for a thrilling sight to the military controllers, who pointed and whispered as it taxied down the runway towards them. The pilot, the son of a Second Word War *Luftwaffe* ace, brought the Learjet 85 to a stop beside the terminal buildings.

The door was opened and the fold-out staircase unfurled. James paused on the top step. The countryside of the southern Urals was covered with a blanket of snow, with a wall of mountains in the distance. Mount Yamantaw towered in the middle.

James was spurred into motion by the icy wind that stung through his coat. He pulled a woollen cap over his head and walked down the steps followed closely by Patrick, who issued short breaths to test the freezing air, convinced of the coldness by the long jets of fog that resulted.

'I've never been in a place this cold,' grunted Patrick. 'Wouldn't want to live here.' He rubbed his hands together and tensed and shrugged his shoulders.

'Let's hope Roger has done the trip in record time,' said James. 'We can all freeze our balls off together.'

The two men made their way through a crumbly old terminal into the parking lot. The SLS was parked in a far corner. They hurried over and got in. Roger grunted in greeting, fired the engine to life and turned the car through the exit of the airport towards Mount Yamantaw.

16
Metro 2
Moscow

The lights overhead buzzed with an electric hum. Fox pulled the military cap down over his ears and rounded the corner of the supplies room without looking back.

His crude Russian might come in handy, he thought as he read a huge blue sign hanging on the wall that announced in Cyrillic, 'Elevator', with an arrow that pointed to the other end of the tunnel. A door appeared a short way ahead with a sign hanging over the entrance: 'Control Room 12'. Fox looked inside. Facing away from the door, a woman sat behind a computer talking into a phone. An easy mark, thought Fox.

A light flickered nervously beside the iron gate of the elevator. As he rung it up, it clanked and chugged until it was high enough for him to enter into the steel cage. He put his hands on the grate to bring it down, but someone grabbed his hand.

'*Tovarishch*,' the soldier said.

Fox's heart stopped, then started again as his crude Russian kicked in, deciphering the word: 'Comrade.'

'*Tovarishch*,' he replied as he forced himself to melt out of a stiff, suspicious posture. He issued a curt smile and a nod and removed his hand from the gate, stepping back to allow the soldier to push his cart into the elevator. The soldier looked at Fox as he pressed minus seven and the elevator began to move down. The light flickered and went out. Fox could feel the soldier's stare in the dark, but thankfully he remained quiet. Finally the elevator ground to a halt at the seventh level beneath the city. Fox pulled at the gate and rung it up. He motioned for the soldier to proceed first with a civil smile. The man grinned and said, '*Spasibo*,' before shoving at the cart to put it in motion.

The sight of the secret train platform was majestic. Double rows of archways towered on either side of a smooth reflective marble floor, stretching some thirty metres to a white wall at the far end. Soldiers milled about, smoking cigarettes. Sentries stood ready with semi-automatic rifles.

A swishing noise made Fox look to his left. A shiny metallic grey train snaked into the station and pulled up at the platform. It looked more modern than regular Metro trains, more like the *Shinkasen* trains of Japan than the clumsy-looking square Metro trains of Moscow. The platform buzzed to life. It swarmed with soldiers pushing trolleys and heaving items through massive side doors onto the train. Fox grabbed a nearby trolley that had military hardware stacked on it and hurriedly pushed it towards the train. He unloaded its contents and followed the other soldiers into a forward cargo compartment on board.

The cogs of time ground to a halt. Anna stood in the darkness of the supplies room and smiled. Fox would lead her to the man who could give her the answers, but now she would have to find camouflage: a female soldier whose uniform she could borrow.

As she waited for Fox to put some distance between them, the seconds turned into minutes and Anna slipped away into memory.

The man flitted beneath a moonlit sky. Past the green onion domes of a late sixteenth-century orthodox church. Over an iron bridge that crossed a river into a small town, its lights dancing like fireflies through the mist. He tracked a path in the snow that wound beside a river, past the church and into the small town's streets lined with streetlamps.

Rounding a corner that led to a gravel road, he paused and searched out the house, a medium-size wooden one with attic windows that peered out onto the road and a post box that bore a dangling number 7.

In the house in an upstairs bedroom, two-year old Anna lay watching the moon-tipped shadows of the moving branches dance on the ceiling: elephants that morphed into unicorns, knights, princesses and fire-breathing dragons.

A loud screeching noise came as the front door was prized open with a crowbar. The man was inside; eyes ablaze, bearing a long knife, wet with congealed blood.

He crept up the stairs and into the room where Anna's father lay ... A long scar on the side of the man's face glowed in the milky light as he lifted the knife and brought the glinting blade down ...

Anna pulled herself together. Every time she saw Fox, she thought about his past, which led her, invariably, to think about her own. She wondered if the man in the dream was who she thought he was. It was a strange feeling, to think that she was edging closer to the one person who could lead her to her mother and father's killer.

The coast was clear. Slinking from the shadows of the supplies room, she slipped along the side of the wall to the edge of the door with the sign 'Control Room 12'. Anna's eyes hardened with determination. Through the doorway she could hear someone speaking.

She peered into the room. A lone young brunette woman of medium build sat facing away from her, talking into a phone. She waited for the right moment. Finally, the business-like words signalled the end of the conversation: '*Spasibo, do svidaniya.*'

Something cold and hard was pressed into the Russian soldier's skull. The woman instinctively raised her arms. Anna instructed her to get up, carefully, and to keep her eyes and her mouth shut. As the woman rose, Anna kept the gun pressed to her head, and a guiding hand on her shoulder. She instructed the woman to walk to the door, close it, lock it and give Anna the keys behind her back, all the while not looking at her. Next, she told her to get undressed. The woman slipped out of her clothes quietly. Anna, keeping the gun trained on her, rummaged in the desk drawers. She found what she was looking for, thick masking tape. First she twisted the woman's arms behind her back and applied several rounds of tape to bind her wrists. Then she told the woman to sit down on the floor and pulled one of her discarded socks around her head, taping it tight over her eyes. She also taped over the woman's mouth and bound her ankles with tape.

It took Anna a few minutes to put on the woman's uniform – grey flannel pants, shirt and a long grey coat with gold buttons and woollen collar.

Finally, she pulled on the cap and slipped on a pair of black gloves, then fumbled in the coat pockets to produce the card that revealed her new identity: Alina Luzkhova, Military Transport Inspector. Anna worked quickly to insert her own photo into the card, and then, leaving the woman lying on the floor, unlocked and opened the door, stepped out and locked it, and walked to the elevator. She pressed the button and rung the gate up.

She prayed that no one would know Alina Luzkhova, or at least that she wouldn't bump into anyone who did.

A grey train, full of soldiers was vibrating in the tunnel when she stepped out onto the platform. Anna slipped into a back compartment.

Fox clutched the railing overhead as the train began to move. At first slowly and then electrifyingly fast, the bullet hurtled through the underground maze, finally evening out with a consistent hum as they headed eastwards towards the Urals.

17
Mossad HQ
Tel Aviv

Ben pored over the file on his desk, a thick black Lever Arch that told the bitter story of an agent's life, an unauthorised biography of a woman who didn't wish to share her true background. Anna had successfully bluffed Mossad about her past, no mean feat, seeing that Mossad's HR department was particularly efficient when checking the background credentials of new recruits. The file had been commissioned, over and above what the agency knew about Anna, by Ben.

Something was turning in his mind. He knew that if the chief of Mossad were to find out about the operation before it could be completed successfully, he'd be in trouble. It was too quickly organised, too risky by Mossad standards. Now the file … it would come in handy.

There was a knock, and his secretary poked her head around the door. She was a mousey woman, with dark rings under her eyes, who lived alone with five cats and a parrot.

'The trackers have been activated, sir,' she said, as Ben looked up. 'Anna is moving at a consistent distance from Fox, heading in the same direction.'

'Heading in a straight line?'

'Yes, sir.'

'So they're on the train. Good. Thank you,' said Ben.

He got up and was about to make his way to the operations room.

'There's something else ...' said the secretary, still standing in the doorway.

'What?'

'*Memune* and his deputy know about the whole operation.' *Memune* was the name given to the Director General of Mossad.

'How?' Ben swallowed to hide his panic.

She shrugged. 'They know everything. They have scheduled a meeting in a few hours, sir.'

Now the file will definitely come in handy, thought Ben as he pushed through his office door.

18
Helambu
Nepal

Ruby-red blood oozed through teeth clenched into a smile, fringing a cracked lower lip, and trickled down like a burgundy river over the chin, turning into an elastic mucous string as it settled, finally, onto Badger's lap.

'You think this is a joke?' Parcival screamed in German.

'No.' Badger laughed.

'Then why the hell are you laughing?'

The Nazi picked up an empty wine bottle, smashed its bottom against the desk and held the sharp broken tip to Badger's neck. 'If I cut just here ...' he pressed the edge against the artery, 'I can put you to sleep. Do you want to go to sleep, you little traitor *bastard*? Or should we kill your Jew brother instead?'

They were in Badger's house beside a waterfall. The Nazis had moved him there from the hilltop stupa where they had first found him.

There was a desk, a chair, a thin mattress, brightly-coloured paintings and wall papers, and a stone hearth in the middle of the room. On the desk was a pile of tattered old books and a candle holder with a box of matches beside it. There were piles of scattered papers on the desk, Badger's notes.

Parcival and his accomplice stood behind Badger, prodding him, pushing him, with a gun stuck into his ribs; slapping the back of his head and laughing.

'This doesn't matter,' Badger said, spitting blood. 'Nothing matters. I've told you everything you need to know. The *dietrich* is at the monastery on Anzer Island. I have fulfilled my debt now, I have paid my dues. Now fulfil your end of the bargain, release me, either to freedom, or to death, and let my brother be.'

Parcival spat in Badger's eyes. 'You *swine*! You are a traitor. You abandoned the *Vaderland* for this hole where you've been grovelling, hiding away from your true Nazi origin. You think that by being a monk, you can become a better person? You think that by me killing you, that you can escape your maker, and your conscience? You better have told me everything there is to know, or else many people here in this stinking little village will die, if not tonight, some other night of the week. I'll cut them all down like flies. Or perhaps, we'll have some fun with them first.' The man looked over to his companion, who was smiling perversely.

'There is nothing more. There are my notes. Take them.'

'Have you been talking to anyone?'

'No.'

'I don't believe you.'

Parcival leaned forward. He brought the point of his elbow into Badger's cheekbone, just beneath his eye and the world faded out.

19
Southern Urals

The SLS pressed through the countryside, around hills, through forests, beside a stream caked with white, frozen over, until the road edged past the shadow of Mount Yamantaw. Eight kilometres north of the mountain, in the thick of a forest, Roger eased the car off the road and wound between the tree trunks until he brought it to a stop about a hundred metres from the tree line. As the three men got out of the car, a deer scuttled into the thicket.

'I hope you've done your homework.' James leaned down to tighten his boot laces. Roger pulled out a camouflage net from the trunk and, with Patrick's help, rolled it over the car. Three bags filled with hard currency were produced, two slung around Roger's shoulders, one slipped on Patrick's back.

'*Jahwol, Mein Führer*, we have done our homework,' Roger finally answered.

'Run us through the plan.'

Roger, both hands on his hips in the way of a boxer or an athlete, emitted short jabs of fog from his mouth.

'We hike five kilometres until we reach the coordinates. There, we will wait for Vladimir's men to meet us. They will give us twelve canisters to carry, of which each of us will carry four, and we will give them the money and then leave the area undetected.'

'Good. I don't want a repeat of Shamrock Bar.'

'Of course not,' said Roger. 'We located a small hill that overlooks the pond. From there, we will be able to watch out for the men and make sure that there are no hidden surprises.'

'Better not be. Keep on your toes, both of you. You never know who might be lurking in these woods, watching us as we speak.'

'We will,' said Roger. 'Although I doubt that they will have followed us all this way. I can't see how they would have made it so far in such a short space of time, or even how they would know where to look. But then, you never know with these Jews.'

The three Nazis crept through the fog-laden woods like wraiths, Roger at point, James in the middle and Patrick behind.

Darkness descended and the night twitched in thickets, the tree branches and a wolf's howl carried on the wind. An angry orange moon peered at them over mountain crests as the woods broke open to a valley lined by a frozen stream, with wooded slopes rising on either side.

They climbed a hill and, at the top, entered an overhang. Roger and Patrick pulled their backpacks off. Roger removed a pair of night-vision optics and handed them to James. Aside from the 'pond' there was little else to look at in the plain below: a few foxes, deer, appearing through the heat-sensitive night optics as small grey blobs.

20
Mossad HQ
Tel Aviv

Three suits sat impatiently behind a steel table. Steven, as he had always done, avoided their eyes, so that thick moist lips, noses, finely-cut suits with shiny ties and pocket-kerchiefs became the focus of his nervous stare while his hands, in front of him on the desk, tapped out a nervous beat.

'Well, where the hell is he?' *Memune* asked.

'Any minute now,' was Steven's reply, which he'd said several times in the last few minutes.

'Damn well better be,' growled *Memune*. He picked at a gold tooth, a glimmer dancing on his cufflink which shone under the bright electric humming light of the meeting room. To his left sat the Deputy Director General of Mossad, with a thick dark beard and a yarmulke. It was no secret he was the *Memune*'s dogsbody and puppet. He belonged to God, but as the head of Israel's religious council that decided on matters of state security, he held his own in these matters.

There was a screen behind Steven, showing an image of Anna. The image was beamed onto it by a projector hanging from the roof, connected to a laptop placed behind a podium. *Memune* had ordered the image to be put up so that there was absolutely no mistaking, as soon as Ben entered the room, what the meeting was going to be about.

Memune had earned himself the nickname 'Bulldog' with more than twenty years' experience in the field, as a *katsa*, and later, as a member of the *kidon*. Once he had reached the age of forty, with an illustrious career as one of the Institute's best agents, he became a strategist, working in Ben's current position as Director of Operations, before the Prime Minister had suggested that he was the ideal man to take over the reins of Mossad. Times were getting tougher by the hour, the PM had told him, 'It's time I have someone I can really count on, someone with balls.'

Bulldog could proudly claim to be the mastermind behind several of Mossad's most notable operations in the last few years, including operations against several of Iran's top nuclear scientists; the infiltration of Iran's Nanatz nuclear plant with the Israeli-made Stuxnet computer virus; and reaching further back in time, involvement in the capture of Adolf Eichmann in the 1960s, as well as involvement in the assassination of the leader of the Black September group, Ali Hassan Salameh, the 'Red Prince', who had masterminded the September 1972 killing of eleven Israeli Olympians.

The temperature in the room had become decidedly hot for Steven, who twiddled his thumbs, beads of sweat collecting on his brow while a crimson rash rode high on his cheeks. Steven adjusted his tie, then loosened it, hoping subconsciously to release some of the scalding heat. Finally, the door opened, and Ben strolled in, a file clutched beneath his arm.

'Need I remind you,' burst out the Deputy Director, 'that you are on probation after the last indiscretion?' Spittle rained and his eyes smouldered as he directed a piercing gaze at the man who had strolled into the room sipping aromatic coffee from a polystyrene cup.

'I'm late. I'm sorry.' Ben shrugged, placing his coffee on the table and pulling out a chair to sit down. 'Right, fine gentlemen, what can we do for you this morning?'

Ben knew that the one virtue that Bulldog liked most in his employees was brazen self-assurance, and if he was to survive this grilling, and escape with his job, this was the way to do it – cocksure.

Bulldog growled. 'This operation involving Agent A and Fox ...' He looked from one man to the other, Steven still avoiding eye-contact, Ben staring full into Bulldog's eyes. 'Whose idea was it?'

'Mine, sir.'

There was an awkward silence. Bulldog settled into his chair, crossed his ankle over his knee, withdrew a cigar and lit it. He inhaled a short puff and blew out. Then he said, 'Brilliant.'

Both Steven and Ben looked perplexed. Bulldog continued, 'I like it ... the way both agents aren't aware of the entire picture in this case, it works well,' he said, his head cocked to the side as he looked straight at Ben.

'However,' anger lurked now, 'due to insufficient planning, we might have a problem, no?' He was staring straight at Ben. 'A major one. And you may need to be held responsible for our agents' deaths, if they don't make it out of this operation alive. I have been told that the kidnap attempt in Moscow has failed. Correct me if I'm wrong, but here's how this operation is being executed … Fox is sent in to capture Trevellian, the most dangerous Nazi in the world …'

Ben was silent.

'Right?' prodded Bulldog.

'Yes, sir.'

'Then, Agent A is sent in after him, to "defeat" Fox and recapture Trevellian, to prove to him that really, she's a Nazi at heart, and that she wants to work for him?'

'Correct.'

'Now … Fox was meant to capture the target from a pub in Shamrock Bar. But we know that the attempt failed.'

'Yes.'

'So now, they are all making their merry way across Russia to the southern Urals, Fox and Agent A travelling by the Metro 2?'

'Yes, sir.'

'And when they get to the middle of nowhere in the southern Urals, following some random coordinates from Badger, Fox will somehow achieve the kidnapping single-handedly, and Agent A will then attack him and rescue the hostage?'

'That's right, sir.'

'Okay soldier, so I have the basics right; now it's time to ask you a few questions.'

'Yes, sir.'

'Shut up,' barked Bulldog, 'that wasn't a question.'

Ben smiled, a brazen attempt to win over *Memune*, but the older man ignored him and poked his cigar into an ashtray on the table.

'Now, one thing I have learnt in my many years here at the Office, is that agents need more than orders, more than money, and more than the promise of comfort, to get them to risk their lives for the Institute. What makes you so sure that these two agents of ours, both of whom are relatively inexperienced, are happy to gamble away their lives for you in such a *badly* organised operation?'

'Sir, may I present some facts?' asked Ben, rising to his feet.

'You may, if it will save your job, and your life, soldier,' said Bulldog, smiling.

Ben got up and walked over to the screen behind Steven. He said, 'I have prepared some files for your viewing. They all relate to Agent A, as you know her. We'll call her Anna, and Anna has a lot of secrets.'

He operated the laptop behind the podium, closed the image of Anna, inserted a flashdisk into the USB port and opened a file that was stored on it. Anna's face reappeared, this time beside listed information: *Female, thirty-four years of age; Hair colour, dark brunette; Eye colour, hazel ...*

'This is a glorified agent personnel file, sir. But it contains even more background information than the usual files, down to Agent A's favourite movie, whether she prefers dogs to cats, her taste in men, what kind of underwear she likes, even what kinds of personal items she keeps in her bedroom drawers,' said Ben, admiring the picture.

'I hope that my exposé of Anna's true past will not get HR into trouble for failing to uncover the real facts behind this mystery agent.'

'Get on with it,' said Bulldog.

'Right.' Ben started to pace. 'As you may know, Agent A graduated top of the class from The Academy, sir, with all of her instructors, myself included, duly impressed by her ability to act. She takes on new identities and constructs covers out of almost anything. In short, gentlemen, give this woman half a leaf, and she'll convince you she's a tree.'

Beginning to get into his stride, Ben walked over to the desk and took a sip of coffee.

'And as you may *also* know,' Ben continued, walking over to the window and looking out over the city, facing away from his audience, 'Agent A passed her psychological evaluations with only a note in the margin from the psychologist to say that she suffers from a mild depression, nothing serious. What we have been fed by her, about her past, is that she, being eligible for immigration, obtained *Alliyah* into Eretz Israel, and that she came from a small town in Russia called Novgorod. There are no formal records of this, sir. She left when she was eighteen. That is all we have on her, and we have believed her, relying on trust, I suppose? Until now.'

Ben returned to the screen and scrolled down the document.

'I commissioned a look into her past – her *true* past, not the lie that she fed to us while being recruited. Agents assisted me with obtaining information, and what I am about to tell you will give you some idea as to why this woman is such an asset in this case, and why such a hastily-thrown together plan might actually work.'

Bulldog shifted in his chair, the red nib of his cigar glowed faintly. He said, 'Good, you'd better be confident. This is an *ain efes* operation, an absolutely no-miss operation. You know,' he added, 'you remind me of the "oy-oy" bird.'

Ben looked puzzled.

'The one that has such huge balls, but a very small brain. Every time this stupid comes in to land, it says "oy-oy", or "ouch-ouch" as it hits its balls on the tree branch. Now you need to show me, soldier, that you can land without saying "oy-oy".'

21
Metro 2

The train wound down to stop beside a second platform. Anna slipped out, adjusted her woollen cap and followed the throng. They were moving towards an entranceway. Above it was inscribed 'Mount Yamantaw'. Two sentries, one on each side of the entrance, checked IDs.

Anna raised herself on tiptoes to peer over the crowd, searching for Fox. It was difficult to make out his figure, but she thought she saw him slipping out of the river of soldiers and exiting through a door with an exit sign.

Anna followed. The door opened to a dark vertical tunnel with a ladder leading up to ground level. She squashed herself into a corner and listened, hearing the faint sound of boots on metal, then peered upwards. It looked like Fox was almost at the top.

Suddenly light poked into the tunnel from above, accompanied by the sound of a hatch creaking open. Anna shielded her eyes as she peered up, and tried to push herself as far against the wall as possible.

Fox seemed to take his time. There must have been something wrong there, or *someone*, thought Anna. Eventually, the trapdoor closed and the light disappeared. She slipped off her shoes, tied the laces together, slung them around her neck and began climbing.

22
Mossad HQ
Tel Aviv

Ben pulled up a satellite image. On it were two dots. One was red, the other blue. There was a third graphic, a yellow star.

'The red dot represents agent Fox, the blue represents Anna and the star is the location of the deal between Trevellian and the FSB men. My task now is to convince you why this will all work out.

'As you can see by the image, our operatives are about four kilometres from the target, which means I have about half an hour, give or take, to convince you why I can land without hurting my balls.' Bulldog didn't smile.

'Right, let's get on,' said Ben, clearing his throat, firing up another cigarette and taking a short pull before placing it in an ashtray and walking back to the podium. He scrolled through the pages of Anna's file until he came to a picture of a handsome-looking middle-aged man with a beard and long dark hair.

'Ludvig Leonov. Father of Anna Leonova. Found murdered with multiple knife wounds in his chest in Novgorod, Russia, two weeks after the body of Skule Leonova, Anna's mother, was found trumped up like a ragdoll in a flowerbed beside a river in Buenos Aires with three bullet holes in the back of her head. Three shots to the head are *indulgent*. Only the Mob does that, and domestic murderers. It has vendetta written all over it.'

Bulldog placed a thoughtful finger over his lips.

'Why in Argentina?' Ben asked rhetorically. 'I don't need to remind you where the "Desk Murderer", Eichmann, was found. So, was Skule's murder the work of an ex-Nazi?' Ben looked from one face to another. 'We need look into her *real* past for the answer.

'Who was her mother, her grandmother, her grandfather? Agent A's story begins in Novgorod, one of the oldest towns in Russia. While World War II was raging and the Germans were making alarming strides across the eastern front, the *Wehrmacht* crossed the Volkhov River and rolled into Novgorod on 17 August 1941. They occupied it.

'*SS Standartenführer* Colonel Franz Wagener was tasked with rounding up the Jews in the town. A young officer of only twenty-seven, he had already developed a formidable reputation as a ruthless *SS Mann*.'

Ben paused to take a sip of the cold coffee on the table, placed his arms behind his back and faced away from his audience.

'One day in 1942, while inspecting a group of people rounded up as suspected Jews, Franz Wagener laid eyes on the most beautiful woman he had ever seen, twenty-eight-year-old Sazje Leonova. He demanded to see her papers, and discovered that she was Russian Orthodox, not Jewish. What he didn't know at the time, however, was that the Russian secret service, the NKVD, had recruited her for her looks, ability to speak German and her quick mind. She was in fact, a Jew. Franz commanded that Sazje be set to work at the local Saint Sophia's Cathedral, spared from certain death in a labour camp.

'In the following months, Franz would visit Sazje often, bringing her extra rations of food and talking to her. It was clear that he was infatuated. Finally, he had her brought in to his offices on the town square. As an NKVD recruit, she was of course interested in getting information on German troop movements in the area. So, she allowed herself to become involved with him and the two began having an affair. Just as Sazje fell pregnant, Franz got an urgent call from Berlin to go on a special mission which would take a few months, touring the concentration camps.

'Sazje gave birth to a baby girl in mid-1943. She named the child "Skule", which means "hide" in Scandinavian. She gave her to a local family to care for until after the war, and they kept Skule hidden in their basement.

'When Franz returned to Novgorod in September 1943, he received an anonymous letter saying that Sazje was a Jew.

'In a fit of rage, he went to the cathedral and pulled Sazje out by her hair. Before he could shoot her, she produced a blade concealed in her clothes, and struck his face, leaving a large scar along his cheek. He then pumped several rounds of bullets into Sazje's head, in full view of a group of people, and he shouted, "One less bloody Jew to bother us!" or something to that effect.'

'How did you get all this information?' Bulldog asked.

'It was recorded by a local man named Ragnor who lived in Novgorod. Ragnor wrote a war-time diary in shorthand, using several different languages to ensure its secrecy. He survived the war. My men uncovered his diary in Russia.'

'What happened to the child?'

'Franz never found the baby. By that stage, the Red Army was advancing on Novgorod. In January 1944, Franz left the town, having been promoted to *SS Gruppenführer*, Lieutenant General. He vanished without a trace after the war.'

The two blips on the screen behind Ben continued snaking eastwards, closer together now.

'So Skule survived the war ...'

'Yes. She grew up in Novgorod, working with the local Red Cross to help to rebuild the community. She met and married Ludvig Leonov and had a daughter, our very own Anna Leonova. Ragnor recalls in his diary that many years after the war he received a visit from Skule, who came asking questions about her mother and father. Ragnor told Skule everything that he knew, allowing her to read his diary. Of course, she discovered the fact that her father was a Nazi general who had murdered her mother, and that this monster, Franz Wagener, had escaped Germany after the war without being brought to trial. Ragnor told Skule that he believed Franz to be one of several Nazis who were setting up post-war operations in Argentina and other South American countries, although he didn't say why he thought so.

'And this, gentlemen,' completed Ben, 'is what led Skule to Argentina. Not so much in search of her father, but more in search of the man who had murdered her mother.

'Anna is in Russia, as we speak, for the very same reason. She is hunting for her grandfather, but again, more importantly she is trying to find the man who murdered her grandmother *and* her mother.'

'But how can you send her in then after Trevellian to "get to know him" ...' the deputy director asked, '... if technically they are related? Half brother and sister, is it?'

'They aren't related at all.'

'How do you know?'

'I have it on good authority.'

'Does Anna know this?'

'Yes, I told her.'

The cigarette in the ashtray had burned to the butt and the blue and the red dots merged on screen.

23
Southern Urals

A fox edged into view at the base of a tree. It sniffed the air, muzzled the ground and pawed at the snow. A Russian soldier in a hillside bunker protecting an emergency exit to the Metro 2 raised his rifle towards the fox, pointing it through a slit overlooking the plain. Through the crosshairs, the soldier saw the fox bury its snout in the snow and nudge at a hole. It dug and sniffed, paused and listened, waiting for its prey to make its move. It took a few steps to the left, tracing the tunnel of the hare or gopher, and then paused again. It began digging.

Heavy metal blasted through the ear buds of the soldier's iPod, his only escape from a mindless twelve-hour shift, along with observing wildlife through the scope of the Dragunov sniper rifle. A few metres to the side of the hidden bunker there was a hatchway that he was meant to be watching. The snow creased at the hatchway. If the soldier had been doing his job, he might have seen the two glints that were observing him from beneath the lid.

Fox immediately noticed the faintly unnatural slope of the bunker's 'roof'. He also saw the barrel of a rifle poking out, a silencer affixed to its end. He had been expecting some kind of sentry watching over the exit, and he was glad to have spotted him undetected. He made out the figure of a soldier behind the rifle, staring through the scope. He slipped out, and wriggled on his belly, snake-like, to the edge of the bunker.

The soldier hummed an off-beat accompaniment before pausing to see the fox collect itself to pounce. He tensed as he watched the fox leap into the air and before it landed, he felt the crushing blow to the side of his head and saw the black and multi-coloured spots that danced on his vision before he blacked out.

Fox worked quickly. He heaved at the bunker's roof and it swung up on its hinges. Snow cascaded down either side as he pulled it up. He slipped into the two-by-two; pushing the soldier aside and pulling the bunker's roof down to let it rest on the catch.

He looked around: the soldier's iPod lay on the rough-hewn shelf of earth and rock in front of him. Track information streamed across the iPod's screen: 'Evisceration Plague' by Cannibal Corpse. The bunker seemed to be lined with some kind of cloth. Thermal netting, very clever, thought Fox. The thin net disguised the man's thermal imprint so that those with binoculars or scopes with thermal optics wouldn't see him.

One ear bud had been jolted out of the soldier's ear and lay on his chest, his head smeared with blood. In front of the soldier and beneath the slit was a rock-shelf table. A half-eaten chocolate bar lay beside a shift register, with the latest entry: 'Date, 15h00 – 21h00: Mikhail'. Poor bastard would have gotten off his shift in a couple of hours, thought Fox.

Fox quickly removed his uniform to replace it with Mikhail's, a flight suit, custom-made to completely disguise the soldier in the snow. A wind raked the east-facing slope and bit into Fox's exposed skin. He quickly pulled on the uniform, slightly too small for him, and leaned over the man to pry the sniper's rifle from his hand, already cold and clenched shut. It was a standard-issue 7.62 gas-operated rotating bolt.

Fox admired it for a second and was pleased to see that it didn't have the usual scope, but a custom-fitted one with night-optics. The silencer fitted to the end of the barrel would mean a loss of power and accuracy over range, but it would definitely be useful in not giving his position away.

Neatly tucked into a big pocket on the inside of Mikhail's coat were a few rounds of bullets. Fox scrutinised them, happy to discover that they were a heavier variant: 178-grain boat tail hollow tip, meaning less sway, greater accuracy, heavier impact.

He poised the rifle through the slit in the bunker and looked through the zoom. His eye danced over the plains, running alongside rocky crags hidden in the snow and trees that poked branches through the mist. A Norwegian elm, English oak and pine forest lined a river twisting beside and around a hill. Fox checked his GPS, and saw that he would have to follow the river.

He drew the rifle in and pushed the roof open. He slid out and dropped the roof onto its catch, reaching a hand inside to manoeuvre the catch of the roof out of its hold. Not a trace of the hidden bunker was visible as it closed shut. Slinging the Dragunov over his shoulder, Fox crouched and entered the mist, wraith-like as he stalked through the trees and made his way down towards the river. He was close now. He grimaced.

The moon rode low over the mountain tips, washing the plains in silver. James and his men lay in silence, nursing their bodies against the cold. James flicked the night-vision optics up and scanned. Without warning, engines roared.

'Scramblers,' said Roger.

Two lights moved over the countryside. James made out the outlines of the men who rode the bikes in his night-optics. 'They're about three kilometres away,' James estimated. 'Stay on high alert.' He lowered the binoculars and watched the lights slip closer.

Roger and Patrick nodded, almost in unison.

James spoke into his coat collar. 'Frieda, come in.'

'Here.'

'Vladimir's men are almost at the location. Any news?'

James imagined her pacing up and down in the Learjet's communications centre.

'Yes, a message from Parcival. The first task has been completed. He has sent a set of coordinates for a monastery located on Anzer Island in the White Sea, north of Russia.'

'Good job. Did he get Badger's notes?'

'Yes.'

'Get a helicopter on standby. Roger and I will fly to Anzer Island as soon as we're back in Moscow. Patrick will see the ingredients arrive safely in Argentina.'

'I'm on it.'

'Oh, and one more thing.'

'Yes?'

'Arrange some Russian orthodox monks' robes for us. Better make one extra large.' James smiled at Roger.

'Consider it done,' Frieda said. 'Parcival also asked me to pass on a clue that he'd read in Badger's notes regarding the *dietrich*. May I read it?'

'Go ahead.'

'"To the east of the Great Temple, the key is buried at the foot."'

'Is that it?'

'Also something about a monk who lives in a wooden cottage. I'll fill you in on the details.'

'What on earth does the clue mean? See if you can dig anything up.'

'All right, thank you.'

The sound of the motorbikes grew louder, and then cut out abruptly. James raised the binoculars again and saw two men about two hundred metres away.

'Patrick, scout ahead.' Patrick rose from his crouched position and slunk off into the trees in the direction of the bikes. 'Roger, cover.' They followed Patrick at a distance of thirty metres. James reached behind his coat and pulled out his Walther PPK. They inched forward until they reached the limbs of gargantuan pine trees at the tree line of the forest, twenty metres from Vladimir's men.

Patrick signalled the all-clear. James leaned back and poked his head out to take a look. Vladimir's men spoke loudly. One was smoking a cigarette. A sniper could easily have plucked the man off, even without a night-optics scope, thought James, Vladimir had sent bloody amateurs.

James whistled three times, each one short and sharp. The men stopped talking.

'Who's there?'

James repeated the whistles and after a pause, Vladimir's men replied with three whistles of their own. James walked out of the edge of the wood towards them.

He pushed the Walther into its holster. Roger and Patrick followed. When they were within three metres of Vladimir's men, James motioned for Roger to toss the bags of cash to him.

'Quantity?' James asked.

'It's all there,' said one of the men in English in a thick accent, pointing to the cans that were tied to the back of the bikes.

'*Betrag?*' A tall lanky man countered, staring blankly at James. His use of German seemed a deliberate taunt.

'Ten million in euros. Cold hard cash, as agreed.'

James held the bag beside him.

'You first.'

The tall man motioned with a clumsy wave of his hand towards the cans. He said, 'You can look, but don't touch. It's all there.'

'You don't trust us?' Roger laughed.

'Don't tempt me,' the tall man said, raising his gun.

'Relax.' James threw the bags of money over to him, landing at his feet. The man took out a torch and sat on his bike. He proceeded to count the money.

'What, *here*? Are you serious?'

'I need to make sure it's all there.'

James watched as the man painstakingly counted the bundles. He cursed Vladimir for sending these two morons.

'Patrick, do a sweep of the area.'

Patrick disappeared into the woods.

24
Helambu
Nepal

Badger was alive, but only barely. He lay in a pool of blood on the rock floor of his cave, unconscious. A woman smeared healing balm over his eye, wrapped his head carefully in gauze and bandages, and took him to her home down in the valley.

25
Southern Urals

Fox paused at the edge of the wood, breathing out starlit jets of fog, and pulled out his phone. He had two kilometres to cover in fifteen minutes. He'd make it in a paltry eight, if he tried, but bracken would crunch loudly underfoot and noise would precede him in the night. He was a fast runner and this fact, coupled with his cunning, had earning him the nickname 'Fox', after the desert foxes of the Negev.

Scraggly winter trees nudged through a carpet of fog, and silver streaks of moonlight fell to the forest floor as if filtering in through an attic roof. As Fox slipped through the forest, he thought ahead. A single shot to the head with the hollow tip. A small entry but a big fleshy exit wound. That would do it. All he needed to do was get close enough to have Trevellian in his sights.

A hill loomed, blocking out the view of the path ahead. He flew up the slope, flitting around the boulders. At the top, he took advantage of the view down the other side of the hill to determine his way. A white disk cleared between trees – the pond.

Anna fell in behind him, racing through the forest. It felt, in the woods, as if suddenly her senses had been piqued. She could see further, smell the sharp scent of pine and hear every last of Fox's footfalls, which she tried to sync with her own to minimise her noise. The silence was oppressive as they cut clear into a space on a hilltop.

Craning forward into the maddening silence, Anna pressed close on Fox's tail, at a distance of thirty metres. In the city it would be ten, but out here there were fewer places to hide.

She hid behind a wide tree trunk as Fox topped the hill and waited, as he stood and assessed the path ahead.

Snap.

Gunshot-like, a twig had snapped under her foot. Anna stopped breathing. Fox waited a full two minutes, roving his head around in the dark to see where the sound had come from. A rabbit bolted out of the scrub and scampered off into the night.

Fox took off. Anna waited, peered down the other side of the hill, and watched Fox, a nimble creature, float down. She followed his tell-tale tracks in the snow.

One and a half kilometres passed in this way until Fox disappeared.

26
Mossad HQ
Tel Aviv

The blue dot stopped and the red dot pulled ahead.

'What the hell just happened, you schmuck?'

Eyes descended on Ben. It had been a long day for him and the night would be longer still, especially if it didn't work out as he hoped it would.

A lighter grated, a cigar was puffed, someone coughed and said, 'How's this going to work out then?'

27
Southern Urals

Fox increased his pace, rushing on for a kilometre and a half, until, rudely, twenty metres ahead, the ground gave way to a cliff.

A fallen tree trunk led all the way up to the edge of a cliff face. Fox jumped and clutched a branch, pulling himself up into a tree. Balancing like a trapeze artist, he danced across the branch's length until he lunged for another, in a neighbouring pine, and dropped off onto the fallen tree trunk at its end. This way, his footprints appeared to disappear from the snow.

Staring over the edge of the cliff, Fox counted this as one of those rare times his climbing experience would come in handy. He lowered himself, feet dangling, to catch a foot on a rock hold. He found hand and footholds as he went, feeling his way and using the moonlight.

He dropped off a remaining three-metre jump. Collecting himself, he made full speed towards the edge of a line of trees, close now, so close that he could almost smell a smoking bullet hole in Trevellian's head. As he neared his target, he found a boulder, the perfect sniper's position, and steadied the gun on the top of the rock. He looked through the scope.

'He is to be captured alive, Fox. Under *no* circumstances should he be killed,' Ben's voice on the phone came back to him, but instead of weighing the words, Fox grunted and felt along the smooth scope to flick the night view on: four men, greyish blobs.

Four bullets, within the space of a few seconds, that's the way it has to be.

He put the rifle down; its butt nuzzled into the snow, barrel against boulder, and he scooped up two handfuls of snow, coning them on the rock like ice cream scoops, a trick he'd learned to enable him to guide the shot more easily into the sweet spot. A bag of soil was ideal for this, but he didn't have one.

One of the first things that Fox had learned about sniping was what were to the naked eye only small movements became, in the lens, the grossly exaggerated gestures of giants. A hand moved up to scratch a nose, obscuring the head temporarily, or the whole frame moved down to tie a shoelace, and the entire body disappeared in a split second. The second thing he'd learned was that bullets do not travel in straight lines. They were swayed by wind and air pressure.

He eased his finger against the trigger. There was an owl's hoot. He squeezed.

Anna had lost track of him. Using his footprints as a guide, she rushed blindly, her feet crushing the silken snow, moving lightly but with a heaviness of heart. She stopped as the ground gave way to a steep fall and found herself peering down a cliff face. To one side, the hill descended gradually.

Picking up her pace, she flew down the hill at the easy, but longer side, but forced herself to stop and observe near the bottom. Ahead of her, a dark figure slipped into the woods and moved towards a boulder, huddling behind it.

Anna crouched as she ran to scoop up a rock; everything was a blur. The rifle whipped, spurting fire. 'I'm too late,' she thought, 'he's killed him,' as she brought the rock against Fox's head.

Anna fell to her knees and cupped Fox's bloodied head in her hands. She pressed a finger into his throat beside the larynx to check his pulse. She felt the beats tickle her cold-stunned fingertips.

Motorbike engines buzzed. Anna picked up the Dragunov, raised it to her shoulder and looked through the scope. There were two grey blobs, moving fast into the woods. Anna's heart jolted as a third grey outline appeared on the outskirts of the wood to her right, getting bigger, and coming towards her, fast.

Whoever it was had spotted her, probably using night optics. She was faced with a dilemma: run or lie? Would the cover that was 'Alina Luhzkova' hold up? She worked quickly to bury the Dragunov in the snow beside Fox and scooped handfuls of snow on top of his unconscious body. She dug down until she reached soil, and rubbed the brown earth together with snow over her face and into her hair. She unbuttoned her coat, ripped her shirt open and, improvising a limp, began staggering off in the direction she'd seen the two grey blobs moving towards, drawing her pursuer away from Fox, no longer Anna but Alina Luzkhova. She invented a whimper and ran, panicked, into the woods.

Patrick pulled up behind a tree trunk. He looked through his binoculars while snow fell in a dark blue-grey haze around the wood. Two grey blobs, three o'clock. They were the unmistakable thermal imprints made by humans; one was moving towards him, the other was motionless and dimmed. He withdrew a knife and lowered the binoculars.

A few moments later, Patrick looked again. The thermal imprint of the other blob seemed less strong. That could only mean one thing, he thought: a cold body. He decided to double around the advancing target, to sneak up on and ambush it, moving in a wide arc until he came up on the oddly shaped footprints. They were regular, if heavy, but spaced close together, with a drag along the ground: the person is injured, thought Patrick. He moved up within twenty metres and saw that it was a woman. She appeared to be in pain, was limping and crying. He moved up ahead of her and hid behind a tree.

As she rounded the trunk, he struck. He placed his arm around her neck, with one hand quickly and firmly clutched against the other. His grip tightened, the body went limp. He leaned her to the ground and undid her shoelaces, which he used to bind her wrists and ankles. He slung the woman over his shoulder and made his way back to James and Roger.

28
Mossad HQ
Tel Aviv

Ben's confidence was buoyed. He, like everyone else, didn't know what was going on, but both dots had made it to the star. Did it mean that both agents were still alive?

29
Southern Urals

When Anna came around she saw the ground rushing by and realised that she was being carried like a sack of potatoes, surprised by the speed they were going.

'*On iznasiloval menya ... On iznasiloval menya ...*' she whimpered.

Patrick said nothing as he slipped in front of James and Roger.

'Jesus, what's that?' Roger asked.

'What do you mean?' asked Patrick.

'Looks like a yeti.'

Anna repeated: '*On iznasiloval menya.*'

'What's it saying?' asked Roger.

'She's been repeating the same phrase. I think it's Russian?' Patrick breathed hard, looked at James. James looked at the woman. Her clothes were ripped and even in the full wash of the moonlight he couldn't remotely make out the features of her face.

'She was in the woods about a hundred metres from here. She was limping and in this terrible state, crying.'

'*On iznasiloval menya.*'

'Is that Yeti she's speaking?'

'Russian. She's saying "he raped me".' James tried her eyes. They were cold. He leaned closer and reached out to search her pockets. Shrieking, she fell to the ground and kicked out wildly.

'Hold her.'

Patrick and Roger moved to secure her. Patrick held her legs and Roger pinned her shoulders.

'*On iznasiloval menya.*'

'In order to help you, I need you to calm down. Tell us what happened.' James stroked a comma of hair that had fallen aside her face and noticed appreciatively that the gesture seemed to have worked.

The woman looked into his eyes pleadingly.

'*Ya ne govoryu po anglĭski.*'

'She doesn't speak English.'

He faced her. '*Da, skazhite mne, chto sluchilos'.*'

Anna related in panicked short Russian sentences and James translated.

'She works for the army. Earlier she was lured into the woods by a general and he raped her. She killed him afterwards.'

'What if she's lying?' asked Roger.

James searched the eyes again. Patrick suddenly remembered how the other grey outline, the stationary one, he'd seen in the woods had been considerably dimmer when he had looked through the binoculars the second time.

'I think she might be telling the truth. Before I tracked her down, I saw *two* human outlines through the night vision, but when I looked again a second time, one of them was much dimmer. The only reason …'

'Is that it was a corpse,' completed James.

'Do we kill her? What if she saw what went down here?' asked Roger.

'No,' said James. There was something to her, he couldn't say what.

'Do you want us to go and search for the corpse?' asked Roger.

'No, too risky, no time,' said James. 'We can't chance drawing any further attention to ourselves.'

'And this mess, this Yeti,' offered Roger, 'is a publicity fest just waiting to happen.'

'We have to get moving,' James said. 'But untie her hands so that she can go free. My gut tells me to let her go.'

Patrick turned Anna over and cut her wrists loose. Her wildness returned and she shrieked. She flung her body onto James. He tried to throw her off but she held on tight.

'*Pomogite mne.*'

'Help you?'

James threw her off.

'Let's go.'

They left her, kneeling, and made off into the woods.

30
Mossad HQ
Tel Aviv

A yellow dot flared up on the screen as the bug was activated.

'That would be our lead,' said Ben, grinning.

'What's just happened?'

'She planted a bug on him.'

'A bug?'

'Tracker and audio, but with a very limited battery life. Product of the nanotechnology research department.'

'Genius!'

The men had heard every last word of a professional agent bluffing her way out of a tight spot. Ben sat through the whole thing smiling. Bulldog's face erupted in a smirk.

'You can keep your job. Keep listening, interpret any clues ASAP. Move your operation to the control room, you have full use of all the analysts and strategists you need.'

'Thank you, I'm on it.' Ben picked up a phone, dialled and spoke: 'Record all audio, notify me as soon as anything intelligent comes through.' He hung up.

'Before you go, sir,' he said.

Bulldog turned around. 'What?'

'There's more to this story.' Ben searched the deadpan faces.

'What is it? I've had enough surprises for one night.'

'The reason Trevellian is in Russia.'

'We know bloody well why he is in Russia.'

'No sir, the *real* reason.'

31
Mossad HQ
Tel Aviv

'Spit it out.'

Ben lit a cigarette.

'All right. I suppose I'll start with the Nazi belief in the occult.'

'The occult?' Bulldog looked puzzled.

'Dark magic, sir.'

'*Ei*, here we go.' Bulldog raised his eyebrows.

'The Nazi high command held strong beliefs in the occult. Hitler too, and Himmler ... worst of the lot. They basically believed that if they could unlock the mysteries of the occult, it would help them to win the war.

'In fact, some of their theories were pretty silly. *Reichsführer* Himmler in fact, saw his SS as the modern-day reincarnation of the Crusade-era Teutonic Knights. He had his own council of twelve knights, fashioned on Arthur's Knights of the Round Table, and set up the SS spiritual headquarters at a place called Wewelsburg Castle, his very own Camelot. There, in a crypt in the northern tower, Himmler reputedly met with his knights. Some believe that dark ceremonies were performed in the crypt, but there is little evidence. Officially, the castle was to be a special school to train SS youth in Aryan history, ideology and "science".

'The delusions were extensive. Aryans were thought to be descended directly from a race of Nordic supermen, *Jötunns*, who came to earth from another dimension. They settled in the North Atlantic Ocean, and their home was called Atlantis.

'The highest Norse god, Odin, had sent the *Jötunn* there himself, and had also given to earth the runic alphabet. The Nazis of course used the *Sig* rune in the makeup of the SS symbol – the double lightning strike.

'The belief was that the superbeings of Atlantis were wiped out in a flood that sank their continent. A handful of *Jötunn* managed to escape via boat to Asia where they settled.'

Ben picked up his cigarette, evaluated it, and took a long drag before placing it back in the ashtray.

'This belief caused the Nazis to send parties to central Asia, such as the Ernst Schäffer expeditions, to investigate further. The "scientists", if that is what they can be called, measured Tibetans' features in an attempt to find successful comparisons with Germans. They set up a society to investigate Aryan history and pseudo-science. It was called the *Ahnenerbe*, and such was Himmler's passion in these projects that he reputedly spent more money on them than the Allies did in developing the A-bomb.

'The master race theory was a powerful, attractive one to the Nazis. Perhaps it made them, somewhere deep down, feel better about killing so many people. It gave them reason to do so. In any case, it would give the masses reason to feel that the killings were justified.

'Himmler set out to recreate the Aryan master race by breeding tall, blond superwarriors, knights of the new order through his *Lebensborn*, "Fountain of Life", which produced 10 000 "superbabies" between 1935 and 1945. More than 200 000 Polish children with so-called Aryan traits were extracted from Poland and sent to live with *Lebensborn* families in Germany.

'But here's where it gets really interesting. Himmler was obsessed, you see, with finding the Holy Grail. A certain man called Otto Rahn had come to his attention for writing a book called *Crusade Against the Grail*, which posited that Wolfram von Eschenbach's work *Parsifal*, which described a hunt for the grail, contained real clues to the grail's location.

'Legend had it that the thirteenth-century Cathars, demonised by Rome as heretics and later persecuted in their millions, possessed the secrets of the location of the Holy Grail. They supposedly held the grail, or the knowledge to its location, at a castle called Montségur in southern France. As Rome intensified its persecution of the Cathars, a force of Crusade knights was sent to crush the last bastion of Cathar hope at Montségur, which did prove very difficult for the Crusade knights to capture. A 10 000-strong army of Catholic-aligned forces was stationed in the shadow of Mount Pog, unable to ascend the castle walls, laying siege to the Cathars. Before long, the castle fell. But before the Crusade knights had managed to secure the castle, three Cathar knights managed to drop down the steep northern slope of the castle, apparently carrying with them the secret to the location of the grail. Rome succeeded in capturing Montségur, but failed to capture the grail, if indeed that is what they were after.'

'So how does Rahn fit in?'

'The archaeologist had been poking around the caves of southern France around Languedoc, and Himmler was quick to support him financially. Before Rahn knew it, he was recruited into the SS and working full time on the grail puzzle.

'But he turned up empty handed time and again, and fell into disfavour with Himmler. In 1939, he was mysteriously found frozen to death in the Alps. Well, so the history books say. But, here's where Badger comes in. The real story, according to Badger, was that Rahn discovered that Montségur was not the place to go looking for secrets about the location of the grail. He also found out that there were a series of clues and tests that needed to be discovered and solved before the grail could be found. It could take years of research, finding and deciphering secret texts. The place with the next clue was apparently Montserrat Abbey, near Barcelona. Himmler had Rahn killed off, according to official history, to protect this clue, and he made a secret war-time mission to Montserrat Abbey in 1940.

'Apparently, he uncovered a secret text at Montserrat that described how to find the Holy Grail. The text contained riddles in Devanagari, an ancient Nepalese script, as well as in Zhang-Zhung, the language of the pre-Buddhist religion, Bön. It became clear that someone with intimate knowledge of these ancient scripts and of Bön religion would be needed in order to decipher the clues, not an overnight thing. Himmler advised Hitler that they should select a child to be sent to the Himalayas, to learn. So, in 1944, they selected an Aryan child born in 1941, and sent him to be brought up by a family in Nepal.'

'Let me guess,' Bulldog cut in, 'Badger?'

'That's right. In time, he was supposed to solve the riddles of the grail and send his notes to Himmler. But of course history intervened in 1945 when the Germans were defeated.

'In December 1944, a secret meeting was held at Wewelsburg Castle. At that meeting, Himmler set up an inner circle of knights, which he named OSSFOW, *Organisation SS für Operation Wewelsburg*, and asked his knights to undertake an oath or covenant, in which they would swear absolute allegiance to the continued Nazi cause. Franz Wagener was among those knights. At that meeting he was elected, due to his fluency in English, his ruthlessness and his age, to lead up the post-War corporation that would act as a front company for the Nazis' business, later named Trevellian Enterprises.

'They planned to use their smuggled war loot, as well as to blackmail certain people high up in British society who had sympathised with the Nazis before the war, to achieve their cause.

'As the advancing Allies drew in on Berlin, Himmler sent an SS unit on a special mission to Wewelsburg to destroy the castle, especially his safe in the western tower – where Himmler's personal study was located – containing his notes and the secret text he'd uncovered at Montserrat Abbey.

'But the SS men failed to completely destroy the castle, or the safe, before the Allies closed in. A group of Allies actually found the safe and blew it up to access its contents. What happened afterwards is unknown to history. The men mysteriously disappeared, along with the papers.'

'So they just *vanished*?'

'Yes sir. But according to Badger, the men discovered Himmler's notes and fled to pursue the grail themselves. These men were hunted down by Trevellian's BEAD agents after the war and they were eventually tracked to Nepal, and killed. Franz Wagener, the new, secret *Führer* of the Fourth Reich and leader of Trevellian Enterprises, re-established contact with Badger and gave him the notes he'd recovered from the eight Allies soldiers to continue his work. He has been working day and night ever since to solve the riddles.

'Badger called to tell me that he has solved the last of the secrets, and that he thinks that Trevellian's men will visit him soon to extract those secrets from him. He told me that Trevellian is in Russia to secure a *dietrich* – that's German for skeleton key – which will enable him to unlock the grail.'

'And you are expecting us all to act on this information?'

'Well, sir, the surface is thin. Sometimes if you scratch in the right places, you will find some interesting things.'

'One question,' Bulldog said. 'Why would Badger cooperate with the Nazis?'

'They have been blackmailing him, telling him that he had a brother, and if he didn't cooperate, they would kill him.'

'And who is this man, his brother?'

'You're looking at him.'

32
Beloreck Airport
Southern Urals

By the time James and his men made it back to the car, each man was sweating and breathing hard.

With the canisters safely packed into the SLS, they sped off towards Beloreck Airport, where they found the Learjet already on the runway, ready for takeoff.

The canisters were loaded into storage, the engines whined and then the Learjet touched off the ground and rose steadily to 40 000 feet.

33
Mossad HQ
Tel Aviv

Ben had moved to the operations room as soon as Bulldog left the building. His secretary had not called him yet, which meant that they had heard nothing on the tiny microphone that had been planted on James.

The room was busy, with three rows of desks behind which sat analysts before a giant screen that took up a whole wall. The analysts stared up at him, awaiting orders and listening patiently to the up-turned speakers.

There were only '*Ja*'s' and '*Nein*'s', commands, scuffled sounds, a yawn and then the electric sound of takeoff before the excruciating hum and constant whistle of the plane at cruise speed.

Ben stood motionless, his head cocked to one side, a finger pressed over his lips, listening.

'Say something, goddamn it!'

After twenty minutes, he was beginning to lose hope. The tiny tracker and microphone would fuse if it came into contact with water, and its battery life was notoriously short.

Ben cleared. 'I want every background noise analysed. Turn the volume up.'

'It's on max, sir,' said an analyst nearest to him.

'I don't bloody care, get in some more speakers then ... what's that?'
Static crackled. At first faint, then louder, the voice of the *Führer* came over the speakers.

34
40 000 feet
Russia

'Get General Husseini on the line.'
'*Secherlich.*'
James swirled his glass of bourbon as the line began to ring on the speakers inside the cabin. An Arab-accented German man replied: 'Head of Public Relations Department, how may I help you?'
'I would like to speak with the White Horseman.'
'Who's calling?'
'Pale Horseman.'
'Hello James!'
'General Husseini! Listen, I read that the green movement is making good progress in the revolts against your enemy.'
'Indeed, James. We are on the brink of revolution.'
'As indeed we are on the brink of launching our naval war machine.'
'I commend you and your people on a magnificent achievement.'
'General, please join us at the launch ceremony in Bandar Abbas.'
'Of course, it will be an honour.'
'Good, I look forward to seeing you.'

35
Mossad HQ
Tel Aviv

'A *marats*! Get me a German-speaker who can interpret this!'
'If I may, sir.' A young, beautiful analyst stared up at Ben, her jet-black hair flowing beside piercing green eyes. She didn't wait for Ben to give her permission. 'I speak German.'

'Good, get me a transcript from the recordings. What's your name?'

'Lucy, sir.'

'Thanks, Lucy, I'll be in my office.'

What did the reference to horsemen mean? Thought Ben as he walked down the short corridor. Most likely just a random code-name. Why was Trevellian speaking to General Mubarak Husseini? Ben closed the door of his office and began to pace the length of the room. He looked out of the window. He shrugged, debating with himself. Was this about an arms deal? And what were they launching at Bandar Abbas, the Iranian port city in the Strait of Hormuz?

He opened the laptop on his desk and connected to Mossad's internal network. He opened a programme that monitored active tracking devices, and watched the Eagle soar over Russia towards Moscow. He listened to the static; no more words were being said, so he turned the volume down. He picked up his phone and dialled his secretary.

'Yes, sir?'

'How far is my medical team in Russia?'

'Agent A and Fox already exfiltrated, sir. They're on their way to us as we speak.'

'Right,' said Ben, relieved. 'Seal off an entire ward at Hadassah Medical Centre. Fox must have proper treatment. How is he?'

'Concussion, sir, fortunately no haemorrhaging or fractures. He should be fine in a few days.'

'That's what I like to hear.' Ben hung up. There was a knock at the door.

'Come in.'

Lucy's face poked around the door, 'Sir,' a curtain of hair fell about her face, 'I have some bad news.'

'What?'

'The Eagle's line has gone cold, the trace has been lost.'

Ben swore under his breath. He looked at the laptop. It confirmed what Lucy had said with 'No active trackers' displayed across it.

'Okay, listen, I have a feeling that the launch, whatever it is, in Bandar Abbas, will be attended by some of the other Nazis, particularly the British lords, descendants of those who had sympathised with the Nazis during the Second World War. Do you know about them?'

'Yes, sir.'

'Good. There's a man in particular I'd like you to check out for me, Lord Clive Codwell. Fetch me his file, along with printouts of all of the latest COMINT, HUMANT and ELINT intelligence intercepted on him.'

'If I may ask, sir, why Codwell?'

'Because we managed to hack his emails.'

'On it.' The door clicked shut.

36
Moscow

When James, his two bodyguards and Frieda arrived back at the Trevellian Enterprises offices in Moscow, a man was waiting for them. The pilot, in full black mercenary gear, stood in the middle of James's office, his feet planted apart and his hands held together behind his back.

'The Dark Horse's engines are running, *mein Führer*, ready to take you to Anzer Island.'

37
Mossad HQ
Tel Aviv

Ben leaned forward and sat on the edge of his seat. The Codwell file was black, indicating that it was top-secret. It had no identification and was immensely thick. Lucy sat behind his desk, silent.

Ben flipped the file open and his eyes danced over the pages, his pulse quickening. The file on Codwell, a retired car manufacturer and the son of a man who had sympathised with the Nazis during the war, might contain some scrap or clue about whatever was being 'launched' at Bandar Abbas.

Ben flicked through the file's pages and stopped at a heading: 'Intercepted messages', the work of a hacker who lurked in an obscure chamber in the bowels of the building. The first batch of intercepts was transcribed phone calls, totalling some one hundred and fifty pages. Everything from Codwell's intimate conversations with old acquaintances, to where and when he should dump his stocks, according to his broker.

The second batch contained intercepted or 'hacked' emails. This was the work of one of the agency's most underutilised agents, thought Ben, a hacker known as 'Cracksafe'. Although Ben didn't understand all of it, he knew that a malicious program called a Trojan Horse had been implanted on Codwell's computer by Cracksafe. The 'virus' had installed a key logger, which recorded all of the keys tapped on Codwell's keyboard, and then it installed a screen-logging programme, which took pictures of the computer's screen each time the mouse was clicked or the enter button was pressed. This way, they had snatched the password to Codwell's personal email account, the contents of which Ben was currently reading.

The information had already been processed by junior analysts at Nuclear Desk, and their hand-written scrawls appeared in the margins. Flags indicated how the information had been categorised. 'Noted' meant that nothing had happened with the information. 'Flagged' meant it had been passed on to senior analysts, while 'Crossed', the rarest type of information, meant that the entire email had been deleted from the inbox before the recipient could read it, and was in quarantine for twenty-four hours while intelligence case officers at Nuclear Desk read it for possible usefulness. Emails with times and dates in the contents especially were quarantined. When this happened, a delayed delivery notification was issued back to the sender, and the team had a strict twenty-four hours to work on the information before the email would have to be placed back in the inbox as unread.

Ben's finger stopped halfway down the third page: 'Crossed'.

It was from a restaurant named 'Bahnbistro' in Bandar Abbas. This was it, thought Ben. The email was in German.

'Translate.' Ben pushed the file over to Lucy. He tapped his finger at the place on the page.

'Dear valued customer,' read Lucy, 'We are celebrating the birthdays of twelve of our newest patrons. To thank you for your patronage we are inviting you to join us for an evening of speeches followed by fine wine and dinner. 20h00 for 20h15. Dress: black tie. The evening will be at zero cost to you. RSVP by return, indicating "Yes" or "No" and any special requirements.

'The address of the sender is "info@bahnbistro.de",' said Lucy after she had finished.

'It has a time and date stamp,' said Ben. 'Quarantined twenty-two hours ago.'

'That gives us two hours.'

38
Anzer Island
Russia

Two orthodox monks shuffled along a track through the woods towards a hilltop monastery. They spoke quietly in German.

'The scout reported that the monastery has next to no security. I wouldn't be surprised if the old monks haven't even heard of gunpowder.'

'*Mein Führer*, with all due respect, I'll only believe that when I see it.'

'In that case, Roger, make sure the safety catch on your machine gun is off.'

'What's that sound?'

Hooves clopped on the gravel road ahead. A cart driven by an orthodox monk came into view. As it passed, Roger waved at him on impulse.

'What the hell are you doing?' James asked under his breath.

'Being friendly to the locals,' Roger answered.

The man hadn't waved back, regarded them with suspicion and flicked the reins, clicking at the horse as he disappeared down the road.

The path climbed to the top of a hill surrounded by woods, a view of the sea stretching out to the horizon, at its dawning edge, a fracture of light. A path in the snow led from the gravel road to a baroque monastery with three black onion domes and white walls. James and Roger scrambled up the path. James pulled off towards a wooden house, surrounded on all sides by scaffolding.

'This is where the monk lives,' James whispered as they neared the front door. He tried it. 'It's locked. We'll have to find another way in.'

They rounded the building. Just above the planks of the first level of scaffolding was a push-up window, left slightly open. Roger crawled onto the scaffolding, opened the window and slipped inside. His face appeared through the curtains a few seconds later.

'All clear.' Roger motioned for James to enter.

James climbed up and slipped inside. They were in a library with floor-to-ceiling bookshelves and old wooden tables with inkpots and typewriters. At the far end of the room was a stairway. James and Roger made their way to the stairs, carefully climbed it and turned right at the top into a narrow passageway. At the end of the corridor, a door stood ajar.

The sound of snoring came from within the room. Roger poked his head around to take a look. He turned back to James.

'Fast asleep.'

'Let's go.'

Roger took a bottle of chloroform and a cloth from a pocket in his robe. He unscrewed the bottle and dabbed the liquid chloroform onto the cloth. James motioned for him to hurry. He put away the bottle and crept to the edge of the bed. In it was an old man.

With James behind him, Roger leaned forward, aiming to grab the back of the monk's head with his left hand and smother his mouth with the chloroform in his right. Too late, he realised the snoring had stopped. The duvet flew up, and the rapport of a gunshot cracked off the walls as the monk sprang out of the bed wielding a .22-calibre Berretta. He went straight at James.

James brought his left fist up against the monk's right arm to ward off the next gunshot, which ripped into the wall behind them. He struck the monk in his neck with a punch. The man reeled backwards into Roger, clutching at his throat and spluttering.

Roger grabbed the monk's right arm, which still held the gun, extended it outwards, held tightly at the base of the shoulder and brought the elbow in sharply. There was a crack as the arm broke. The gun clattered to the floor and the monk crumpled in a heap of sobs.

Monastery bells began to ring. Roger looked out the window.

'Shit, monks with machine guns headed our way!'

Roger kneeled to grab the old monk's head in his hand, gripping tightly against the sparse line of white hair.

'Where is the key? Speak now and we'll let you live.'

The monk merely sobbed.

'Where is it? Where is the key?'

He reached for his semi-automatic and placed the butt of the weapon against the monk's head.

'If you want to live,' he hissed, 'you will tell us now!'

The monk cowered. He pressed his head into the wall and muttered, 'I can't tell you, I am sworn to an oath protecting the *dietrich*, even at the cost of my own life.'

There was a noise from the scaffolding outside. A plump monk appeared at the window, crouching. He threw his arm into the room and a spurt of bullets rippled into the bed. James and Roger ducked.

Crouching, Roger moved closer to the window. He waited for the right moment and opened fire. The hollow-tip bullets threw the man off the scaffolding.

James leaned down towards the monk, speaking to himself.

'To the east of the Great Temple, the key is buried at the foot.' He stared into the monk's eyes. 'Is this monastery the Great Temple?'

'He's not going to talk,' said Roger.

The monk groaned and shook his head.

'*Mein Führer,*' urged Roger, 'there are at least thirty Bible bashers with guns outside just itching to spray us with lead! We need to act quickly.'

'That's it!' exclaimed James, 'the Great Temple!'

'What?' asked Roger.

'The Great Temple is the human body. The body is the temple for the soul. To the east of the temple, that means the left-hand side, is buried the key at the foot, which means this man's foot …'

James pulled out the monk's left leg and slipped his bed sock off. He felt around the ankle.

'Here it is!' shouted James. 'Feel here …'

Roger felt the bump in the skin between the Achilles tendon and the bone of the ankle.

'There's definitely something there,' he said, standing up. 'And it's not bone. Must have been sewn into the skin somehow. We'll have to get it out.'

James nodded. 'We need to find a knife …'

James got up and began searching the room. Roger looked doubtful. It would take too long to cut the key out of the foot. He had a better idea. There was an axe lying outside on the scaffolding. He went to the window, stuck his arm through the opening and stretched out as far as he could, until his fingers touched the axe handle.

James turned and saw Roger, too late, in front of the monk with the axe raised above his head. A crashing sound came from downstairs as monks tore into the house.

The axe came down with a thump, cutting the monk's foot off clean above the ankle. Blood pooled on the floor. The old man howled and passed out from the pain.

Clutching the severed foot, Roger rushed to the window and climbed out onto the scaffolding, gun first, followed by James.

'They've left the outside exposed, they all rushed into the house through the front.'

They slipped off the scaffolding and landed on the ground, sprinting as fast as they could for the tree line of the woods. A hail of bullets splintered into the bark of the trees around them as they disappeared into the woods. They were only one kilometre from the clearing where the helicopter was waiting.

Roger pressed his finger into his ear and said, '*Kapitan*, start her up, we've got company.'

As they ran, James shouted, 'What the hell did you do that for?'

39
Mossad HQ
Tel Aviv

'How much time do we have left?'

Lucy looked up at Ben across a sea of papers on his desk.

'Half an hour, sir.'

'Keep going.'

They sifted through wads of ELINT (electronic intelligence), COMINT (communication intelligence), and HUMANT (human-gathered intelligence) records on Lord Codwell. So far, their searches had revealed nothing of interest to connect Bandar Abbas, Trevellian, General Mubarak Husseini and the 'launch' they had spoken about.

'Sir,' said Lucy meekly. Ben looked up and issued a growl in response.

'If I may ... when last were you home? You look tired.'

Ben nodded. 'Monday.' He shuffled papers, tapped his pencil on the table and searched the system archives. Lucy noticed that his collar was starting to brown. He was slouching, tired looking, his head cradled in one hand.

'So Iran Desk has nothing for us?' asked Ben, desperately for the second time.

'Nothing, sir – no mentions in any ELINT or COMINT of the meeting, and nothing relating to the fake restaurant's name. I've even had David, you know ...'

'The code breaker ...'

'The one who cracked the German cable from Istanbul last year. I asked him to take a look at this earlier. All he said was "Nada".'

'Lucy ...' Ben didn't look up as he spoke. 'Do me a favour.'

'What is it, sir?'

'Don't call me sir, call me Ben.'

'Yes, sir –' said Lucy before she could stop herself, '– I mean Ben. What's the favour?'

'That was it,' said Ben.

Lucy was blushing. The moment passed and several minutes of silence settled between them as they continued searching. Ben's shout almost sent Lucy out of her chair.

'I knew it!'

'What? What is it?'

'The phone numbers at the bottom of the email.'

Ben slid the page over to her. He had written what appeared to be coordinates beside the phone numbers of the restaurant's email sign-off.

Lucy stared at the coordinates Ben had written: 27°8'54" N and 56°12'18" E, and then looked back at the phone numbers.

'But how ...?'

'Look closely at the numbers. Especially the zeros and the ones.'

'Some of the ones look different. They look more like the letter I, and the zeros look like capital Os.'

'Precisely,' said Ben. 'They stand for "minutes" and "seconds" used in coordinates. The plus at the beginning of the number indicates a positive direction away from the equator, meaning north, and the plus in front of the second number indicates an eastward movement away from the Greenwich Meridian.'

'Ah, I see now,' said Lucy. 'And the zeros stand for "degrees".'

'That's it!'

'Where do they point?'

Ben was already typing. He tapped the 'Enter' key and leaned back, his hands behind his head. 'Bandar Abbas Iranian Naval Base,' he said, grinning.

'A stroke of genius,' said Lucy, 'the Iranian military's nerve centre.'

'This is good. Now that we know where it is, we need to find out a way to get an agent in there …'

The solution hit Lucy as she looked over the desk. 'It's staring right at us, sir,' she said.

'What is?'

'*She* is,' said Lucy, pointing at the up-turned picture of a beautiful blonde woman, Liz Codwell, daughter of Lord Codwell who, Ben had gleaned from the file, was currently in Tibet on a 'spiritual retreat'. Although blonde, Liz Codwell bore a striking resemblance to Anna, though Anna's brown eyes were wider, more beautiful, thought Ben. Liz had been in Tibet for a few years already, so the cover was ideal as no one would claim to have an intimate knowledge of her appearance aside from Clive Codwell.

'The resemblance is remarkable! Get Cracksafe to draft a fake reply from Codwell saying he regrets that he can't make the celebrations but that his daughter will be attending instead. The message needs to be coded, so work with that old dog David to draw something up. The emails can now be permanently deleted from Codwell's machine, including the invite and the new sent message, of course. I also want all the info you can get me on Liz.'

'Right away, sir,' said Lucy. She turned to leave but Ben stopped her.

'And Lucy …'

'Yes sir?'

'Call me Ben, pretty please?'

Lucy turned scarlet.

40
Moscow

This time it was a Trevellian Enterprises-employed doctor who was waiting for James to return in the Moscow office.

'Glad you could make it at such short notice, *herr dokter*,' said James.

'Only an honour, for you, *mein Führer*,' said the small man with an eccentric shock of white hair.

James handed the doctor a bag with a grimace.

'It's in there. We went to quite some lengths to secure it, and Roger took some initiative of his own to do so.'

James glared at Roger who averted his eyes. 'There was no other ...'

The doctor gasped when he opened the bag. He took a moment to collect himself. 'As far as I understand it ... you would like me to extract a *key* from the human foot?'

'Yes, *herr dokter*, a very valuable artefact, I believe.'

'Certainly, *mein Führer*, to hear your command is to obey you. I will need a scalpel and a clean working surface, if I may. I didn't have a chance to collect my tools.'

'I'm afraid we have neither,' said James, 'but there's a pair of scissors in Frieda's drawer and a bathroom through that door.'

Five minutes later, the doctor stood before James's desk, his white gloves bloodied, breathing like a man who'd committed a despicable act, brandishing a long ancient-looking golden key. It had four blades that spun off at right angles, in the way of old keys used to open the intricate mechanisms of treasure chests.

'It is rather heavy, *mein Führer*. I would even venture a guess ... given its colour and weight,' he turned it around to catch the light. 'That it is made of solid gold.'

'There you would be correct,' said James, taking the key from the doctor and placing it in a small satchel which he hung around his neck.

Frieda entered and showed the doctor out.

It didn't take long for James to fall asleep, his head resting on his desk, exhausted from the long adventure in Russia. He would wake up to the sound of an alarm clock, a blanket draped around his shoulders, and a note from Frieda: the time his plane was to take off to Bandar Abbas.

41
Burj al Arab
Dubai

Anna closed her eyes as the popping bubbles tickled her skin. It was a rare treat, a luxurious bath. She couldn't recall when last she'd had one. She knew that she should be trying to enjoy it more. But her mind worked overtime as she reprogrammed herself as the blonde Englishwoman, Liz Codwell.

Anna tried on Liz's accent: 'My daddy is Lord Clive Codwell. Yes, that's right, the ex-car manufacturer, one of Trevellian's most generous benefactors. He's supported the cause since before the War. Huge fan of Adolf, of course.'

Freshly returned from Russia, Anna had barely set foot in her homeland before she'd been whisked away by private chartered airplane to Dubai, and given a new identity. The time she had to try on the new persona was dangerously short. It was far from ideal, and Mossad would never have operated under such conditions were the situation not so desperate. Still, it annoyed Anna.

'Hi, I'm Liz. Liz Codwell ... Yes, that's right, Lord Clive Codwell of CC Motors. Yes, well, I've also heard so much about *you*, *herr Führer*. No it's not *herr*, it's *mein, mein Führer*,' she corrected.

The Panorama Suite of the Burj al Arab was immaculate. The hotel was, if the brochure was to be believed, the world's only seven-star hotel. The Panorama Suite had two floors. On the lower level, a gigantic living area sprawled out towards floor-to-ceiling windows that eyed the Arabian Gulf, a tan strip of beach clinging to an azure sea.

Lucy, a Mossad analyst, had really done her homework. Not only was a thick file on Liz Codwell provided to Anna, but also audio and video files of Liz Codwell.

She got out of the tub and dried herself with a heated towel. She stood in front of the mirror and pulled her dyed-blonde hair to one side, dabbing at it. She allowed her eyes to dance over her body, imagining how someone else might see it if they were looking at her for the first time.

Her breasts were modest, but shapely, perking up to small brown tips. Spindly brown legs stalked to neat round buttocks and silky cheeks. She hadn't known whether to shave *there* or not. It had been a very long time since she had been with someone, and the question had provoked her into thinking about what the job would entail. But in the end, she'd decided that she should.

Anna slipped into a bathrobe and made her way down a spiral staircase to the lower level. The sun was setting over the Gulf. Sailing ships and ocean liners docked close to the shore. Anna sat at a breakfast nook table beside the enormous windows and poured out a cup of aromatic Turkish coffee. The phone rang.

'Hello?'

'Hi Anna.'

'Dr D, is that you?'

'Yes, Anna, just checking in. A "hello, how are you" really.'

Dr D was a Mossad psychologist.

'Did Ben put you up to calling?'

'Well, I would be lying if I said no. But I was thinking about you, if that's any consolation. My favourite agent.'

'Ah, but I know you say that to them all. Associate F told me you say the same things to him.'

Dr D laughed. 'Okay, you've got me. This is a full time job. So how are you?'

'May I talk specifics?'

'Yes, the line is secure.'

'Well ...'

Anna opened a briefcase beside the table as she talked, pulled out a file and placed it on the table in front of her. Across its front was written, 'James Trevellian, Russia, Priority'. She began to flick through the pages.

'It was pretty short.'

'Badly planned?'

'Terrible.'

'Was it a success, in your opinion?'

'We failed in one way, but succeeded in others.'

'In what ways?'

'Well, first contact, for one. Plus, a major one: he's still alive, wasn't assassinated by F. And, of course, if we hadn't gone, I wouldn't be here in Dubai waiting to fraternise with Nazis at their "launch" across the strait in a few hours.'

'How do you feel about going in?'

Anna's pulse quickened as she looked at a picture of James on the next page.

'Mixed. I've being asked to do anything necessary.'

'And you're worried about what that might entail?'

'Yes. How are you supposed to feel when your country indirectly asks you to sleep with your arch enemy?'

'A difficult question that, if you don't mind, I'll let you answer for yourself, as I've never been in a situation like this and can only imagine. All I can say is: don't do anything that you really don't want to do, and don't get in too deep. You always get in too deep, Anna.'

'Trust me, I won't.'

'Good. Listen, I have to go. I'm glad to hear you're okay, and Anna, I look forward to having breakfast with you when you get back.'

'Thanks doc, take care.'

Anna hung up and sipped her coffee. She flipped the pages to look at James, a mixture of paparazzi-style photos taken of him as he, she presumed, left or arrived at meetings with clients; warlords and military top brass. As she stared at the pictures, she felt betrayal stirring in her groin. Anna folded one leg over another, and stared at the rugged features, thick black hair and the still-muscular frame. What was it about him? Her mind raced to the woods. Why had he not killed her then? She was a witness. If anyone had to ask 'Alina Luhzkova' if she'd seen three men in the woods carrying canisters, and if she really was the Russian soldier she was then pretending to be, she could easily have blown the lid on him.

Because he had saved her, she realised, there was something to him. Now, as she stared into a blow-up picture of his face, she could see a flicker of … what? What could she see in them? Was it compassion? Or perhaps, Anna thought, she was projecting. A tingling sensation arose between her thighs and, as she felt her cheeks warming, she couldn't escape the unmistakeable moistness, sickening betrayal.

'What would Dr D say? Ah,' Anna said to herself, 'She would say that the reason my body is betraying me is that Trevellian represents the biggest challenge I could ever sink my teeth into. She would say that I like fixing people, and he's the biggest mess I've encountered in my life. She would say, be mindful of your own desires. *Don't get in too deep.*'

Regaling herself, Anna snapped the file shut, rose quickly, carried the file to the electric fireplace and threw it in the grate, turned the knob and watched evil blue flames spring to life and devour the pages, nibbling at the red-coal edges. Orange flames took over to finish the job.

Wiping her hands on the bathrobe, Anna turned and ascended the stairs to the bathroom and bed level. She left the bathrobe in a puddle of creased silk on the floor as she slipped into a crushed velvet dress, the kind Liz Codwell would wear, and fastened the hook of a white pearl necklace behind her neck. Next were the diamond earrings, make-up applied more carefully than usual; stark black lines around her eyes to create a nostalgic 60s look. She dabbed perfume on her wrists, and behind her ears, styled her hair to create a curling wave of blonde above her right eye. Liz Codwell had quite a retro feel, Anna thought, as she rushed over to the bed, slipped vintage black Louis Vuitton shoes on, before shuffling down the stairs into the hallway, catching a departing glance at herself in the mirror as she leaned down to smooth out a crease in a shoe strap. A strange, *gorgeous* woman stared back at her. The sight momentarily caught her off guard before she pressed out her dress, left the room and made her way to the heliport where she would meet a Mossad agent who would fly her across the Strait of Hormuz and land in Bandar Abbas, near the naval base. A Rolls would take her the rest of the way.

42
Hangar Q
Bandar Abbas Naval Base

In a charcoal-grey suit with a slim black tie, the company symbol on his jacket pocket and a red, white and black armband with a swastika around his left arm, James stepped out of a Mercedes-Benz onto a red carpet.

He walked towards the twenty-storey hangar. Two guards, squashed into tuxedos, with semi-automatic machine guns slung over their shoulders, stood guard at an entrance. They made the '*heil*' salute.

'*Aben, mein Führer*,' one guard said, stepping forward. 'They are waiting for you.' He opened the door and moved aside for James to step into the hangar.

As James entered, a deafening roar arose from a crowd of black-overalled Trevellian Enterprises engineers and workers in hardhats, and white-capped *kriegsmanne*, naval officers. There was a platform in their midst, with a podium adorned with the Nazi emblem. Red swastika banners streamed down the sides of the walls. On the side of the hangar's wall, about ten metres up, was a balcony for the VIPs. A group of men and women chattered excitedly. There were about thirty seats, all taken up. James could scarcely see the faces, but he made out a few of his *kameraden*.

James hadn't prepared a speech, but he knew exactly what he was going to say. It had after all been drummed into him over forty-eight years. The crowd parted to let him through. The air was electric with excitement as he swept up the stairs, waving to the crowd, unsmiling. Silence descended on the hall and, as suddenly as he had entered to a massive roar, a pin-drop could be heard as a sea of upturned faces looked expectantly at him.

He turned to look at the black-overalled workers with admiration. They were the men and women who had left their homes to work and live here. Menace crept into James's eyes as he began his verbal tirade, which rose from a low growl to a vibrating crescendo: '*Unseire weid word kommin*! Our time is coming!' His fist was raised. The expectant crowd erupted in cheers, and then quietened.

'While our enemy sleeps, we have been very busy.' Scanning the faces again, his voice bristling with excitement, James continued. 'We have been busy building the greatest naval war machine known to mankind. We have been building an elite force of superwarriors, the likes of which the world has never seen before.' Heads nodded, some swayed as if in a trance; others remained resolute.

'As you well know, each of the nuclear-powered submarines that we have here makes less noise than a baby dolphin. These silent hunter-killers can technically stay underwater for twenty-five years. They are capable of manufacturing their own oxygen and drinking water, and the radar system is so sensitive that it can pick up an enemy ship's movement more than 5 000 kilometres away. A new age is upon us, and it is Aryan persistence, it is Aryan strength, and it is Aryan ingenuity that has carried us this far. No other nation or people could accomplish such an incredible feat in such a short space of time. Finally, here are submarines that can compete with the Royal Navy's Avante-class, and we have far more than they could ever have dreamed of having.'

James's knuckles turned white as he clutched the podium and shouted his sign-off: *'Sieg Heil!'* and the crowd responded with *'Sieg Heil!'* and erupted into frenzy.

43
Helambu
Nepal

An assembly of golden Buddhas smiled down at Badger when he awoke. He found himself in the bed of a beautiful woman, in a stone and thatch elfin cottage tipped on the edge of a wall of mountains.

His eyes stung, his vision was blurry. His head was split with pain and it took him a while to recognise the bright million-colour *thangkas* – embroidered silk artworks the woman was so good at creating – and the Buddha statues of Lhama's house.

Gentle hands moved over his scalp, massaging, healing, and a wet sponge was dabbed on his forehead. What hurt most of all was his eye, the one he had been hit beneath. He was grateful for the scent of sweet apples, freshly picked from the river gorge, and the smell of incense.

He looked up into a set of emerald eyes. Lhama, meaning 'goddess', was the only other half-Westerner in the hilltop community. His mouth felt shut against the immense pressure that weighed down on his jawbone. No words came out, only a stifled croak. A bowl was tipped to his lips, and he took the fiery liquid in, *raksi*, a local brandy made of wheat.

'Shhh, rest now. Be at peace.'

Badger tried to lean forward, but stopped short in agonising pain. He managed to open his mouth wide enough to whisper through his clenched teeth: 'Come closer.' Lhama leaned in, her ear just above Badger's mouth to listen to his muted instruction.

She hesitated for a moment, in half a mind to tell Badger to shut up and go back to sleep, but rose instead, took a pencil and notepad from the desk and leaned over his mouth to listen and take notes.

She tore the page she'd scribbled on out of the notebook and walked to the door. She paused to see Badger lapse into sleep once more, took her sheepskin coat off the rack, put it on and stepped out of the stone cottage into the rhododendron forest.

She stood for a while, reading the note aloud to herself, trying to decide if Badger's injuries had damaged him mentally. 'Phone Ben. Very important. Tell him cakes are being baked in the eyes of salt.' She stopped short of reading the phone number, which had an international dialling code she didn't recognise and which Badger had recited from memory, and hid the note in a pocket.

44
Mossad HQ
Tel Aviv

'The cakes are being baked in the eyes of salt? What on earth does "eyes of salt" mean?

'Just the fact that Badger got someone else to call makes me know that Trevellian's men must have paid him a visit. Why couldn't he call himself?'

Ben was crumpled over the desk, stooping into misery. Lucy stared at him. As Ben mulled over the words "eyes of salt", it hit him.

'Ojos del Salado!'

'What?' Lucy regarded him with a puzzled expression.

'"Eyes of Salt" in Spanish, the second-highest peak in Argentina.'

'A mountain?'

'Yes, look it up, and search the tour operators in the area, perhaps we can find some clues.'

'Here's one ...' Lucy looked up. 'Enterprises Expeditions. Their homepage is in German. They organise climbing parties up the mountain.'

'And I wouldn't be at all surprised if it's a front company for the Nazis.'

'Well, just because they speak German, or at least have their website in German, that doesn't mean …'

'How many other tour operators in the region?' Ben interrupted.

'Not many. All their websites are in Spanish.'

'Good, that sounds a little more promising then, at least. How is Fox?'

'Just woke up, sir. The doctor tells me he should be ready for visitors in a few days.'

'Good. But that's too long. Call the doctor on duty and tell him I'm on my way.'

'But he's just woken up …'

'Do it. And book him on a flight to the nearest international airport to Ojos del Salado, wherever that is, and arrange the necessary transport – bus or car or *sayan* or whatever – to get there. I have the perfect cover for him. He'll travel with a top-class Turkish passport. As far as everyone's concerned, he's a wealthy businessman called Younan Sahin. Get him booked on a climbing party with Enterprises Expeditions. He's going in to sniff around for clues.'

'But sir, he's only just woken up.'

'He's tougher than you think.'

Part II

1
Hasaddah Medical Centre
Tel Aviv

Light seeped in through Fox's eyelids, temporarily blinding him after a week of lying in a private medical facility bed. Dull pain throbbed behind his eyes. The concussion made him feel drunk, then extremely tired, and disorientated.

The room was brightly lit. Rays streamed in from a large window overlooking the sea. A breeze floated in through it. Obscure shapes finally began to take on familiar outlines: furniture, domestic objects such as a kettle, a jug of water and a television, paintings on the far wall.

Fox reached out with his hand, feeling along the cold sheets. His fingers played around beneath the pillow, where his gun would usually be, but there was nothing. He pulled up and looked around. It was a plush bed, with a crinkly duvet and voluptuous pillows, like those in a guest house room perhaps.

He rubbed his eyes as they adjusted to the light. Out, beyond the window, the ocean was visible. Then he recognised the smell drifting on the breeze: salty, inviting, reminiscent of childhood holidays, but also of that dark day. He must have been several storeys up in some kind of building. A hotel?

No, a prison? Was he being kept by someone here so that they could interrogate him? An age-old interrogation trick was to begin gently. Promise the subject freedom. Promise the subject everything. Then grind him.

The events of Russia came flooding back to him with a jolt. Was Trevellian dead?

Sleep was coming back, and coming fast. A familiar voice hovered above his head – Ben from Nuclear Desk?

Fox awoke several hours later in a sweat. This time, opening his eyes was easier, but the pulsating pain was still there. He noticed that the open-plan suite had an en suite bathroom, a kitchenette and a small reception area with dark leather couches and a coffee table. There was a flat screen TV on the wall and a bowl of fresh fruit on the windowsill.

Two remotes were on the bedside table, one for the TV and the other for the adjustable bed in which he lay. Beside the remotes was a brochure. He picked it up and read: 'Hasaddah Medical Centre'. The printed Hebrew was reassuring. 'At least,' thought Fox, 'I am in Israel ... Hasaddah is in Tel Aviv.'

But if he was home, and Trevellian was dead, this was going to be his day of reckoning. Mossad agents were never court marshalled. What was likely to happen, Fox thought, was he would appear before a private tribunal of sorts, and be meted out his punishment: assigned to some tedious job at HQ pushing papers in a dusty office.

The door swung open. A man in a suit walked in.

'Agent Fox. In case you haven't gathered yet, you are alive and well in a private clinic in Tel Aviv.'

'Ben.'

Ben took a seat on a couch facing Fox across the room and, in spite of several non-smoking signs, took out a cigarette, lit it and got to the point.

'You've just come out of a severe concussion. Now, in case you can't remember, let me fill you in on the details of the operation.'

Fox let his head fall onto the pillow and he stared up at the ceiling.

'You went after Trevellian in Moscow. In spite of my instructions to capture him, you opened fire on him and his FSB contact. First breach.'

Fox was silent, he closed his eyes tightly.

'Right?'

'Yes, sir.'

'Good, glad to see we have our memory back. Now,' Ben stood up and walked over to the window, staring out over the sea. 'After that first bungled attempt, you chased him to Mount Yamantaw. Your orders were to capture, *not kill*, Trevellian. As far as I understand it, you managed to secure a high-powered Dragunov rifle off a Russian soldier hiding in a lookout bunker in the hillside. He has been reported dead. Do you realise the possible consequences?'

Fox offered a weak, 'Yes', and Ben continued.

'Lucky for us, however, they are unlikely to make any noise about these deaths, even if they knew it was us, as they took place near one of their military secrets. You then proceeded to the meeting point, where you attempted to assassinate Trevellian with the rifle.'

Ben tapped ash from the end of his cigarette into a vase on the window-side table. Fox opened his mouth but Ben went on. 'You jeopardised years of Mossad work on this case because you let your personal feelings interfere with your Mossad objective. Your hatred is *wild*, Fox, untamed, and that is *not* how we carry ourselves as employees of this institution.'

Ben paused again and took a deep drag on his cigarette. 'Are you hearing what I have to say, soldier?'

'Yes sir,' Fox gazed at the ocean behind Ben's outline. Here it comes, he thought.

Ben's eyes narrowed. He exhaled deeply and scrutinised Fox.

'Even so, soldier, don't ask me why, but I still have faith in you. You have passion. With some work, you could be the best kind of agent – motivated not only by religious and patriotic zeal, but also by personal vendetta. You need to learn to channel these energies.'

'I have failed you.'

Ben sat in the chair again. He put up his hand to indicate that he wasn't finished. 'For the reasons stated, and also because I think you've learned some valuable lessons in Russia, I am going to give you a second chance.'

Fox leaned forward. Ben threw his cigarette butt into the vase and it fizzled out with a hiss.

'Let me fill you in on what happened.'

He began to pace again as he explained that Agent A had been following Fox on Ben's orders. At the precise moment Fox had pulled the trigger, Agent A had knocked him clean out with the rock, which had caused his concussion. His shot had gone wide and Trevellian was unharmed, and had gotten away with the plutonium. He explained how Agent A had planted a bug on Trevellian, and how they had identified the next clue – a launch in Iran. Then how the intercepted email had pointed them in the direction of the naval base, where Agent A was being sent in under the cover of Liz Codwell, the daughter of a rich Nazi sympathiser, to get close to Trevellian. Finally, Ben explained that Badger had delivered a final message – the location of the secret Trevellian Enterprises base in Argentina: Ojos del Salado.

'All we have is a broad location. A clue,' said Ben. 'It's the second-highest mountain peak in Argentina. I'm guessing that the base is underground. Call it a hunch. We've established that there's a company at the mountain that organises climbs to the summit. It is called Enterprises Expeditions, and I'm betting it's a front company. Listen, how's your head feeling?'

Fox managed a weak smile. 'It's painful as hell.'

'Good, you deserve it. You're on a chartered flight to Argentina first thing in the morning.'

'You're sending me back into the field?'

'To infiltrate the base, hopefully. Or at least to poke around and see what you can dig up. You better not screw this up, or this time you *will* be fired.' Ben's smile faded. Fox noticed the deep panda-like rings beneath Ben's eyes. Probably hadn't slept in days, thought Fox.

'Thank you, sir!' Fox leaned forward in the bed and tried to get up, but a sharp pain struck him between the eyes and he quickly fell back, clutching his head.

'Easy does it, soldier. As far as you and everyone else is concerned, your new name is Younan Sahin. You're a wealthy businessman from Turkey who has made it big off sleaze – you own a string of strip joints and adult video stores in Istanbul. You're an adrenaline junkie who travels the world in search of the highest peaks and the lowest, darkest caves to explore. You've already been booked on a climbing expedition up Ojos del Salado with Enterprises Expeditions and you'll have to work from there. Once inside, you will find a way to permanently disrupt the warheads, if in fact, that is where they are being produced, which is another hunch of mine. Failing that, you are to provide information on their attack plan, any scraps you can lay your hands on.'

'In honouring me with this mission, sir, I will not fail you, even at the cost of my own life.'

'Spoken like a true son of Zion.' Fox smiled.

'Tell me, sir, the Turk, Sahin, he exists in real life?'

'Yes. He's currently in Argentina on holiday, enjoying the finest prostitutes and mountains of South American cocaine. We had him checked out. There's a full file on him and everything you need in the case …' Ben motioned to the door of the bathroom where Fox saw a suitcase.

'From passports to suits and business cards, it's all there. I've prepared some video footage stored on a USB stick which you can view on the laptop. That should help you get into character. Right now, I'm going home to get some sleep.' Ben stumbled towards the door. As he opened it, he turned and added, 'And Fox ...' he looked at the bed, eyes bleary, 'don't think you can get away without writing your usual, meticulous report on the operation you've just failed. I want every last detail, down to what the Eagle's head looked like in the view of the scope and how you were feeling. *Everything*, as usual. There's a notepad and pen beside you.' Ben didn't wait for an answer and disappeared behind the click of a door. Fox looked at the bedside. He didn't care that he would have to write the report. He wondered how Agent A was getting on as Liz Codwell.

2
Bandar Abbas

Undercover, Anna only became herself when she had fallen asleep, in her dreams. Liz was a criminally rich playgirl, an anti-Semite and, to boot, had a posh British accent. She went against every grain of who Anna was. Anna had never been rich. She was an orphan child of a genocide caused by anti-Semitism, and her accent was usually quite neutral, with a hint of Middle Eastern mixed with Eastern European.

Sitting in the third row of the cordoned-off balcony for VIPs above the podium, her gaze was rapt on James Trevellian. He shook with passion as he spoke. She had never seen anything like it. Although she knew now what he looked like in real life, she was curious to know what he'd be like up close.

The crowd erupted as he rounded up his speech. An old lady, Sarah Dwyer, one of the Fourth Reich's richest supporters, was helped by two *kriegsmanne* onto the platform. She would christen the submarines about to be launched in the tradition of 'lady luck'.

Anna gazed up at the snout of one of the subs. They must be at least a hundred metres each in length, and easily ten to fifteen stories in height, she assessed. They were black, aside from a swastika inside a white circle against a red rectangle at the front.

Trevellian was surrounded by bodyguards. Anna guessed that the man to James's left, in a crisp uniform, was the captain of one of the submarines about to be launched. To his right, Anna identified General Husseini.

It was time to act. Anna stood up, pressed out her dress and held her purse. She smiled at an old man sitting beside her as he shuffled his legs back to make room for her to push past him into the aisle. At the edge of the balcony near a spiral staircase, a guard unhooked a red cordon and Anna slipped out of the VIP section. At the bottom of the stairs, she walked along the hangar wall.

James and the group of men had disappeared into a doorway about fifty metres ahead. As Anna paused and looked up, they appeared in an open iron-cage lift heading up along the side of the wall to the hatch of the submarine. Anna headed to the doorway and slipped through. A stairway, right. She began to rush up, going as high as she could, fifteen levels. She entered the corridor just in time to see the group rounding a corner, up ahead. But there were voices in the passage.

A ladies', thank god, Anna thought. She took the sharp turn into an adjoining passage, following the bathroom signs. As soon as she was inside, Anna slipped into a cubicle and closed the door. She leaned with her back to the door, and let her head fall against it.

She took a deep breath and pulled out her phone. Where were James and his men going? She needed a lifeline. Time was running out, and the only way she could get close would be to take a gamble, she thought, and follow Trevellian. If she got caught, she might say that she was lost, looking for a decent bathroom.

Anna sent an encrypted email to Ben. 'Hangar Q, Iranian Naval Base. Nazis launching state-of-the art nuclear-powered submarines. In pursuit of Eagle, to meet …' There was a noise outside the cubicle and Anna pressed send by mistake.

A woman was humming. Anna typed a quick follow-up message. 'Details to follow', put her phone in her purse, cleared her throat, flushed the toilet and waited a few seconds before exiting the cubicle.

The woman was about mid-fifties, Anna assessed. She was touching up her foundation. She had on an expensive suit with black trimming on the collar, pockets, cuffs and lining. Anna identified her as

Lady Chalmsford as she collected herself and approached the wash-basin.

'*Aben.*'

Chalmsford turned to take the sight of Anna in.

'My dear God, is it Lizzy Codwell?'

Anna smiled and nodded.

'I haven't seen you since you were five years old. My, how you've grown up! Look at you, dear, what a gorgeous creature you are.'

Chalmsford gave Anna the up-and-down. Anna turned to her and held out her hand, blushing. Chalmsford shook it once, moving it down slowly, her eyes transfixed on Liz Codwell's eyes. The drawn-out greeting over, Chalmsford turned to the mirror and continued.

'You wouldn't think that after all the money I've thrown at them they would make me go up fifteen floors to find a decent lady's room. The worker's ablutions downstairs are ... *simple.*'

'Quite,' said Anna, 'and might I say that you are very beautiful, even more so than I remember, and your suit is lovely, what is it?' Anna produced a tube of lip gloss from her purse.

'Ah,' Chalmsford laughed, 'I see you're just as charming as your old man. It's Chanel, dear. How is the old devil?'

'Well, it's lovely. And the old devil asked me to send his love to you. Very busy of course. Asked me to come instead.'

'You know,' began Chalmsford, turning back to the mirror, 'if it wasn't for your siren of a mother, who knows if I'd still be a widow to this day? We had eyes for each other once, your father and I, but then your mother came on the scene and I was forgotten in an instant. What a beautiful man ...'

'I love him more than anything,' completed Anna. 'Still hunting like crazy. Still cursing at the news ...'

'Ah well ...' said Chalmsford, 'they'll never change, these men. If they aren't killing people or Jews or inspiring insurrection in Islamic countries, they're killing pheasants or foxes in the English countryside with buckshot.'

Anna laughed. This was her first real test, but she recognised it as an opportunity. Chalmsford belonged to a clique of families and individuals who had sympathised with the Nazis during the war. They, or their descendants, would have inside information on the Nazis' plans. The Nazis, Ben had told Anna, had documented everything, and used the evidence that they had collected to blackmail some of the families, those who weren't still willing to assist, into helping the cause in whatever way they could.

'Tell me,' Anna ventured, feigning indifference. 'I've been out of the loop for a while. I've been away … I don't want to appear misinformed, and I wonder if you could bring me up to speed with those *monsters* out there in the hangar.'

'Of course, dear,' said Chalmsford. 'Tibet, is it? Five years?'

'Has it been that long?' Anna shrugged.

'Don't worry, dear, I will link you in. I can't believe they've created twelve of those things. Toys for the *Führer*, really, and all equipped with nuclear warheads, so pretty dangerous for toys. They've been building them here in Iran in secret for a good couple of years. Gave one to the Iranians, as their price for using the hangar. It was one of Trevellian's conditions that only his men could be allowed in here.'

'As you said,' Anna smiled, 'always trying to kill something.'

'Between you and me, I sometimes feel as if I'm getting too old, too mellow, for all this hatred. Since my husband died, I've realised the small things are so important. Happiness, having someone to love and be loved by … and I'm not getting any younger …'

'Is there anyone in particular you're hoping to impress tonight?'

'Ah, I see you're perceptive, just like your father. Well, as a matter of fact there is. A certain gentleman named Caxton.'

'Good choice!' Anna grinned. Anna knew him to be one of the sympathisers, an ex-pilot and aircraft manufacturer. 'In that case, if I may …' Anna waved the lip gloss. She leaned over slowly, gently towards Chalmsford. 'You would look even more beautiful if I could just …' Anna began to apply the lip gloss to Chalmsford's lips. It was a bold move, but one that Anna hoped would pay off. Chalmsford froze, with a look of gentle surprise.

'Oh well, thank you!' she stuttered when Anna had finished, turning her head about to study the effects of the younger woman's devices on her appearance.

'They make your lips look luscious, fuller, very … *inviting*,' said Anna.

'Well,' said Chalmsford. 'Well indeed, they do look … lovely!' she beamed. 'Thank you.'

'Not at all. It's only a pleasure for you, my lady,' Anna did a curtsy, before putting her eyeliner and lip gloss back in her purse.

'How are you getting to the celebration dinner?'

Anna stopped herself from asking, 'What celebration dinner?' and instead replied with, 'Oh, I'm not sure I'll be going ... I'm dreadfully tired after all that travelling. I haven't even arranged transport in any case.'

'Nonsense! You can't possibly miss it. It would be doing your devil-of-a-dancer, whisky-swilling, smooth-talking father an utmost disservice. And you'd be missing out. The *Führer's* yacht is *magnificent*. Besides, I could use the company on the trip over and I have my personal helicopter and pilot waiting outside the hangar as we speak.'

Anna feigned opposition. 'But I haven't even packed a bag. How will I get back to the Burj al Arab?'

'Well dear, when you see the magnificence of the stateroom aboard the *Führer's* yacht, equipped with absolutely everything you need, down to designer dresses, even designer *bathrobes*, you'll soon understand that you'll want for very little aboard.'

Anna allowed herself a smile. The door was left slightly open, she sure as hell was going to push through.

'Well, I suppose, if it's not too much trouble ...'

'Not at all. Come, dear.' She took Anna by the arm as they walked towards the bathroom door. 'Tell me,' Chalmsford leaned in stared at the floor, 'do you have any more tips for me to win Caxton's heart?'

'Well,' said Anna as they entered the corridor, 'it's not his heart you should be looking to win. It's his pelvis.'

Chalmsford gasped, then giggled.

'And tricks,' added Anna, 'I have many. I practically wrote the book.'

'Oh my,' Chalmsford laughed, blissfully unaware that she'd just been recruited to work for Mossad.

3
Dubai Marina

The night skyline was sublime. Skyscrapers crowded around the 150-metre yacht docked in the marina, the lights dancing on the water's surface, deep red, purple and blue. A helicopter hovered like a dragonfly above the bow. Anna was nervous, her thumbs twitching as the buildings grew taller and the disk of the yacht's helipad larger. The window seat afforded a magnificent view of the yacht as the helicopter locked into position and began to whir down. Crew scurried about the deck, tending to tuxedoed and ball-gowned guests on the polished wooden decks between several well-lit swimming pools.

The helicopter touched down and immediately the yacht's captain stepped forward to give Anna and Chalmsford a hand. Both women held their hair against the air generated by the blades and hurried out of its reach.

'Lady Chalmsford, Miss Codwell, an absolute pleasure to receive you on board.' The captain grinned. It took Anna a few seconds to readjust herself to his German. He added, 'Your personal assistants for the evening are, for you, Lady Chalmsford, Kate and for you, Miss Codwell, Lily …' the captain gestured towards two uniformed women standing nearby with their feet together and hands behind their backs.

'Should you need accommodation for the night, or anything at all, you need only request it from Kate and Lily. I trust you will thoroughly enjoy your stay aboard the *Aegir*. Kate, if you would lead these lovely ladies to the top deck …'

'This way, please,' Kate said.

They walked down some stairs and across a deck, around the boat via a side passage and up a flight of stairs that led up five levels. Some of the passengers may have considered it a long way to walk, but Anna took advantage of the opportunity to take in the sights.

At the top deck, a fringe pool lit by amber lights led to a polished wooden deck and a bar. Through a set of double doors, a dining room table stretched along the length of a room. The cutlery and china sparkled beneath the chandeliers. It had a very nostalgic feel to it, Anna assessed, as if it was borrowed straight from 1940s Germany.

'If you ladies want for anything,' said Kate as they neared the bar, 'merely ask for us and we'll be with you promptly.'

The two assistants left the bar area and a waiter appeared with a tray of martinis. Chalmsford took two, handing one to Anna, and held her glass up in salute.

'To men.'

Anna drew out the olive by its toothpick, raised her glass and saluted, 'To men.'

Chalmsford downed the entire drink, smacking her lips. 'If only all were sailors.' She was eyeing the Trevellian Enterprises soldier who stood guard at the railing, in mercenary gear with a machine gun in his hands.

Anna smiled in reply. They sat down in some leather couches near the bar. Another waiter appeared with more drinks and as Chalmsford took another and devoured it, Anna knew that she wasn't going anywhere tonight. She would have to stay on the yacht.

Anna waved to Lily.

'I think I'll need that accommodation tonight.'

'Certainly, Miss Codwell. A stateroom has in fact already been prepared for you. Here is your key.' It was on a solid gold key ring, with the number three on it.

'It is amidships one deck down from us. To get there, go down one flight of stairs, the same stairs we came up, and take your first left. It's the third room on the right.'

Chalmsford began a running commentary of the new guests. Anna didn't care much for the rest of them. She was trying to pick out James from the crowd.

4
Helambu
Nepal

A fire-tailed sunbird danced on its forest perch. It appraised the man who slept on a stretcher bed in the middle of the forest, its golden chest pouting, its burned red tail feathers hanging over the branch.

Badger's face was badly disfigured. His one eye was swollen, his face was mummified with bandages and his lips were cracked. As he opened his eyes, the sunbird took off. The sound of a waterfall drifted from nearby. It took him a few seconds to realise that the tall brown columns were tree trunks. The canopy above him was a blazing red ceiling of rhododendron flowers.

Bells chimed and the soothing song of midday prayer came from a monastery. He lifted his head, splitting with pain, as if he had the worst hangover of his life, and tried to figure out why he was in the middle of a forest.

To his right, a small stone cottage, with a Chinese-style roof, a thin line of smoke escaping from the chimney and the smell of freshly baked corn bread and lentil soup.

To his left, the voice of a woman, and children's laughter. Lhama was telling a group of children a story, a hushed group of wide-eyed listeners sitting on rocks or on their haunches. Lhama was in the middle.

Badger rested his head and smiled as he listened to the story. The children yelped, gasped and laughed. Badger closed his eyes, glad to be alive. He felt his tummy growl and realised that he was ravenously hungry, and that he probably hadn't eaten anything substantial in days. Lhama finished her story and chased the children off. She clapped her hands. 'Right, off with you lot – go play!' There were giggles as she chased the children. Badger knew they would be running up the gravel path that led to the monastery on top of the hill. He imagined the village. Mothers sitting in their doorways stitching and sewing garments. Chillies and garlic on the mats in the windowsills of the two- and three-storey houses built one on top of the other. Men, porters, carrying large loads of barley from the valleys on their backs. Goats, cows and old Indian motorcycles. The images were comforting.

The sound of leaves crunching underfoot brought him back from his reverie. Lhama's hair brushed his cheek as she leaned over him and sat down. He opened his eyes and stared straight into the depths of her opal globes. She smiled softly as she worked a damp sponge over his forehead.

'Hello sleepy.'

In spite of the enormous effort, Badger smiled, comforted by Lhama's aura.

'I thought you could do with some air, and look, it has woken you!'

Badger kept quiet, afraid that if he spoke it would betray the depth of his gratitude to the goddess who had taken care of him.

'A tiger was here last night,' Lhama said. 'It stalked the forest and scared the goats. The people are saying that the beast of anger symbolises the violence of your injuries.'

Badger closed his eyes as he spoke. The thoughts of what had happened to him were disturbing.

'It is not past violence, Lhama, but future violence, that the tiger represents.' A pause sunk in. 'Did you send the message I asked you to?'

'Yes, I sent your crazy message. What on earth did it mean?'

'There is great evil afoot, Lhama. Foreigners will soon come in search of an artefact of immense power. It can be used for great good, but in the wrong hands, the artefact can be the most powerful weapon known to man.'

A butterfly with light blue wings flitted down and landed on Badger's big toe. He opened his eyes to look at it. It took off and disappeared into the forest.

'Is this artefact related to those men who did this to you? Is it related to what you have been working on?'

'Yes, Lhama, it's all related.'

'Badger, you're far too weak to do anything.' She assessed him, trying to figure out where he got his strength and longevity from. Although she knew him to be at least sixty, he didn't look it. She found him surprisingly fast, incredibly agile and bright in mind.

'You have no idea how dangerous these people are,' said Badger. 'You see what they did to me. I am living proof. And this is only the beginning.'

'Who are these men?'

'Nazis who will crush all other races in their pursuit of world domination.'

'Where is this artefact they are looking for?'

'Lo Manthang.'

Lhama gasped. 'The forbidden kingdom?'

'Yes, and I need your help.'

'Me? How can I possibly …'

'The artefact is in a cave near the old city, in a mountain. In order to get in, I will need a climber to help me. Will you?'

Lhama thought about it for a second. 'I don't believe in these things, Badger, but if it's that important to you, I will. When do we need to leave?'

'As soon as possible.'

'Fine. But first, do me a favour …'

'What?'

'Shut up, close your eyes and listen to the forest breathe. Enjoy the peace for a while, clear your mind while I prepare you a lunch of delicious corn bread, lentil soup, dhal curry and rice.'

'Now that,' said Badger, 'I can do.'

5
Fiambalá
Argentina

'This is your first climb up Ojos del Salado, Mr Sahin?'

The strawberry blonde in a tight-hugging Enterprises Expeditions company T-shirt slid an indemnity form across the table to Fox. Hers was a faint German accent. His, a thick Turkish. The office was cramped, the town dusty.

'Yes. Listen,' he leaned across the table and stroked the stubble on his chin, 'do I really need to fill out all these bloody papers? What's the meaning of all this?'

'I'm afraid so, Mr Sahin.'

'Do you know who I am?'

'Yes, Mr Sahin. We are well aware that you are a successful businessman with a string of, erm, *entertainment* venues ...'

'Strip clubs.' said Fox, leaning back in his chair, grinning. 'And let me tell you,' he said, appraising the woman's breasts, 'you would make one hell of a –'

'Mr Sahin,' the woman appeared stern. 'As I was saying, we are aware of who you are and I can't stress enough how much reverence we place on you as a client, we are very honoured to have you climb up Ojos del Salado with us, but I'm still going to need you to sign these indemnity forms.' She looked exasperated, thought Fox, but she'd held up well under the pressure. She leaned forward and tapped the form towards the bottom. Fox smiled and took advantage of the view of her cleavage.

The woman sat back in her chair quickly and folded her arms, catching his dirty look. Fox's smile was unholy. It spoke of a thousand acts he wanted to do to her, perhaps even on the same desk that separated them. He picked up the pen, made a quick scrawl on the bottom of the form, threw the pen sliding on the table and sat back with his arms folded behind his head.

He was getting this cover right. He was surprised by how naturally it was coming, even though he wasn't *naturally* a womaniser. He'd spent the entire plane trip over from Istanbul to Rio studying the file and the videos that Ben had prepared for him on Younan Sahin. The real Sahin was holidaying in Argentina, and Ben had insisted that Fox follow the exact same flight route that Sahin had, from Istanbul to Buenos Aires. From there, he caught a flight to Copiapó in Chile, and had driven into Argentina over the breath-taking San Francisco Pass.

The fake passport he'd been given had exactly the same stamps as the real Sahin's would have. Now, he sat in the office of Enterprises Expeditions, in dusty, wine-growing Fiambalá.

'Tell me, sweetheart,' said Fox, 'what does a girl such as you do for fun in this god-forsaken place?'

'Mr Sahin, I am very close to my work.'

'You mean to tell me,' said Fox, grinning his most chauvinistic smile, 'that a girl as gorgeous as yourself is all work and no play? Tut-tut … that would be a shame.'

'I work very hard, and I enjoy my work,' the woman said, staring down at the paperwork.

'I'm sure you do.' Fox produced a packet of cigarettes and offered her one. She shook her head.

'Besides, I like to climb. There are the mountains …' She motioned to the wall behind her. There were framed pictures of the major peaks in the Andes: Aconcagua, Cerro Bonete, Mercedario, Pissis and finally, Ojos del Salado.

'And, there's no smoking in here, if you don't mind.'

'I don't mind at all,' said Fox, lighting up his cigarette. 'Of course, yes, there are the mountains.' Fox nodded, exhaling. He leaned forward. 'Tell me, if hypothetically speaking, I were to ask you out to dinner say, on my return from Ojos, what would you say?'

'Well, sir, it would be against company employee code.'

'*Really*,' said Fox, still smiling.

'I might even get fired, Mr Sahin.'

'If I may be so candid, Miss …'

'Contreras.'

'Ah, Argentinean?'

'Yes.'

'Interesting. An Argentinean with, dare I say it, Miss Contreras, a German accent …' He was pushing his boundaries, fishing, but he felt as if he was getting the cover spot on, and he was within his limits.

She shrugged. 'I went to university in Germany.'

'I see. If I may be so candid, sitting here, looking at you Miss beautiful Contreras, I can honestly say that there's nothing that I would like more than to have dinner with you after a very difficult climb up that lovely mountain of yours. I will carry that dream with me all the way to the very top, on those bitter slopes, and then back down again.'

Miss Contreras blushed and looked down at the desk. She spoke softly. 'Mr Sahin. You are very handsome. Believe me, I'm flattered, but …'

'You have a boyfriend?'

'Yes, Mr Sahin, I have a boyfriend.' She was glad for the lifeline.

'Well good, I like a good challenge.'

'I am not a mountain, Mr Sahin.'

'No, Miss Contreras, you are not. You are far more forgiving, I hope, than that cruel mistress, Ojos del Salado. And far more beautiful.'

'Speaking of which, Mr Sahin,' she began, business-like. 'I'm obligated to tell you about the dangers involved in climbing the second-highest peak in South America.'

Fox smiled and nodded. 'Any excuse to sit back and listen your sweet voice.'

6
Dubai Marina

James paused in front of the full-length mirror in the owner's suite bathroom and adjusted his tie. He ran a finger down his cheek and considered shaving. Giving up on the idea, he walked into the main room, to a wooden cabinet, above which was a window spanning the length of the room that eyed a private swimming pool and deck. Beyond, the Dubai skyline tipped over the waters of the marina.

He slid the panel open, removed a tumbler and bottle and poured himself a drink. He took a fiery sip that burned the back of his throat and ambled over to the phone beside the bed. He dialled the bridge.

'*Kapitan*, this is James ... Set a course around Dubai's pretty lights. Did you receive the coordinates for tomorrow's journey? I sent them via your assistant ... Yes, to Chittagong in the Bay of Bengal. We will make our way inland from there to Nepal ... That's good. How long should the journey take? ... Six days? ... Good, that gives us enough time, I think, to stop over at the cabin ... Excellent, *danke*, *Kapitan*.' James hung up and dialled Frieda.

'Frieda, report on Patrick's movements, *bitte*.'

There was a short pause while Frieda made contact with the base in Argentina. James heard her asking a few questions before her voice came back on the line.

'Patrick has delivered the materials. The scientists are working as we speak.'

'Will they be ready in time?'

'*Jahwol*. I double checked this. It should take a few days for the submarines to reach the west coast of Chile near Copiapo, where they will be loaded.'

'*Danke*, Frieda. Now, please stop working and join us for a drink on the top deck.'

'I will see you up there soon.'

James put the phone and his drink down, exited the suite and walked up towards the top deck. He stopped in front of one of the nearby stateroom doors and knocked three times. Roger appeared quickly, alert and smart in a tuxedo.

'Accompany me.'

'Right away.' At the last moment Roger tore off the tuxedo jacket, unbuttoned his top collar and closed the door. James was smiling at him.

'Those things are a bloody nuisance,' Roger said as they entered an elevator.

As they stepped out onto the top deck, James was greeted by a throng of supporters. He peered past the smiling faces and the empty handshakes to a leather couch beside the railing at the far end of the fringe pool. Something had caught his eye. Chalmsford sat at one end, but that was not who James noticed. He was transfixed by a beautiful blonde in a crushed velvet dress. Her face, tinged with amber light, was disguised by a curtain of honey-golden hair. As she brushed her hair aside, James saw that she was smiling, talking to a man in a single couch beside her.

'Roger, who is that gorgeous creature?'

Roger followed his gaze. 'Ah that ... that must be ...' Roger pulled an assistant over to him. 'Who is that, *mein herr*?'

'Liz Codwell, sir.'

'Codwell?'

'*Ja, mein Führer.*'

'No. That can't be her. Are you sure?'

'Positive.'

'That is not possible at all. She is gorgeous, is she not, Roger?'

'Yes, very pretty, very pretty.'

'Where has she been all this time?'

The assistant answered for Roger. 'In Tibet. A few years.'

'She's a goddamn Cleopatra.'

Her eyes were wide, her smile dazzling. Roger tried to probe James's apparent interest. Who could possibly catch the eye of a sworn bachelor?

'What is it about her?'

'I ... I'm not sure, Roger ...' James was transfixed.

He found himself thinking. Yes, in fact, he was sure. There was an animal magnetism. She could bring empires crumbling to dust. Men would raze cities and crush continents, squeezing for the diamonds, gold and precious jewels and treasures of the world, and they would search for centuries and not be able to find enough to pay homage to her.

James walked over in a daze.

Out of the corner of her eye, Anna saw a man approaching. She stopped talking. It was *him*. Her heart was in her throat. How was she meant to do this? She would have to be deferent, yes, but she needed to catch his eye. Why was he coming over? Not knowing what else to do, Anna stood up and bowed.

'*Mein Führer* ...' She focused on his feet.

'Liz Codwell?'

His voice was unnerving.

'*Jahwol, herr Führer – mein, mein Führer …*'

She bowed slightly and held out her hand. James stepped forward, took it and an electric jolt run up Anna's hand as he kissed it softly.

'I cannot believe that it is you. When last did I …'

'Many years ago, *mein Führer*, I have been …'

'In Tibet,' completed James.

'You've grown up, Liz.'

'Thank you.'

Anna looked up and stared straight into his eyes without intending to. A shock ran up her spine, whether in fear or otherwise, she couldn't tell. His eyes were stormy. They spoke more for him than anything else could. His outward appearance, his position in life or his job title, spoke of a man wanting to accomplish greatness through destruction, she thought. But his eyes betrayed him. They told her that his real greatness lay inside, accomplished rather through 'tiny' acts of love and kindness, perhaps.

'Liz …' He seemed lost for words. She snapped out of her dream and stared at her feet, the moment that had seemed like many lifetimes had passed.

'Let's catch up on Clive, shall we?' As he touched her shoulder another jolt rippled through her skin at the point of contact. He led her gently over to the railing and suddenly, they were alone. The world faded out.

'I must confess, you've taken me completely by surprise, all grown up.'

'Thank you, I think,' smiled Anna.

'If it's not too forward …'

'Yes?'

'I would like to catch up with you afterwards. After …' He'd forgotten all about why they were on the yacht. '… Dinner.'

He seemed to regain some composure as he shook his head.

'Join me for a private drink.'

'I would love that.'

Without realising that he was doing so, James slipped his hand along the small of her back as he led her to the crowd, conspiratorially whispering into their flute glasses and trying not to make it look too obvious that they were staring at the couple approaching them.

James leaned close to Anna's ear and she thought she heard him whisper, 'To hell with all this', as he disappeared into the crowd.

7
Ojos del Salado
Argentina

Fox sat on a bench outside the Enterprises Expeditions office, making sure that his climbing gear was in order. After he had been briefed on the dangers that he would face – gale-force winds carrying bullets of ice and gravel and temperatures of up to minus twenty-four degrees, above High Camp, at 6 000 metres – he and his Enterprises Expeditions tour leader Siegmund Baum had pored over satellite images of the mountain.

It was not a difficult grade climb, especially the summit, accessible by scaling a small cliff face, but the risk would be in not acclimatising quickly enough. Siegmund had disappeared into a back room and Fox had made his way outside. He tightened the laces of his boots and, making sure that no one was watching, rummaged through his backpack to make sure it was all there. Three things in particular. The unusually large-spike crampons. Then, a modified pick axe with a special blade called a stiletto that flared out towards the tip and then narrowed again. It left no exit wounds or blood. Finally, customised gloves that were more like scissors that could be used to cut a man's throat in half. Blades were concealed in slipways along the thumb and forefingers. When manoeuvred out of position, they acted as pincers. Fox moved a blade out and smiled as he ran his finger along the sharp edge. He put it back just as Siegfried appeared in the doorway.

'Ready?'

'Let's go,' said Fox, hauling his thirty kilogram rucksack onto his back. They entered a back parking lot. As Fox passed the front door, he looked in and winked at Miss Contreras, who pretended that she didn't see him. Siegfried led around the building to a specially modified 4 × 4 vehicle with enormous tyres and a monster engine. The Jeep was the same model that a Chilean team had used to reach the high-altitude record for a vehicle, on the slopes of Ojos del Salado on the Chilean side of the border a few years back, Siegmund told him as they got in.

The engine burst into life and they cruised out of the dusty streets past Cazadero Grande *refugio*, an emergency sleep-over shack with a corrugated iron roof. A track led off the road into the infant slopes of the mountain. The Jeep wound through a narrow ravine over slippery moon-like landscape, mostly in first or second gear. Fox watched the slopes pass by. The rocks were green, purple and yellow, caused by mineral deposits by the ever-present wind, Siegmund commented. *Vicuñas*, small antelope-like creatures, nuzzled at the rocks in search of something to eat. Siegmund told Fox how the Incas had a law that only royalty could wear the wool of these magical creatures. Small clusters of *penitents*, spears of ice, appeared on the higher slopes as they neared 6 000 metres. The more tourist-like facts Siegmund told Fox, the more the Nazi's voice grated on his nerves.

'We'll camp overnight at High Camp, a short climb from where we'll ditch the Jeep and make an attempt on the summit in one day, weather permitting, and then we'll return to High Camp for another overnight stay before making our way back to the vehicle.'

Fox didn't answer. Siegmund's German accent set him on edge. As the Jeep made steady progress up the slopes, Fox could feel it getting colder. The wind whistled around them and the landscape became more unforgiving. Dryer, and colder, with more ice and snow. The peak of Ojos del Salado grew steadily larger. He began to feel dizzy, nauseous, the first effects of altitude sickness.

Finally, a small makeshift camp came into view over the crest of a ridge. The vehicle climbed up and over the ridge, tracking the ravine. With about a hundred metres to go to the camp, which was snuggled in a natural wind tunnel, Fox and Siegfried got out, slung their backpacks on and began climbing. The wind was deathly cold and tore through Fox's scarf. Shards of ice and snow hurtled at them, thrown maliciously by the wind.

Then Fox saw it: a small *refugio*, known as High Camp, nestled in the shelter of a giant boulder. It had four walls and a roof, but seemed to be divided into two parts. Siegmund produced a key, opened the door and they slipped inside.

It was a simple room, with an adjoining bathroom, and a place to make a fire in the middle with wood, coal and anthracite for all-night warmth. There were a few pots and a cupboard with medical supplies and food.

The wind howled in a high pitch as the night pressed in. The *refugio* rattled like a box of teeth at 6 300 metres above sea level. A contemplative Fox stood at the tiny pane facing the crest of the mountain and watched curtains of snow falling in the gathering gloom.

Siegmund was on his haunches, bent over a wigwam of firewood, cursing as he tried to get a ball of kindle to catch light. The lighter was faulty. Its grating sound was the only noise in the hut, along with Siegmund's expletives.

'Temperature is now well below freezing,' Siegmund said, gritting his teeth and huffing. 'We are in for a *very* cold night.' He leaned back as the kindle caught light and a ball of flame burst into life. There were two stretcher beds pressed against the walls of the four-by-four metre shack. Fox moved over to the fire and warmed his hands.

'What's in the other room?' he asked bluntly.

'What other room?'

'The one adjoining this one.'

'Oh that one?' Siegmund pulled a pot over, opened a five-litre bottle of water and poured some in. 'Supplies.'

'Supplies? Why's it bigger that this one?'

'Well,' Siegmund fanned the flames. 'I'm not sure. Lots of stuff, I suppose.'

'You suppose?'

Orange flames began to tickle up to the highest point of the wigwam. A thin line of smoke drifted to the ceiling, escaping through a special layer that insulated the hut by keeping warmth in and letting smoke out. If there was one thing Fox was going to do tonight, he promised himself, it was to get into that other room. His head began to spin.

'I need to use the bathroom.'

'Right through there,' said Siegmund, and Fox lurched towards the basin. A hot jet of vomit shot up his throat, but Fox bit down in time to lean over the basin and empty the contents of his stomach into it.

'Alright in there?'

'Fine,' Fox answered, realising that it was the effects of the altitude. 'I need some oxygen, do you have any?'

'I'll find the tank.' The voice filled him with rage. It was a naïve voice. One of a child, an arrogant child who thought he was better than everyone on the playground. The domesticity of it all, bunking with a Nazi, sickened him to the core. He was struggling to keep himself together. He stared at himself in the mirror. His vision was going blurry, but he was determined to find any clue he possibly could. And no, he told himself, not this time. He would not kill, not this time.

Fox wiped his mouth with his sleeve and left the bathroom. As he re-entered the cabin, his mind played tricks on him. Siegmund was a bloodied corpse huddled next to the fire. Fox tried to shake the image out of his mind, and sat down beside the fire, but as he looked up at Siegmund, the illusion was still there. The face was fleshy, full of running cuts, rotting in places with yellow and dark red skin hanging off it. An eye was half hanging out of its socket. Fox closed his eyes for a full minute. When he opened them, everything had returned to normal.

The fire was well on its way, with small blue flames cresting the top of the wood. Siegmund lay back on his stretcher bed, warming his toes near the fire.

'There's the oxygen tank,' Siegmund said, pointing to Fox's stretcher bed, adding: 'That should make you feel better. I am making us some dinner, which should help too.'

Fox looked at the pot beside the fire. It looked pitiful, it made him angry. The pot itself *looked* like Siegmund. It was smug, cosy, domestic.

'Thank you, *Sigy*.'

Fox closed his mouth and ground his teeth. His head was painful as he walked over to the stretcher bed where the oxygen tank lay. He placed the mouthpiece over his head, positioned it, turned the knob on the tank and inhaled deeply. It was bitter.

'I might need another one or two nights to adjust to the conditions,' mumbled Fox through the mask. He was buying time. Instead of a body being found the next day, it might take two days. No, he reprimanded himself; he was not going to kill Siegmund.

'I think that is wise,' Siegmund replied. 'I've seen what happens to climbers who don't adjust properly, and trust me, you don't want that – visions, day-mares, headaches that make you feel as if your head is being ripped off your neck ... been there myself.'

'Been there yourself.'

Fox's teeth pressed together like rock on porcelain, and ground down until he could feel the powdery substance of his teeth on the tip of his tongue. Siegmund leaned forward and fumbled in his backpack for a radio. He turned it on, held down the speaker button and spoke.

'Base Camp, this is Climb Leader One, come in ...'

Fox echoed Siegmund's voice in his mind, but in a whiney imitation of it. Radio static filled the room.

'This is Base Camp, state your position, over.'

'Climber will need more time to acclimatise. Possibly looking at two to three days, over.'

Fox mimicked the voice in his head again and moved his lips at the same time. Siegmund was staring at the ground and didn't notice. Why didn't the clown just speak German? Fox thought as the prattle continued.

'Affirmative, Climb Leader One. Are there enough provisions? Over.'

'Yes, there are sufficient supplies. Over.'

'Over,' Fox echoed.

Siegmund looked up at him, strangely.

'Thank you Climb Leader One, I will notify Front Desk. Weather is expected to clear within twenty-four hours, so in fact your situation is ideal. Over.'

'Thank you, Base Camp. Over and out.'

Ideal, thought Fox. He smiled and sucked deeply on the oxygen. A glint had caught his eye: a bunch of keys dancing in the light of the fire, attached to Siegmund's belt. Were they for the adjoining room?

Fox suddenly began to feel a lot better. Each death, after all, led him closer to Trevellian like a moth to a flame.

8
Dubai Marina

Anna's heart was pounding in her ears as she stood and watched James Trevellian disappear into the crowd. She could not believe that he was a monster. Something glowed behind those troubled eyes. Perhaps a troubled past.

The soft melody of a six-piece orchestra invited Anna into the dining room. She drew in a deep breath, pressed her hands against her dress and moved forward. She felt her shoulders tense and her stomach tighten into an iron knot. Why was she so unnerved? Her knees felt like jelly. It was as if she'd forgotten how to breathe and the world had sunk into a haze of slow exaggerated movements. She'd come face to face with her arch enemy and yet she found no beast.

Chalmsford appeared at Anna's side and linked her arm in. 'So dear … what was that about?'

'Oh,' said Anna, 'just some business to do with Clive.'

Chalmsford smiled and laughed. Her breath was alcoholic and bitter. Anna recoiled, but stopped herself from unlinking her arm.

'I'm sure dear, just business with Clive.'

The table sparkled with cutlery. Beside it, servants stood in uniform behind high-back chairs. The guests took their seats, looked around the table and exchanged pleasantries with nervous excitement. Anna sat beside Chalmsford and an old man who Chalmsford introduced as Lord Buxton.

He must be more than sixty years old, thought Anna. He smiled non-stop and bowed to his male colleagues, but ignored the women. Across the table, Peter Crouch, the editor of a right-wing tabloid, the *Daily Insight*, exchanged pleasantries with the distinguished-looking German ambassador to Iran who wore a monocle and a finely cut suit. His wife wore a strapless grey dress, her breasts pushing out above the folds of the vintage piece that made her look like an Austrian princess, with her blonde hair in neat curls.

The banter died down as James stood up. The captain of the yacht, on James's right, faced the table with his chest out, gold buttons glinting, and raised his right arm in the *Führer*'s salute. '*Heil, Führer!*'

The crowd responded: '*Heil Führer!*' and sat down.

'Friends,' James began. He couldn't keep his eyes off Anna. 'Friends ...' He seemed to hesitate. Anna deflected her eyes at the table. James collected himself and tried again.

'*Kameraden*, we share tonight, around this table, a sense of excitement that has been lost to us for decades. We have, all of us, since our glorious leader died, been chased to every far-flung corner of the five continents, pursued like wild animals by men who do not deserve to go by that title.

'Tonight, we celebrate the eve of victory. You, *kameraden*, are the future kings and queens of a new order. I am glad that you are here with me, to share in this triumph, to celebrate the launch of the greatest naval war machine ever constructed – in secret, no less – a fleet of twelve world-class submarines that will carry with them our final hopes and dreams. The submarines will be equipped with nuclear missiles and we have ensured that they will be ideally placed to strike at Israel's soft belly – its coast line. They will also carry troops, the likes of which the world has never seen, of perfect Aryan warriors.'

Anna's heart skipped a beat. Israel, Eretz Israel? Of course, she knew that Israel was a prime target, but she would have thought that the Nazis would have first struck at America or England. Their ideological zeal obviously outweighed the need for revenge against the old Allies. Anna realised that she hadn't yet transmitted an update to Ben. She would need to soon, but had to remain calm.

'We have reached Phase 2. Now, we forge ahead with the final phase of the attack. I am aware that not all of you know the details of the plan. It has been deliberately kept among the War Council as a closely guarded secret.

'But for those of you who do not know what will unfold, I can assure you: victory will be swift, and it will be absolute. But now, let me not keep you from your food and drink. This evening is one for celebration. Raise your glasses with me to hail our victory. As we do so, we pay homage to those who have made this possible. Not only yourselves, who have contributed financially, intellectually, even with your bodies and souls, to this cause, but also those who have gone before, and to my father, who is ill and cannot be with us here tonight. *Prosit!*'

All the guests stood and raised their glasses in salute. '*Prosit!*'

They resumed their chatter as they sat down. Waiters took orders for an eight-course meal. The famed southern German wine, Moselle, flowed. Anna watched James call a servant over. He seemed to give the man detailed instructions before the man nodded and took off towards the kitchen.

A servant came over and allowed Anna to sample some wine. She nodded with approval. He poured, and when Anna looked back down at the table, a napkin was spread out in front of her. There was writing on it, small but legible: 'Meet me at the bow, ten minutes. J.'

9
Ojos del Salado

There was something not quite right about Younan Sahin, mused Siegmund Baum as he lay on his stretcher bed listening to the wind. Perhaps it was that he hardly smiled. And when he did, it seemed to come from a place of pain, almost a sadistic type of smile. Perhaps, thought Baum, it was in the way Sahin left questions unanswered. And also in the questions he had asked about the adjoining room. Perhaps it was in the strange way he had repeated the word 'over' when Siegmund had said it on the two-way. But that was not it. It was in the vacant, glazed-over eyes that were colder than glacier winds. Baum was a good judge of character. He lay, wide awake in his stretcher bed, clutching a hunting knife.

That was how Siegmund Baum fell asleep, clutching his hunting knife, sensing danger and naïvely ignoring his instincts.

There was something not quite right about Fox. Something in the way he thirsted for blood. Once a victim, an orphan of hatred, Fox had turned the tables, unable to let go of his need for vengeance. Now Fox lay deathly still and listened to the wooden window rattle like old bones against the fury of the snow blizzard that raged around the hut. Very rarely did the opportunity present itself, and so sweetly, for Fox to take matters into his own hands. It would be the only way to get at the keys on Siegmund's belt, he convinced himself.

Fox had watched Siegmund climb into bed, making out his half-shadowed face in the glow of the dying embers. Siegmund hadn't removed his pants, hadn't unbuckled the belt, or even removed the keys from his belt. Fox had listened to the stilted breathing of the man until they rattled off into the deep even breaths of an exhausted sleep. Fox lay on his side and reached down to feel the cold steel of his pick axe. He moved deliberately in his bed, to test if Siegmund was still awake. There was no reply movement or sound.

He would do it quickly. He would jump up and spring on him, bringing the axe down into his chest or his head, over and again until there was nothing left. Or he would do it slowly, deliberately. He would slit his throat, watch the blood and air bubble; listen to the pathetic gurgle of the pig!

10
Dubai Marina

Anna excused herself and got up. She asked a waiter where the ladies' room was. He pointed her in the direction of the front of the ship, further into the dining room. She walked in the direction he had pointed, searching for an exit, finding a doorway opening to a deck. Anna glanced back at the table quickly before slipping through. No one was watching her. The servants were too busy, and the guests were already well on their way to getting horribly drunk.

The surface of the deck was shining, catching the wash of the moonlight. Making her way towards the bow, the deck ended in a stairway that led down, it seemed to Anna, all the way to the lowest level. She navigated the turn-back stairs clutching her purse in one hand and holding onto the railing with the other.

Her mind began to race. Was she proceeding straight into a trap? Had Trevellian been tipped off? Then again, there seemed to be genuine chemistry between them a few minutes ago. James had mentioned some business to do with Clive Codwell. That was probably what it was about, thought Anna as she took the last step off onto the lower-most deck's wooden surface and headed towards the bow, her high heels clacking on the wood.

Helicopter blades came into view first and then, as she got closer towards a set of steps that led up to the helipad at the bow, the full sight of what Anna recognised to be a Trevellian Enterprises-built Dark Horse 12 helicopter came into view.

A servant stood beside the helicopter and motioned for Anna to get in. She was completely at Trevellian's mercy, she thought, as she climbed the set of portable stairs that led up to the helicopter's back seats. Hiding her fear, she settled in to a window-side chair in the back-most row and put her purse in her lap as the door was pulled closed and the blades began to whir.

11
Ojos del Salado

Siegmund was snoring. Fox had decided to make it silent and quick, and with as few visible wounds as possible. Slipping out of the stretcher bed onto his hands and knees, he used the dim light of the coals to make out the shape of Siegmund's head. The German was lying on his back with his head facing up. Fox slid his hand along the pick axe's handle and gently picked it up. The wind howled like a chorus of baying wolves. Crouching, he placed one foot carefully in front of the other. He paused, towering above Siegmund, and wielded the axe until it crested a wide arc. Fox smiled as he brought it down. It whistled through the air and entered the head through the eye socket with a moist plop. Fox knew immediately that something was wrong. The blade hadn't gone deep enough to sink into the brain. He had discounted the fact that the width of the blade was probably more than the diameter of the bone sides of the eye socket. Siegmund jerked involuntarily out of sleep like a roaring giant, piercing screams followed a second later. Fox felt a sharp pain in his foot and looked down to see a knife blade sticking in his flesh, a fresh pool of blood collected around the outlines of his foot. Siegmund was turning the blade and trying to get up at the same time, clutching at his eye with his other hand. Fox jerked the pick axe out of Siegmund's bloodied head and a marshmallow-like object came away with it. Fox buried the pick axe deep into Siegmund's rib cage.

He yanked the knife out of his foot and plunged it into Siegmund's throat, baring his teeth.

Siegmund sprung out of the bed, stunned by the violence and the shock. He spluttered as the blood and air mixed to form bubbles.

'Listen to the pathetic little pig gurgle!'

Siegmund struck out with his fist, smashing Fox flush on the ridge of his nose. Clutching at his face more out of surprise than pain, Fox's hands slipped on the smooth bloodied skin of his cheeks while Siegmund crashed through the door of the hut, holding his neck and gasping, flailing like a wounded animal full-on into the blizzard.

The wind stunned Fox into moving. He crouched to grab one of his boots with the giant-sized crampon blades in his hand, and he pursued Siegmund in the snow.

'Your time is up, you stinking little Nazi rat!' shouted Fox. Siegmund collapsed in a heap. Fox flipped him over and used his boot with its extra-large crampons to hammer away at Siegmund's face, smashing it into a collage of blood, skin and bone as he lost all self control.

Fox did not remember taking the keys off Siegmund's belt. He did not remember dragging the body a hundred metres to a concealed natural crevice. He did not recall throwing the body into the gloom. His hands full of blood, his breathing quick and shallow, Fox only came around standing in front of the bathroom mirror of the *refugio*, clutching the bunch of keys and staring at a madman who shook with uncontrollable laughter.

12
Dubai Marina

A soldier appeared on the helipad, poking a semi-automatic machine gun around. He shouted something in German, Anna couldn't hear what it was against the whine of the helicopter's blades, and then James Trevellian appeared on the platform.

He crouched beneath the wind of the blades while the soldier slid open the door and he got into the helicopter, taking a seat beside Anna. She was trying to act as if it was all normal, but decided that it wouldn't be *normal* if she wasn't surprised.

James was smiling. The hatch door was closed, the shrill whine of the engine grew louder and the helicopter lifted off the ground. It turned about five metres up, towards the Dubai skyline, and then began to lift quickly.

James handed Anna a set of headphones, which she pulled over her head. As soon as James also had his on, he turned to her and smiled.

'What's going on?' Anna asked.

'You'll see. Just enjoy the scenery.'

James uncorked a bottle of wine and handed it to her.

'Do you mind the bottle?'

'Not at all,' Anna said, taking a swig. It was sweet, delicious.

The helicopter climbed to half the height of the buildings. The yacht faded to a small spec of white bobbing on the marina as the lights of the city glowed all around them. The helicopter picked its way between the skyscrapers, seeming to be headed in the direction of one particularly tall building that Anna recognised as Burj Khalifa, the tallest building in the world.

As the 800-metre building came into view, the helicopter descended, and touched down on a helipad.

James tore off the headphones, opened the door and motioned for Anna to step out.

'Come, I have a surprise for you,' he said as he took her hand and helped her out, and then delicately kissed it, sending bolts of electricity racing up her arm.

13
Ojos del Salado

Fox was immensely cold. He shuddered against the icy wind of the open door. 'Bloody Nazi scum deserved it,' he said to himself aloud. He slammed the door closed against the wind and ice whipping off the mountain slopes and began scrubbing the floor of the hut with his shirt to get rid of Siegmund's blood. He had a job to do, and he knew he couldn't let Ben down again, although he realised that he already had. Killing a Trevellian Enterprises agent was no way to be inconspicuous. He threw on some clothes and his boots before exiting the hut, once more into the heavy blizzard, to walk along Siegmund's trail of blood, covering it over with fresh snow as he went kicking with his boots. He hurried back to the door of the room adjoining the hut, fumbled with the keys that he'd taken off Siegmund, trying several before he felt one grating the lock open. There was a click and he opened the door and took in breath through his teeth.

The room was empty aside from a circular hatchway in the middle. Fox scrutinised it with a flashlight that he had picked up in the other room. It was a green thickset metal door, a bit like a manhole cover, but thicker. There were no handles or holes. He tried pushing it, but it didn't budge. There was no way one could use anything – a crowbar, or any lever – to force it open, but there was a small panel beside it, with a blinking red light. It seemed to be an access-controlled entranceway, but to what? And how did it work? Fox hurried back into the hut, and looked for further clues. He dug in Siegmund's bag, finding a set of extra clothes, and finally, in a front pocket, a small tag that looked like an access card.

Tearing off his clothes, placing them in a neat pile at the back of the cupboard, Fox pulled on Siegmund's Enterprises Expeditions gear, including a black beanie with an iron eagle embroidered on the front. From his climbing backpack he produced an emergency disguise kit and took out a pair of coloured contact lenses. He hurried to the bathroom mirror and put the contacts in, staring into cold, blue German eyes instead of his usual brown. He washed the blood off his face and felt his nose. It wasn't broken. Only then did he remember the blade that had been stuck in his foot. He leaned down and touched it where the wound was. There was no excruciating pain, a flesh wound, and he would be able to ignore it. He hadn't felt it when he walked and he would be okay.

Fox had one last thing to do. He took his and Siegmund's backpacks, ensured that all the zips were closed and that there were no clothes lying around the *refugio*, then he ran outside and threw the bags into the crevice that Siegmund's body lay in. Panting, he locked the hut and slipped into the adjoining room, locking the door behind him. He swiped Siegmund's card next to the hatch and held his breath. There was a pause, then a small buzz, and the light changed to green! The hatch door swung up, to reveal a ladder that disappeared into the bowels of the earth.

14
Dubai Marina

James led Anna into the foyer of the Burj Khalifa and almost immediately into a lift leading off to the side. A group of tourists stood, arguing with a guard about having a tour they had already paid for that had been cancelled at the last minute.

A hotel employee welcomed James with a wide smile as they entered the lift. He asked what floor, James answered, 'All the way', and the lift began to hurtle to the top.

When the lift came to a stop with a beeping sound, they stepped out onto the observation deck of the Burj Khalifa, more than eight hundred metres above the ground.

There was no one around. Across from the elevator, at the floor-to-ceiling window, was a table. James had set up a private table for two overlooking the dazzling night lights of Dubai. Anna couldn't help but feel a little impressed.

15
Ojos del Salado

The ladder descended into darkness, about two hundred metres, assessed Fox, as he had counted out at least three times that number of steps. Finally, the ladder's rungs gave way to air and Fox searched the floor with his flashlight. It was a cave, deathly quiet. The darkness seemed to suck everything in, but Fox felt at peace.

There was a sound. What was it? A sneeze? He switched the light off and crouched. A tiny speck of red light appeared, shooting up like a thin laser beam from the floor of the cave onto a rock jutting out of the wall several feet above it. Fox crawled over to the light and brushed some dust away from its glass surface.

It was an access pad! Just like the one that protected the hatchway above. Whoever was beyond this one was most likely guarding the entrance, in the same way Mikhail had been guarding the emergency exit tunnel near Yamantaw.

Whoever it was, thought Fox, he needed to be taken out. Making sure that there was a space to crouch into along the wall, he produced Siegmund's tag and pressed it near the light. There was a click as the hatchway opened in the cave's floor.

'Who's there?' A thick, Bavarian accent.

Fox waited. A large head poked up through the hatch and looked around. It was a mistake. Fox's blade flashed. Blood gurgled from the guard's throat and he fell back downwards with a heavy thud. His face was pale blue by the time Fox climbed down through the entrance.

The guard had been alone in what appeared to be an alley, with cobbled pavestones and grimy yellow walls. Fox grunted as he dragged the dead body behind a tower of wooden crates. It was a massive corpse, about six-foot-two, with blonde hair and blue eyes. Fox removed the dead man's clothes and put them on, completed by a *stalhelm* and a rifle. The clothes looked ridiculously large on him. It was unnerving.

What is this place? he thought.

It was a short way to the end of the cobbled alley, which opened up to a vaulted chasm. Steel walkways, iron grills with imposing stairways, led up the walls, above a thriving subterranean town on the floor of the cave. No ordinary town, if any underground town could ever be called ordinary. It was bristling with steepled, traditional alpine German houses with smoking chimneys, cobbled streets lit by old-style streetlamps and bicycles. The men in the streets wore jackets and hats, the women wore frocks. Dogs and children played in the streets.

It looks bizarrely like a 1940s German town, thought Fox as he stared in horror at the red banners with swastikas streaming down the sides of the steep, high cave walls that led up to a blunt ceiling, so high that it felt dizzying to look at. Soldiers marched in step through the small streets to the adulating gaze of women and children who stood on the pavements. Fox pulled out his phone and took high-res pictures, but when he checked for signal, there was none.

In a daze, Fox climbed down one of the ladders leading to the floor of the town.

16
Burj Khalifa

Anna sank her teeth into the most tender rump she'd ever had, and washed it down with a smooth red wine that had a delicious chocolate aftertaste.

'How much of the language did you pick up?' James asked.

They were discussing Liz's spiritual retreat in Tibet that had happened to last five years. Anna was playing along. It was like trying to walk gingerly through a minefield with elephant feet.

'Well, I wasn't much interested in the language, but I've been learning a lot about Eastern philosophy and religion.'

'Ah,' James answered between mouthfuls. 'Did you know, Himmler used to carry a copy of the Bhagavad Gita around with him during the war. Or at least, some pages from it.'

'They were fascinated by eastern religion, weren't they?'

James smiled. 'Ah yes, the old guard. You know of their beliefs?'

Anna had read about it. 'Oh yes. They believed that the Germans were originally from Asia. I've read Lord Bulwer's *The Coming Race*, about the *vyril*, the magical substance. Do you believe any of that?'

This line of questioning was really for Anna to cast out feelers. What kind of potential there was to get information out of him.

'I'm not sure,' admitted James. 'I know I'm supposed to. It's sort of an open secret within the organisation, that we've spent a lot of money searching for Himmler's artefacts. I mean, a *lot*.'

'You mean, like the Spear of Destiny?'

'Among other things. Anyway ...' Here goes, thought Anna, he was about to shut the door closed. '... I would rather talk about you.'

Anna allowed a pause to sink in. She wanted him to make all the moves. That way, she was innocent.

She wondered if Liz was just a diversion for him, an escape, whether or not he knew it, from the pressure of planned mass murder. Or was there something more?

She knew that he was unmarried and had shown an almost complete lack of interest in women. But surely, she thought, there was something different to this situation she found herself in, at the top of the Burj Khalifa, alone with James Trevellian. It was more than an anomaly. Why had he said, 'To hell with all this', under his breath earlier and why had he abandoned the dinner to spend his evening with a woman he hardly knew?

'What would you like to know?' The ghost of a smile played on her lips.
'Everything.'
'Well!' Anna laughed. 'That could take some time ...'
'I have time.'
Anna was taken aback. Why was he being so forward?
When they had finished eating, James led her to a door, climbed up a ladder, followed by Anna, onto an open platform with a breathtaking and scarily high view of Dubai unfolding around them. James sat on the edge of the platform with his feet dangling over. Anna joined him after a moment's hesitation. Only a rail separated them from a fall of almost a kilometre. They sipped from a bottle of the sweet chocolatey red, sharing a comfortable silence on the platform. For a long time, James seemed far away with his thoughts.

'Liz ... do you ever feel like your life doesn't belong to you?'
His question surprised Anna. Short and simple, it struck a chord with her. She realised that it pretty much summarised her life. She worked for an organisation driven by a strong national and religious zeal that, in a sense, wasn't her own. Some might call her a traitor for thinking that, but she believed she was really just being open minded.

Anna leaned her head to one side and stared out over the dancing sea of lights.

'Yes, I do. In fact, you're more right than you think. Is that how you feel?'
'All the time.'
A pause sank in.
He'd revealed another side to him that she really hadn't expected. It was disarming; humbled her assumptions about him.

James added: 'You realise that your life belongs to someone else, or *something* else, when you're forced to make a decision that tests every ounce of what you've been taught to believe in.'

'Like what?'
'Well, for example, if you are taught, as a child, that Jews are the enemy. You accept it and you believe it. Then one day, say, a Jew saves your life, and in an instant your whole world view is called into question.'

Was he hinting? Did he know about who she was? Was he deliberately leading her on and letting her in, only to expose her, having a bit of fun with her before feeding her to the sharks? Anna clutched the rail and tried to believe differently.

'Do you believe that all Jews are the enemy?'

'I've been taught that my whole life. I've heard nothing else. Israel is the enemy ... but ... lately I feel that there's something wrong with this whole philosophy. One minute I am inspired to be my father's son, but the next ...' He shook his head. 'I don't know anymore.'

Maybe it was the wine, or maybe he needed to offload; this quiet time alone was allowing him to open up.

'You mentioned an instant that can change your life. What did you mean?'

'I think you know. One of those moments. Perhaps the first time you lay your eyes on someone.'

He was looking at her, and she at him, and they both knew then that one of those moments had just happened.

17
Ojos del Salado

Fox walked through the streets of the German town, starry-eyed and dazed. A column of soldiers passed by. Each soldier in the unit was *exactly* the same in appearance as the one next to, in front or behind him. Fox thought he must be hallucinating.

Statues of Aryan gods lined the street: bronzed eagles, eight-legged horses and warrior kings. A street sign read '*Prinz Albert Strasse*', the same, mused Fox, as in Berlin during the Second World War, where the headquarters of Himmler's SS had been stationed. A poster glued to a red-brick wall caught his attention and he drew up to read it, producing a cigarette from the soldier's pocket, lit it and, even though he didn't smoke, inhaled sharply.

The banner read: '*Kämpft, vir Führer en Volk*'. It showed a battalion of soldiers marching beside ultra modern-looking battle tanks with red standards of swastikas held high, a smouldering city in ruins in the background. In the foreground submarines with swastika insignias on them shot torpedoes at warships. Fox recognised the poster as an updated version of Second World War Nazi propaganda.

Beside the streets were cafés with round tables where 'civilians' of the Fourth Reich smoked, ate, drank and greeted passersby warmly, stepping out of 1930s-style cinemas and dance halls. There were dress shops, hardware stores, appliance stores, bars and restaurants, all teeming with patrons. Some even sang German war songs. And there were high-vaulted hallways with runic symbols, outside churches of the Fourth Reich, which recognised neither Christianity nor anything else except Nazism. Fox could never have imagined something of such a colossal scale.

A group of young children played a game of soccer under a street lamp. A lone child sat glum, away from the group. Now was the time to get some answers.

'Hey you! Hey boy!' Fox shouted. The child looked up. His eyes were wide with excitement at seeing a soldier call to him. He pointed to his chest as if to say, 'Who, me?'

'You boy, come here!'

The boy bounded over to him. Fox ruffled his hair and then produced a knife.

'Do you like this knife?'

The boy nodded enthusiastically.

'I'll give it to you.'

'Really?'

'A genuine soldier's blade.' Fox ran his finger along the edge. The German was coming easier than he thought.

'Can I really have it?'

'Only if you play a game with me. You like games?'

'Yes, *herr soldat.*' The boy looked down at his shoes.

'Good. You need to pretend that I'm not from this place. Pretend I'm from another world and I just arrived here in my spaceship. Now you need to tell me all about this place, so that I can know all about it. Does this sound like something you can do?'

The boy nodded.

'Good. I want to see how well you can describe it to me. Let's sit down.' They sat, cross-legged, on the cobbles.

'Tell me about this place, everything you know. Remember, I don't know a thing, so start with its name.'

'*Drachenfeld, herr soldat*, it's called *Drachenfeld*, Dragon's Rock.'

'Good, now tell me more.'

'And you will give me the knife?'

'Yes, I will give you the knife.'

The boy began to tell Fox all he knew about his world, as if relating a great wonder to a stranger, his eyes averted, his cheeks rosy, skin exceptionally pale. He spoke of a great war in a long-distant past, heroes like Otto Skorzeny, Adolf Hitler and Hans-Ulrich Rudel … Heinrich Himmler and of James Trevellian.

'So tell me,' Fox interrupted. 'This leader of yours, James …' he waited for the boy to finish.

'Trevellian. His real name is *Adler*, because he soars like a mighty eagle above ground, where he runs Trevellian Enterprises, the arms company.'

'*Ja*, Trevellian … This man Trevellian, he is truly a great man?'

'The greatest man alive. He builds massive bombs and submarines, and he has built the greatest army on earth.'

'He's an impressive person, your leader, James Trevellian,' said Fox, nodding his head. 'Now tell me, these bombs that Trevellian builds … what kind are they, and where are they made?'

'That is the best part.' The boy brimmed with excitement, and kept stealing glances at the blade. 'It's just like in the movies … just like the bombs that the cowardly Americans dropped on Japanese cities, except my uncle Göttfried tells me they are at least ten times more powerful.'

'I see, indeed! And tell me …' Fox cocked his head to one side. '… Where are these bombs produced?'

'My uncle says … my uncle says that, even though it is supposed to be a secret … they are made in Factory 12.'

'Factory 12, you say?' Fox tried for 'pensive', with his chin clutched between his thumb and his forefinger.

'And where is this Factory 12?'

The boy looked uncomfortable, his eyes and head drooped. 'I'm not supposed to say, *herr soldat*.'

'Excellent answer!'

The boy looked up, and Fox ruffled his hair again. 'You see,' began Fox, 'I am actually no outsider. I came here directly from head office.'

Fox had struck gold, and was mining the seam.

'Head office?' the boy asked, excited.

'Yes. Head office, above ground. You see, I was sent on a mission by the same man you were telling me about just now, *Führer* Trevellian himself. I report directly to him.'

'You do?' the boy's eyes lit up.

'Yes, and this was a test. I also work in a very important department. Can you guess which one?'

The boy thought for a while. 'You're a secret agent!'

'Correct.'

'You work for BEAD?'

'Yes, I was sent here to make contact with you. We have special plans for you, and I was sent to test you.'

'Did I pass?'

'With flying colours. You didn't reveal the secret location of Factory 12. That was your test.'

The boy looked overjoyed. Fox produced a cigarette, lit it and inhaled.

'I have another test for you.'

'What is it?'

'We need to test how smart you *really* are. Because, you see, BEAD agents need to be very smart.' The boy nodded. 'You need to tell me the real location of Factory 12, so that I can see that you're not bluffing. I need to know whether you actually know the secret. Otherwise it wouldn't be a secret, would it?'

The boy didn't hesitate. 'Level Five.'

'And you have been there?'

'No, *mein herr*. But my Uncle Göttfried works there.'

'A soldier?'

'No, a scientist.'

'Good.'

Fox rubbed his chin. This was working out nicely. 'And how does one get into this secret factory, Factory 12?'

'With special cards that you swipe.'

'Ah. And Göttfried has one of these special cards?'

'Yes, *mein herr*.'

Fox let silence fall between him and the boy, until the boy, writhing, finally said, 'Did I pass?'

'Not yet. One more thing.'

'What is it, what do I have to do?'
'A final test.'
'Anything!' said the boy.
'That card you told me about ... the access card.'
'*Jahwol*, what about it, *herr soldat*?'
'You need to steal it for me. Can you do that?'
The boy nodded.

18
Burj Khalifa

It was turning out to be a very strange night indeed. Anna couldn't believe her luck. First, she'd thought she was being trapped, that James had discovered her true identity. Then, she was whisked off to the tallest building in the world to have a private dinner date with James Trevellian, the very man she was sent in to 'get to know'.

There was just one problem, thought Anna. She felt herself losing control. The more the wine flowed the drunker she got, and the more James talked, the more she let go. She felt herself slipping, and didn't know if she had the strength to hold on.

19
Drachenfeld

The boy came bounding along the path ten minutes from the time Fox had watched him run off, a massive grin spread out on his face, breathing heavily and doubled over with the effort after he handed the card to Fox.

'*Herr soldat*, here it is! I got it!'
'You have surpassed our expectations. And did anyone see you?'
'Not a soul, *herr soldat*.'
'Good, that is very good. Tell me ...' Fox began.
'More tests?' the boy levelled up, his breaths coming easier, a look of puzzled disappointment on his face.

'Yes, some final small ones, which I have no doubt you'll ace.' Fox ruffled the boy's hair and smiled. 'Do you remember the game we played just now?'

'Yes, of course *herr soldat*, the one in which you were a foreigner and I was telling you about *Drachenfeld*, about our *Vaderland.*'

'Yes, that's the one. Tell me, as a foreigner, how would I get to Level Five?'

'The access is restricted, but you can go in those lifts that go deeper into the ground.'

The boy pointed across the wide main avenue to a dark glistening side of the cave where an iron lift cage was guarded by two soldiers with guns.

'I go down there?'

'Yes, *herr soldat.*'

'You are a very clever little boy. And tell me, do they allow "normal" soldiers like me down there?'

'No, *herr soldat*, not normally, but they do sometimes.'

'When?'

'To deliver messages to important people working down there.'

'Like your uncle?'

'Yes, like my uncle Göttfried.'

'And tell me, what is Göttfried's family name?'

'Junge, *herr soldat.*'

'Ah, well!' Fox said, clutching the boy's shoulder, 'You've passed this test, soldier, here's your knife.'

'Wow!'

The boy swished the blade through the air.

'You'll make a fine secret agent one day.'

'*Danke schoon, danke, danke, herr soldat!*' The boy made a Hitler salute, '*Heil Führer!*'

Fox didn't reply to his salute and clenched his teeth together.

'Now listen, if anyone asks you, and I mean *anyone*, about the card you gave me, what are you to say?'

'Nothing, *herr soldat.*'

'That's right, you are not to utter a word.'

The boy shook his head, his eyes purposeful and wide.

'Now go back to your game. If anyone asks you about the blade, tell them you found it.'

The boy nodded.

'Good boy, run along now.'

The boy skipped away. Fox walked to the lift as quickly as he could. When one of the two guards on either side of the lift stepped forward to halt his progress, he shouted, 'Out of my way, you imbecile! I have an important message for Göttfried Junge, one of our most esteemed scientists. A message from head office!'

Fox knew that Göttfried Junge was at home, and this was risky, but today he was in a gambling mood. He'd first thrown the dice a few moments – although it seemed like years ago – when he'd murdered Siegmund. The man slunk aside. Fox entered the lift cage and pressed minus five.

20
Strait of Hormuz

Anna awoke in the owner's suite of the *Aegir* to the sweet scent of strong coffee mingled with a fresh sea breeze washing into the room from the large bay windows that overlooked a the sea, sparkling in the morning sun. Or was it afternoon? Her head was splitting with pain, and she was naked. What had happened last night? The last thing she remembered was sitting on top of the Burj Khalifa. Had she blown her cover? She started to feel panic but forced herself to remain calm. James sauntered into the room, bare chested, and she clasped the duvet around herself shyly. His torso was tanned and Anna admired the lean muscles, wondering how he could possibly be forty-eight years old.

'What time is it?' asked Anna, trying to sound nonchalant as James placed the tray down on the bedside table. On it was a coffee plunger, two mugs, a bowl of sugar and one of cream, and delicious-looking fresh croissants with tubs of butter and jam. Anna's stomach grumbled and she realised how hungry she was.

'Twelve o'clock,' answered James, sitting down beside her on the bed, pouring out a cup of coffee.

'Thanks,' Anna said.

'I'll give you some privacy to get dressed.' James fetched a beautiful black silk robe from the cupboard and placed it next to Anna. 'Join me outside on the deck,' he said, picking up the tray and disappearing through the doors into the bright sunlight.

Anna slumped her head back on the pillow and forced air through her lips. How drunk had she gotten last night? What had she said? How did they end up back on the yacht, and what happened then?

She mulled over the questions as the world began to spin. She felt dizzy and nauseous, but swallowed hard and forced herself to get out of bed, quickly slipping into the gown. She stood briefly before the en suite bathroom mirror and tidied her hair, returned to the room, found her bag, fumbled in it for her dark shades and joined James on the deck. He lay on a deck chair beside the azure swimming pool, his hands clasped over his chest, staring out over the sea.

A wave of panic hit Anna as she realised the boat was moving. She looked up to the horizon and saw the distant shoreline. No Dubai Marina, no tall skyscrapers. She sank down in the deck chair beside James, trying not to panic. James smiled at her, a reassuring grin.

'Are we out at sea?' she asked.

'We're set on a course to the Bay of Bengal and, before you panic …' James looked up and smiled. 'I took the liberty of kidnapping you, while I tossed the others out at midnight. We're sailing towards Chittagong in the Bay of Bengal. I thought, as you were returning to Tibet in any case, you could hitch a ride.'

'But,' said Anna, frowning, 'what about my things?'

'I sent an agent round to the Burj al Arab to pick them up.'

Anna's mind raced. Had she left any items that could incriminate her at her suite? She was immensely glad that she had destroyed the file on James in the fireplace, but what about the files on Codwell? She recalled stowing them away in a hidden pocket in her suitcase. She hoped that it hadn't been searched. She was skating on very thin ice.

'I'll arrange your transportation from Chittagong to Tibet once we're there. You will find no need for visa stamps, as you'll be travelling almost as a diplomat would.'

'How will you manage that?'

'I have my ways, and my friends,' said James with a grin that broadened into a wide smile.

'Is that so,' said Anna, trying to appear thoroughly displeased.

'Are you in the habit of controlling people's movements, or is this just a once-off? Did you think I'm such a pushover that I wouldn't mind?' Anna glowered. But she didn't manage to put James off his stride, not one bit, she noticed.

'It's a once-off thing,' said James.

Anna allowed her feigned anger to melt. A smile crept onto her face. She looked out over the bright sea, watching the faint blue outline of oil tankers moving through the Strait of Hormuz.

'Can I ask you a question?'

'Go ahead,' said James.

'Last night, after the Burj Khalifa … I don't remember much … what did we do?'

'Do?'

'I mean, did we …' She averted her eyes. 'You know …'

'Sleep together?'

'Yes …'

'Yes.'

Anna's heart sank. James noticed the look on her face.

'Don't worry, it's not what you think,' he said. 'When we got back here, we had a few drinks. One thing led to another, but then you passed out on my chest. I fell asleep shortly afterwards.'

'So nothing happened?'

'Well, I suppose.' James looked a bit hurt. 'If you call that nothing, then yes, nothing happened.'

Anna sighed. She was genuinely relieved, but half of it was an act. She could feel the chemistry between them growing, but she wanted James to think she was a goody-two shoes who wasn't in the habit of climbing into any man's bed. She wanted him to find her worthy, attractive.

There was a faint knock on the inside cabin door. A voice called out, *'Mein Führer?'* James sighed, got up, went into the cabin and opened the door.

'What is it?' she heard James ask.

'Your father … his condition is worsening.'

Anna decided to use the opportunity to get closer. She went into the cabin, took her bag from the bed and snuck into the en suite bathroom, leaving the door open slightly to listen.

'How bad is it?'

'A few days.'

Anna gasped. If he was dying, it meant that, along with him would be buried any chance of revenge.

'The doctors have been saying that for weeks. But I will make some calls right away. Listen ...'

Anna had to lean closer to hear James whisper.

'Did you find anything amongst her things?'

'*Nein, mein Führer.*'

'That's good, you may go.'

The door clicked shut. Anna carefully closed the bathroom door. Now she would have to pull out all the stops to make sure he really believed her, if he doubted her credibility. She hoped she was up to the challenge. She pulled out her satellite phone from her bag, locked the door quietly and began tapping away on the phone. Ben would be pleased with the results, but somehow the thought of sending the message made her feel guilty. Strange emotions she couldn't identify fully were tugging her deeper into a trap.

21
Drachenfeld

The lift ground to a halt at minus five. Fox shuffled out, exhausted. His foot was starting to pain slightly, but he ignored the feeling and pushed on, entering a long tunnel, following the signs for Factory 12. The tunnel seemed to go on forever. Finally it forked in two directions. Fox followed more signs and entered a bathroom which he presumed to be near the factory. He would need to get a new disguise, somehow.

Voices erupted from the tunnel, and Fox jumped into a bathroom cupboard. He decided to wait there, hoping for a scientist to come within striking distance. He let the voices die down, crouching in the wide cupboard, and without intending to, fell into a deep sleep.

22
Arabian Sea

In the shower of the en suite bathroom on board the *Aegir*, Anna turned the water pressure up and closed her eyes. Jets of hot water massaged her skin and steam floated like a cloud, fogging up the mirrors. Between scrubbing her back and lathering soap over her body, Anna reflected on her situation, hoping it would help her to put things in perspective.

James's father, Franz Wagener, an escaped war criminal, her parents' killer, was tucked away in a Nazi base somewhere, dying. Instead of confronting his so-called son, the leader of the Fourth Reich, James Trevellian, she'd slept naked with him, aboard his giant private yacht, now cruising the Arabian Sea off the coast of Pakistan.

She should try to get to Franz before it was too late if she could, but for now, she was trapped. The yacht would wind around the coast of India, just north of the Maldives, and into the Bay of Bengal, before docking in Chittagong. She could disembark there, but then what? James was expecting her to go to Tibet. She couldn't very well take off in the opposite direction.

It was too much to think about. She allowed herself to zone out. The apple-scented body scrub smelled delicious; the coral sponge's cleansing effect was cathartic. She felt like she had to get James out of her skin.

Her shower done, Anna returned to the bedroom. She sat on the edge of the bed and James came in from the deck. He found her wrapped up in the black silk gown, drying her hair with a towel.

'Liz, I have some business to tend to,' he said. 'It will most likely take up most of my day. Will you join me for dinner tonight, on the top deck, at seven? You'll find an evening gown in your stateroom when you return there. I'll be in the conference room on the second deck.'

Anna stared, open-mouthed, deciding whether or not to protest about being told what to wear, but decided against it and said, 'Who else will be there?'

'Only you, only me.'

23
Ojos del Salado

It was an Argentinean porter who first followed the faint traces of scuffled footprints to the entrance of the crevice in which Siegmund's body lay, and peered down to make out the purplish neck and the mangled and bloodied face of the murdered climb leader.

The porter called out to his boss, Sanchez, who was leading a climb party up the slopes of the mountain.

'Boss, you'd better see this.'

Sanchez sighed. It was not the first time he'd heard those words, nor would it be the last. Too many climbers were too stubborn to take heed. Too many of them, he thought, wanted to defeat Mother Nature, and most wound up in the foetal position, frozen stiff on the slopes or in crevices such as this one. But this body was different.

Sanchez reached his porter, breathing hard, frowning.

'What is it, Miguel?'

'There, sir.'

'Dear Jesus.' Sanchez genuflected. 'Mother Mary and Joseph.'

A few hours later, Miss Contreras would gasp for air and cup her hand over her mouth, biting down hard as the bitter taste of bile crept into her mouth. The sight of Siegmund's barely recognisable face and prostate body lying naked and cold against the hard steel of the morgue slab was too much for her. She hunched over to the side and threw up on the floor.

The morgue worker, a university Medical School drop-out, stood on the other side of the slab. Disenchanted, he looked up from the mangled face, the likes of which he had never seen.

'So that's him? Siegmund Baum?'

Miss Contreras wiped her mouth with the back of her sleeve and gave him the most contemptuous look she could muster. Did he have no sympathy? This Hispanic *untermenschen* didn't deserve to live, she thought. Finally she mustered the courage to look at the body again.

'Yes. I think so. What's left of him.'

She broke into a sob. The death-worker, unperturbed, folded the sheet over the face and turned to leave, gesturing towards the door, 'Thank you,' he said.

'No,' Miss Contreras protested. 'I need a moment.'

She calmed herself, wiped her eyes and pulled out her phone as the man left the room. She dialled a number and waited for Frieda to answer.

24
Arabian Sea

Roger rapped on the door of James's study. He knew that Frieda was inside.

'*Bitte?*'

'*Fraülein*, it is *herr* Roger.'

'A moment.'

Frieda appeared at the door, opening it only a slither, looking out suspiciously. 'What?'

'May I come in?'

Frieda closed the door in his face. He heard rummaging inside the office before the door was re-opened and Frieda stood staring at him, tapping her foot impatiently.

'Did you receive a reply from Codwell's secretary?'

'No. I've left several messages with her. Lord Codwell is a very busy man, *herr* Roger.'

Roger rounded the desk and sat smugly in Frieda's chair.

'Yes, I understand,' he said, picking up a pencil and acting the part of an investigator. 'But you know …' he leaned towards Frieda who was still standing beside the door, glaring at him. 'It's just that I don't trust her, this Liz Codwell character.'

'For once, I agree with you,' Frieda snapped. 'I'll try again, I'll send emails, text messages …'

'Failing that,' Roger leaned back in the chair, 'we could even try the lodge that Liz Codwell stayed at in Tibet. To check whether or not our mystery woman is there.'

'Good idea, *herr* Roger. For once.'

Suddenly Frieda's bright red telephone rang, a shrill sound that spelled danger. Only a few individuals had access to the number. Frieda hurried over and picked it up.

'*Ja?*'

Frieda hit the speakerphone button as she waited for the reply.

'Frieda?'

'*Ja*, it is me. Who is this?'

'Contreras, Enterprises Expeditions front desk. We have an emergency that we need the *führer* to advise on.'

'Go on.'

'Code red.'

'What?' Frieda's face was pale.

'An intruder, at *Drachenfeld*.'

'*Onmochlich!*' said Roger.

'An *NSS Mann* in-training, Siegmund Baum, was found murdered on the slopes of Ojos del Salado. The so-called tourist with him, a Mr Younan Sahin, is nowhere to be found. We believe he may have infiltrated the base. We suspect he is an enemy agent of the highest priority.'

'Highest priority' was code for Mossad. Roger stood up, possessing a new-found mantle of authority.

'Listen, Contreras, this is *herr* Roger. I will notify the *Führer* right away. You are not to sound any alarm of any sort. Notify BEAD agent Patrick immediately of the situation. He will hunt your man down as he is currently at *Drachenfeld*. If you raise any alarm, this man will get away. Do I make myself clear?'

'*Zu behefl.*'

Roger turned to Frieda. 'Phone Sahin's secretary. Establish his whereabouts. Do you know who he is?'

'Yes, *herr* Roger, the Turkish businessman.'

'Good.'

Roger stormed in search of James.

25
Arabian Sea

Roger burst into the conference room. James was in the middle of a call, his face etched with anger and surprise at Roger's unusual intrusion.

'What the bloody hell?'

'There's a Code Red, *mein Führer.*'

James spoke into the phone: 'I'll have to call you back', and hung up.
'Where?'
'*Drachenfeld.*'
'When?'
'About an hour ago.'
'What agency?'
'Priority.'

There was a long pause. Roger knew that it would make James furious that Mossad could be involved. James drew in a long breath.

'*Sheiße!*'

'Patrick will be onto the intruder, *mein Führer.*'

'Good. Has he been notified?'

'I'm on it.'

'Find the man. Hurt him if you have to, but don't kill him. We can use him as collateral. And I want to know how this cock-up happened.'

'*Zu behefl.*'

Roger turned to leave, but James halted him again.

'Roger, I think it's time to bring out the dagger.'

'Operation Hidden Dagger?'

Roger smiled. James had spoken the words that would put in motion a chain of events that would decimate Mossad.

26
Tel Aviv

Two junior Mossad officers were parked in an olive-green Ford pickup truck across the street from a restaurant in which Steven was enjoying a meal with his mistress.

'You're sure they'll take his car home?'

'She doesn't have a car.'

'What does she do?'

'She's a dancer. From France.'

'How did *he* get someone like *her*?'

'He pays.'

'How did you find this out?'

'He told me once, after a couple of drinks.'

'So ... if she goes too, will there be repercussions?'

'Repercussions? Of course there'll be bloody repercussions. But she's no one's daughter, if that's what you mean. She's a low-life piece of trash. Came in from France on her father's whim. Abandoned at the age of eight to make a living for herself. Paying off a student loan by dancing in the clubs around Tel Aviv.'

'Such a pity ...'

'Wait till you see the body on her, then you'll see what a pity it is. But it's wasted on him ...'

'Absolutely. Listen, I have to ask again. What if he doesn't crank it, or what if he doesn't notice it, or if he just leaves it alone?'

'Don't worry. He will crank it. He'll be drunk, always is when he's with her. Has to compensate for what an idiot he is sober. He's amused by small things. You'll see ...'

The Deputy Director of Operations and his mistress Sylvaine stumbled onto the street. He was laughing, drunk, and she supported his weight. They walked to a Toyota Corolla.

She pulled his keys out of his pocket, unlocked the front passenger door and slumped him inside. She rounded the car and got into the driver's seat. She always had to drive them to her apartment where, usually, he would fall asleep on her couch while she made coffee or fixed him another drink, which was preferable to him ordering her to strip and dance for him. But in order to be paid anything, she would have to try and coax enough rising interest out of him, a difficult job, in order for them to have sex. Sylvaine didn't know why he even bothered.

As she got in she noticed a colourful box on the dashboard.

'What's this?' Steven slurred, fingering the crank on one side of the box. 'It wasn't here before, was it?'

'Don't touch it,' she said, aware of the kind of work he was in to. 'It could be a trap.'

He didn't listen, and began to wind up the crank, slurring some words she couldn't make out.

A childish song she recognised as 'Pop goes the weasel' began to play from the box with the sound of small gears turning inside. It was what she knew as a '*diable en boîte*' – French for 'boxed devil' – or, as the English called it, a 'Jack in the box'. When the song stopped, a clown figurine shot out, dangling on a spring. Sylvaine gasped. The glass fuse had been broken and the current connected.

The car exploded with such force that the agents across the street felt their truck sway in the bomb's wind and they instinctively covered their faces. Metal from the wrecked car clanged against the walls and on the sidewalks. Passersby screamed and crouched and held their hands around their heads.

Their job done, the two agents sped past the scene, en route to their next assignment. The agent in the passenger seat of the Ford pickup was already on an untraceable line to *Haaretz* newspaper as an anonymous 'angel of justice', claiming responsibility for the murder of a high-ranking Mossad officer in downtown Tel Aviv. He also had pictures of him with a mistress shortly before his death, he said.

27
Ojos del Salado

Patrick whistled an anthem as he turned the water off and stepped out of the shower. After drying himself he wrapped a towel around his waist and walked, feeling the softness of the lounge carpet between his toes, to his living room area.

He sat down, plucked a grape from a bunch on the coffee table and dropped it into his mouth. The phone rang in the hallway of his private, 40s-style German bunker. He sighed.

'*Ja?*'

'There's a code red.' It was Frieda.

'Where?'

'*Drachenfeld*. Most likely a Mossad agent. Suspect has murdered an *NSS Mann* and gained entry into the base.'

'When?'

'About an hour ago.'

'*Danke*, I will take care of him.'

He dialled a number and waited.

'Surveillance? ... Yes, *herr* Patrick here. We have a code red. Pull out all of the CCTV footage from the cameras for all entry and exit points to the base within the last hour. Look for anything unusual. I'll be there in ten minutes.' He hung up and walked to the bedroom, quickly dressed in jeans and a Trevellian Enterprises shirt, tucked his Walther PPK into his belt and exited the bunker.

'Rewind ... pause. There ... do you see him?'

Patrick stood behind the Chief of Surveillance's chair.

'Play it.'

On the screen, Fox slipped out of a hatchway after a guard had tumbled out of it, clutching at his throat. They watched as Fox removed the man's clothes and put them on.

'Print his photo for me. Can you trace him from there?'

'*Ja.*'

The controller pulled up the town cameras, pausing and zooming in to identify the intruder climbing down a ladder and stepping off into the town's streets. A man in an NSS uniform stopped near a group of children.

A child came over to him and admired his knife. They seemed to talk for a long time, after which the child disappeared and the man loitered around smoking cigarettes.

The child appeared a few minutes later and handed something to the man, who gave the child the knife in return and made his way over to the lifts beside the wall.

'Is it too much to ask to do your job for once?'

The head of Surveillance apologised profusely.

'Is there any more footage of this man after he entered the lift?'

'*Nein*, he disappears.'

'Find out who the boy is, let me know on my phone. I'm going to sort this whole mess out.'

Patrick clutched the picture of the enemy agent and made his way up several levels to the ground floor. He questioned the guards at the lifts, who told him that the very same man had passed by. Patrick got into the lift and pressed minus five.

28
Drachenfeld

In a white overcoat, a clipboard slung around his neck, Fox hurried down a tunnel towards Factory 12. He heard the trampling of marching boots before the first of the soldiers came into view. Led by a giant man of about six-foot-four with broad shoulders, cold blue eyes and high, wide cheekbones, the soldiers marched as if to the beat of an invisible drum.

After waking up in the bathroom cupboard, Fox assaulted a scientist, who he'd strangled to death to get his white lab coat. As the unit of soldiers neared, the general called out in a deep voice: '*Soldat, salute!*' The units turned towards Fox, raised their hands to their *Totenkopf* hats and saluted, staring at him from pitiless blue eyes.

Fox stared from one pair eyes to the next. Each face was identical! He'd not been dreaming when he thought he saw identical-looking soldiers on the streets above.

The bodies too, were all tall, broad-shouldered and muscular. How had they managed to do this? Fox wondered as he raised a hand in a Hitler salute and said '*Sieg Heil!*' as the last six-foot-two giant super-warrior brushed past him.

The entrance to the fifth-level nuclear research labs and factories, a non-descript grey portal, appeared to Fox's right. A sign above the door read 'Factory 12. *Verboten.*'

Fox produced Göttfried's access card and held it against the machine on the side of the iron door. A green light glowed, the door opened and he slipped through.

Inside, the massive factory buzzed with scientists, workmen, men behind computers and, in the centre, circular dents in the floor, where tips of missiles were poking out.

Fox walked along the side wall until he found the men's bathrooms. He went in, closed himself into the lone stall and waited for another fly to be drawn to the spider. A scientist came in, alone, unzipped and stood in front of the urinal. Within seconds, Fox was behind him.

He held a knife to his throat, demanding to be taken to his office.

Across the oceans, Operation Hidden Dagger kicked up a notch.

29
Tel Aviv

Schlomo Yatom, at first glance, was an ordinary man. He worked in a diamond polishing factory as the master polisher for a man called Motti Lav.

His boss worked for Mossad, as an analyst specialising in Africa. The payslips he brought home for his wife to file were stamped 'Prime Minister's Office', but his wife didn't ask, so he didn't tell. The diamond factory was his official occupation. It was the reason he didn't have any down payments on his DB9.

Schlomo was one of the few people who knew the real reason for Lav's wealth: blood diamonds. He sat late at his bench that night, a diamond pressed hard to the polishing wheel and his thoughts turned to how he would do it, and then to the wife and two daughters Lav would leave behind. Schlomo knew them well.

The distinctive sound of expensive Italian shoes came from the hallway. Lav and Yossi, Lav's business partner, were slightly early for their nightly meeting.

They sauntered past, chatting to each other and greeted: 'Hi Schlomo'. He greeted back and kept his eyes on the wheel. The two men continued to the boardroom, a massive square room with glass walls in the middle of the factory. Inside, they sat on either side of a long table, on which was a teleconference phone. Had Lav and Yossi seen that the telephone was currently in call, they might have shifted the conversation to the pony Yossi had bought Lav's eldest daughter for her thirteenth birthday. Instead, they spoke business.

'Why's production down this week out there?'

'A small riot by the workers, nothing serious. Quelled by the militia within half a day.'

'How many dead?'

'Five Liberians, two Angolans. Easily replaceable.'

'That's no reason for them to stop working. Get the militia to crack down on any remaining dissenters. Pay the armed men a little extra. That should work. If it doesn't, we can call in the South African mercenaries. Worked like a dream last time.'

'*Ei*,' Yossi shook his head at the memory, and said, 'you're right, don't worry, leave it to me.'

'Now ...' Lav leaned back in his chair with his hands behind his head. 'Tell me about your wife. Did my trick work?'

'Singing to high heaven. It worked like a charm.'

'I told you.'

Both men laughed and silence settled over the room. Lav's smile faded as he looked up towards the glass door. Schlomo was standing in front of it pressing a newspaper against the glass and pointing. He was trying to say something.

'What is it, Schlo? Come in.'

Schlomo opened the door. 'Did you see what's in tomorrow's paper?'

He beamed from ear to ear, but his hands were shaking as he handed the paper to Yossi. To Lav's annoyance, Schlomo turned and walked out the door, closing and standing behind it, watching them.

'What's this clown doing?' Lav said under his breath.

'Why on earth would we know what's in the early edition when it's not due out until a few hours time?' said Yossi, turning the paper over in his hands, putting his reading glasses on and focusing on two snippets of text encircled with red Koki pen.

'The obituaries? What the hell is this?'

Yossi read on in silence, the look of confusion on his face sharpening with every word.

'What is it?' asked Lav.

Yossi handed him the paper, shaking his head and removing his spectacles. 'I'm not sure, exactly, some kind of joke.'

Lav read aloud: 'Motti Lav, smuggler of Liberian blood diamonds ... *what the?* ... and alleged Mossad agent, killed last night in blazing office inferno in an industrial section of Tel Aviv, aged fifty-five. Survived by a wife and two children.'

He read a similar obituary that had been posted for Yossi, then looked back at Schlomo, thinking it must be a joke. Lav shouted, 'What kind of crap joke is this? Do you know how many calls I'll be receiving tomorrow?'

'None,' said Schlomo as he turned the key in the outside lock. He produced a lighter and flicked it a few times, looking at Lav, his eyes hardening and his smile fading.

'What the hell?' said Yossi, looking down at the sole of his raised shoe, and then at the carpet. 'The floor's wet, Motti. I thought I smelled something in here, is that petrol?' He sounded panicked. 'What the hell's going on?'

Schlomo lit a strip of carpet leading under the glass door to the boardroom and watched the fire quickly spread over the heavily-doused carpet, rippling, a fast-moving wave of trembling flames. Lav and Yossi jumped to their feet. Lav bared his teeth, shouting, 'Let us out, what the hell is this?' he banged on the reinforced glass uselessly, at first weakly, then harder, and then with his full weight, shoulder first, he crashed into the door but bounced off the glass. Schlomo laughed.

Schlomo Yatom, real name Werner Müller, watched with perverted satisfaction as the two men caught alight. When he was happy that they were burnt beyond hope, he turned to leave, pleased that his job as part of Operation Hidden Dagger had finally been completed. The sound of exploding glass filled the air as the lift doors closed behind him.

'*Sieg heil*' he whispered as he exited the building. He would leak the tape of Lav and Yossi's conversation to the press in a few hours.

30
Drachenfeld

'Let's start over, shall we? Name and position.'

They were in a cramped office overlooking the factory floor. On the table in the room was a computer, phone, books, notepads, scraps of paper and diagrams of warheads.

The scientist was slumped, defeated, against the door of the office. His hands were bound behind his back and his legs were stretched out in front of him on the floor. He looked like a rag doll, Fox assessed: his left eye was red, bloodied and swollen. His right eye gaping open, the lids above and beneath the eye were held open with two large black paper clips. Fox sat in front of him, leaning forward in Ulrich's chair. He held a pen in his right hand, centimetres from Ulrich's right eyeball.

'Ulrich Schwartzkopf. Nuclear Physicist. I have done nothing to you.'

Ulrich breathed quick, panicked breaths.

'Shut up!' growled Fox. 'I ask the questions, you answer. I decide if the answer is good enough, or if I think you're lying. If so, the pen does the talking.'

Fox clutched Ulrich's curls, clamping his head against the door. He smiled. He was enjoying himself. It was more fun, he thought, than Siegmund Baum had been, more drawn out, more involved.

'The plan, *in brief.*'

Ulrich shook his head. 'I don't know anything.'

'Come now, Ulrich, you're a nuclear physicist of the Fourth Reich. Surely you must know *something.*'

'I don't.'

Gripping the pen in a closed fist, the tip pointing out from the pinkie-finger side, Fox grabbed harder at a handful of Ulrich's curls and pulled his fist backwards towards his chest. He jerked the pen forward, deliberately wide of Ulrich's eye. It poked through the flesh, opening up a slight tract of red flesh. Ulrich let out a sob.

'Ah, there,' chided Fox, 'who's a big boy? You're lucky I missed that time.'

He stroked Ulrich's curls and sat back in the chair. Ulrich's breathing was coming thicker and faster now.

'Now,' Fox was removing the clips. He placed them carefully in place above and below Ulrich's left eye. 'It's time for you to sing. This time, I won't miss.'

Something unexpected happened. Fox had seen it many times before, but he hadn't expected it to come so soon in this case. There was a certain point, breaking point, at which subjects in interrogations did an about-turn. Suddenly, they couldn't be more cooperative. In more intelligent men, Fox had observed, this point came sooner. It made more logical sense. Loyalty, particularly unquestioned or illogical loyalty, Fox had reflected, was a trade perfected by imbeciles. Where the subject of the interrogation worked a less 'ethical' job – one that might involve murder, say, or mass murder for that matter – breaking point was reached sooner, helped along by a good dose of guilt.

'I'll talk.'

Fox waited. It would come gushing out of him now.

'Twelve thermonuclear warheads will be loaded onto submarines, which are to travel ... loaded with troops, to the Mediterranean Sea. The nukes will be deployed against major Israeli cities and military strongholds.'

Ulrich was like putty in his hands now.

'Date of the attack?'

'21 December 2012.'

'Time?'

'Midnight on the twentieth.'

'How many troops are there?'

'About one hundred thousand of the most elite fighting units ever to grace a battlefield, better even, more disciplined, more ruthless in attack and better in defence, than the *Waffen-SS*.'

'Why do they all look the same?'

'The soldiers?'

'Yes, of course the goddamn soldiers you fool, what else would I be talking about?'

'They are the products of a process called mononuclear reproduction, perfected here in the Mengele Medical Research Centre labs on Level Four.'

'That swine Dr Josef Mengele engineered this project?'

'It was the reason the great doctor was so fascinated with twins. He was trying to breed the perfect Aryan warrior, over and over again.'

'What that man did was disgusting. Nothing can justify how he experimented on twins. He was no doctor. He was an amateur. Call him a great doctor again and you lose an eye,' barked Fox. 'What does this mononuclear reproduction entail?'

'It involves replacing the nucleus of an ovum with a genetically-enhanced body nucleus, with chromosomes that will ensure preferred features in the infant.'

'Speak English,' said Fox.

'Put simply, we have been *cloning* future generations of the perfect warrior.'

Fox's mouth hung open for a split second. It was exactly as it had been in Ira Levin's *The Boys from Brazil*.

'These troops that you saw, tall, blond, muscular and perfect in almost all aspects, they are the result of mononuclear reproduction, all born in 1987, perfect soldiers each one: strong, obedient, sharp, agile and intelligent.'

'And the generals? The tall one – who is he?'

'Otto Skorzeny, Hitler's general, most probably the best German fighter in the Second World War, a guerrilla commando genius. Rescued Mussolini's mistress and led troops to victory against far-superior numbers of General Tito. Reproduced thousands of times over to lead perfect columns of Aryan supermen on the battlefield.'

'Who else have you scumbags cloned?'

There was a noise outside the office.

Fox snarled. 'Seems our time is up. You've hit a bit of luck, or perhaps that shall still be decided. I've enjoyed our little chat. How do I make an international call from this phone? Get it right and I won't kill you before they get in here.'

Voices outside the door, shouting, 'In here!'

'Dial 311 and the number.'

Fox drove the pen in so deep that only a short stub poked out like the stick of a toffee apple, the rest had gone straight through the brain. He gurgled, sputtered, and died. Fox grabbed the phone's receiver and dialled Ben's emergency line, prefaced by 311. It was answered on the first ring, and all that Fox had time to say was: '21 December 2012, zero hundred'.

Fox left the phone lying sideways on the desk so that Ben would be able to hear what happened next, and he stared into the eyes of the man before him and said slowly, deliberately, 'So, we meet at last, *herr* Patrick.'

31
Bay of Bengal

Anna stood in front of her stateroom bathroom mirror and touched up her lipgloss while her mind raced. Surely, something had to give. She couldn't go on pretending forever. James would find out soon enough who she was. The conversation she'd had with Dr D while still at the Burj al Arab came back to her. 'Don't do anything that you really don't want to do,' Dr D had said. 'Don't get in too deep. You always get in too deep, Anna.'

Was it too late? Anna wondered. After her conversation with Dr D, she had realised that Trevellian presented something that she couldn't resist: a giant problem that needed to be fixed. Now, Anna thought, the problem was that she saw a way in. The door was left slightly open. She could change him.

The dress that she'd found lying on the bed of the cabin room was a sleek black number. At five minutes to six, there was a rap on the door. Anna, dressed up, and with her make-up done, opened the door to Roger.

'This way, please.' He gestured down the hallway and Anna exited the stateroom. Roger overtook her and led her up a set of steps to the top deck. With no other passengers on board except for the staff, the boat was quiet aside from the lapping of the water and the faint hum of the engines.

Roger led Anna through the dining room where the celebration dinner had been held, and out onto the deck. Beside the pool, a soft rug was splayed out. On top of it was a low table, and around the table, cushions.

'Take a seat.'

Anna removed her high heels and padded over the rug. She sat down, her legs folded beneath the table top. A waiter appeared, offered wine for tasting. She nodded and he poured out a glass.

James appeared through the doorway of the dining hall, wearing a light-blue collared shirt, top buttons undone, and sandals and black pants. He looked at ease as he slipped his shoes off at the edge of the rug and sat down, smiling gently. But Anna could see something bothered him.

'Are you okay? You seem ... frustrated,' Anna said.

'Some business with intruders, nothing serious.'

Anna decided not to push for information.

'You like sushi?' he asked.

'I do.'

'Good.'

A thin blue line clutched to the horizon against the steadily advancing navy dome. The evening star, breathing back and forth, stronger and weaker, lighter and brighter, advanced up the sky.

Bizarrely, thought Anna, this was the closest thing to a 'date' that she had had in a while, aside from last night. She was tense at first, expecting to be tripped up by some question only Liz Codwell could answer, but she managed to steer him away from dangerous ground. They talked and laughed together, playing the gentle game of giving and taking. Rounds of sushi never seemed to stop coming and the wine flowed.

Tonight, thought Anna, she'd find out the cause of James's unease with his Nazi side. If she pried enough, she'd be able to lift the lid and discover what was making him privately reluctant. If she understood the source, she might be able to play things in her favour, and turn him. She didn't think of it this way, but this was exactly what Mossad agents were best at doing: recruiting unsuspecting players to a cause, spiritually, mentally, or usually, by offering sex and money. This was different though, thought Anna as James spoke; she was already invested emotionally, but at least she recognised that. Although revenge still ticked inside her against the old man, James's father, she saw no point in blaming James for it, and equally thought it worthless to hold an entire system against him.

The staff had gone to bed and the yacht was quiet as a mouse as it gently pushed its way beyond the distant shapes of the mountains on the horizon. They had finished eating, and now shared a bottle of wine, drinking straight from it. A pause settled in after James had explained the intricacies involved in running a multinational arms company. Anna took advantage of it to ask a question.

'It sounds like you're really good at what you do. But last night, you seemed … unhappy. As if you were not living your own dream, but someone else's.'

James stared out over the ocean.

'I do. I've always felt though, that I have an unexplored creative side. And yes, it would have been nice if someone actually took the time to stop and ask me, when I was young, "So James, what do you want to be when you grow up?" Instead of always, "James will make a great leader one day", and "James is learning well, you see".'

'I think I know what you mean,' Anna replied. She thought of her own experience as a Mossad agent, and allowed emotion to colour her words. 'I've never really been allowed to be Liz Codwell. I've always been Clive's daughter. All the social engagements … all of the godforsaken smiling, nodding and pretentiousness. I'm not sure I was cut out for it. I had no idea who I really was. I thought when I went to Tibet, that I could get away from it all, but you never can,

can you? It's as if all your life you've been pushed to do something you're told is right, and that it's your destiny. I suppose that's how you must feel too. Somehow, your nation's destiny becomes your own, and there's nothing left, no space to fit yourself into.'

'How do you know this?' He seemed surprised.

'I suppose ...' she leaned closer, took a sip of wine, passed him the bottle and put her head on his chest. His heart ticked faster, began to boom against her ear. 'I suppose it's because, as I said, I'm never quite Liz ... I'm always, and always have been, Lord Clive Codwell's daughter. Sometimes I wish ...'Anna trailed off, staring into his eyes ...

'I know how that feels.' James reached up and brushed a comma of Anna's hair aside. He let his fingers wander over her neck, to nestle in the soft, downy hair at the nape. A chilly wind blew up off the sea, in the distance: thunder, icy white streaks across the sky. Anna leaned closer.

'Tell me about your mother and your ...' Anna hesitated before finishing, 'father.'

'My father is dying.'

Anna felt sick.

'I'm sorry to hear that.'

'It started as prostate cancer, but it's spread to his whole body now.'

'How old is he?'

'Ninety-eight.'

That made him twenty-seven in 1942, Anna thought.

'That's older than I want to live,' she said. 'And your mother?'

'Died when I was sixteen.'

'What about your childhood?'

'Well, I grew up in a castle, as you know ... a very old castle.'

'With your father?'

'Yes, I grew up with the best German tutors, professors, doctors, wise old men. I loved drawing. I drew everything, from landscapes to people, animals, especially dogs, but my father didn't encourage it, and I was persuaded that my true calling was in business and war, weapons and death. I took over the company from a fairly young age. By then I was persuaded that it was my life's work to run an empire, and to make weapons to use against our ideological enemies, and to provide these to allies who fought against Israel and America. And now, here I am, on the brink of the historic rise of the Fourth Reich, sitting here sipping wine with you.'

'I admire you.'

'Why? I'm no more than a product of my father's will, I sometimes feel …'

'No. You're much more. I can tell that. You have a heart.'

James smiled. 'I'm glad to hear you think so.'

'Have you ever considered marriage?'

'No. I suppose you could say, I'm married to the cause.'

'Like Hitler was.'

'Yes, and that worked out very well for him, didn't it?' he laughed. 'What about you?'

'Me?'

James nodded, took a swig from the bottle as Anna spoke.

'Well, I struggle to trust … and I like to fix people.'

'Fix people?'

'Like broken things. I have this urge to patch them up, make them whole and then send them on their way …'

'Ah,' James stared into her eyes, 'Then you leave them alone.'

Anna was quiet for a moment. 'Yes. Then I leave them.'

'I'm the same,' said James after a pause. 'You know … have you ever tried to die your hair brown? I think it would suit you better.'

James took her chin on his curled finger, drew her in. They locked into a second-long gaze before giving in to the slowly building tension that had lasted the whole evening. The kiss happened just as drizzle began to fall and thunder brawled far away.

There was a long pause after they'd kissed. James was imagining her nude, piecing together what he had felt in the dark last night: long silken hair, pert, perfectly shaped breasts, a taut stomach, handle-grip hips, the small of her back and perhaps the little dimples above …

32
Drachenfeld

Fox sat with his head drooped, his hands tied behind his back, on a steel chair in an interrogation room. He was blinded by a set of incredibly bright lights that shone directly into his face. A string of red mucous dangled from his bottom lip. The room had a steel table, two facing chairs and a one-way glass window. He hadn't put up a fight. The game was up, now it was a case of trying to throw the man off, feed him misinformation.

Patrick had been followed into the room by three men, identical soldiers. They bound Fox's hands, gagged him and then forced him to shuffle along with Patrick two levels up to an interrogation room. As they had waited for the door to be unlocked, Fox had pretended to fall over. He was shouted at and kicked, told what a useless swine he was, and as he was getting up, he slipped his fingers gingerly into the sock covering his right foot. When they came out, they clutched a small capsule, which he managed to slip into his mouth as he pretended to cough.

They tossed him into the room and forced him to sit on an aluminium chair.

'Unbind his hands.'

A soldier came over and undid the knots.

'Cigarette?'

'No.'

'Suit yourself.' Patrick lit one up. 'So, who do you work for?'

It was obvious to Patrick that Fox was Mossad, but he hadn't indicated so, officially, and forcing Fox to admit it would be the ultimate humiliation.

Fox stared blankly at the table. Finally, knowing that Patrick knew who he was, and that he wasn't going to get out of this alive, he decided that to hint to Patrick who he was would be more a victory than a defeat or humiliation. He'd managed to breach their security, and he wanted Patrick to know it.

'Israel first, Israel last, Israel always.'

'I don't know why you insist on that meaningless phrase,' Patrick growled. 'It's only a matter of time before your beloved nation burns to the ground. How much do you know? How much did you feed to your Mickey Mouse organisation about our attack? If you answer correctly, I might spare you a very painful, slow death.'

'Israel first, Israel last, Israel always.'

Patrick spat into Fox's eyes and swung his right first straight onto the ridge of his nose, where Siegmund had hit him previously. The bone cracked, and rivers of blood trickled down to mingle with the mucous in his mouth. Fox spat blood onto the floor.

'I asked you a question, you swine.'

'Israel first, Israel last, Israel …'

Patrick's left fist connected flush with Fox's jaw.

'Speak.'

'I have nothing to say.'

'Then I'll have to try my best to answer for you.'

He fetched a shining metal police baton from beside the door.

'Do you know how many hours of cleaning it will take to get your filthy Jew blood out of the walls after I'm done with you?'

Patrick leaned closer, teeth bared, and he growled, 'Let me tell you something. I can make your death very easy. We both know I would never let you live in any case, so what's the use of struggling? I can put you out of your misery in an instant. All you have to do,' said Patrick as Fox moved the capsule from under his tongue towards his teeth, 'is tell me how much information Mossad has on our activities.'

Fox remembered Siegmund Baum, and wondered if Patrick too, one day, would picture Fox's own face before his death. He bit down on the capsule.

'I see that this is how you want it, very well …' said Patrick. 'I am leaving this room now, and will come back in five minutes. I am going to fetch some instruments that I think you will find very engaging. Think about that very carefully. When I get back, you are going to tell me everything.'

He smashed the baton down onto the table, causing the soldiers to jump, and leaving a large dent in the metal. Then he left. The soldier's stood, staring blackly at him. Fox registered that these were the 'imbeciles' with unquestioning loyalty that he was thinking about before.

Fox whispered a final goodbye to Anna, and recited a prayer in Hebrew. It was the *Vidui*, for those facing death: 'Almighty God, forgive me for all my sins and transgressions …'

Minutes later, Fox's breathing became bitter. He began to shake and froth at the mouth, then he passed out. His brain was dying from the cyanide. Next would be his heart. As he lay there, slumped in his chair, bleeding profusely, his skin turned cherry red. As he spasmed in his chair, the only thing crossing his mind was that his life had been reduced to a date: 21 December 2012. Finally, his head slumped on the desk in a final caricature of sleep.

33
Mossad HQ
Tel Aviv

'It can't be!'

Ben slammed the phone down as it went dead on the other end.

He cradled his head in his hands and closed his eyes. Images of Fox came rushing in, Fox as a recruit, standing in front of his desk at the Office, with so much dark promise.

He'd lost an agent, and one of his best at that.

Nothing felt worse, Ben thought. He'd lost a few, but for some reason this one really stuck. He needed to speak to someone. He picked up his mobile and typed an encrypted email to Anna, then poured himself a tall glass of whiskey on the rocks.

34
Bay of Bengal

Anna's phone was vibrating.

She tried to ignore it, but knew she couldn't. She slipped out of her clinch with James, apologetically, hurried into the bathroom and pulled out her phone.

An encrypted message from HQ made her cup her mouth with her hand as her honey skin turned ashen.

> Business Associate F has resigned from the organisation. Call me to discuss options.

She turned on the shower and dialled Ben.

'Hello?'
'Ben?'
'Yes, Anna.'
'You sound terrible. Are you okay?'
'I guess. You got my message?'
'Yes, what happened?'
'He made it into the Nazi base in Argentina. He called me a while ago.'
'What did he say?'
'A date.'
'What was it?'
'21 December 2012. The date of the attack. He died for those numbers, Agent A.'

He sounded horrible. Terribly drunk and perhaps crying.
'Then what happened?'
'Patrick. James's man. Heard it on the phone.'
Now there was definite sobbing.
'Calm down, Ben.'
It took him a while. He seemed to collect himself, cleared his throat and then said, 'What am I thinking, this is dangerous, us speaking on the phone like this. Run an update. Make it quick.'
'Okay. On a yacht, cruising the Arabian Sea. On our way to the Bay of Bengal. I'm not sure where to for T after that.'
'You?'
'Supposedly back to Tibet.'
'No, stick with him.'
'Follow him?'
'See where he goes.'
'Thank you, get some rest, Ben.'

Anna clicked the phone down and slid down to the floor. She covered her eyes with her hands and tried to bite back the tears.

35
Tel Aviv

A few hours later, Ben was desperately trying to put Agent Fox's death behind him. It was the only thing he could do, if he were to keep things ticking. He'd immersed himself in research, cooped up in the study room of his bachelor's flat in Tel Aviv.

The walls were littered with newspaper articles, mostly about operations he'd been instrumental in, but one would have to read between the lines to know that Mossad was involved. Even then, nothing was what it seemed.

The bookshelves heaved with thick volumes on the Second World War, particularly titles about Himmler's *Lebensborn* project, racial superiority theory and eugenics, Nicholas Goodrick-Clarke's *The Occult Roots of Nazism* and Trevor Ravenscroft's *Spear of Destiny*. All of the books, which he consumed prolifically in his own search for the Holy Grail, hoping to help his brother, contained more riddles than answers.

He could be dead, for all Ben knew. In a sense, his life was caving in. Everyone seemed to be dying around him. Steven, Motti Lav, Fox, and now possibly Badger was gone too …

Ben had gone home after speaking to Anna, throwing himself into analysing everything he knew about the grail. He had asked Lucy to keep an eye on things for him at HQ. Bulldog had called several times to ask how the two *kidon* unit agents were progressing. Ben had mentioned Fox's date but avoided his death. He knew that Fox had most likely died a slow, torturous death, for those three snippets of information. Twenty-one. December. Twenty-twelve.

The guilt was overwhelming, so he discussed Anna's movements instead, her transmissions about the Nazi submarines, and his follow-ups with Naval Intelligence. Apparently, nuclear submarines were very hard to detect, and nothing had been uncovered.

It was a matter of time before Ben would have to call a meeting with all of the heads of intelligence, and then he would have to let everyone know that he'd lost another one. He tried to dissolve into the pages of his history books, to forget that he was responsible.

'That can't be right,' he muttered. He was half-reading Nigel Graddon's *Otto Rahn and the Quest for the Holy Grail* which alluded to Otto Rahn's belief – one shared by Rudolf Hess – that the grail could be at the Rosslyn Chapel in Scotland.

There was a knock at the front door. Ben got up, scratching his beard, and opened the door recklessly to a beautiful face: wide green eyes, perfect skin and flowing black hair. 'I brought you dinner.'

'Thank you. Unnecessary, but thanks.'

Ben walked back to his study, leaving the door open for Lucy to close it and follow him down the passage. Her skirt was a little too short, revealing spindly tanned legs, and her white shirt pressed against her breasts tightly to create an attractive profile. She sat down on a couch near the window, looking around. Ben averted his eyes.

'You know,' said Lucy, putting the food down on the table beside her, 'you really ought to take better care of yourself.' She stared pointedly at his worn trousers and collared shirt, the top buttons undone, revealing soft hair on a brown chest. He was in slippers.

Ben muttered something vague in response. Lucy tried a different approach.

'So,' she cupped her hands in her lap, 'you heard the rumours about Lav? About his diamond mine?'

'Yes, I heard about Motti.'

'I'm not sure whether to believe it or not. Do you really think it was blood diamonds? I mean, the voice recording that was released to the press … it sounded a lot like they were talking about a blood mine.'

'They did have a blood mine.' Ben stared at the page of his book, unable to think straight or to take anything in. Lucy was eroding his concentration, which had been waning for a while.

'How did you know?'

'I've known about Motti's little side business for a long time now. I had him followed and had listening devices installed in his factory and his car.'

'Huh,' Lucy grunted and leaned back in the sofa. 'Who do you think is next? It could be any one of us.'

'Could be. But I know who is next.'

'Who is, Ben?' There was a strange look in her eyes, almost suspicious. He hadn't noticed it before, but there it was.

'I am next, Lucy,' Ben replied. 'At least, I'm meant to be.'

'What? How do you know?'

Ben finally stopped staring blankly at the book and looked up at Lucy. 'Because, Lucy, I know who is behind the attacks.'

'Is it an agency?'

'In every sense of the word. It's the Nazi's BEAD department.'

'But how do you know all this? More importantly, how do you know you're next?'

'My brother, Badger told me, many years ago, about a planned Nazi operation. I didn't know whether to believe him or not, but he had been told by the Nazis that they could kill his brother, *me*, at any time. There was a double agent close to me, apparently, that would get the job done.'

Lucy shifted a leg over another. 'You stress far too much, Ben.'

'I can't afford not to.'

'You need someone to take care of you.'

He looked up at her and then back down, almost guiltily.

'You need a good woman,' Lucy said.

He closed his eyes and a few seconds later he felt nimble hands massaging his neck. He grunted; it felt good. She carried on talking.

'You need a strong woman who is good for you, who knows how to really take care of you, to *please* you.'

Her hands slipped under his shirt and worked over his back, his eyes momentarily shooting open but then, giving in, closing again. He felt his erection grow, filling up the space in his pants.

'Shhh,' she bent down and whispered in his ear, 'Just relax and enjoy this.'

She nibbled his ear, then swung him around in the swivel chair and straddled him, her skirt pushing up to reveal her thighs, his hands on them, stroking up. She kissed his face, then down his neck, and then slipped off him.

'I want you to watch.'

He opened his eyes and watched her undo her shirt buttons, slowly, deliberately, leaning towards him. It was agonising. She shrugged out of her shirt, turned away and giggled, undid her bra and then leaned down to wiggle out of her skirt, revealing a black thong beneath her arched back.

Ben's groin pained. Lucy teased him as she slipped her panties down around her ankles, where they stayed above her high-heels. She turned to face him, a neat dark triangle pouting.

'Oops! I've lost my clothes!' she giggled.

Ben was up on his feet. He picked her up, her panties slipping off onto the floor and her legs wrapped tightly around his waist as he carried her over to the couch and lowered her onto it. He played along. He flicked the light off and slipped out of his shirt and pants. As he levelled up to her to kiss her, his tip brushed gently against soft hairs and she moaned. She kissed back. He got up.

'Where are you going?'

'Protection.'

Ben walked over to the table drawer, rummaged in it, and returned to her. He pinned her down with her wrists held together in one hand above her head, brought his glistening tip to the brink of her, a bead of moisture strung out between them, and just as she thought he would push inside her, she felt something cold and hard pressed into her neck.

'What're you doing …?'

'Drop it,' he commanded.

She unclenched her fingers. A blade clattered on the floorboards behind the couch.

'Did you really think I didn't know who you are?' he asked. 'What is your BEAD name, Nazi scum?'

36
Helambu
Nepal

Badger lived in a cave high up on the mountainside. It was accessible by a path that climbed through forest, beside a waterfall and over a swing bridge between two ledges, over a chasm. As Lhama and Badger entered, stooping through the doorway, Badger lit candles that were arranged on shelves of rock. Lhama looked around. A bright mandala-patterned rug formed a centrepiece, beside a stone slab hearth with fresh firewood piled on it. On the walls were bright red *suavastikas*, ancient eastern versions of swastikas, painted on yellow wallpaper. They were the signs of the Bön religion, known as yungdrungs. Bön was the pre-religion of Tibet and Nepal, and considered by many to be a dark art, shunned by mainstream Buddhists as shamanism. The religion had been almost completely eradicated through Buddhism's own 'crusade' against Bön beginning in the seventh century.

In a far corner of the cave, there was an altar with statues and prayer wheels. *Thangkas* depicting the Bön deities of peace, four in total, were hung up above the altar. Near the door, Bön's wrathful deities presided, clutching weapons and trampling people to death. There was a table in the corner opposite the altar. On it were maps, weathered yellow folios from ancient manuscripts written in Sanskrit, an orange cloth and a *shang* bell, different from the mainstream Buddhist prayer bells in that it had a flat edge and was held upwards and not downwards, as with the usual Buddhist bells.

Badger lit a fire, and Lhama sat on the mandala rug beside the hearth, silently, trying not to appear judgemental, but unable to mask her surprise. Badger threw juniper leaves onto a wigwam of branches and pungent columns of smoke arose to the chimney above the hearth. His face glowed green in the fire. It was still bruised around the eye and his lips remained cracked, but he was much better and Lhama had been surprised by the speed of his recovery.

'Why didn't you say something?'

'Say something? What good would that have done?'

'You're right. It wouldn't have gone well with the community.'

Badger remained silent, heaping more leaves onto the fire.

'If they'd have known you were a Bönpo, they'd have chased you down the hill and far away.' Lhama rubbed her hands in front of her, bringing them closer to the fire.

'I'm a bit of everything, really.' Badger tucked his feet behind his knees, lotus-style. He pulled over a thick book from the desk. Its pages curled at the edges and were a faded yellow. Badger opened it and Lhama saw that it was inscribed with many languages. On the pages were geometric shapes, mathematical workings sketched in the margins and photos that had been glued down, with captions written beneath them. Badger flicked through the book until he came to a page with a large black-and-white picture of a Western man. Handsome-looking, Lhama assessed, with dark hair and eyebrows. The caption read 'Otto Rahn, 1939'.

'What do you know about Bön?' Badger asked, looking up at Lhama.

She shrugged. 'A little. The Bönpo argue that Gautama Buddha was not the first Enlightened One, but a reincarnation of him ... that around 18 000 years ago, the first Buddha, a prince, Tönpa Shenrab, had given up his wealth and luxurious existence to pursue, and ultimately attain, enlightenment.'

'Good, the basics. Now I want to set something straight. For centuries, Bönpo have been persecuted. One would think that of all the world's religions, Buddhism would at least allow for more understanding and tolerance. Not so. Bön is recognised today by the Fourteenth Dalai Lama, yes, but it still has this stigma attached to it. Buddhists think that Bön is a sham religion. Based on too much superstition, a dark religion devoted to evil practices. If I am to explain to you what this is all about, I need you to know that those views are false. Bön does involve what you might term 'superstitious' practice, yes, but it is equally based on compassion and an end to suffering.'

Badger paused and looked up. Lhama simply nodded.

'And it has much more of a connection with the past. It's much older than Buddhism. Its secrets reach much further back. Now, on the business of why you're here and what this is all about ... you will need to keep an open mind.'

'That, I have,' replied Lhama.

'Then I will need you to *bend* that open mind.'

Badger took a kettle off the floor, scooped water into it from a bucket and placed it on the fire.

'It starts with this man.' He pointed at the photograph. 'Otto Rahn. I presume you don't know who he is?'

'No.'

'He was an interesting man, much like a real Indiana Jones of his time, who took interest in an artefact that is commonly known as the Holy Grail, in German, *der Heilige Gral*.'

'You speak German?' Lhama's brow crinkled into furrows.

'I'll come to that part.'

Badger slid a book along the floor over to Lhama who picked it up and read the title: *Otto Rahn and the Quest for the Grail*, by Nigel Graddon. 'That is a great book that speculates about Otto Rahn's fate.'

The kettle began to hiss.

'The grail was supposedly part of Solomon's Treasure. Legend has it that the treasure was taken from Jerusalem when the Romans led a successful campaign against Jewish Jerusalem in 69 AD. They took the loot to Rome, which was sacked by Alaric the Visigoth many years later, in 410 AD. Alaric took the treasure to Carsaconne in Spain, near southern France.

'Rahn's search for the grail began with a German opera called *Parsifal* by Wolfram von Eschenbach. It was about the search for the Holy Grail. Rahn interpreted the opera as fact, which led him to believe that the grail was located in southern France, in a series of caves in the Sabarthés, near Languedoc.

'Rahn's belief was that the ancient Cathars, who flourished in Europe in the twelfth and thirteenth centuries, became the custodians of the grail. The Troubadours or knight-poets of the Cathars were also called Minnesingers, because they sang the praises of the grail or "Minne" in their spoken poetry.

'Their HQ, so to speak, was at the fortress of Montségur, on top of Mount Pog in southern France, near the caves of the Sabarthés. The Catholic Church denounced them as heretics and persecuted them, in what would become one of the first genocides of modern times. One million of them were killed.

'And a further five to six million witches were subsequently hunted down and slaughtered by the Church,' Badger completed. 'Some say the real reason the Church persecuted the Cathars was for Rome to lay claim to the grail. But that's a tenuous claim without any proof to back it up.

'In 1244, the Church sent more than 10 000 Crusade knights to lay siege to the castle of Montségur, where they thought the grail was held by its keeper, Escarlamonde, sister of Richard Raymond of Foix.

'After a long siege, the Cathars negotiated with the Crusade knights. They had no choice, having run out of supplies. According to the Crusade knights' terms, those who denounced their faith as heresy would be free. Those who were not willing to denounce their faith would be burned alive. But a few nights before the negotiated surrender, Richard Raymond had four men lowered down the inaccessible northern slopes of the mountain, carrying the grail to safety.'

'So the Church never got the grail?'

'No, not if Rahn, and others, are to be believed. The grail was given to a man who concealed it in the caves around the region, deep in the forest. Rahn wrote a book about this called *Crusade against the Grail*, which had first brought him to the attention of *SS-Reichsführer* Heinrich Himmler. It was read by Gabriele Winckler, "surrogate" daughter to an eccentric character named Karl Maria Wiligut, a diagnosed schizophrenic and megalomaniac who later would become Himmler's high priest and chief exponent of occult magic.

'It was alleged that an order called the Black Swan even tried to experiment with time travel, to go back to a time when the grail was available and bring it to the future for Hitler and Himmler's use. In a bizarre experiment in 1923, according to Graddon's book, the Nazis tried to open a dimension to another world, creating a rift in space/time known as the Kali Rift. Hitler even established a special SS unit to protect his time-travel project.'

'Strange,' was all Lhama could muster. The kettle was nearly boiling. Badger took it off, and poured out two cups of tea, handing one to Lhama.

'It gets stranger. Karl Maria Wiligut, or "Wiesthor" as he was known, read Rahn's work *Crusade against the Grail*, on Gabriele's suggestion, and suggested it to Himmler, who also read it and was duly impressed. He was on the lookout for anything that could help him and his society, the *Ahnenerbe*, unearth mythological artefacts such as the grail.'

'Interesting. But I still can't make the connection between the Cathars, Rahn, the Nazis and you ...'

'By the end it should be clear. All you have to understand at this stage is that Rahn had been hunting for the grail that the Cathars had stowed in the caves of southern France.

'During the 1930s, Rahn was hard on his luck and out of money. After writing *Crusade Against the Grail*, he received a mysterious telegram that promised him a thousand German marks if he wrote a sequel. The message included an address in Berlin. Rahn arrived at the address to find that the benefactor was Himmler, who asked Rahn to join the SS and to work for Karl Maria Wiligut.'

'So the Nazis recruited Rahn to find the grail for them.'

'Rahn joined Himmler's personal staff in 1935. His work was officially called "sacred geometry", because he was apparently good at finding sacred objects and pathways. Himmler's grail hunt, begun a few years earlier, had received the boost it needed.'

'I can't believe the Nazis actually believed all this. So Rahn was sent to find the grail?'

'Well, *clues* to where the grail was hidden, around the caves of the Sabarthés.'

'Was he successful?'

'Many think so, at least in part. Many believe his successes to be the reason for his apparent "suicide" in 1939. But Graddon, for one, speculates that this might not be the case.'

'What happened to him?'

'I'll get to that.'

Lhama looked at the photograph of Otto Rahn on the cover of the book, and saw in his visage a peacefulness. 'So did Rahn find any clues?'

'Yes, he did. He spoke often about a *dietrich*, which in German means "skeleton key", necessary to unlock the grail. What he found in southern France, among other things, was a clue to the location of the *dietrich*. Some think that by *dietrich* Rahn referred to a spiritual key, the ability to look inside yourself and to unlock the path to spiritual enlightenment, but what he actually discovered was a clue to the location to a physical key, a skeleton key made of pure gold, a way to cheat spiritual enlightenment and access the grail.'

'Where was it, where was the *dietrich*?'

'Let me finish first. In 1937, according to Graddon, Rahn went to Rennes-le-Château, where he met the housekeeper of the deceased Berénger Saunière, the Compte de Saint-Germain, who was part of an order dedicated to the protection of the grail. The housekeeper gave Rahn Saunière's papers. Rahn also went on secret missions, in 1938, to areas of sacred geometrical importance. These locations were only known to Himmler, and on Rahn's return from his 1938 missions, Himmler received a report from Rahn that was highly confidential.'

'What did the report contain?'

'Rahn had been deciphering the work of a French mathematician and sacred geometry expert, Gaston de Mengel, who discovered an "axis" of great power near Europe, possibly the location for the *dietrich*, or even the grail.' Badger flipped a few pages.

'De Mengel wrote that he had found the axis in Murm, Lapland, at thirty-five degrees east and sixty-eight degrees north, near Russia. A place in Finland.'

'Is that where Rahn went on his secret missions?'

'I think so.'

'Did he find anything?'

'No. The coordinates were wrong. Gaston de Mengel was off by a few degrees.'

'So where is the real axis?'

'Well, this is what I've been trying to discover for many years, and finally, last week, I discovered the real coordinates by cracking an ancient mathematical problem. It turns out De Mengel only had the longitude wrong. It is actually sixty-one degrees north of the equator, not sixty-eight.'

'So where is that?'

'Anzer Island in the White Sea.'

37
Tel Aviv

Lucy transferred her body's energy to her limbs by arching her back and stretching out. Her knee struck Ben's groin, bull's-eye. He recoiled with a howl, but the pain quickly morphed to anger and he charged at her like a raging bull.

Lucy's claws were out, digging into his back. She bit into the arm holding the gun, almost causing Ben to drop it, but instead he struck out with a hand blindly to land around her throat. Tightening, he brought the Beretta's barrel to her temple.

'Give me half a reason!'

He felt her body, defeated, loosen beneath him. She knew the game was up. There was no fighting this man who was evidently, even though committed to an office all day long, surprisingly strong. At least, thought Lucy, if she couldn't confront him on an equal footing physically, she had to find a way to unbalance him with her tongue.

'Hands behind your back, now!'

He rounded the couch with the gun to the top of her cranium. Lucy complied. Ben switched the light on with his free hand.

'Get dressed. Move so much as an eyelash in the wrong direction and I'll paint the walls of this study with your brains.'

Lucy threw on her collared white shirt and the short excuse for a skirt. Ben forced her towards the desk, instructing her to fish a pair of cuffs out of the drawer and put them on. Cuffed, Lucy was forced back onto the sofa.

'Those bangles suit you.' Ben searched the drawers for another pair of cuffs and slapped them on Lucy's ankles. 'These too.'

Ben threw on a dressing gown and began to pace the study room, fingering his Beretta.

'Now,' he said, agitated, 'you will tell me the location of the grail.'

'The grail?' Lucy seemed genuinely puzzled.

'Don't act like you don't know what I'm talking about. I need the location of it. In fact, more specifically, the location of Agent Badger.'

'I don't know ...'

Ben pressed the gun against her head. 'I know you do!' he shouted.

'I don't know anything about what you're talking about. All I've been fed information on is Operation Hidden Dagger. You were my assignment. That's all. As operatives of Hidden Dagger, we have been deliberately cut off from HQ. Trained for years and then sent to live in Israel. I wouldn't even know how to contact them if I wanted to. Plausible deniability.'

'You think I'm blind? Why would they send a low-level agent to kill the Director of Operations? Surely, they would have told you something.'

'I know nothing about any "grail".'

'I'll put one bullet in each limb, then one in your stomach.' Ben snarled and bore the barrel of the gun into her skull. 'Tell me about the submarines.'

'What submarines?'

'Don't play games! That's it.' Ben moved in front of Lucy. He checked that the silencer was screwed on tight, he hadn't used his gun in a while, and lowered it to Lucy's bare foot. There was a quiet whip, and a hole sprouting dark blood appeared in the middle. Lucy didn't, couldn't believe, that the wound was real. Then pain seared up, at first dully, and then excruciatingly, as she began to sob.

'Please ...'

'That's one limb.' He pointed the Beretta at her other foot.

'Okay, I'll tell you about the submarines.'

'Sing.'

'There are twelve of them.'

'Where?'

'Remote, deep, *very deep* oceanic blind spots. I don't know exact locations. The final two have just been launched.'

'And they're equipped with warheads?'

'Not yet, but they will be. They'll strike against Israel.'
'What is your BEAD name?'
'It is Lucy, too.'
'Family name?'
'Von Bismarck.'

'Ah, your royal highness,' Ben snarled, moving the gun up to point at her left arm, 'sorry to trouble you, your majesty, but I'll be needing more information. Tell me what you know about 21 December 2012?'

Lucy's nose crinkled. 'What about it?'

'Fox called it in. Answer the question,' Ben snapped.

'The date is significant because of its numerology.'

'What do you mean?'

'All the twelves in the date, and one inverted twelve. Twelve is an important number in occultism. It is also the winter solstice in the northern hemisphere. That's all I know …'

Ben drew slid the barrel across her cheek. 'Tell me more. What do you know about the grail?'

'The grail, as far as I know, is an emerald,' Lucy replied. 'A stone of one hundred and forty-four facets …'

'Twelve squared …' Ben said. 'Go on.'

'That is all I know. And the only reason I know that is because I've read half the books on your shelf there.'

Ben forced the barrel of the gun into Lucy's right eye socket.

'I'll report you,' said Lucy, 'for sexual harassment. Do you think you can get away with shooting me? Do you think they'll even believe you with such a wild tale about holy grails and double agents? They'll never accept the mighty Mossad has been infiltrated.'

'I'm going to feed you to Bulldog. I'm sure he'll know what to do with you.'

'How are you going to prove that I'm a double? You have *nothing*.'

'Ah, there you are wrong.'

'How in hell are you going to prove it then, Ben?'

'I'm lucky, you see,' said Ben, 'that my apartment is bugged. I'd like you, Lucy von Bismarck, to say hi to Bulldog's men, who are listening to us as we speak. They should also know that I demand a meeting of all the heads of intelligence.'

38
Maldives

A gorgeous creature in a white bikini lay face-down on the top deck of the *Aegir*. A breeze rippled across the sea, stirring a forest of small white hairs in the nape of her arched back. Light bounced off a slow bead of sweat that glided down the curve, rushing, with a force of its own, to settle in a tiny pool and mix with the beads of sunscreen.

A turquoise dragon fly hovered just above her head. Beside her, a tube of sunscreen lay, cap open, a dribble pushing out of the opening, trickling and melting onto the wood. On the other side, a man in knee-length white cotton shorts slept, bare-chested.

Anna's response to Fox's death had been exhaustion. The tiredness that seemed to cripple her body had followed despair. Most of all, she kept thinking that his life was such a waste. All he knew, even up to his death most likely, was hatred and revenge. If only he'd not been so stubborn, he could've been saved. He didn't keep that option open, of being able to change things, change people. Strangely though, Anna thought, she didn't blame James for any of this.

'Here we are. Heaven.' James had stirred. Anna opened her eyes to a breathtaking view. The yacht pushed past white-beach islands that fringed a sparkling sea with endless blue horizons.

'Where are we?'

'In the lowest country on earth, the Maldives.'

'Already?'

'We're passing through the North Atoll, heading south west.'

The sound of water gently lapping against the yacht was soothing. She closed her eyes against the indigo paradise and wished to return, as in her sleep, to not pretending to be someone else, yearning to be on this yacht with this man under a completely different set of circumstances. Yes, she admitted, she might be with him.

She reached for her drink, a Southern Comfort and lime, ice clinking and beads of perspiring residue dripping down the sides of the glass. She sipped through a straw.

'So you've dived before?' James asked.

'Mmm,' Anna answered dreamily, 'I've done a bit.'

'What level?'

'Advanced PADI.'

'A bit? That sounds like a lot. We won't go further than thirty metres, but trust me, you don't have to go far down here to see some amazing things.'

'You've dived here?'

'We operate a small operation around Hanifaru Bay, Baa Atoll. Part of our global network of front companies.'

A portly man in slops, bright blue board shorts and an island shirt appeared on the deck. He looked Maldivian.

'We're nearly there, sir. Twenty minutes. Suit up?'

'Yes, Max, we'll be down in a minute. Is the equipment ready?'

'Yes, sir.'

'Scubacraft ready?'

'Yes, sir.'

'Good, lower her in.'

'Right.' Max disappeared.

'Let's go,' James said to Anna. She grumbled and turned onto her back to stare up at the sky.

James got up, towered over her and held his hands out. She leaned up and let him pull her to her feet. They climbed down a ladder onto the fourth deck, and then another to the third and, around a winding staircase, made their way to the bottom deck with a blue pool and more stairs leading down to the launch area. A yellow Scubacraft that Anna recognised to be part submarine, part speedboat, bobbed in the loading bay. Two stacks of equipment were piled on a bench beside the pool. James took a seat beside one, smiled and patted the bench beside him.

'Suit up!'

He took a three millimetre Lycra wetsuit and dipped it into the pool. Anna took off her sunglasses and did likewise. When the suits were sufficiently doused, they pulled their clammy outfits on. James zipped Anna up, then spat into his goggles, smearing the liquid around inside, to prevent them from fogging up, and then gave them a quick wash and put them beside his Buoyancy Control, BC, and air tank on the bench. Anna zipped James up. The zip caught halfway, and there was an awkward moment before it glided to the top. They put their BCs on. James clipped Anna's ten kilogram air tank onto her BC and then made sure her shoulder straps and tummy buckle were clipped tight. It was a delicate, almost intimate gesture. Anna reciprocated.

They tested their regulators to check that bitter-smelling oxygen trickled out, and that there were no leaks, and ensured that the lug for the regulator pipes around their shoulders were secure. Max took their flippers and threw them into the Scubacraft.

'Ready?' asked James.

'Let's go!'

This was what she needed, Anna thought, as Max started the engines. A distraction. Something to get away from Fox's death.

The Scubacraft was small, but nippy. The 500 hp engines whined to life and Max unfastened the rope, got back behind the wheel, ensured his passengers were safely inside, and took off with a lurch.

Fringe islands with swaying palm trees and light blue waters passed by either side. They went about three kilometres before the boat geared down and glided to a bobbing stop.

Anna peered over the side into the turquoise waters, where the reef was visible at a depth of about twenty metres. Giant grey sea creatures swirled.

'Manta rays,' said James, putting his flippers on. 'They're feeding.'

Anna squashed her feet into the flippers, put the goggles on and bit down on the oxygen regulator. Max cast out a red buoy, attached to a long nylon line that would be fed out by James as they progressed along the reef. James offered a last muffled 'Ready?' through the regulator, and Anna tried a smile that she knew would be lost and gave the diver's 'Okay' signal.

They sat, backs to the ocean, on the side of the boat, and James pushed back and fell backwards with a splash into the water, followed closely by Anna. James signalled 'down'. Max replied with a thumbs-up and a smile and Anna and James pulled the release cords that deflated the air pouches on their BCs, letting the weight belts pull them slowly into the light blue world.

39
Helambu
Nepal

'Has anyone ever gone to Anzer Island to find the *dietrich*?'

Lhama looked up at Badger, wrapped around the incredulous narrative of crazed Nazis, a real-life Indiana Jones and the hunt for the most prized mythical object she knew of, the Holy Grail, and couldn't make sense of it all.

'There was a final riddle, a literal one: "To the east of the Great Temple, the key is buried at the foot." That was included in the notes that Trevellian's men stole. They need to take that clue with them to Anzer Island and solve it, in order to get the key.'

'Do you know what it means?'

'Not entirely. As with any riddle, it would depend on the context.'

'Badger, I've been meaning to ask you. *Why* have you been collaborating with these evil men?'

'Have you ever heard of the Second World War *Lebensborn* programme?'

'No.'

'It was a programme created by Himmler to try and "manufacture" as many pure Aryan soldiers as possible. SS men sired many children with different mothers.'

'How does it relate?'

'Well, I was one of those children, born in 1943, a few years after Rahn supposedly committed suicide. Himmler, encouraged by Rahn's work, determined that a young Nazi child should be sent to the Himalayas, to undertake research on the grail, to be fed clues and information on the grail by the *Ahnenerbe* and any of Himmler's mathematicians working on Gaston de Mengel's "axis" problem. That child was me. Apparently I'd shown extraordinary aptitude for languages and maths at a very young age, and this was the reason I was chosen.'

'But why are you still going along with it?'

'I have a brother, Ben. He works for Mossad.'

'Israeli intelligence?'

'Yes. At first, I had no idea that I had a brother. My mother, a staunch German who survived the war, gave birth to him, but her guilt was too much. She decided to give him up for adoption. She insisted that it must be a Jewish family. He was given to a woman immigrating to Israel. He has lived there ever since, and he ended up working for Mossad. One day, the Nazis came here, when I was very young still – in my early twenties – and at that time I was looking to quit this business. I was beginning to form political opinions of my own, and they knew that I was wavering. They told me that I had a brother who worked in Mossad, and that if I dissented, they would kill him. They told me they had agents planted in the organisation, and that they could kill him at any time.'

'Is that him?' Lhama pointed at the picture on the page facing the one with Rahn of a handsome, dark man in his twenties.

'Yes, that's him.'

'But this could be the fate of the universe we're talking about. Surely it's worth risking the life of one man, your brother, who you've never met?'

'It could be the fate of the universe, but then again, the grail could be some dusty old cup or faded emerald lying somewhere gathering cobwebs, no more than an empty vassal of high-flying myth.'

'But what will the Nazis do without the actual location of the grail?'

'I was coming to that part. I have also been working on that, and I believe I have found the location through decoding allegories in ancient Buddhist and Bön texts.'

'Don't tell me the Nazis have that, too.'

'All in my notes. The ones they took with them.'

'Hell!' Lhama issued a rare curse. 'Badger, I'm beginning to make sense of this. Rahn was hunting for the grail in southern France. He discovered some secrets about a skeleton key necessary to unlock the grail. But he was only scratching the surface. Much more scholarly work needed to be done. A man needed to be sent to Nepal with the single focus of finding not only the location of the key but also the final resting place of the grail. That man was you. You were blackmailed into cooperating under fear of your brother's murder. Now, you've solved both problems: the location of the key and also of the grail …'

'Full marks.'

'And a while back you told me that the men would come *here* to search for the grail. That means it's in … *Nepal?*'

'And an extra star for you.'

'We're almost on the same page. Phew, this is some business. But you still haven't told me what happened to Rahn.'

'After his secret missions in 1938, he undertook one more mission the following year, to Saint-Cillien, where he witnessed things that affected him very badly. It is not clear what these things were. At this time he was running out of favour with *SS-Reichsführer.*'

'Why?'

'Because he was gay, and to be homosexual and an *SS Mann* at the same time was the kiss of death. Himmler apparently even had his own nephew executed on suspicion of being gay. Rahn had already been caught having sex with a man twice, and leading into 1939, he was caught a third time with a *Luftwaffe* pilot, and was condemned by Himmler and given the choice of death in a concentration camp or suicide.

'On 13 or 14 March 1939, just before the 16 March anniversary of the Cathars' massacre at Montségur, he was found in the Tyrolean Mountains, propped up against a tree trunk, forty kilometres from Hitler's *Berchtesgarten*, with two phials of sleeping pills beside his frozen emaciated body.

'But the circumstances surrounding the death leave too much doubt, according to Graddon. He was too important to the Nazi high command for them to kill him, and by faking his death he could take his search for the grail underground, far from prying eyes. His close friend, Antoin Gadal, claimed that the real Rahn died in a car crash in Iran in 1959, at least, again that's according to Graddon.'

'So he could have unearthed more about the grail?'

'Could have, but he disappeared; no one really knows what happened to him. I need your help. We need to get to the grail before Trevellian does.'

'Where exactly is the grail?'

'There are caves near Lo Manthang where British adventurer and climber Peter Athans and his team found ancient Bön texts, at a place called Marjhang.'

'How did you work all this out?'

'I had some help from a friend,' Badger smiled. 'He didn't die in

1939, or in 1959. He disappeared after visiting Nepal sometime around 1960, and I've been tracking him ever since.'

Lhama's eyes opened wide. 'Otto Rahn!'

40
Maldives

The two divers descended slowly to pressurise correctly. At five metres beneath the surface, Anna's world of despair disappeared, to be replaced by one full of the bright colours of forgetfulness and peace. It was truly spectacular.

A whale shark with a gargantuan white-spotted dark blue hide nearly bumped straight into them.

Following James's lead, Anna resisted the temptation to swim alongside it, and they descended until, a metre above the reef, both divers checked their buoyancy. They'd stay at this level and track the reef.

A lion fish, with spears and spikes poking out of its orange back, flirted with the coral, scuttling away from Anna's hand as she reached out.

They glided past an overhang, steadily making their way towards a swirling cloud of manta rays, like stealth craft of the deep with their mouths open to skeletal throats, catching the plankton. Anna looked up towards the surface and saw a mass of circling manta rays, almost in sync as if the delicate dance had been choreographed.

When, travelling no faster than the up-reaching bubbles to the surface, they finally poked their heads above the water, Anna was speechless. The dive had only lasted close on thirty minutes, but it had seemed like hours. On the boat back to the yacht, Anna crawled closer to James and pressed into him and said, 'So, where to from here?'

'The beach!' James grinned like a schoolboy.

41
Helambu
Nepal

Badger and Lhama pored over maps of Nepal, spread out on the floor of Badger's cave. Lo Manthang, Lhama knew, was in the upper reaches of Mustang, a Nepalese region formerly known as the Kingdom of Lo. In some senses, it was a mystical Shangri-la, closed to foreigners from the 1950s until 1991 when a limited number of tourists were allowed into the country by the king.

Badger traced his finger along the map, pointing out the route they would need to take. She could see he had been planning the trip for a while already, most probably ever since he'd cracked the location of the grail.

They would travel by scooter, Badger explained, from Helambu to Pokhara. There, they would trade the scooter for sturdy and fast horses from someone Badger knew in the area called Old Mother. Then they'd begin the 130-kilometre journey to Lo Manthang, sweeping along the deepest river gorge in the world, the Kali Gandaki River gorge, crested on all sides by the mighty Himalaya.

They would travel by daylight and would be able to cover at least forty kilometres a day, which meant that the trip to Lo Manthang would take a few days altogether.

'In Lo Manthang,' Badger said, staring at the glowing embers of the fire, 'we'll travel to Marjhang and enter the caves. There, we will need to go through nine chambers that lead underground. Each chamber will present us with a challenge. Only those with utmost knowledge of the ways of Bön, and those who have studied the ancient texts and have solved the nine riddles will be able to pass.'

Lhama looked surprised. 'There are riddles we need to solve to reach the grail?'

'Did you expect it to be easy?'

'No ...'

'Along with solving the location for the grail, as I explained to you, by deciphering allegories in the ancient Bön texts, I also unearthed a series of nine riddles. These need to be solved to gain access to the grail.'

'When do we start?'

'First thing in the morning. You can sleep here. I'll lay down on the floor.'

Lhama looked around at the swastikas, and took a moment's hesitation to decide. 'Okay, but I'll need to pack a bag and come back. I presume I need to pack climbing material – ropes, and everything else?'

'That's half the reason I need you, you're a great climber.'

Badger rose, and sat at his desk, pen in hand, and began to scribble in his notebook. He didn't notice Lhama leave his cave as he copied maps, and wrote out for the hundredth time the answers to the nine riddles, speaking to himself as he conjectured their possible interpretations. He wondered where James Trevellian was, at that moment, and if he knew what lay in store for him at Lo Manthang. More importantly, he wondered if Ben was still alive, but he'd decided that he would no longer transmit anything to his brother.

42
Maldives

On the eastern edge of the Baa Atoll, on the beach of a private island in the Maldives archipelago, a table was laid out for two in front of a wooden hut, built between palm trees that stretched over the sand and almost touched the light blue water with their fingertips. It was sunset, a mixture of dark oranges, reds and purples pushing off the sea. Rolling clouds like battleships sailed on the horizon.

Besides the private chef who lived in a separate hut deeper in the palm forest, Anna and James were the only two people on the island. They had spent most of the day on the beach, drenched in sun, enjoying cocktails, and at one point racing two baby turtles across a stretch of sand, betting each other with cowrie shells. ('The Maldivians used to use these as money,' James had told her.)

Although Fox's death was ever-present in her mind, the day was helping her forget. As the sun sank behind the clouds, the smell of coconut curry from the wood fire of the hut's kitchen drifted on the slight breeze, drawing them from the beach to the wooden hut, to take separate hot showers in secluded outside stalls in the forest.

Anna slipped into an open-strap dress and pushed a red lotus into her hair above her right ear. She sat barefoot at the table, listening to the ocean wash the shore, sipping a glass of South African wine called *Rust en Vrede*.

After a few minutes James appeared on the wooden walkway that led down to the beach. He was barefoot, in rolled up black pants, a black jacket, and a collared shirt with the top buttons undone.

'Thought I'd make an effort,' he said, smiling. 'You look absolutely gorgeous.'

'Thank you. So do you.'

James took a seat, and uncorked another bottle of wine. He offered a small taster to Anna who nodded, 'delicious', and he poured out half a glass for her and then for himself.

'I don't know why you don't just live here,' Anna said.

'I would, but there's too much to do. I'm always travelling.'

'Don't you feel worried someone might find you here, attack you?'

'It has crossed my mind … But I'll take my chances. This place is so remote. Hardly anyone knows about it. Only my friends get to come here.'

Anna wondered briefly who his friends were, and what they spoke about when they were together, but she refrained from asking. The day's drinking had left her feeling a little tired, and tipsy. Her thoughts drifted. 'That dive was like nothing I've ever experienced. Those manta rays were hauntingly beautiful.'

'I first visited with my father in the seventies, and I've been hooked ever since.'

'Will you see him soon? Your father, I mean.'

'I've got some business to attend to first, but then I will travel to see him.'

'Business?'

'Yes, business.'

'What could be so important?' Anna asked, looking out over the orange mirror of ocean, hoping not to appear too interested.

'When you go to Tibet from the Bay of Bengal, I will go to Nepal.'

'It's such a remote country,' Anna offered.

'That's right, it is.' His eyes sparkled with enthusiasm. 'The region I'm going to is the remotest region in central Asia.'

'Whereabouts?'

He gave her a look and then paused, as though he was debating something with himself, but eventually he said, 'Lo Manthang.'

Anna had struck gold, but she disguised her excitement. The chef, a rotund Maldivian with a chef's hat, white apron and a sweaty face, appeared beside the table bearing a wireless telephone.

'Call from Frieda,' he said, breathing hard.

'Just a moment,' James apologised to Anna. Instead of getting up from the table, he allowed her to listen in.

'Yes, *fraülein*? ... Ah, he's on his way? ... Did he secure the coordinates? ... Oh, that is excellent. Have Roger look into the location, and if we can fly there by helicopter ... Good. Prepare a stateroom for Parcival ... Clues? ... We'll have a look as soon as he's landed ... *Danke schoon* ...' James handed the phone to the chef who carried it away.

Anna had been about to ask, 'What's in Lo Manthang?' but she thought better of it and changed the subject.

'Do you think the weather will be bad tonight?'

'The clouds are rolling in, it might rain.'

James put down his wine glass, brushing her hand. An electric exchange sent a stab of current racing through each of them.

'Will we spend the night here?'

'That depends,' answered James, 'the hut is something of a honeymoon suite.'

'There's only one bed?'

'Yes.'

'In that case, we'll have to pretend.'

43
Helambu
Nepal

The time had come for Badger to bring out the jar stuffed to the brim with US dollars. He'd changed Nepali Rupees for the dollars with a local man who ran a transport business between Helambu, the capital of Nepal, Kathmandu, and China and India. Curiously, it was the same transporter to which Badger took his dollar bills.

A knock on the old man's door produced a small round woman behind a half-opened door.

'Dakuuuu!' she screamed, 'Visitor!' eyeing Badger.

When there had been no response a few seconds later, the woman wiped her hands on her apron, smiled at Badger nervously and repeated her shout, this time louder, 'Dakuuuuu!'

The old man, crooked but surprisingly energetic, appeared with the broadest smile of glowing white teeth and welcomed his visitor.

'Ah, Badger, tea?'

'That will be nice.'

'Come upstairs.'

Daku commanded his daughter to make tea, then bent over as he tackled the stairs to his 'living room'. The ground level, a typical Nepalese house, was for the livestock, and for cooking. The upper level was for sleeping and living.

'So, my friend, what good winds bring you?'

The old man sat lotus-style, his posture suddenly more erect than Badger thought possible as he took a seat on the mat.

'A Piaggio Vespa Ape.'

'Ah,' said Daku, grinning broadly. 'To rent or to buy the old scooter van?'

'To buy. By the time I come back, it might not be in one piece.'

'Where to, where to?'

Daku looked genuinely interested, his face cocked to one side and his eyes crinkled with worry.

'Kingdom of Lo.'

Daku's smile fell. He nodded, open-mouthed. 'What business in the sacred lands?' He stuffed tobacco into a pipe and lit it.

'You heard about the men who came for me?'

'Yes, very unfortunate, very unfortunate. I see you still have bruises.'

Badger was quiet. He touched his face involuntarily.

'You know ...' Daku inhaled deeply, and released a puff of smoke that seemed to hang in the air for several minutes, curling up the sides of his face, around his clean-shaven head and disappearing beyond a beam of sunlight that fell across the room from the high window. 'The others, they – *talk*. But this business of yours, it's none of mine.'

'Thank you, I respect you even more for that, Daku. But it is with these men that I have dealings in Lo Manthang.'

'Ah,' said Daku, 'and now you need guns.'

'Wheels and guns,' said Badger.

'Those,' he straightened his head and nodded, 'I have. What guns?'

'What do you have?'

'All sorts. Two sniper rifles, Russian make. A couple of semi-automatics, a few *dunali* sawn-off short-barrel shotguns … and an RPG.'

'I won't ask where the last item came from, but I'll guess Pakistan.'

'Seeing as you didn't ask,' smiled Daku, 'I won't tell you that you're right. What takes your fancy?'

'The sawn-off shotguns.'

'The *dunalis*?'

'Yeah.'

'Right.' The old man tapped his pipe to loosen the tobacco and shouted in a shrill nasal whine, 'Mingmaaaa!'

A boy appeared, listening to his iPod, all sixteen years of him chewing gum and leaning against a column. 'Huh?'

'Fetch *dunali*. And bring rounds.'

Mingma vanished and reappeared a few minutes later swinging two sawn-off shotguns in either hand.

'What did I tell you?' Daku scolded. He sprang to his feet with alacrity that surprised Badger, and that seemed to surprise Mingma too, and clipped him around his head, 'Not toys!' as he grabbed the two shotguns. 'Get out!' Mingma slunk off dejectedly and Daku sat on the floor and smiled broadly.

'So, mister Badger, here are *dunali*. Lots of rounds too. You like?'

'How much?'

Badger weighed one in his hand. They were cleaned up, he could see, and trusted that Daku would have done a good job of checking they were legitimate, fired correctly and that he had filed off the serial numbers.

'Two hundred dollar.'

'For two.'

'For one. Five rounds.'

'No good,' said Badger, passing the gun back to Daku. He made as if to get up, and Daku relented.

Badger had always been decent to him and had always accepted lower exchange rates than they both knew to be current.

'Okay,' Daku said. 'No rush, mister Badger. A hundred for two, but no rounds.'

'One twenty-five for two with rounds.'

Daku sucked air in through his teeth. 'One fifty.'

'Done. How much for the scooter van?'

'Five hundred.'

'With fuel?'

Daku took a moment. 'Okay.'

'Good!' Badger smiled and got up. He pulled out hundred dollar bills, counted and handed them to Daku.

'Mingmaaaaaa!' The boy appeared. 'Bring 1963 Piaggio Vespa Ape van round front. And barrels of petrol and all rounds of *dunali* ammo we've got.'

Mingma disappeared without a word. A few minutes later, a light blue, ancient-looking, bug-eyed scooter van was outside Daku's house, the engine whining softly. Mingma finished loading it and sauntered off sullenly. Badger got behind the wheel, smiled and waved once before taking off.

'Crazy dude!' said Daku, twirling his finger around his head.

44
Maldives

The storm clouds had rolled in and the night quickly became gloomy. Anna and James had been forced into the hut by the rain.

James crouched beside the fireplace, tending to a fire that was starting to take off. Anna had wrapped herself up in a rug, and was sitting beside the fireplace, sipping from a bottle of wine. She was long past tipsy. At first, she'd struggled against the heady effects of the alcohol, trying to keep her attention focused and her mind clear, but the more they drank, the more she gave in. 'Let's have some fun,' she'd thought a few hours back when she'd decided that it was useless to try to resist, and in any case, James was pretty drunk himself, and not likely to notice, for example, any minor slips in her accent or behaviour.

'Let's go for a swim,' she said, grinning.

'What, now? Are you crazy?' But Anna could see by the glint in his eye and his return smile that that was the exact reason he didn't think it was a bad idea.

'Now,' Anna confirmed. 'Butt naked.'

James laughed. 'You don't play around, do you!'

Anna got to her feet, stumbling a little as she tugged at James's hands. 'Come!' she pleaded.

'I'll race you.'

They ran into the pouring rain, peeling their clothes off and rushing into the water. Anna was a few metres ahead, and just as she thought she'd made a clean break, James caught her around the waist and picked her up with surprising strength. He swung her over his shoulder. She twisted around onto his back and play-attacked him, trying to pull him into the water, taking both of them down.

They came up gasping for breath against their laughter. James took hold of her thighs; her legs wrapped around his waist, and the laughter faded as they looked into each other's eyes. Her arms pulled tight around his neck, and they kissed.

By the time they re-entered the hut, the fire was roaring in the grate. Kisses and hands gently searched as they fell down onto the rug, droplets shimmering all over their bodies in the light of the fire.

45
Aboard the *Aegir*

'Anything from Codwell?'

'Not a word.'

'And from the lodge in Tibet?'

'Nothing. The line is engaged, seems down, I've tried so many times.'

Roger looked peeved. 'Anything else we can try?'

'Nothing but wait.'

46
Helambu
Nepal

As Badger pulled up outside Lhama's home in the three-wheeler, she asked, 'Where did you get *that* from?'

Badger smiled. 'Daku.'

'Should've known.'

'Hop in.'

It was still dark. Lhama had packed a small canvas bag of food, kerosene for cooking and a tent, and another filled with mountain climbing equipment. She wore a light blue windbreaker, faded jeans and old sneakers, her 'Western' getup when travelling.

The tiny Piaggio's shrill engine hampered conversation. They wound down small tracks of dirt road out of the valley until they reached a plateau, and made their way towards the Araniko Highway, which would take them to Kathmandu. From there, it was the Prithvi Highway to Pokhara, and then it would be horseback to Lo Manthang. Badger had kept an extra three hundred dollars handy to purchase an extra horse in Pokhara to lug their equipment through the wide gorge of the Kali Gandaki, the river known as 'the Black One'.

47
Maldives

She was asleep, wrapped up in his arms.

It was a strange feeling.

He hadn't been with a woman for a long time.

He had put work ahead of everything else, for obvious reasons. Besides, he wasn't getting any younger, and he had never found anyone he wanted to be with. It wasn't that there was no one, it was that he didn't trust any of them ... until now.

Was it guilt? he wondered, as he listened to her breathing softly in his arms. Did Hitler or Himmler perhaps feel this way too towards the end of the war?

Maybe, he thought, that was why they had spent so much money on finding the Holy Grail and trying to prove the existence of an ancient Aryan civilisation that had dominated the world. To make up for the lack of happiness in their lives?

Somehow, she had made him realise this.

He craned his head to look at her, gorgeous and comforting as dawn crept in.

Palm leaves swayed in the breeze. An infant sun pushed through dark rolling banks of clouds.

Barefoot, island sandals in hand, and with fifty metres still to walk, Roger waded in the shallow waters. It had been one hell of a monsoon storm. At least, the clouds appeared to be clearing, he thought as he edged along the crystalline beach, towards the hut his *führer* had slept in with Liz.

He didn't trust her. There was something off about her body language. Either Liz Codwell was slightly too self-conscious, ill at ease with herself but not so much so that *everyone* would notice, or she was a complete fake. Roger thought the latter.

He reached under his shirt, which was open at the top showing a thick carpet of chest fur, and fingered the warm steel barrel of his Walther PPK.

Pacing up the wooden deck stairs that led onto the hut's patio, Roger leaned close to the door and tried to listen. He didn't want to interrupt his leader's morning glory, he reflected. No sound, except for faint popping from the fire; no snores either.

He tapped with the barrel of the gun against the wood. When there was no answer, he made his way around the hut to one of the steamed-up windows and cupped his hand against the misty pane. James lay prostrate on the floor, bare-chested, with an arm flung out to the side, facing the window, and with a deathly pallor on his face, his eyes closed.

Roger swore. He banged on the glass and looked again through the hazy window pane. There was no response. She's poisoned him, he thought in horror, banging again and shouting '*Mein Führer!*'

The chef appeared on the porch of a small hut behind the main one, yawning and scratching his bulging tummy.

'What's the matter, sir?'

Roger ignored him and made around to the front of the cabin. He positioned himself two metres from the door and took two steps, body lowered as if in a rugby tackle, and smashed clean through. He stumbled into the room and pounced on James, slapping his face, '*Mein Führer!*'

'What the bloody hell is wrong with you, Roger?' shouted James, trying to sit up but failing against Roger's weight. Embarrassed, Roger backed off hurriedly. The blanket came away to reveal the naked back of Liz Codwell, who stirred, panicked, and grabbed up the blanket to cover herself.

'I'm sorry, I had no idea …' Roger mumbled.

'What, you've never seen me hungover?'

'I thought you were …' Roger looked from James to Liz's puzzled face.

The chef was at the door, looking sheepish. 'Is everything okay, sir?'

'Roger here, thought I was dead,' James grunted. 'I actually feel like the living dead. Chef! Can you make breakfast for a couple of zombies? Liz, what do zombies eat?'

'Human organs … brain omelettes for breakfast with a vial of blood.'

'Sounds fantastic. Chef, you heard the lady, go work something up.'

'Sir.'

Roger, still looking embarrassed, gave a small cough. 'I'll just be off then.'

'You!' said James, pointing at him in mock anger. 'I'll deal with you later.'

'Sorry,' said Roger again, practically curtseying as he left the room. Anna sighed and pulled James back into the rug as the door clicked.

'So much for privacy,' she snorted.

'Sorry,' said James, stroking her.

'Anyway, now that we're awake,' she purred, 'fancy another turn in the hay?'

48
Nepal

The valleys were misty as Badger and Lhama rattled down a choppy road winding towards the small village of Dolalghat. They chugged over the Dolalghat Bridge, over the Indravati River, and puffed through the valley road towards Kathmandu that seemed pressed like a ribbon into clay, winding up and around terraced farmlands and houses built one on top of the other.

Broken-down cars littered the sides of the Araniko Highway. Badger thought the old Piaggio, not for the first or the last time, had seen its final hill as they crested a town with the curious name of Zero Kilo, then crawled along a plateau and through the village of Panchkhal with its lush green fields.

It was the time of Dasain, a festival celebrating the victory of Lord Ram in a battle with evil demons. Pots of barley shoots grew outside houses and the children walked around with red marks, *tika*, painted onto their foreheads. The road climbed the hills towards Kawa. Colourful trucks, with writing on the insides of their windscreens, and screaming scooters filled the roads. Then, opening to a plateau of crumbling multiple-storey houses and bustling streets around Dulikhel and Banhepa, they entered Kathmandu, the capital city of Nepal.

Green fields fringed city blocks in pastel colours, around elegant Buddhist and Hindu monasteries in the hills. The road wound beside Tribhuvan International Airport, billboards advertising cell phones and televisions, with smiling Bollywood stars. There were roadside stalls with vegetables and hot food everywhere.

Then the Piaggio, with a brave captain at the helm gritting his teeth against the odds, climbed out of the busy city streets and into the mountains, edging towards Pokhara.

49
Maldives

Perched on James's private deck aboard the *Aegir*, Anna was surprised how well the hangover was treating her. Decidedly kindly, she thought. She was more dazed, even smitten, than hungover.

They were eating pancakes at the table next to the pool. She glanced over at James and tried to figure out his expression. He definitely seemed changed, somehow, not so businesslike. She had scratched the surface, and found a person inside. But now, she reflected, he was slightly aloof, shutting emotion out, withdrawing into his shell. Or more likely, he felt guilty and wanted to return his full attention to his work.

Her thoughts were interrupted by the on-board chef. 'Coffee or tea?'

'Turkish, very strong, black,' replied James, glancing at Anna who smiled and nodded.

Anna waited for the chef to disappear. 'Can I ask …'

'Fire away.' He smiled briefly.

'The other night, you mentioned that you were married "to the cause".'

'What of it?'

'Well, I was thinking,' Anna hesitated for a moment. 'Thinking that it couldn't have been the only reason …'

A corner of white tablecloth crinkled up in the breeze while James thought about his reply. The sun was out now.

'You're right, Liz.' He sighed. 'A very long time ago, something happened …'

Anna was expectantly quiet.

'Do you really want to know?'

'Yes,' Anna replied.

James reached out and traced his fingers over her hand. 'It involved a little girl.' He hadn't told anyone this story before.

'When I was eight years old, all I knew was the castle I lived in with my father. Everything in it was old, stuck in the past. I didn't have any friends, and I wasn't allowed to go anywhere outside the castle grounds. One day, my father needed to travel inland to the town to visit an old friend, a lawyer. I was desperate to go with him. It was very cold that day, and it was sleeting. My father told me it was too risky, that I was more important than I realised, and that I couldn't go. But I kept on begging him …'

A servant arrived with coffee, set it down, sensed the mood and scuttled off. James filled two espresso cups and handed one to Anna on a saucer. Creamy foam floated on the dark surface.

'Well, eventually he gave in, and told me I could come. So we travelled by boat to the small garage where he kept his cars – all German, of course – and we got into a classic old wartime Merck and he drove us to the village. It was the 70s, and everything was colourful, and the people looked happy and busy, and there were televisions in the shop windows … and little children playing soccer in the streets … nothing like my life in the castle. I had never seen anything like that.'

As James paused, Anna realised why he was usually so cold. He'd been a very lonely child, like an emperor confined to a palace.

'Hippies, long-haired men, were hanging out with girls on street corners, dancing and listening to music. There were milkmen and postmen and newspaper boys. It all looked so natural … more natural than my perfect existence at the castle. I'd only read about that kind of thing in books. But then, we came to the lawyer's offices, at the other end of the town. My father left me in the living room and went into the study to talk business. He took so long. I was bored. There was a grandfather clock in the room, I still remember it; I watched it tick for what seemed like hours. I wanted to go out and make friends with the children in the town, but I knew my father would be angry if I left the house. Eventually, I went to look out the window. There was a river outside, and I watched it flow past. It was deep; it hadn't frozen over yet, but it looked cold. And then I saw a young girl, well she was probably eight or nine, pulling a sleigh behind her, far away on the other side of the river. I watched her come all the way closer to the house, and I was going to wave to her from the window. I thought maybe she could come inside and speak to me.

'But instead, three huge boys came from somewhere behind her and started bullying her, trying to take her sleigh. They pushed and taunted her, but she didn't let go. One even punched her in her face! Eventually, they took the sleigh and ran away. I felt like I should have run after them or done something, but I was too scared.

'She sat there for a long time, opposite the house. I tried to wave to her, but she didn't see me. Eventually I found my way out, over a bridge and sat next to her and asked if she was okay. She looked up, and I saw she was trying very hard not to cry. She told me her name was Rachel, and she was supposed to be at synagogue. I asked "Where's that?" and she said "It's where we pray," so I asked, "Where who prays?" and she said, "Us Jews".'

James stopped and passed his hand over his eyes, shaking his head.

'If I had just– but I was small and stupid, so stupid – I got a fright; I wasn't supposed to be there, and now with a Jewish girl; I tried to run back over the bridge, but I tripped and fell into the river. My German tutors were the best in the world, they taught me philosophy, mathematics, music and languages, but they never taught me how to swim, in that ridiculous fortress of a castle. I was drowning …' he stopped again.

'Then what happened?' Anna prompted, after a long pause.

'She saved me.'

'The girl?'

'Yes, Rachel … she must have been a good swimmer … she grabbed me, pulled me up, but I was panicking and kicking and punching out with my hands … I knocked her unconscious … ' he shook his head.

'What happened to her?'

'She didn't make it. My father came and pulled me out. He could have saved her, but he knew somehow that she was Jewish, he told me afterwards, and he let her drown.'

'Oh god. That's so sad.'

He nodded bleakly. 'And you know … the strangest thing is that you remind me of her.'

'Rachel?'

'Yes.'

James squeezed her hand.

Suddenly Anna saw James in a whole new light. She'd noticed in his speech during the last few days that there was a reluctance to his cause. He'd questioned whether one should, without *thinking*, take up the cause of a nation. The individual, she'd thought as he explained, needed to have room for a choice.

A seaplane glided in off the breeze. It flew low over the water, touched against the smooth surface, and then came to a skidding halt. James's eyes were suddenly wide with excitement. He shouted for Max to get the Scubacraft in order, jumped up and flew down to the loading bay, leaving Anna sitting at the table.

Anna watched as the small craft buzzed out to meet the plane. A few minutes later a man stepped down from it and boarded the craft, which nipped back to the loading bay. She was all but forgotten as Parcival stepped onto the *Aegir*. He and James had a hushed conversation, then brushed past her on the way to James's study.

'James?' Anna murmured.

'Yes, Liz? Sorry, I've just got something to sort out ...'

'May I stay in your cabin?'

'Of course,' he said.

'I'll be waiting for you.'

He came over and kissed her. She did wonder what could be so important.

50
Pokhara
Nepal

The old Piaggio coughed into Pokhara with a puff of grey-black smoke. The sun set the white peaks of Annapurna and Dhaulagiri on fire. The sky was lilac, spelling a bitterly cold dusk. The Piaggio, which Lhama had taken to naming Slug, provided scant relief from the afternoon winds. She put her hands on the dash board and scrutinised the town, a first-time visitor.

Like other Nepalese towns, Pokhara was built around tourism. Cramped, shoddily built shops hung over the main road on each side, with millions of faded signs crowding out the sky. The shops – Internet cafes, restaurants, craft and textiles shops and climbing equipment stores – seemed like matchboxes piled one on top of the other, with lock-up garage doors or flimsy walls with windows that looked out onto dusty, sad-looking streets.

Packs of dogs roamed, scavenging for trash while the odd lazy water buffalo or cow sauntered across the street dejectedly. Whole families on motorcycles, without helmets, sped by smiling into the night, on their way home to the eastern side of Pokhara over the White Gandaki River. The western side of the city was reserved for tourists, the lifeblood of the city, with the beautiful Lakeside district around the paradisiacal Phewa Lake, and the World Peace Pagoda that overlooked it.

Overflowing vegetable carts and hot food stalls with cooks disappearing behind wisps of steam littered the roads. Honking horns and corner-chatter filled the space that was left, while bicycle rickshaws laden with overweight tourists pulled through the buzzing streets, stopping occasionally to be blessed by fake monks who marked the tourists' foreheads with *tika*. Above flat rooftops, thousands of colourful paper kites, flown by children, flitted like sails that could pull Pokhara into the sky.

The Piaggio kept going, beyond the western edge of the city and into the foothills that rushed up rudely around it. The dimly-lit halls of monasteries tucked into the hillsides glowed, with bronzed Buddhas peering out from the cliffs and surrounded by thousands of butter lamps. Inside, frescoes of Buddhist gods and the karmic wheel of life adorned the walls, while bookshelves were stacked with mantra books in colourful silk bags. The drums, trumpets and temple horns blasted human spirits and gods to a crescendo of harmony while the eaves of the temples were decorated with ornate carvings in wood, painted over with bright gold, and prayer lines stretched between the stupas and multiple-storeyed houses.

Finally, the Piaggio crested a green hill heading out of the city and came to a stuttering halt outside an ancient-looking yellow house with swastikas painted on the doors and windows. Lhama knew that a Bön shaman would likely live here, the woman Badger had mentioned.

'She probably knows we've arrived,' said Badger as he jumped down from the Piaggio onto a dusty driveway, 'but it's best if I go first.'

'Okay,' said Lhama, and wrapped a scarf around her neck. Badger walked up to the front door and knocked once. A woman who seemed at least a hundred years old answered. She cast a look of disdain at Lhama when Badger motioned towards the Piaggio, but it seemed she relented and produced a small wave that Lhama returned. Badger gestured for Lhama to come to the house.

It was stuffy inside, but warm, an open-plan downstairs with a kitchen crowding round a fire, a few beds in the corners of the living space, and in one corner, the most impressive altar that Lhama had ever seen.

'Tea?' the old woman asked.

'Beer?' answered Badger.

'I see it has been a long day.' She displayed two rows of crooked teeth.

'Old Mother,' said Badger, 'this is Lhama.'

The crumpled woman nodded. 'I know.' Her voice sounded like song.

They sat around the fire in the kitchen, drinking and talking.

'I need at least two good horses.'

'Those have been prepared for you,' she said. 'Don't fret over the trivial things.'

'Thank you,' Badger said. 'Please, you can take the old scooter. I don't need it anymore.'

'That old thing?' She laughed. 'No. But I will give it to someone in the valley. Far too much pollution. It will anger the *Tsen* spirits of the air. Not to worry, we will appease the spirits later. Now, to the important business.' The old woman got up and made her way to the altar, and began lighting butter candles and incense.

'We need to consult my *Pawo* at once.'

Badger noticed that Lhama looked uncomfortable.

'If you don't want to be a part of this, Lhama I fully understand.'

'No, it's okay. Just tell me what's going on ...'

'Of course. Old Mother's *Pawo*, her spiritual guide, is called Azura. He is a powerful Bön ancestor. Azura shows us the light in times of darkness. We need to divine whether and how we should travel to the location of the grail and whether the ancient Bön masters have any advice for us on this matter, also, how far Trevellian is, and so on.'

'You will stay here for the night,' Old Mother said.

'We are most grateful.' Badger bowed.

'I might be utterly exhausted after this,' she said, 'so you are to make yourselves comfortable.'

'Thank you.'

Old Mother handed a drum to Badger and a heavy-looking bell to Lhama. She placed three mirrors in different parts of the room close to the altar.

'Have you been to a shamanistic ritual before?' asked Badger.

'Of course. But nothing like this,' Lhama said.

'The mirrors are for Old Mother's own spirit, her *namshe*, to leave her body to visit one of the three realms alternately: sky, earth, or the underworld. There she will make peace with the nature spirits, to ease our passing through the countryside as we make our way to Lo Manthang along the Kali Gandaki River. As you know, the land is sacred, and filled with daemons.'

'Ah,' Lhama tried to understand. What Westerners might regard as superstitious rituals such as these were by no means uncommon among Tibetans and Nepalese, even among mainstream Buddhists, but the Bönpo took it to another level.

'While Old Mother's *namshe* travels among the spirits, her body will be possessed by her spiritual guide Azura who will consult with us – with *me* – on our journey into Lo Manthang and the caves at Marjhang.'

Old Mother began to move in an ecstatic way. 'Start drums, start bell,' she said, and danced around the altar. She moved to the rhythm of the drum, which Badger seemed to bang expertly, motioning to Lhama to chime.

'Louder,' Old Mother said, almost shouting.

They formed an off-beat melody. Some minutes passed. Gradually, Old Mother's body spasmed into uncontrollable movement, guided by a hidden force, and shrieks issued from her throat. She continued dancing for a while, before collapsing in a heap on the floor, breathing heavily. She spoke in a low, alien voice.

'You seek entrance to the most sacred caves of Marjhang,' the voice growled.

'It is a quest for which I am prepared to die, but I seek guidance on how to enter,' answered Badger.

'A bad daemon is also on the hunt for the object.'

'This is the reason why I must travel to Marjhang. The daemon has stolen the key …'

'He shall not have it of his own accord. Only one who is pure, *you*, and you alone, may possess it.'

'Then I have nothing to fear!' Badger's voice was shrill, excited.

'You may yet have something to fear. The stone will be his, in time.'

'He will possess it?'

'Do not question; this is your karmic destiny. You must travel like the wind. Three nights from now, he will be at the cave.'

The Old Woman began to sob. The voice was gone. She lay whimpering on the floor.

'Is it over?' Lhama asked.

'Yes,' said Badger, kneeling down to help Old Mother. He cradled her head in his lap, as she looked around the room, lost.

'Thank you,' Badger said. 'Thank you, Old Mother.'

When Old Mother had reoriented enough to get up, she went straight to bed in a corner of the room and collapsed without saying another word.

Badger and Lhama ate a delicious meal of dhal bhat curry with rice and vegetables. Badger tore off a piece of *gunrung*, a thick tortilla-type of bread that usually made for excellent breakfast with honey, and began to explain, looking gravely at the wooden table.

'The first day we travel to Beni. Sixty kilometres. Then on to Kagbeni, on the border of Lo Manthang. That will be about fifty kilometres. Then the final leg will take us to Lo Manthang and beyond. That will be about sixty kilometres. We need to be there in three days, as you heard. We'll stock up on food tomorrow.'

They finished their dinner and fell asleep, wrapped up in blankets near the fireplace, almost as soon as their heads touched down.

51
Aboard the *Aegir*

Anna had the rest of the day free. James had been cooped up in his study all morning with the new arrival. She'd heard James call him 'Parcival'. With the sky cleared up, she spent most of the morning beside the pool reading Bond novels. There was a complete collection of them, first editions, in the impressive library on the third deck.

Around six in the evening, James returned to his suite and found Anna halfway through *From Russia with Love*, marvelling at the interplay between the SMERSH and MI6 agents.

'My favourite,' said James. Anna looked up and saw him smiling.

'Mine too!'

'Listen. Sorry I've been so busy.'

'Any luck with whatever it is you're up to?'

'No.' He looked genuinely displeased. 'I should have filled you in. It concerns something I've been looking for for a very long time.'

'Oh,' Anna said, closing the book and placing it on the bedside table. 'What could be so important to the man who has almost everything?'

'Everything? Well, not until now ...'

'Do you have any time for *me* tonight?'

'That's what I've come about. Dinner and a movie at the yacht's very own cinema.'

'Sounds lovely. What movie is it?'

'Anything you like. If I don't have it, I can ask Frieda to download it.'

'Hmmm ...' Anna thought. 'How about ...' she twirled her hair around her finger, 'From Russia with Love?'

'Excellent choice. Sean Connery at his prime, ha.'

'I just like the plot. Simple, realistic ... no nuclear bombs or lost objects ... or dangerous warlords who steal innocent girl's hearts.'

'I wouldn't know anything about that.' James smiled, kissed her on the head, and left.

52
Pokhara

Old Mother stood in the doorway and waved Badger and Lhama off around four thirty. They'd made a quick but delicious meal of *gunrung* and honey, and packed their bags with provisions, mainly yak cheese, *gunrung*, *raksi* brandy and rice, now fastened to the sides of the horses. There was no time to talk, and less time to admire the scenery. They had to cover sixty kilometres of dusty, crumbling roads that flanked the Kali Gandaki. As they headed westwards, a wall of mountain closed in, the river gorge sunk deeper and the distant cityscapes of Pokhara and Kathmandu gave way to small pagodas nestled in the hills, and colourful rice and millet paddies.

The road narrowed through forest paths. They crossed a long swinging monkey bridge and stopped at an old farmhouse, at around twelve o'clock for lunch, in the middle of an apple orchard.

As the sun began to set, Badger and Lhama cantered into the small village of Beni, found a cheap teahouse and shared a meal of left-over curry. Badger left the room saying he had to make a phone call, and returned a few minutes later. They tucked into their beds and fell asleep almost straight away. The next day's journey would take them to the border of the ancient Kingdom of Lo.

53
Tel Aviv

A thick cloud of smoke hung in the air. Beneath it, glum faces glowed in cigar-coal light. Mossad was in the worst state of disarray it had ever been in. Ranged around a poker table, in a basement safe house deep in the industrial part of Tel Aviv, the heads of intelligence bickered over who was to blame for the murders of some of its top-ranking men. Some blamed the Palestine Liberation Organisation. Others said that it was Iran.

'Who will be next? You think they won't target our families?'

Voices were spiked with fury. 'They'll stop at nothing! This is the 70s all over again. It's Golda Meir's war on the Red Prince, except it's happening backwards!'

'Yes, but why Mossad only?' asked the head of Aman, army intelligence.

'Gentlemen, gentlemen ...' Bulldog spoke. 'Yes, our organisation has been infiltrated ... at the lower levels, I have to stress. My Director of Operations, Ben Hariri,' Bulldog tipped his cigar at Ben, 'has told me that he's caught one. A real live Nazi. Haven't you, Ben?'

Ben looked around the room, from face to face, unsure of where to begin.

'An explanation is overdue,' said the head of naval intelligence.

'I agree. What the hell happened, Hariri?'

Bulldog nodded. 'Go ahead …'

'Gentlemen. It is true. I caught an agent who was about to kill me.'

'What agency?' The head of Aman sprung the question after a puff on his cigar.

'BEAD.'

'I thought that was a joke,' said the head of the Israeli Defence Forces.

'The existence of BEAD is every bit as real as the CIA or MI6, gentlemen. Some of you know that well enough.'

The head of Aman nodded in agreement. 'It's true. We know that James Trevellian, and his father Franz, have been supplying Hamas with weapons for many years.'

'Yes, but a secret service?' asked the sceptical head of the Israel Defense Forces.

'Yes,' said Bulldog. 'Let him get on …'

'Now,' Ben continued, 'one of their agents had been working in the research department at the Institute, and was assigned to this case to work closely with me.'

'What case?' asked the head of naval intelligence.

'Operation Eagle Chase. The Nazis are planning something, and we've been following them,' Bulldog answered. 'Go on, soldier.'

Ben nodded. 'Operation Eagle Chase has been one of the shortest and most dangerous operations in our history. As some of you know, we learned that Trevellian was travelling to Moscow a few weeks back, and we had to act fast. We sent in two *kidon* agents to capture Trevellian. The plan was to infiltrate his ranks.'

'We used a honey pot, Agent A; some of you are familiar with her,' Bulldog chipped in.

'Agent A has gotten close to Trevellian. She's learned some unsettling facts. The Nazis are far more organised than we thought. They have a huge secret underground base in Argentina. Near Ojos del Salado, the mountain close to the border of Chile. We sent in the second *kidon* agent there, Agent Fox, although the details are not confirmed.'

'What happened to him?' asked the head of Aman.

'Communication was limited. He only managed to make one transmission.'

'What was it?' The head of naval intelligence this time.

'The date of a planned assault against Israel. 21 December 2012.'

The head of Aman nearly choked on his whisky. 'Like the movie? 2012?'

'Well,' Ben said, shrugging his shoulders, 'the point is that the Nazis believe it.'

'How exactly are they planning to attack?'

'With nuclear submarines.' Bulldog's answer cut the air like a blade.

'And, I believe, vast, well-trained armies. Let us not forget that Trevellian Enterprises has manufactured some of the deadliest war machinery ever built,' said Ben.

The head of Aman chipped in. 'Gentlemen, this is no joke. I can tell you what they've produced for our enemies. They have, of course, never supplied our armed forces. We believe they helped develop a new type of hypersonic stealth craft that can exit the earth's atmosphere and enter low-earth orbit and re-enter halfway around the world, completely undetected. It's equipped with what is known as "scramjet" engines that kick in after a certain altitude, once the airplane has reached the speed of sound. Mossad helped us find that out,' he casually saluted Bulldog. 'A prototype has been bought by Iran. Then there are amphibious tanks that can cross oceans to attack a distant country's shorelines. They've developed Spybots and high-energy laser beams ...'

'And not to forget the cyber war we believe they've been funding against the CIA,' cut in Bulldog. 'We suspect they sponsored Assange's WikiLeaks for a time, and encouraged teams of hackers to use DDoS against US government and military websites. In case you didn't know, those are Distributed Denial of Service attacks, which work by inundating websites with so much traffic that they crash.'

'Assuming that they do have these nuclear submarines,' the head of naval intelligence began, 'how many do they have and where are they? And what proof do you have that they exist?'

'They have twelve submarines, each equipped with a nuke.'

The head of Aman whistled softly. 'Does the PM know about this?'

'Yes,' interjected Bulldog. 'He's asked for minutes of this meeting which, you'll all be glad to know, is being closely monitored.' That stopped any errant whispers around the table. Ben continued.

'As I was saying, gentlemen ... regarding the recent attacks, BEAD has been behind them, through a secret operation known as Hidden Dagger. Lucy, the one we now have in a holding cell at the Institute, was one of those Nazis who successfully managed to infiltrate our ranks, and she was going to kill me.'

'We should find out what we can from the Nazi.' The head of Aman shouted eagerly. There were murmurs of consent around the table.

'I doubt we'll find out much,' said Ben. 'These agents were deliberately kept in the dark regarding all Nazi developments. They were *specially* trained for this job, and some have been living in Israel for most of their lives. I believe that their communication with Trevellian has deliberately been curtailed, to ensure plausible deniability if they were ever caught.'

'How do we know you're not making this up?' barked the head of naval intelligence.

'Simple,' replied Ben. 'I have proof. Lucky for me,' he shot a look at Bulldog, who knew what was coming and avoided eye contact, 'my apartment has been bugged, and my little exchange with Lucy was recorded.'

Ben hit the play button on his iPhone and the recorded conversation played.

'So now that we've cleared that up, and thank God for surveillance ... I'll move on to the next part of the story. Agent A has found out that Trevellian will travel to Nepal, and it is my full intention as Director of Operations, to let her see this operation to the end.'

'Why don't we go into Argentina and bash the daylights out of this secret base,' fired the head of the IDF.

'You've already lost one agent, haven't you?' said the head of naval intelligence. 'Why should we risk another?'

'Surely you know better than I do that it would escalate to all-out war, and yes, I take responsibility for Fox's life.'

'He was one of our best,' the head of IDF said. 'A true son of Israel.' A sad, crushing silence settled around the room, felt more acutely by Ben than anyone else.

He gathered himself. 'It is imperative as Mossad that we do what we do best – gather intelligence through recruiting people. Therefore, Agent A should stay on Trevellian's tail.'

'I must admit,' a rare comment from the head of *shin bet*, Israel's internal security service, 'you've managed to get a lot of loot already.'

'Thanks to Ben,' said Bulldog.

'But now,' said Ben, 'the floor opens to you, as we need to decide on a course of action. As I remain firmly rooted in the intelligence gathering community, I offer only a humble opinion. That is that all stations, intelligence as well as embassies and military posts, go on daylight, full alert, and that we secretly ready our troops for war without alarming anyone, and also that we involve the US Sixth Fleet in combing the seas for the nuclear submarines.'

'Couldn't have suggested a better course of action myself,' said the head of naval intelligence.

'Me too,' agreed the head of Aman.

'We'll all do our bit,' added the head of *shin bet*.

54
Bay of Bengal

The *Aegir* had slipped into the Bay of Bengal, cruising at a surprisingly fast speed over twenty-four hours. Anna was blissfully and deliberately ignorant of the fact that the trip would come to an end soon.

On the fourth day, the distant shoreline of Bangladesh loomed at sunset, and the boat slowed and bobbed lazily on the sea. Anna took a stroll to the bridge and struck up a conversation with the captain.

'Why have we stopped?'

'We haven't stopped, *fraülein* Codwell, we've slowed down drastically. By morning we should be in Chittagong.'

'So that there, on the shoreline,' she pointed, 'is not Chittagong?'

'No, that's further south. You'll know when the waters start getting lighter, we're close.'

'Ah, I see, thank you *Kapitan*.'

Anna returned to the owner's suite. James appeared, looking somewhat dishevelled, thought Anna, most likely due to what he was researching with Parcival, and they had dinner out on the deck with the sun setting over a beautiful orange horizon. He softened up as the wine flowed, and they found themselves talking about each other's lives. Anna borrowed from her own experiences, cast in a 'Liz' mould.

They spent the evening in front of the fireplace, drinking wine, and listening to a crackling old record of Myra Hess, a German wartime singer. They made love in front of the glowing fire and fell asleep warmed by the embers until the light flickered and a storm cackled into life with raging force.

55
Bay of Bengal

Rain assaulted the cabin windows. Lightning threw the choppy seas, visible from the cabin's windows, into white relief. Anna clutched her knees close into her chest in the chair near the window. The source of her restlessness lay sleeping, silent aside from the sweeping sips of air he sucked in. She wished things were different. She wished many things were different, but most of all, she wondered why simple beliefs and ideas could alienate people, nations and religions to the point of one wanting to wipe the other off the face of the earth. Although Anna didn't think of herself as some kind of 'hippie' with highfalutin but useless ideas, she was sure there were practical solutions.

'You're not so different, you and I,' Anna whispered in the wake of a thunder crack, noticing the lights of Chittagong blaze through the haze of the downpour. 'We must be close now,' she thought. She sat on a sofa in James's cabin, curled up in a blanket. The events of the last few days went completely against the grain of what she had thought she believed in. Who had she become? What was she still going to have to do? The walls began to close, her breaths became shallower, each one harder to reach, and her chest tightened. James stirred, turning over, but thankfully he did not wake up.

Would she be able to save this man, as she had hoped? How would she do it, how would she break the news of who she was to him? Surely, Anna thought, he would do something rash.

There was a noise. What was it? A deep grumble. The growl of a man, in the passageway, trying to whisper. She slipped quietly into the bathroom, and got up onto the sink, placing her head closer to the open window. It was Roger, James's bodyguard, talking to Frieda.

'Should we wake him?' Frieda's voice was soaked in concern.

'*Secherlich*! She could kill him.'

'But what if we're wrong?'

'*Fraülein*,' Roger's cold voice again, 'how can we be wrong? Clive Codwell himself phoned you to say that he was disappointed about the launch.'

'*Ja*, and I invited him myself. I made sure of it. I even received the reply confirming Liz's attendance.'

'Something's wrong. You phoned the lodge in Tibet?'

'Right after Codwell phoned. The receptionist went to get her, and then their lines went down again.'

'I'm telling you,' said the gruff voice, 'I don't know who is in there with him, but it sure as hell isn't Liz Codwell.'

There was a shuffling sound. Anna panicked. Someone was about to come into the room.

'Wait,' said Frieda.

'For what?'

'Are you sure?'

'Sure? How could I *not* be sure?'

'Even if she isn't Liz Codwell, if she wanted him dead she would have killed him already.'

'Listen, I'm not about to sit around ...'

Anna was out of the bathroom, across the room and at the sliding door before the sentence was completed. She had disappeared by the time the ray of light from the opening door shot into the cabin room. Half naked, battered by the rain, she scaled two levels of railing and reached the bow, hurling over it and falling, feet dangling in mid-air before plunging into the ice-cold water, gasping for air as she surfaced, at the shock of the cold; swimming for the far-distant lights.

56
Aboard the *Aegir*

Roger barged into the room, flicking on the lights, blinding James out of sleep.

'What the hell!' James shouted, jumping up from the bed, his eyes set on Roger. He pulled on his boxers, scowling. Frieda stood in the doorway, averting her eyes.

'I'm very sorry for the interruption, *mein Führer*. That woman,' Roger pointed to the bed, 'that woman is a spy!'

James checked the bed and saw that it was empty. 'What? What are you on about?'

'Tell him, Frieda.'

'*Mein Führer*. Sorry for the intrusion. We have reason to believe that Liz is not who she says she is.'

'What do you mean? How do you know?'

'Lord Clive Codwell phoned me earlier this evening, asking why he wasn't invited to the ceremony.'

'Well, why the bloody hell didn't you invite him?'

'She did, *mein Führer*.'

'I sent the email, and I even double checked after he called. The invite was definitely sent. I received a reply from him saying that Liz would attend instead. I also phoned the lodge where Liz Codwell said she was staying.'

'And?'

'They went to fetch Liz to come and speak to me, saying that she was around; had been sun tanning beside the pool all day! But then their phone lines went down. They've been out for more than two weeks. They seem to be down more than up.'

'You didn't actually speak to her?'

'No. But they insisted she was there.'

'So then who is she?'

'I have an idea …' said Frieda, '… that the email invite that was sent to Lord Codwell was intercepted. A fake reply was drafted to say that Codwell's daughter would attend instead, and a spy was sent in her place.'

'*Unmöglich!*'

'Mossad work, *mein Führer*,' offered Roger.

'First *Drachenfeld*, now this?'

'No one else could have done this …'

'But how?' muttered James. 'Where did she go?' He turned to the windows to watch the rain's assault. It was unthinkable she would have escaped the yacht already, but his first thought was whether or not she was safe.

'Search the place.'

'*Zu befehl.*' Roger slunk out of the room.

'I know her.' James was looking intently at the cabin floor.

'Apologies, *mein Führer*?'

'The woman in the woods. Alina Luzkhova … she's … she was there … I remember the eyes. Her face was smeared with mud. I couldn't see her face in the dark, but I saw her eyes. I thought there was something familiar about her, but couldn't put my finger on it till now …'

James took a few minutes to come to his senses. He had appeared angry, but in reality, he was more hurt. The thing that plagued him most was whether she had felt *anything* at all, as he had. She had gotten to him. Could she have been in it without developing any feelings? If she was an agent, he thought, it meant that she most probably hated his guts, hated him for being a Nazi. Had he really slept with a Jew? The thought made his stomach churn. His father had told him that SS men were decapitated if they were caught sleeping with Jews. He pushed the thought out of his mind as he tried to concentrate on being practical. He stormed into his study, calling Roger and Parcival in.

'Roger. She must have been transmitting somehow back to her headquarters.' James sat in his chair behind a desk. 'Get our Mems in Russia to use the yacht's coordinates and check them against signals received and transmitted.'

'On it.' Roger dialled a number on his phone, spoke for a while and rang off. 'They'll get back to us.'

'Okay, I have a job for you. How far are we from Chittagong?'

'The *Kapitan* told me yesterday we're about thirty kilometres from the shore.'

'Good, I doubt that she'll get very far. Take out the Scubacraft and find her. Bring her to me, alive. Do *not* harm her, do you understand?'

'On it right away,' said Roger.

'Call Frieda in on your way out,' James shot.

'Yes sir.' Roger disappeared. Frieda stood in the doorway.

'How can I be of service, *mein Führer*?'

'Make special contact with Schlomo Yatom, his real name is Müller, isn't it?'

'Yes sir.'

'Tell him that Ben Hariri must be next.'

Frieda nodded.

'Is there anyone in Chittagong we can call on to find the woman?'

'I'll look into it, *mein Führer*.'

'Excellent. As I told Roger, do not harm a hair on her head. Put two million greenbacks on it.'

57
Chittagong

Dawn was a thin crust of white heaving against deep purple as it broke over the horizon. A small glimmer of hope, the white gave way to orange and then a dazzling golden brown.

Anna's arms held tightly around a small piece of wood, the remnants of some shipwrecked fisherman's canoe. She was drifting with the current, fading into the deep blue. The storm's anger was spent, and had finally withered and collapsed. No matter how much she tried to swim towards the shore, the current kept tugging her back like a bully pulling at her ankles, and she found herself further away than when she'd started each time. Her arms stung, her legs were numb. A final push might take her close enough, but she was exhausted.

Anna's eyes were closing. She was drifting to sleep, when a blob appeared against the sky. It must be a mirage, she thought, as it grew in size. Finally, as she realised what it was, she became fully alert and waved her arms and screamed wildly. The blob grew into a tatty, medium-sized fisherman's boat with flaking white and red paint, broad smiles and white gleaming eyes aboard. One man, net in hand, pointed and told the operator of the motor to kill the engine. The prow turned and excited chatter grew louder until the small boat was beside Anna. Hands hoisted her on board.

When Anna had climbed into the boat she was bare-chested. The fishermen were embarrassed, Anna could see, but undeniably curious. One took off his coat, got up and draped it over her shoulders. Another handed her a bottle of water. All of the men smiled and nodded in greeting, handling her like a prize mermaid catch. The apparent captain, a frail old man with white hair poking out of his beanie, tatty clothes and a broad grin, handed Anna a raincoat. She threw it on and was glad to see that it covered her body almost all the way down to her ankles.

'Where?' the captain asked.

Anna pointed to the shore. 'Chittagong?'

'*O-key.*'

The boat's prow turned into a fresh on-coming sea breeze and made for the shore. As the boat hurtled towards the shore, Anna thought back on the last few hours. She'd jumped off the *Aegir*, panicked, and swum like hell for the lights. At one point, she'd seen the lights and heard the engine of a motorboat. When it had come into view she realised that it was the Scubacraft, but she'd ducked under the water and held her breath long enough for the boat to disappear.

They neared the shore. Anna didn't wait for the boat to jetty, anxious to get onto land and feeling nauseous. She climbed out into waist-high water, turned and pushed against the water with her back.

'Thank you,' she shouted to the captain. He made a wave with his hand and smiled. All of the men waved as Anna waded through the water closer to the beach where a group of children stopped their game as she walked up to them.

'Phone?' Anna asked, her teeth chattering against the cold. She made the universal sign for telephone. One brave soul, about thirteen and probably the oldest of the group, said, 'Come, come', and took her hand and led her into the city.

The boy tugged Anna's hand as he led her through a maze of streets that were already bustling with activity, into a marketplace, up a flight of stairs and to a corner where, beside a public coin phone a blind beggar sat, her legs folded beneath her, chanting a prayer and rocking gently backwards and forwards. Anna ruffled the boy's hair and said 'Thank you.'

The boy lingered. He wanted money, of course, thought Anna. This was the subcontinent, where tourists were never left to themselves for more than a few split seconds.

'No money.' Anna shrugged.

The boy simply smiled and nodded, but stayed at her side. Anna walked over to the beggar and leaned down. She waved her hand in front of the woman's face. She didn't budge. Anna hovered her hand over the beggar's pot of coins. Again, the old woman didn't flinch. Anna detested herself, but there was no other way. She faked a sideways cough and lifted a coin at the same time. The woman offered a blessing, but thankfully didn't seem to notice. She repeated the routine and lifted another two and then four coins altogether from the pot before walking over to the phone. The boy stared in awe, as if he'd been taught a new trick.

She dialled Ben and spoke quickly: 'Call Boleyn back on this number,' and she read the digits from the side of the phone. She waited. A few seconds later, Ben's voice came over the line.

'Anna! Are you okay?'

'B, we must be quick, I think someone's following me.'

'You're in Bangladesh? I saw from the code.'

'Yes. I need help. Listen, T is on his way to Nepal. He's hunting for something.'

'I know.'

'I don't know where he might be going. There's not much I can do here, B …'

'Listen, soldier, you've managed to stay alive this long, and you got us the information about the submarines. You've done really well …'

'Thanks B, but …'

'Did you find anything else out?'

'Well, there was one thing that I overheard on the yacht.'

'What was it?'

'Someone arrived on the yacht yesterday. He was talking to T and they had some notes of some sort that contained a location to somewhere, something …'

'As mystical as it sounds, I know what you're talking about, go on.'

'Well, T said something like, "What about the curators? Will they be a problem?" I mean, he was asking the other man.'

'And what did he say?'

'He said something like, "The curators won't be a problem. Easily silenced. It's the youth hostel that's going to be the problem".'

'Curators and a youth hostel?'

'Pretty cryptic. Do you think it refers to the place where they're going in Nepal?'

'Doubt it,' said Ben. 'Where they're going ...' Just then Anna heard another phone ringing. 'Badger!' said Ben excitedly. 'Sorry, hold the line, A, I have to take his now. I can't believe who this is ... don't go anywhere ...'

She listened to him taking the call. 'Can't tell you how happy I am ... I thought you were ... You know where he's going? ... Lo Manthang ... The ancient kingdom in Nepal? ... When will you be there? ... Listen, I'm sending you help ... One of my agents ... Could you meet her at Jomsom Airport? I'm looking at a map ... Excellent ... Look out for the most beautiful brunette, oh, wait, blonde is it now? Whichever it is, I'm not sure ... Well, look out for the most beautiful woman you've ever seen ... Ask her if she's looking for something and she'll answer, "A stone." ... Good, my brother, I can't tell you how happy I am you're alive!'

Ben rang off and came back on the line. Anna could hear the excitement in his voice. 'Sorry, breaking code and all that, but this line is secure. Here's the plan. I'm going to fill you in with the essential details, because we don't have time. Here goes. Firstly, what is T searching for in Nepal? Sounds crazy, but the answer is the Holy Grail.'

'What?'

'Secondly, in order to get his hands on the grail, he will need a *dietrich*, German for "skeleton key". I believe he may have it by now. He'll try to use it to get the grail. You need to work with Badger to stop him.

'Now, you need to get to the international airport in Chittagong. Meet a man there named J.B. Steenkamp, a South African who runs a transport company between Bangladesh, Nepal and China with a small aircraft. He'll fly you to Jomsom Airport near Lo Manthang.

He's one of the only people with an open 'passport' to fly as he pleases between countries. Knows the right people in the military and at the airports. He'll also help you out with any supplies you need. He owes me one. You're to meet Badger at Jomsom. He'll ask you if you're looking for something …'

'Yes and I'm looking for a stone,' completed Anna.

'We need to know now is what this curator and youth hostel business is all about. Where are they headed after they get the grail, if they get the grail, and what are they going to do there? But actually more importantly, stop him at all costs from getting his hands on the grail. Don't kill him though, he's the key to this whole mess and he is the only one that can stop what has been put in motion.'

Hearing Ben talk about him in this way made Anna regretfully recall the events of the past few days, and that James was, in fact, the enemy. She didn't even know where and what to start thinking about this 'grail' business.

'I'm on it. I'll do my best, but I'm unsure whether I'll be able to glean anything unless we capture him. And if he sees me now, who knows what he might do. Any word on the submarines?'

'Nothing yet, but I'll keep you posted.'

Out of the corner of her eye, Anna noticed something. *Someone.*

'Listen, I have to go.'

'What's happening?'

'I'm being followed.'

58
Chittagong

Anna peeled away from the public telephone, clutched the boy's hand and slid out of the market onto a bustling street.

'Bad man?'

Anna was taken aback not only by the boy's English, but also his awareness that they were being followed.

'Yes! Bad man! Need to go to airport.'

'Okay, follow me.'

They pressed close to the sidewalks that overflowed with fruit vendors and rickshaw drivers who milled around smoking cigarettes and reading newspapers. They were walking along a main road in what Anna thought must be an easterly direction. He led her into a side street. The alley was narrow and grimy, fringed by an industrial shipping container yard on one side and a flaky apartment building on the other. They jumped the fence to the shipping yard and began to zigzag through colourful stacks of containers. Finally, they reached the entrance and ran past the startled men at the guard post.

'This way!'

The boy led Anna into another alley. This one was crowded with drying laundry. It led to a street across which was a modern building with big, bold signage on the facade that read, 'Perfect Jeans Inc.' Ironic, thought Anna, given the Nazis' crazed obsession with 'genes', as they twisted through the street into a field bordered by mangrove trees. The way was blocked by a solid wall of factory buildings. They made along a fenced edge to a main road that bristled with rickshaws, yellow buses and taxis. Nearby was a painted sign: 'RICK-SHAW'.

'Here!' said the boy excitedly as he grabbed hold of the handle of a rickshaw and climbed onto the back seat. Anna didn't think twice, jumped on, steered clear of some vendors on the pavement and started the slow grind that got the bicycle in motion. They edged along the main road towards the airport, a highway that throbbed with buses and cars. She looked back. Their pursuer had also stolen a rickshaw and he was gaining ground. The boy pointed to the side of the road and said, 'Stop there.'

Anna pulled up and jumped off. Her legs were stiff, and her muscles loosened up after only a few metres, as they sprinted into a field, the boy leading by a few metres and the man closing in on his target. They entered a wooded area. The wood thinned to a row of trees that hugged a road. Overhead, an airplane whooshed down and disappeared. They were close now, thought Anna thankfully.

A yellow taxi cab was parked in the road. Its door was open and its owner leaned over a nearby fence, talking to a woman. The engine was running. Anna rushed to it and got behind the wheel, waiting a second for the boy to climb into the passenger's seat before burning rubber in a spectacular pull off, leaving their pursuer in a cloud of smoke and dust that caked his face.

They covered the rest of the way in less than five minutes. As they drew closer to Shah Amanat Airport, Anna noticed the ugly fake lakes that had been built around it before pulling into the parking lot.

59
Nepal

Badger and Lhama mounted their horses and set off from the teahouse in Beni to the sound of birds welcoming the dawn. They pressed through the Kali Gandaki gorge, edging north until they reached the town of Tatopani Myagdi. After rounding a bend in the valley, the imposing massif of Annapurna, previously hidden from view, glowed white against the sky.

They pressed on beside the river, over hills and through rice paddies surrounded by mountains. After Lete, Dhaulagiri loomed around another hill. Although the route was not built for cars, it thrived with local porters carrying loads of harvested crops, apples or other wares to sell in the cities. Mule caravans passed like trains as the valleys grew deeper.

As they neared Jomsom in the late afternoon with a cold wind pressing hard from the south, the landscape became drier and grainier, more like a desert.

At around six o'clock, the team of two stopped in a field beside Jomsom Airport, exhausted. Badger left Lhama to rest, with the horses tethered to a thin tree, while he found a bench beside the airport's terminal and sat and waited for the 'beautiful woman'.

60
Chittagong

Anna had no idea where to look. All she had been given was a name, J.B. Steenkamp. The boy was still with her as she walked into the main terminal building. Anna saw the 'information' sign and they made their way over. As she pulled up to the counter, the woman behind it turned around and her smile fell as she took in Anna's bedraggled appearance.

'I'm looking for J.B. Steenkamp.'

'Steenkamp Freight?'

'Yes,' said Anna, wondering how many businesses in Bangladesh went by the name 'Steenkamp'.

The woman pulled out a map of the airport and pointed. 'Yellow airplane.'

'Thank you,' said Anna and shuffled off, holding the boy's hand. They made their way out into the dazzling sunlight and Anna turned towards a smaller terminal with some offices. A yellow plane that looked like a Cessna was parked beside a corrugated-iron hangar. On its side was painted, 'Steenkamp Freight'.

As Anna and the boy neared the plane, a broad-shouldered, bearded, mountain of a man emerged from the hangar in a yellow overall, wiping his hands against it, a cigarette dangling from his lips. He didn't notice them and leaned over a box of tools.

'J.B. Steenkamp?' Anna asked as they were within a metre of him. He turned, eyed Anna and whistled.

'*Jis Janie! Kyk wat het die kat ingesleep!* Janie, look what the cat dragged in!' He smiled. Anna recognised the language as Afrikaans. Mossad had a history training the old forces of apartheid, and this was most probably how Ben had met this South African man.

Steenkamp wiped his hands on his overalls and reached out to shake Anna's hand as another man, equally huge, emerged from beside the airplane, also wearing a yellow overall.

'You must be Anna,' said Steenkamp in a characteristic South African accent. It wasn't flat, as some said, but clear, almost half-way between an American and a British accent.

'Yes, you must be J.B.?'

'Like the whiskey,' he smiled. Anna didn't catch the reference. 'This is my business partner, Janie.'

Anna smiled in greeting. 'Did Ben call you?'

'Yup. I've been doing work for him for many years.' He stood with his hands on his hips. His face was smeared with grease. He was handsome, thought Anna, but perhaps not her type. Janie clutched a bottle of whiskey that he tipped into a glass of Coke. Along the bottle's side was 'J&B' and Anna caught Steenkamp's earlier joke.

'Listen, I hear you've had a rough time. Good news is that I can get you anything you need. We've got a shower in there, in our offices, and lucky for you I've got some clothes from an ex-girlfriend that will fit you perfectly. Ben told me you are travelling to Nepal?'

'Yes,' said Anna, suddenly conscious of her faint middle eastern accent. 'Jomsom Airport.'

'Good. Ben told me there's no time to lose, so let me show you around.'

'Good, have you got some food ... for the kid? And for me I guess.' She realised how hungry she was.

Steenkamp looked down. The boy hadn't taken his eyes off the giant the whole time. 'The kid. He coming with?'

'No, but whatever you can give him ... He's homeless, and he helped me a lot today. Saved my life. Did Ben ask you to give me any money?'

'Greenback, no less.'

'Good. Could I have the cash now?'

'Sure, come inside.'

They entered the high-roofed hangar and stood in front of a desk. Steenkamp's secretary, a pretty brunette, handed Anna notes of hundred dollar bills. Anna turned to the boy and gave him five. His eyes lit up and suddenly he burst into tears. Anna hugged him and said, 'Thank you', as she looked into his eyes. She knew he'd most likely never seen so much money in his life. He clutched the money and disappeared through the doors of the hangar.

Anna showered, got dressed in the clothes that had already been laid out for her in the bathroom – jeans that fitted snugly, light running shoes and a black coat – and emerged a different woman, a backpack filled with provisions slung over her shoulder.

'Ready?' Steenkamp asked.

Anna nodded. She was tired, but she didn't think twice as they made their way out of the hangar, got into the plane, taxied into the queue, waited their turn and then sped down the runway.

61
Tel Aviv

The sniper rifle was perched on a gun stand on the windowsill of a flat across the road, opposite Ben's apartment. The butt was pressed against Ben's shoulder. He was staring out of the window. Bulldog sat in a chair that creaked in the corner of the room.

Ben had had a hunch that someone might be on their way to kill him, and he was right. He'd camped out in the flat opposite his own, across the street – which was rented by Mossad at all times exactly for this reason, to be able to see who might be watching Ben's apartment – and had patiently hunched over his sniper rifle, looking through the scope from time to time at his apartment or walking around the room, talking to Bulldog who had taken to visiting him.

'What does the reference to the curators mean?'

'Obviously, it's some kind of museum. But Lo Manthang in Nepal is practically made up of dust and gravel. I doubt there will be any museums or youth hostels there.'

'It obviously refers to something that's going to happen after Nepal.'

'Yes, I think the ritual, or whatever it is that they need the grail for, is going to happen elsewhere, at a museum of sorts.'

'We've got a live one!' Ben pressed his earpiece in and said, 'Agent One, look sharp, trouble headed your way.'

Bulldog got up with an effort and made his way to the window, careful to crouch as he looked down into the street below. An electrician's van had pulled up outside the apartment building and a man emerged from it, looking every bit like an electrician and carrying a clipboard. He walked up to Ben's front door and rapped on it. A few moments later a man looking very much like Ben, the agent known, for the time being, by the codename 'Agent One', answered the knock. Ben listened through his earpiece.

'Ben Hariri?'

'Yes?' Agent One answered.

'I received a complaint from your neighbours. It seems an electrical fault stemming from your flat is causing their power to be out.'

'No problem, do you need to come in?'

'I'm afraid so. I'll just need you to sign this consent form, if you don't mind.' The man reached into a back pocket. Here it is, thought Ben as he played the sniper rifle's cross hairs over the 'electrician's' head. But the man produced a pen and handed it to Agent One.

'Come in,' Ben's double said. But the man paused.

'There's one other thing.'

The electrician reached behind his back and Ben noticed the glint off the gun's handle. Before Müller could move the gun around, a shrill whip accompanied by a small burst of fire from the end of the nuzzle of Ben's gun issued from the apartment window across the street.

'Got 'im!' shouted Bulldog, as the man crumpled to the floor.

'That was too easy,' said Ben, putting the rifle down. Ben pressed the earpiece down and said, 'Agent One, come in.' Ben saw his double, standing in the street below, press his earpiece in.

'Agent One here. Go ahead.'

'Is the target dead?'

'Yes, sir, but there's …'

'Down!' Bulldog shouted. A hail of bullets ripped through the apartment. The electrician had been bait, realised Ben, to draw his position. He crawled to the edge of the window. The rifle had been knocked down and was lying on the floor. He picked it up and made a mental note of where he thought he'd seen the fire erupt from in the street below, and he crawled over to the bathroom as a fresh volley of bullets riddled the room's walls with dents.

'Are you all right?' Ben shouted.

'Yes,' said Bulldog.

Ben stood up on the toilet seat to peer out the window. People were coming out of their houses. Ben scanned the streets, but he couldn't pick up any trace of the Nazis in the street below. Then he caught a faint glint of light – from behind a dumpster. He acted on instinct, guided more by memory of the sound of the guns blazing in the street below than by sight, and he swung the gun's barrel through the window, pulled the trigger and hit the mark in the head.

'Good work, Hariri!'

Bulldog slapped Ben on the back as they stood over the body of the Nazi who'd called himself Schlomo Yatom, in the street below the apartment that Ben had sniped him from. They'd foiled the Nazis' attack. Police and ambulance sirens wailed in the distance. Ben's double had taken a bullet to the stomach from the man who had opened fire with the machine gun, but he would be fine.

'Now,' said Bulldog as the ambulance pulled away from the front of the building. 'Let's get to business in your study.'

The two men shuffled into Ben's cramped study room. Bulldog produced another cigar and lit it up. It was Ben who spoke first.

'How are the Sixth Fleet and Naval Intelligence coming along on those subs?'

'Not a single trace, but I'll keep you in the know.'

'Okay. Back to that business of the youth hostel and the museum … to be honest, sir, I just can't fathom it, I have no idea where the Nazis are going or what they're going to get up to.'

'It will come to you, I'm sure.'

'Perhaps. I'm just glad that my brother and Anna are alive. I wish I could say the same for Agent Fox.'

'Me too, but, we are warriors, and it comes with the territory. When this whole mess is over, we'll find the base in Argentina and bring his body back to be buried where Mossad agents deserve to find rest. We'll have the added bonus of rounding up all the other Nazis.' Ben picked up his phone and dialled a number.

62
Jomsom Airport

Steenkamp answered. 'Hello?'
'You picked her up?'
'Yes, sir.'
'Listen, I need you to take the cargo further.'
'Where to?'
'All the way.'
'Lo Manthang?'
'Yes. Can you do it?'
'It might be a rough landing, but when I refuel I could find a suitable patch of desert to come in on. I have a lot of satellite maps of the area.'

'Great, and another thing …'
'What?'
'There'll be more passengers.'
'How many?'
'Two more. Can you handle it?'
'No problem. I'll make a plan.'
'I have no doubt. And you'll be paid, with interest, for your troubles as soon as I know the cargo's safe on the ground.'

The Cessna banked and landed. Badger watched the plane come in and knew that it was the one he was looking for. 'Looking for something?' he asked Anna as she climbed out.

'Badger!'

Anna flung her hands around his neck and rained kisses on his head.

'Oh, and yes, I almost forgot, I *am* looking for something … a stone.'

Badger smiled and detached himself from her. 'Good, good, we must get going. I've just purchased another horse …'

'No, Badger, we need to get there quicker than horseback.'

'How?'

Anna smiled and nodded at the airplane. 'Just refuelling.'

Badger looked mortified.

'I promise it won't be as bad as you think,' said Anna. 'Is anyone with you?'

'Lhama. Over there,' he pointed to a tree with two horses tethered to it and a woman who sat in meditation nearby on a small patch of grass. Behind her, the Himalayas formed an impressive white curtain of rock and snow.

'We must get going.'

Anna watched Badger shuffle off to Lhama. He seemed to explain to her that they would fly the rest of the way and pointed at the plane. Lhama nodded and loosened the horses from the tree, took the saddles off and let them free.

Steenkamp appeared beside Anna. '*Jislaaik!*' he exclaimed, 'they've got a lot of stuff.' He walked over to give Badger and Lhama a hand. When they were all loaded up and refuelled, Steenkamp sat in the cockpit and analysed his satellite maps on a computer screen for a few minutes, Anna in the co-pilot's chair.

'We can probably land there.' He pointed to an open part of land that he'd zoomed up on. It was some distance away from the city of Lo Manthang, at the edge of the plateau on the fringe of the foothills.

'Can you give me the coordinates again?'

Badger recited them, and Steenkamp punched them into his map. 'That close enough?'

'Yes, seems okay,' replied Badger. 'The important thing is enough daylight to get into the caves, and that should give us about two hours to get in.'

Soon enough, they were in the air. Badger and Lhama fell asleep almost instantly after their long journey. Anna hoped that they'd make it to their destination before James did. She wondered if any of his thoughts were of her.

63
Off the coast of Chittagong

James *was* thinking about Liz. James sat in his study with his fingers steepled, a tumbler of bourbon on the table in front of him. He couldn't get her out of his mind. He was like a schoolboy madly in the throes of first love who'd just found out that his girlfriend had cheated on him.

Frieda sat opposite him, unsure at first of how to act, but when he started talking, she kept quiet and simply listened, letting him say what was on his mind. It was a very rare occasion, she thought, to have James speaking his mind, so she let it go uninterrupted. He was a little drunk, but that was probably helping him to think through the issues.

'Have you ever been in love?'

The question startled her somewhat.

'In love?'

'Yes, you know ...'

'*Nein.*'

'Not once, not ever?'

'*Nein.*'

'Then you don't know how it feels.'

'To lose someone?'

'Yes, in the blink of an eye to have everything snatched away from you, worse than death. Death comes in the night and robs you. It takes someone away from you. But being betrayed ... it's worse.'

'With all due respect, I don't think you have to have been in love to know what it's like to lose someone.'

'I'm sorry, that was insensitive, I forgot ...' Frieda had lost her two-year-old son a few years ago.

'Apology accepted. You know ...' Frieda leaned closer to him. 'Do you know what your problem is? Permission to speak freely.'

'What?'

'Your problem is that you shut everyone out. You make out as if you're this ... ice block ... but the trouble is that eventually you're going to melt, and when you do, it's *disastrous*.'

James started laughing.

'What?'

'I'm sorry ...' James shook his head. 'It's just that ... you're completely right. And I had no idea about this problem of mine, until now. It's just that,' he became serious, wistful even; 'She really opened me up. And I don't know how to explain it to you, but it had nothing to do with how she looks. Don't get me wrong, she's bloody gorgeous. But that wasn't it. There was something to her. And the reason I know this is because I could sense that even in the Russian countryside, when I couldn't see her face.'

'*Mein Führer*, you are undoubtedly ...'

'I know what you are going to say. You're going to say I am smitten and biased, that my judgement is clouded.'

'You wouldn't be wrong. I was going to say something similar.'

'Frieda, I respect your opinion, but this is something only I can know. There is something about that woman that just ... she drives me mad, makes me want to give everything up.'

Frieda understood. This was more than infatuation, but she decided to tow the hard line.

'Fine. But, *mein Führer*, we have work to do ...'

'Yes, you're right, I need to stop this. Has the alert gone out?'

'*Ja, mein Führer.*'

'Any bites?'

'Lots, some ex-military, some street thugs.'

'Good. Make it clear again that if any of them harm her, they won't live to see another day.'

'*Ja, mein Führer.* I understand the situation.'

'Helicopter ready?'

'Yes.'

'Good, call Roger and Parcival. We leave in five minutes. Where's my pilot?'

An overalled man appeared after Frieda shouted through the door.

'Dark Horse ready?'

'*Jahwol, mein Führer.*'

'I don't hear the engines …'

'I'll start her up.'

The pilot clicked his heels together and disappeared.

'How long will the trip take?' James asked.

'Four hours,' Roger, who had appeared in the doorway, replied. James heard the engines of the helicopter start up. The three men made their way to the helipad at the front of the boat and watched servants lug some final equipment on board. When the pilot gave the signal, they hopped in. The Dark Horse reared up and they sped off towards Lo Manthang.

James sat in the co-pilot's chair and allowed himself, without knowing it, to be sucked into meditation. He saw her smile, her wide eyes glinting, her silken blonde hair floating in the sea breeze as they sat on the owner's private deck of the yacht. For some reason, he thought of Rachel, the girl who had died for him, and his thoughts drifted to his father. He could picture the old man on his deathbed, and a pang of guilt struck. Why was he dallying with simple-minded, weak thoughts about a woman? The nagging feeling on his shoulder was Roger tapping him. He leaned back.

'*Ja?*' James said through the mouthpiece. He didn't realise that Roger had been speaking to him through his headphones.

'Frieda would like a word.'

'Of course, put her on.'

'Here, *mein Führer.* I've just heard that Agent Müller was killed in a trap set for him by Ben Hariri. The Mems told me all his trackers went dead. They must have "dry-cleaned" the body to remove them.'

'*Sheiße*! And we have no idea who 'Liz' really is?'
'*Nein.*'
'*Danke.*' He was more dejected than angry, Frieda assessed.
'Anything else?'
'*Ja*, the twelve knights. Have they been notified?'
'*Nein.*'
'Get on it. And I've been thinking up a little plan how to throw them off ...' James explained his plan to Frieda as, finally, the sharp white teeth of the Himalayas began to rear up.

64
Kingdom of Lo

The Cessna cut through a thin veil of mist. Mountain peaks pushed through, glowing auburn in the setting sun. Anna knew that only a handful of tourists were allowed into the kingdom each year. They were privileged to be among those who entered it now, albeit without climbing permits or visas. It was a risky move. If caught and identified, Anna could have provoked an international diplomatic 'incident'. If nothing else, it would be a massive embarrassment to the Israeli government.

In the back seat, Badger stirred. He yawned and rubbed his eyes as Steenkamp gave a status update: 'We'll land in twenty minutes, people.'

Badger drew in a breath that reached all the way into his deepest chakra, and exhaled. Anna thought that it was more out of peacefulness than terror, as she turned to look at him in the back seat. He offered some kind of prayer – a *puja* – to appease the ghosts that lived in the air or perhaps the ghosts that whispered between the cold blue mountain chasms. Anna's stomach churned as they made their first big drop in altitude. The plane banked, whirred around and came in to land.

'Brace yourself,' said Steenkamp, 'we're in for a *very* bumpy landing.' Everyone stiffened except Steenkamp. The plane seemed to float above the surface for a few drawn-out seconds before it touched the ground and bounced up on the first attempt.

'Hold on!'

On the second attempt, the wheels stuck. Stones and loose gravel flew up around the plane before it finally came to a skidding halt, engulfed in a cloud of dust.

With their nerves slightly frayed but their bodies thankfully intact, they stepped out into an otherworldly landscape dominated by chalky sandstone cliffs, desolate plains and majestic peaks in the background. It was undoubtedly one of the most beautiful places Anna had seen. The distant cliffs towering over the Kali Gandaki river were washed with yellows, blues and reds.

Badger came over to Anna and saw that she was captivated by the sight. Anna hunched her shoulders in and turned her coat collar up against the cold wind from the south. Steenkamp busied himself piling their backpacks near the tail of the plane.

'Beautiful, isn't it,' Badger said.

'It's ethereal,' said Anna. 'I've never seen cliffs like that. The colours are just ... so vivid.'

'If you ask the locals, they'll tell you that the place where we're going, Marjhang, was the site of a great battle between two religions, Buddhism and the Bön. A great Buddhist master fought a demon woman who represented Bön, and killed her, spilling her guts all over these cliffs. The blue, supposedly, is from her liver and the red is her blood, the yellow is her bile.'

Badger's face crinkled into a smile.

'Delightful!' said Anna. 'Don't you like how they made Bön a *woman*? Ridiculous. Right up there with Eve.' Badger laughed and nodded.

They pulled their backpacks over their shoulders. Steenkamp came over to give Anna a satellite phone. 'You'll be able to send encrypted messages from it.'

'Thank you.'

Steenkamp shrugged. 'It's my job. Listen ... Ben didn't ask me, but won't you need help getting out of here?'

'Yes, we will. Must have slipped his mind.' Anna looked at Badger. 'We shouldn't be more than a few hours?'

'A day at most,' Badger whispered.

'How far are we from Lo Manthang? The city, I mean?'

'About four days' walk, I think,' Steenkamp replied.

'I know it's a lot, and you've done so much for us already, but is there any chance you could you wait for us?'

'*Ja.* It's fine. I'll stay here. Punch the coordinates into the phone … just in case. My number,' he brandished another satellite phone, 'is saved under "Steenkamp Mobile".' Anna flicked through the phone's contacts and found it. 'Thanks, here it is. We best get moving. Again, I can't thank you enough.'

'That's okay, I owe Ben. In any case, I'm working, this is a job. Good luck out there.'

Steenkamp waved them off. They began their trek over the plain.

Ten minutes later, the gravelly path began to lead up into the hills, backgrounded by a curtain of white peaks. The path struck into a bluish chasm. Within half an hour, they had crossed a turquoise icy cold river and stood before a crumbling sugar-loaf shaped hill.

'There it is,' Badger panted through purple lips. He gazed up, mesmerised, fog issuing from his mouth. 'Marjhang, home of the Manni.' Badger traced a finger up along the edge of the cliff to a cave about a third of the way up. 'That's where we need to go. Look difficult?' he asked, turning to Lhama.

Lhama assessed it quietly. 'Relatively. Not too high. The problem is the material. Look how it flakes to the touch.' She broke off a piece of wall that came away with ease in her hand. 'It isn't ideal climbing surface, but I'll go first and secure holds in the rock. We'll set up a pulley system that will allow each of you, in turn, to get up easily enough.'

The sun was setting behind the mountains. In the distance, Annapurna and Dhaulagiri were like purple-grey phantoms poking through the orange clouds.

'We'd better hurry,' said Anna, 'James and his men could be here any minute.'

Lhama took off her backpack and put on her climbing shoes. She began to carefully scale the wall. It was a climb of at least fifty metres of sheer cliff face which she accomplished with spider-like efficiency in half an hour, flakes of rock peeling off the walls at various intervals where she hammered holds into the cliff. Finally, she neared the cave, waved down and disappeared.

Badger and Anna held their breaths. Badger dropped to the ground and rummaged in his backpack. He brought out an orange cloth, which he placed on his head, and a *shang* bell. He sat down, chanting a ceremonial offering to appease the deities while ringing the bell and making flicking movements with his upturned hands. A few minutes later, Lhama emerged from the cave above and shouted: 'Anna, here comes the harness.'

'Go ahead!' She shouted back.

It fell to the ground with a clutter. Badger repacked his backpack, pulled it over his shoulders, picked up the harness and secured it around his waist, with his shoe firmly in a foothold.

'See you inside,' he said as he began to climb up.

Anna hauled herself up over a ledge and into a pitch-black cave. A thin line of torch light licked over the walls, revealing ancient frescoes. They looked a lot like those found in the Buddhist monasteries all over Nepal, but the colours were washed and faded. Bön and Hindu deities scrutinised the intruders from the walls; the evil gods were surrounded by fire and brandishing weapons, trampling humans or cutting them down with swords, while the peaceful deities sat in meditation.

'This is the top level of the cave complex.' Badger stood with his hands on his hips. His breathing was slightly laboured from the climb. 'The Bönpo built caves into these cliffs in Lo Manthang. The top level is the monastic level, where the ancient Bönpo used to pray. There are several levels beneath us.'

Lhama rummaged in her pack to produce headlamps. She handed them out to Badger and Anna, who strapped them over their heads.

'Each level will represent a challenge to us,' Badger continued. 'The ancient texts tell of nine levels – spiritual as well as physical – tests, if you will, that will need to be passed in order to gain access to the object that these caves protect.'

'The grail stone …' Anna whispered.

'Yes. Each level corresponds to one of the nine "vehicles" or "ways" of Bön religion.'

'The nine ways to enlightenment?' Lhama had heard of them. 'They'll be difficult to get through.'

'But you have discovered the answers to all of the riddles, haven't you Badger? You said you had worked them out.'

'Theoretically. I have spent my whole life finding out what the questions are ... and then trying to figure out the answers. But just because you know the questions and in fact even the answers, it doesn't mean that you will know how to interpret them in context.'

'Bit like an open-book test,' said Anna, but her companions didn't quite understand her meaning.

'How did you know where to look?'

'The riddles to the grail's location were hidden in secret texts, known as *terma* to the Bönpo. Small clues that point to other clues – some are in Wolfram von Eschenbach's *Parcifal*; others yet are in ancient Occitan. The most resourceful, though, have been the ancient Bön *terma*.'

'How long have these caves been deserted?' asked Anna.

'Some think a thousand years,' said Badger.

'What happens when we reach the final level?' Lhama asked.

'As far as I could tell from the texts, there is a vaulted chasm at the lowest level. In it lies the grail in a box that can only be opened with a skeleton key, the *dietrich*.'

'The one Trevellian has ...'

'Exactly. We need to get to it before he does, and take it away from this place. The time has come for the grail to find a new home.'

'Where was it before?'

'Rosslyn Chapel, in Scotland.'

'Where do we start? How do we go down to the next level?' Anna turned her head to focus the light around the walls. It seemed completely devoid of any kind of way down. Badger scuttled off deeper into the cave and crouched at the wall. He began to heave at the edge of a stone. Anna and Lhama helped him and a dim light began to appear through a crack.

'It's a tunnel!'

The opening led to a tunnel about five feet long and just wide enough to let a human through. The tunnel led to another cave. They squeezed through and Anna got up and smacked her hands together to get rid of the dust. She looked up and was awestruck. The light beams of their headlamps criss-crossed on the ceiling, revealing a dome on which a navy blue night sky had been painted, little stars glittering in the torchlight. It was immaculately preserved. A grating sound reverberated around the chamber, as if rocks were being ground together.

'What's happening?' Anna asked.

'Look!' Lhama pointed towards the dome of the cave. There seemed to be a second level of rock that was moving behind the painted sky. There were holes in the sky, about one foot each in diameter, at four points of the room, through which the second level of rock was visible, turning round and round as if on a disk.

Pictures had been painted onto the revolving disk. Figures passed through the holes as it turned: animals, Buddhist gods, snippets of ancient script that looked Chinese to Anna, and numbers.

'Badger, I don't like the look of this. What are we supposed to do?'

'This is the first test. A good place to start is with the first riddle: "Our Lord's birth animal".'

'Whose lord?' Anna asked.

'Tönpa Shenrab, the founding father of Bön religion,' Badger answered, staring up at the revolving pictures flashing through the holes.

'What is Shenrab's birth animal?'

'He was born in the year of the male wood mouse.'

Anna and Lhama looked up at the ceiling through the holes. Different animals appeared through the hole furthest away from them – tigers, dragons, oxen, monkeys and others.

'There,' said Anna, pointing to the hole, 'that one has animals.'

'Yes, but what about the others?' Lhama asked.

'Through that hole,' Badger pointed to another one, 'can you see the script?'

'Yes,' Lhama replied. 'But I have no idea what it says.'

'That's because it's Zhang-Zhung.'

'Ancient pre-Chinese script?'

'The script of the Bönpo.'

'What does it say?'

'Different months of the year.'

'So which month was Shenrab born in?'

'The first.'

'And the other holes?'

'That one there is the year,' Lhama pointed at the hole closest to them.

'And I presume it should be the first year?' Anna asked.

'Correct. The first year, 18 000 years ago, when Bön came into existence.'

'What is behind the fourth hole? It looks like it's also script.'

'That one,' Badger squinted at it, 'seems to be the names of the birth animals.'

'And we're looking for "male wood mouse"?'

'The trick is …' Badger began to stroll around the cave, sliding his hand against the rock of the wall, 'how does this whole thing work?'

Lhama offered: 'I think we need to get the canvas behind the night sky to stop with the correct numbers, animals, months and words in place in the correct holes.'

'Clever, Lhama, I think you are right. But how do we …'

'There!' Anna pointed to the opposite side of the cave. Something was protruding from the wall. It seemed like a wooden crank with a handle jutting out. Badger rushed over. 'Carefully now …' he said as he eased the crank round. It turned a cog behind which seemed to be connected to a shaft, inside the wall, that controlled the turning disk.

'It's slowing down!' said Anna.

'Now, there must be a way to stop it at just the right moment,' Badger said. 'Lhama, help me to search the walls.'

Lhama ran her hand up and down over the cave's walls. 'Wait, what's this … it feels like a button.'

'And I'll bet if we push it down, the canvas will stop moving.'

'What happens if we get it wrong?' Anna asked nervously.

'I think we will be trapped inside. This place was designed to stop anyone with evil intentions. I wouldn't be surprised if the chambers are riddled with death traps. Spears … footholds … falling rocks.'

'Well, that's a comforting thought,' said Anna.

'Now,' Badger lifted his torch to illuminate one of the holes, 'shine your lights on the holes so that I can see.' The torches and head-lights washed the holes with light.

'Sure as hell hope these batteries last,' Anna muttered to herself.

'Come and take over, Lhama, I need to push the button.'

Lhama made her way to Badger and began to wind the crank. Badger swapped places with her at the other side of the cave where the 'button' in the wall was. 'Slow it more.' Lhama increased her rate of pull and the canvas slowed down. 'More …'

'That's as much as it seems to want to go.'

'Alright ...'

Badger rubbed his hands and looked up. He placed his hand over the button again and closed his eyes.

'Badger, why are your eyes closed ...?'

Snap. Badger had pushed it.

The roof stopped moving and there was a grinding sound. It took Anna a few seconds to realise that the sound was coming from the entranceway they had come in through. It was closing.

'We're being trapped!'

'No, I don't think so,' Badger said. There was silence for a few moments and then there was a small 'click' sound and a ring of blue light glowed in the centre of the floor.

'A doorway?' Lhama drew in a deep breath and sighed. Anna could almost hear her smiling as she said, 'Badger, you did it!'

'No time to waste, the challenges only get more difficult,' Badger pulled up the hatch for Lhama and Anna to climb down into the second chamber. Just as Anna slipped through, she thought she heard the faint beat of a helicopter.

Anna landed on her haunches like a cat and rose up to her full height. Slowly, deliberately, she took in the sight of the chamber. The hatchway above had completely closed, trapping them in.

'I've seen nothing like it ...' Lhama murmured. She glided her hand smoothly along the edge of a mercurial wall that seemed to be made of glass. Behind it, colours were swirling. Bright, beautiful patterns formed and vanished as soon as they appeared.

'How on earth did they make this?'

'I have no idea!' said Badger. 'But it's majestic ...'

In the middle of the room, rising from a cobble-stone floor was a rock structure like a raised basin. They moved towards it. In the middle of it was a bronze bowl. Its sides were dented with pock marks. There were tags lying on the edges of the basin. Anna picked one up, weighed it in her hand and asked, 'What do you think these are?'

'Like name tags,' Lhama said, picking one up.

'More like keys,' Badger replied. 'Each one has a Bön god's name on it, written in Zhang-Zhung.'

'What is the second way of the Bön?' Lhama asked, running a finger across the tag's engraved surface. Badger watched the swirling colours. His gaze seemed to be locked on a specific part of the wall.

'The second way of the Bön is the "visual manifestations of the gods".'

'What does that mean?' asked Anna.

'It means the ways that the Bön gods show themselves in our world. It also has to do with the need for appeasing the gods, an important part of Bön religion and, indeed, Buddhism.'

'You mean like offering them gifts?' asked Anna.

'Precisely. More like bribes sometimes! The clue to this one is: "Eyes to burn you with, fingers to tear at you, toes to dig into your side, and legs to trample you with, I have one hundred and forty-four all together."'

'How is that supposed to help us with this wall of swirling colour?'

'Well ...' Badger scratched his stubble. He crossed his arms and cocked his head to one side as he looked at the wall. 'The answer is Walchen Gecko.'

'Walchen who?' Anna was puzzled.

'Walchen Gecko, a Bön deity,' Lhama replied.

'How on earth did you get that?'

'The clue mentions "eyes", "fingers", "toes" and "legs". Then it says, "I have one hundred and forty-four together."'

'So let me have a guess ...' said Lhama. 'If you count the number of eyes, fingers, toes and legs the Bön god Walchen Gecko has ...' Lhama picked up one of the tags again and held it out in front of her, 'you get one hundred and forty-four. So we should be looking for the name tag, or key, that says "Walchen Gecko"?'

'Correct. Can you see him in the walls?' Badger asked, gesturing around the room. Anna squinted around.

'I can't see anything. You, Lhama?'

'Nothing.'

'He's there ... don't worry, I can see him.'

'So what do we do now?'

'I believe we should insert the correct tag here,' Badger motioned to the bowl. There was an indent right in the middle, like a slot. Badger picked up a tag that said GECKO on it and pushed it into the groove. Nothing happened.

'Are you sure that's the correct one?'

'Positive,' said Badger. 'Why is it not ...'

'Maybe it's the wrong way round,' suggested Anna.

Badger removed the tag, flipped it around and slotted it back in. 'Clever, thanks.' A deep grumbling sound shook the walls, which began, slowly, to twirl inwards, like layers of curtains turning around and around, closing in on them.

'How are we supposed to get out?' said Anna. 'Are you sure you got it right?'

Badger merely smiled and nodded. 'We'll see.'

Anna felt her chest tighten. She could feel her heart pounding in her eardrums.

'Badger, what's going on?' asked Lhama, as the rock closed to within two metres. Badger was quiet. 'This is no time for meditating!' Lhama's voice was almost a scream. Badger wasn't budging. His eyes seemed to have half-closed and a vacant expression came over his face. His breathing was even and controlled. Still, the walls closed in, and Anna and Lhama began to panic.

'Badger!'

The walls were within a metre of them.

'There's no way out,' Anna shouted, 'we're going to be crushed!'

Badger was seated lotus-style and began to hum. The walls were half a metre away. Suddenly, the grating noise let up, to be replaced by an oppressive silence. The walls had stopped. Anna gulped a deep sigh of relief, but the grating sound returned almost immediately. This time though, instead of the walls moving, the floor on which they stood, a small circle of cobbled stone, moved downwards in a spiral towards the third chamber.

The circular pedestal came to a halt. On each side, a tunnel curled down and around to a room below. The room was dark, with cobbled walls on which were mounted terrifying faces that hung over a well. Large drops of crystal-clear water fell from the moist grey-green ceiling and plopped with bright sound onto the surface of the water. Across from the well, Lhama's torchlight made out a statue of a Bön god, Anna didn't know which one, and near it was an ancient-looking chest.

'What is this place?' Lhama asked, her voice echoing around the chamber.

'The clue to the second way of Bön is: "Knowing that what you see is an illusion, is the key."'

'There's a chest over there,' Lhama said. 'It looks like a treasure chest of some kind.'

'Is it open?' Anna asked.

Lhama made her way to the chest and tried it.

'It's shut tight. But there's a keyhole ...'

'We'll need to find the key,' Badger said.

'The well ...' Anna said. 'It must be in the well ...'

They peered down into the deep waters. Yellow-white torch beams searched the sides and the bottom of the well.

'There!' said Anna. 'Move your light back, no, towards the left, there! Can you see it?'

'Yes!' Lhama said excitedly. A golden key shimmered in the light, towards one side of the well at the bottom. Anna tore off coat, shirt and jeans. Without waiting for Badger or Lhama to stop her, she climbed onto the ledge, pressed her fingers closed around her nose and plunged into the water. She surfaced with a deep gulp of air and without hesitating, made a turn and swam towards the bottom.

'Bloody crazy!' said Badger as they watched her grope around the floor of the well. A few seconds later, she broke the surface and drank in a massive gulp of air. Her lips were purple and her skin pale.

'There's nothing there!' she said as she'd managed to catch her breath.

'What do you mean there's nothing there?' Lhama said, helping Anna out. They all looked over the sides and Badger flashed his light over the golden key that still, despite Anna's best assurances, seemed to be lying at the bottom.

'I don't understand,' said Anna. 'I felt all around the floor. There was definitely nothing there. Maybe I should try again ...' Neither Badger nor Lhama protested, so Anna got back into the well and dived down, once again returning empty-handed.

'I'm not making it up,' she stammered as she surfaced. Her teeth were chattering. She stuttered: 'There's ... definitely ... nothing down ... there.'

'I think I know what the problem is,' Badger said as Anna got out and began to put her clothes back on.

Lhama took off her jersey and helped to dry Anna. 'What is it?' she asked.

'The problem is that we *think* because we see the key there, at the bottom of the well, that it is there. The clue says, "Knowing that what you see is an illusion, is the key", so that would be a good starting point. The key is not there.'

'Then where is it?' Anna panted, pulling her clothes back over herself, glad for the faint warmth that still lingered in her jeans and shirt.

'Here.' Badger reached into the well, but ran his hand along the edge of the wall. He pulled a golden key out.

'How the hell …?'

'I have no idea,' Badger replied cryptically.

He hurried over to the chest, leaned over it and inserted the key. He turned it and the lock opened with a click. Lhama and Badger peered inside.

'Juniper leaves?' Lhama asked. There was a pile of leaves, and a rock and flint inside the chest. Badger carried some leaves over to the statue, leaned down, and began to strike the flint against the rock just a few centimetres above the pile of leaves, which he bunched on the floor. A long time seemed to pass but no sparks caught.

'Here, let me try,' said Lhama. On her first attempt, a stream of orange sparks fell onto the leaves and a small flame licked up.

'More leaves!' shouted Badger. Anna hurried to the chest and brought bunches of leaves clutched in her hands. In the light of the flames, Badger noticed a strange-looking button engraved with an inscription on the underside of the statue's chin. He got up and pressed it. A hatchway sprang open in the wall, leading into a pitch-black tunnel.

'It's fresh, *mein Führer.*'

'How long ago?'

James stared up the slippery surface that led to a cave about fifty metres up.

'I don't know, perhaps an hour?'

'Look,' it was Parcival who spoke. He pointed up. 'They inserted climbing rods into the walls right at the top there.'

'Are you sure these are the right coordinates?' James asked.

'To the button,' Roger replied.

'Make no mistake,' James began, 'this is no coincidence. Whoever is in there now is after the same thing we are.' He turned to Parcival. 'Are you certain Badger is dead?'

'Yes, *mein Führer*, positive.'

'Do you want us to go in?' Roger asked. 'The easiest way for us to get into the cave would be for the men to be lowered in by chopper.'

'No. I have a better plan. Parcival, follow these tracks –' James shone his torch onto the ground, pointing out the footprints that led away towards the river '– Roger and I are going to have a little surprise in store for our grail robbers when they come out.'

'You will wait here for them to come out?'

'They're sure to come out the same way they went in.'

Anna squeezed through the tunnel and popped out at the other end, crawling into a massive chamber. She shone her torch around as she emerged. She couldn't see any ceiling.

'And this room?' She joined Badger and Lhama a few metres in front of her. Only when she drew level with them did she see that they were standing on a rocky ledge, below which, a few feet out, the ground gave way to nothing but an endless pit with strange columns of rock poking from up the abyss.

'Oh my ...' Lhama shone her torch down into the void. The light became fuzzy around the edges and produced a stunted tip without touching a finite end.

'What's that?' There were the tops of column beams floating in the void, each no wider than a foot in diameter. The closest one was flush with the ledge, like a stepping stone into the darkness. Lhama's torchlight played down, finding that the surface was the top of a column. About a metre further down were the tops of a multitude of other columns.

'There are about eight of them surrounding the first one.'

Further out, a criss-crossing nightmare of columns became visible under Anna's light.

'They look like beams of rock ...'

'Columns that we have to cross,' Badger added.

'We have to go over these?'

'I don't see any other way.'

'But they're each no wider than a foot.' Lhama said.

'What is the fourth way of the Bön?' Anna asked.

'The fourth way of Bön is to help the dead, who are trapped between the world of the living and the afterlife, to find their way to the light. I suppose what these columns symbolise is finding a pathway in the darkness.'

'What is the clue and the answer for this chamber?' asked Lhama.

'The clue is: "Use your first and your next to make nine".'

'That makes no sense at all,' Anna said.

'Look,' Badger shone a light onto the first stepping stone. There seemed to be something engraved on it.

'What's that on it?'

'A number,' Badger said.

'First and your next to make …' Anna thought. 'Use the first number and add the second to make nine?'

'That's right,' said Badger. 'Can you see the other columns around this first one?'

'Yes.'

'They each have numbers too, but some of them must be fake columns or booby trapped in some way.' Badger walked to the side of the cave and picked up a rock.

'Hold my ankles,' he said.

Lhama and Anna each held tightly onto an ankle as he leaned over the ledge to place the rock onto one of the columns. As soon as it had touched down on top of the column, it crumbled into gravel and dust and disappeared from sight. Anna and Lhama held tight as Badger moved backwards onto the ledge on his stomach.

'Did you see that?'

'The column just disappeared …'

'What's the first column's number?' asked Anna.

'Two.'

'So …' Anna shone her torch around the tops of the other columns below. 'That one …' the torch's light remained fixed on a column with 'seven' engraved on it. '… That must be it?'

'Yes,' Badger said. He got onto the first column and jumped. Although he seemed old, Badger was surprisingly flexible. When his full weight landed on the 'seven' column, it slid down as if it was a hydraulic shaft and he stepped onto the next one marked 'two'. The first column slid back up.

'Sevens and twos all the way!' Badger shouted. 'Follow me.'

Anna stepped onto the 'seven' pillar and held her breath as it whooshed down into the darkness.

Anna's feet touched down on solid ground. She'd jumped the last metre from the final column onto a ledge. All three were safely across the nightmare of beams. A tunnel opened in the side of rock wall that rose up to a dizzying height. Beside the entrance of the tunnel were rock carvings of patterns that looked like curly bits of fire, dragons and tiger's heads.

Badger got onto his hands and knees and led the way, crawling into the tunnel. It took some time to open up to the chamber that corresponded to the fifth way of the Bön. The chamber was lit faintly by tiny streams of light that filtered in from a high ceiling. A sloping embankment of stone led to a floor with five rows of two holes each, side-by-side.

'And the fifth way of the Bön is …?'

'The fifth way outlines ten ways of the layman, according to the Bön tradition. Ten basic guidelines for how ordinary followers of Bön, those who aren't monks, are to live their lives.'

They crowded around one of the holes and peered down. All of the holes snaked away at an angle and disappeared into darkness.

'What are we supposed to do now?' Anna asked.

'I think we're meant to choose one and jump into it.'

'How do you know?'

'I don't,' Badger said. 'Call it a leap of faith.'

'There seem to be ten holes,' Lhama pointed her torch over the rows. 'How do we know which one to choose?'

'I have a feeling it's this one.'

Badger disappeared.

'Badger?' Lhama threw her torch light around.

'Where is he?' Anna asked.

'I think he must have jumped into one of these god-forsaken holes.'

'Which one?'

'I'm not sure …'

Lhama's light danced over the two holes closest to them. 'It could only have been one of these.'

'Well, there's nothing for it,' Anna said. 'We have to go. We have to choose.' She stood above one of the holes and prepared to lower herself in.

'Wait.'

Lhama picked up a rock and came back to the hole. She dropped it in and they waited. It made no sound. She tried with another stone in the other hole. They waited for a long while before a faint splashing sound came.

'Water!'

'It must be that one,' Anna said. She threw herself into the hole.

Lhama held her breath. There was a faint 'plop', louder than the sound the rock had made. 'I'm coming!' she shouted and lowered herself in. She took a deep breath before letting go of the sides, quickly tucked the torch into her pants and shot downwards like an arrow.

A few seconds later she emerged through the end of the tunnel and fell, sinking fast, into the water. Just as she thought she could hold her breath no longer, she surfaced, and she felt Anna's hands pulling her up. Anna tugged her to the side of the well and pushed her up before following her onto a ledge.

They rushed through an arched entranceway to a brightly lit chamber. All around them, on ledges, were small Buddha statues. Each one had a swastika on its chest. They sat in rows like terra cotta warriors, no more than a foot high. Small candles in their laps burned with an unnatural purple-blue flame. Their eyes, peering through small slits, glowed red.

Badger was standing in the middle of the room, staring at the audience of Buddhas.

'Thank god you're okay. We weren't sure which hole you'd gone down!'

'Shhh!'

They joined him in the centre of the chamber. On the floor, there seemed to be an indent. A groove into which something could be pushed.

'What is the sixth way, Badger?' asked Anna.

'The way of the monk.'

'What is the clue?'

'"One of us is left."'

'One of us is left?'

'Their chests,' Badger said.

'Yes?' Lhama replied, confused.

'They all have swastikas.'

'So?'

'I think one of the swastikas is turning left, like the Nazi's swastika did, and not right like the yungdrung swastika of the Bönpo.'

'There seems to be a groove in the floor here,' Anna said, flashing her torchlight onto the non-descript indent. 'Do you think one of those Buddhas will fit in here? I mean the bases of the statues …'

'Perhaps.'

It seemed a near-impossible task to find the left-turned swastika – there were at least two thousand statues on the raised ledges of rock, and their chests were partially obscured by the flames. But Badger walked forward, picked one up from the third row directly in front of where they'd been standing, and slid it into the groove. Again came a grating sound, and a doorway opened in the side of one of the ledges. Badger passed through, stooping through the arch, without waiting for Lhama and Anna.

'He's bloody good that one,' Anna offered.

Badger was seated lotus-style in the middle of the next room. His face was lit by a strange blue glow, as if he were a porcelain doll. His forefinger was pressed over his lips, to show Lhama and Anna that they needed to be quiet. He motioned for them to sit down. As they sat, Lhama played her light over the walls. They were covered with rows of upturned bells. Each one was see-through, like delicate lotus flowers made of glass, attached to the walls by nearly invisible wires. In the light of the torch, the bells began to quiver, and a humming sound reverberated through the room. Badger held a hand over Lhama's arm and pressed it down. He whispered so softly that the two of them could only just make out what he said.

'Light off. Keep quiet.'

He pointed up. Above them was a ceiling of spikes, ready to collapse in, it seemed. Anna and Lhama understood that sound would provoke the ceiling into falling down. Badger began to hum, and drifted into deep meditation. His humming sounded strange to Anna. It sounded as if it were made up of two octaves; one made her feel tired but the other octave, slightly higher, was rejuvenating.

After about a minute, Badger's hum was taken up by the bells and rose to a deafening crescendo. The floors and the walls began to shake. Anna and Lhama cupped their ears. It felt as if their eardrums would burst. Without warning, the floor that they were sitting on shattered like a sheet of glass; thousands of shards flew about in every direction as it gave way, and Badger, Lhama and Anna fell with a thud into a deep, dark chamber.

'None of our lights seem to work well down here,' Lhama said, tapping her torch against the ground of the chamber. There was a faint glow that came from it, but the light seemed to be sucked into the darkness.

'It's as if the dark is eating the light. What is this place?'

'The chamber of the eighth way of Bön, which speaks of the need for great Bön teachers.'

'Never mind this place,' Anna said, 'what was that *last room* all about?'

'The seventh way deals with how to attain perfect pitch while humming in meditation. You saw those spikes above us?'

'Pretty scary, could've crushed us to death easily.'

'If I got the pitch wrong, I believe the ceiling would have caved in before the ground gave way. An old Bön technique involves training the voice in a special way so that the monk is able to hum in two octaves at the same time. The lower octave, I have read, is even lower than that of the greatest opera singers. Scientists still are not able to prove how Bön monks can accomplish this feat. The clue for the seventh way is: "The clear high voice that is produced in a low place, like the black dog's barking."'

'Padmasambhava Buddha wrote that himself in one of the ancient texts …' said Lhama.

'But how can you hum in two octaves at once?' asked Anna. 'I've never heard anything like it.'

Badger chuckled. 'Practice.' He groped around on the floor.

'There are holes in the floor,' Lhama observed.

'It's a grid,' Anna added.

'Here. Seems to be a bag of small round pebbles. I think they're meant to go into the holes.'

'How, and in what order?'

'We need to make the shape of a right-turning swastika. The swastika represents the nine ways of Bön and the need for great teachers to help students to practise them.

'Turn off your lights,' said Badger, 'light is likely to cause more harm than good in here. Sit back near the wall. Let me put the pattern in place.'

Anna and Lhama moved backwards and cleared the middle to let Badger work. Anna whispered to Lhama: 'I'd like to have seen anyone else get through this!'

'There's no way …' said Lhama. 'Not unless you've studied these things your whole life, like Badger has.'

'Especially the chanting – only a trained monk could have done that.'

Suddenly, Badger stood up and dusted his hands. 'Ready? One piece to put in place, and I suggest you join me here in the middle.' Anna and Lhama crawled over to him.

'Here.' He caught their hands and brought them closer, then leaned down and he put the final pebble in place. The floor burst open like two swinging saloon doors and they tumbled into a room with a vaulted ceiling and three tall, spinning prayer wheels that took up the entire side of one wall. The massive drum-like structures seemed to have writing on them, or at least characters, like syllables, thought Anna.

'The ninth level!' Badger said. "We've made it this far!'

'What's the clue for this level?'

'The clue is "The jewel in the midst of the lotus".'

'I know this one …' Lhama said. 'It's the end part of the universal chant, *ohm mani padme hum*. It's the *mani padme hum* part: "The jewel in the middle of the lotus"!'

Lhama walked towards the prayer wheels. A screech stopped her in her tracks. Anna stood over a skeleton that was propped up against the wall, sitting down and staring ahead, its jaw hanging off its skull. It seemed well preserved. A hat was on its head and it wore what seemed to be a military uniform. Lhama and Badger came over for a closer look.

'Here you are!' said Badger.

'Who was this person?' Anna asked.

'This, can you see? It's an SS uniform,' said Badger, 'I had no idea that he'd come this close, only to die in the ninth level!'

'I know who he is,' said Lhama.

'Who?' asked Anna.

'It's Otto Rahn, Himmler's grail hunter, isn't it?'

'Right!' said Badger. He kneeled before the skeleton and offered a prayer. 'Must've thought the uniform would help him in some way down here. I can't believe he would come this far only to die here. How come he didn't solve the final clue? It seems obvious,' said Badger. 'The prayer wheels – three in total – need to be turned so that *"mani padme hum"* shows on the front of them. At least, that's what I think.'

Badger rushed over to the prayer wheels and turned the first one until the symbol for *'mani'* was facing forward. He shuffled to the second and turned the wheel with a squeak until *'padme'* was showing, and then he moved *'hum'* into place on the third. He stood back and waited, but nothing happened. The seconds became minutes, and then finally Badger spoke. 'Why isn't it working?'

'I think I know why,' said Lhama.

'Why?'

'Look behind us, near the top of the roof.'

Anna and Badger swung round to see what Lhama was talking about. There was a mirror tucked on a shelf of rock above and behind them. There were three squares, and in them were reflected the three symbols that Badger had moved into place.

'They're facing the wrong way. It should go in reverse,' Lhama said.

'Yes, and I suspect,' added Badger, 'that those mirrors are only visible for a very brief time of the day, they're fading. That's most probably why Rahn never figured it out.'

'Quick.'

Badger turned the prayer wheels so that *'hum'* started the progression and *'mani'* ended it.

'No, they've changed now,' said Lhama looking up at the mirror. 'I have no idea how, but they've changed again. Move the middle one to *"mani"* and the right one to *"hum"*, then the left to *"padme"*.'

'I'm not surprised Rahn didn't figure this out!' Badger moved them into place. A deep, grating sound issued and a slither of golden light curved into the room, as two massive arched doors swung out of the wall.

The chamber glowed with every conceivable kind of precious metal Anna could have imagined. Jewels sparkled, crowns littered the chamber, diadems and royal-looking staffs lay on cushions and divans.

'Where did all this come from?' Anna said.

'King Solomon's treasure,' Badger answered.

'No, it can't be!'

'Well, only a small portion of it. I suspect some of the less important objects, those without "power".'

'Why? Why here?'

'Buddhists – and old Bön masters – as you may well have noticed, like to offer treasures and "ransoms" to the gods and also to hungry spirits and ghosts, to appease them, to keep them happy but more importantly, to keep them out.'

'Ah!' said Lhama. 'The treasure is here to appease the gods so that the grail – the artefact that they will want most – is forgotten in all this splendour.'

'Precisely. And I wouldn't touch any of it, if I were you.'

Anna put a diamond encrusted gold band back on top of a pile of gold. Badger led them through the room, around the horde of treasure to a bare chamber. In the middle was a raised shelf of rock. There was a box on top of it.

Badger dropped to his knees before the rock pedestal and issued a chant. He said the word *'mani'* several times, and then got to his feet. Before he picked up the box, he said, 'Are you ready to run like hell?'

'Why?' Anna asked.

She got her answer soon enough. As he moved the box off the shelf, the walls began to shake. A tiny hole appeared in the wall behind the pedestal and Badger, Lhama and Anna slipped out just before the chamber collapsed behind them in a heap of stones.

They were in a tunnel. At the far side, straight ahead, was a hopeful slither of light. They sprinted towards it.

'A part of the mountain's caving in on itself!' Lhama shouted.

They stumbled out of the hole in the wall just in time, as part of the mountain fell away, booming, causing clouds of dust to spiral upwards. Coughing, Anna, Badger and Lhama found themselves on the moonlit plain.

'We need to go, *now!*' said Anna. 'While we were in there, I heard a helicopter. That was as we entered the first chamber …'

'Trevellian …'

'The good news is that he's probably waiting for us at the entrance to the cave. Unless he was stupid enough to try and go through the chambers himself.'

'Which direction do we go in?' asked Lhama.

Badger looked up at the stars. 'This way.' He led them into a chasm between two walls of mountain as a whole section of the sugar-loafed mountain they'd been in a few moments back cascaded off the sides and collapsed into a heap of rock with a loud sound. Each of them ran at three-quarter pace. After fifteen minutes they rounded a bend and Anna pointed, 'There!'

'The plane!' Lhama said excitedly. They sped up, running towards it. As they neared, Anna noticed a man in a chair next to the plane. It looked like Steenkamp, slumped forward.

'Something's not right …' Anna said, but it was too late. Guns were pointed at them, before Badger had a chance to remove the *dunali* shotguns from his bag. A group of men surrounded them. Parcival stepped forward, walked up to Badger and shot him in the stomach.

'Here, I'll take that.'

Anna and Lhama were tied up and forced to watch Badger bleed to death as the men ran off into the gloom. Anna looked up at Steenkamp and noticed that behind him, the engine of the airplane had been destroyed. She saw the charges of the bombs lying on the ground.

'J.B?'

There was no answer. He was gone, and they were at least four days' walk from Lo Manthang, with no food or water.

65
Tel Aviv
One week later

Ben sat in his office and stared out of the window. He'd heard nothing from Anna or Badger in a week. Steenkamp's offices hadn't heard from J.B. either and Janie had taken another plane to Lo Manthang to mount a search. There was a possibility that the plane had gone down in the Himalayas, Janie had told Ben.

He had nothing. No clue as to where Trevellian might be headed, and now he'd lost track of the best agent he had left. And to top it all, Ben had been notified that a Jewish girl had been kidnapped from Jerusalem a few days ago, possibly by BEAD agents. She was deaf and blind, and had been last seen at Ben Gurion airport with an unidentified man. It was suspected that the Nazis were involved, but no one knew what was going on.

He picked the phone up before it had a chance to complete its first ring.

'Hariri?'

'Ben.'

'Anna! Is that you?'

'Yes, it's me, listen ... Badger's dead.'

'What?'

'Badger is dead. He was shot by Trevellian's men.'

'No ...'

'We did what we could, but it was too late. We left him on the plain to have a sky burial. It was what he would have wanted. Lhama tells me its customary for the vultures to eat the body, and that way, it is redistributed to nature.'

Ben was quiet for a full minute. 'Did they get the stone?'

'Yes, Ben, they did. They also killed J.B., blew up the plane and took off. Lhama and I hiked nearly four days and then collapsed. I spent the other two asleep, woke up about five hours ago.'

'Where are you?'

'Lo Manthang.'

Her voice sounded raspy. His heart was sinking even deeper. Now his brother was dead, too. He had died trying to defend the grail. It was all entirely his fault. Why didn't he listen to Steven in the beginning when he said that they should kill Trevellian? He thought back to that meeting they had held in the office on the seventh floor. It seemed like a different universe that he'd lived in then, such a long time ago. Anna's voice came over the line.

'We almost died out here, Ben. We were saved by some porters. They gave us water and carried us the last ten kilometres that we would never have made ourselves.'

'Thank god,' said Ben. 'If I had lost you too …'

'You may as well have.' Her voice was filled with anger. 'Look, Ben, too many people have died. I'm sorry about your brother … But this whole thing is just wrong. You make these decisions that kill so many people, and you don't stop to think of consequences.' Anna paused.

'I *am* … *sorry* …' Ben's voice faltered. He knew there was nothing he could say.

'Tell that to the families of all these people,' Anna said. 'At least, those who still *have* families. Get me out of here, Ben, I want to come home. And consider this my official resignation.'

The phone slammed down in his ear.

66
Wolfschanze

The wind howled a deathly prattle as waves crashed against the outer walls of the castle, a salty breeze drifting in from the slits at the top of the war chamber in the *Wolfschanze*. James's twelve were seated around the table, his chosen few.

He'd flown straight back to *Wolfschanze*, vowing to put the events aboard the *Aegir* behind him. His father was dying, and he realised now more than ever that he needed to fulfil his father's dream. The woman was a slip up, and he wouldn't allow it to happen again.

He paced up and down. Roger, one of the twelve, watched him closely. James had changed completely once he got his hands on the grail. He wore it on a chain around his neck. He seemed agitated most of the time, but he spoke in a measured voice that seemed strangely precise. Ever since they had returned from Nepal, he had locked himself up in his study, or spent the time in his father's chambers. And the strangest thing, was the green glow in his eyes. It freaked Roger out a little. He couldn't explain any of it.

'As you all know,' James finally began to speak, 'We were infiltrated by those bastards.'

A pause, and then: 'That excuse for an intelligence service called Mossad. You know, Mossad was once a really formidable institution. Even though we've fought them tooth and nail, I held respect for them once. But now? It's a different story. We infiltrated their ranks. We killed several of their top people. We led them to the grail, but they got it for us and handed it to us on a silver platter. They are but a shadow of their former selves, a ghost express rattling on the fumes of yesteryear's glory.'

He started to pace again. 'As you all also know ...' He looked around at the twelve. Each wore a black Death's Head SS uniform and a *Totenkopf* hat with a metal skull set in the middle, above a castle with the word 'Wewelsburg' etched below it.

'They did have some minor successes. Let me put the rumours to bed once and for all. They sent an agent to the launch ceremony at Bandar Abbas Naval Base. Some of you even met her. That night, she was Liz Codwell, Clive's daughter.'

There were murmurs of agreement.

'But it was a Mossad agent who was really there, that night, not Liz. Lord Codwell's email invitation was intercepted. The Jews decided to send one of their own under cover as Codwell's daughter. That is what we think.

'The damage caused was minimal, however. We managed to weed out, at the same time, an agent that had infiltrated *Drachenfeld*. We killed him. We also killed several top-ranking agents through an operation known as Hidden Dagger, a spectacular success. One of our finest heroes, a man named Müller, killed the Deputy Director of Operations, an unprecedented victory for any agency working for any government around the world against Mossad.'

A voice interrupted, '*Mein Führer*, excuse me but some of us have been wondering.'

'What is it?'

'Why was the agent not killed? The one under cover as Liz Codwell.'

James seemed stumped. He fumbled for an answer. 'I ... we ... left Parcival in charge of retrieving the stone. He was pressed for time, and left her and another woman unharmed.'

No one answered. James gathered himself and continued.

'Now, let me assure you, gentlemen, we are putting measures in place to draw them out further. We want their Director of Operations next. We are going to misdirect them. They are desperate, and they will clutch at anything.

'I just got off the phone with our chief scientist at *Drachenfeld*. He assures me that the warheads will be ready on time, within five weeks. Our man Patrick will deliver to me, personally, a briefcase that contains the codes for detonation. Let me remind you, gentlemen: the magical number is twelve, and there are as many warheads. But the most important thing ...'

James stopped pacing, and turned to face half of his audience. His voice lowered and Roger thought he caught the faint green glow in his eyes. 'The single most important factor is that we now possess the stone.'

The room erupted with murmurs of consternation.

'It is true. I have in my possession the stone that Himmler sought for so many years, that Otto Rahn and Himmler's *Ahnenerbe* failed to find. The stone, *der Heilige Gral*. Now, each of you will need to be at the final ceremony. I cannot disclose the location to you now, for safety's sake, but I will send messages to you ...'

Just then there was a loud bang on the vault's door. James walked over and opened it. It was Frieda.

'What?' he asked, irritated.

'*Mein Führer*, your father ... *herr dokter* says to come right away ...'

'Excuse me, *kameraden*.'

The room in the northeast tower was cold. The light from the fire had gone out and, like it, the fight in his father lying on the bed had begun to slip away.

'Father,' James said as he leaned over Franz, patting his forehead with a damp cloth. Franz turned to face his son. His face was a pale, fleshy white. Red slabs of skin hung off his cheeks and dark rings encircled his eyes. It was the face of someone who could easily have chosen to die, even a few weeks ago, but had fought off death with a bony hand and had managed to hang on long enough to see the fruits of his life's labour.

'James ...'

James had to lean in with his head right above his father's mouth to catch his next words. 'I have something very important to tell you ...'

James moved his head up, picked up a cup of water on the bedside table and brought it to the fringe of Franz's lips. The old man took a sip, enough to keep him going through what he had to say.

'The time has come to tell you the truth.'

Franz paused and coughed. His whole body shook.

'I can feel myself slipping James. I'm getting dizzy ...'

'Hold on, let me call the doctor,' said James, getting up to leave. Franz's hand caught his forearm with such strength that the old man's bony fingers pressed into his flesh and hurt.

'No, James, not now ... I am dying, and I need to tell you this. Listen to me.'

James settled down and leaned over Franz's face.

'You remember when you were here a while ago, I told you that you would be faced with a choice.'

James nodded.

'And that there was a final secret that would be revealed to you at the right moment.'

He nodded again.

'Now, James, my precious son, the son I have brought up to be my own, the very strong boy who I love more than anything on this earth, even more than my own life. Now, my son, it is time for you to hear the truth.'

Lightning struck the surface of the ocean. There was a blinding flash of white light through the window overlooking the sea.

'You know well that the great doctor Mengele perfected mononuclear reproduction.'

'Yes.'

'There was one other important man, who was cloned I mean ...'

'Who?'

'James,' Franz clutched his hand and forced him closer.

'The greatest German leader of all time. The most terrifying orator, the single man who nearly succeeded in conquering the whole world ...'

'Is it who I think it is?'

'Yes, now do you see?'

James remained quiet.

Franz uttered his last words as his final breath escaped through his lips: 'I am not your real father.'

His head rolled and James knew that he had finally gone.

Part III

1
Wenceslas Square, Prague
Six weeks later

The target was thin as a rake, a waif that cut through the streets like a midnight blade. Tall, with brown hair and stringy legs and arms, the man slipped beneath the streetlights and took a quick right into an alley. He had two shadows on his tail.

'Subject is heading towards Wenceslas Square.'

'Mobile One keep that distance and don't look back,' Mobile Two, who was trailing the man, advised Mobile One, who was ahead of the target.

'On it,' Mobile One's voice was a whisper.

'Subject seems to be heading up towards the National Library, about a hundred metres away from the statue of Saint Wenceslas.'

'Which one is that?' asked Mobile One.

'The one rearing up on the horse. Wait, there's a change in course, he seems to be moving left towards a garden up ahead of you, Mobile One. Change course to eleven o'clock.'

The target, with one Mossad shadow behind him and one ahead, veered towards a garden in a centre aisle towered over by the brightly lit buildings of Wenceslas Square. He slowed as he entered a sidewalk.

'He's slowing down, Mobile One, take up an observation point. Look busy.'

'On it.'

Mobile One dropped to his haunches to tie his shoelaces. He carried a paper bag filled with mangoes. He let the mangoes tumble out of his bag and cursed as they rolled on the sidewalk.

'He's making his way over to a newspaper dispenser, Mobile One. Stay down, it's near your position. I'm moving in.'

Mobile Two approached a bench, sat down and flung open a newspaper. He peered over the top in the direction of the target.

'The newspaper dispenser must be a dead letter box,' Mobile Two said. 'I bet the next newspaper to come out of it will contain the invitation with coordinates to the location of Trevellian's ritual, Ben.

Looks like there's only one paper in there. The man we're following must be the guy who runs this letter box.'

Ben, who was listening in from Tel Aviv said, 'Good, get in there before him. Get that newspaper.'

'Got any coins, Mobile One?'

Mobile One whispered: 'Spent my last dime on mangoes ...'

'Then I'm going in,' said Mobile Two. 'Distract him.'

Mobile One struck up a Czech song, still picking up the mangoes that had fallen out of the bag. He rose from his crouching position and turned to the target. 'Excuse me, sir, don't I know you?'

He spoke in Czech, and saw that the target hadn't a clue about what he'd just said. Mobile Two stepped between the target and the newspaper dispenser, slotted the requisite number of coins into the machine and waited for the thud of the paper falling to the bottom of the hatch. He opened the drawer and removed the paper, passed the target and Mobile One on the sidewalk and smiled.

'One thousand euros on Barcelona for the Champions League!' Mobile Two waved the paper as he passed the two men and scurried off across the street and disappeared into an alley.

'I have fifty on Bayern, but god knows this'll be the last bloody time,' said Mobile One, and hurried away in the direction Mobile Two had disappeared in.

'Good work,' Mobile Two whispered, 'fade out.'

The two Mossad agents made their way back to the safe house in downtown Prague, doubling back several times to ensure that they weren't being followed.

2
Tel Aviv

'Good work, Mobile One and Two,' Ben congratulated.

Mobile One's voice came through the speaker phone: 'Thank you, Ben.'

'Anything unusual about the newspaper?'

'You're going to like this ... Everything's normal aside from one thing that kind of slipped out.'

'What is it?'

'Appears to be a postcard of some sort. Or a really cheesy advertisement that looks like a postcard. I'm sending you a scan in an encrypted email. Two attachments, one is a picture of the front of the card and the other is a picture of the back.'

'Here it comes,' Ben said. watching the images load on his computer. Anna rounded the desk and stood behind Ben, leaning onto the table and squinting at the screen. Ben had managed to convince her, after a few weeks at a spa in Tel Aviv and a few sessions with Dr D, not to quit Mossad after all. She had mostly recovered and had returned to work on the case.

Mobile One described what they were looking at.

'It looks like one of those novelty adverts. On the front there's a picture of the Alps with a small village, it looks like a resort of some kind. It says, "Wish you were here …" But on the back, sir, that is where the money is …'

Ben opened the second attachment and read out loud. Strangely, it was in English, perhaps, thought Ben, for the benefit of the British sympathisers. '22:00. Greetings from the gorgeous Alpine village of Bad Aussee! Join us at Bahnhof Hotel to celebrate Winter Solstice on 21 December 2012. One night only limited offer with special prices! Join us for our special ceremony as we enjoy the most important ancient rite of the year. Book now to avoid disappointment on the numbers below.'

Anna's eyes flashed at Ben. 'Coordinates!'

'Just like the email we intercepted that led us to Bandar Abbas,' said Ben. 'And …' he typed them into his computer and pressed the Enter key, 'they point to the town of Bad Aussee, in Austria.'

'Isn't that where all the Nazi gold was sent at the end of the war? The Allies found it all stashed in an abandoned salt mine.'

'Yes, except it wasn't the Allies, it was the Austrian Resistance that found the treasure. It was worth about 2.5 billion US dollars. And it contained all sorts of things of worth such as paintings, gold bars, and even the gold teeth of executed Jewish prisoners. The Reichsbank was planning to smelt down the teeth to produce gold via a company called DEGUSSA. Then the gold would be smuggled into Italy and disguised as roof slates in the houses of the southern Tyrol. Goebbels called the town of Bad Aussee an "Alpine fortress", and many Nazis flocked there at the end of the war, a last stronghold as the Allies closed in around them.'

Anna couldn't contain her excitement. 'So that's where the ceremony is taking place! That's where they're taking the girl!'

The CCTV tapes from the airport had been obtained and Mossad had confirmed that the man last seen with the girl was a BEAD agent.

'That's where the twelve knights will be headed,' said Ben.

'But what about the clues?' said Anna.

'About the curators and the youth hostel?'

'Yes, don't they mean anything?'

'Well, I think that they refer to the Kammerhof Museum in Bad Aussee,' said Ben, reading off his computer screen, 'and the youth hostel ...' he Googled it, 'is right there – there's one in Bad Aussee.'

Ben stood up. 'Anna: get a crack team to go in ahead of us to Kammerhof Museum. Ten at most, I think, with backup to follow. And pack a bag, we're going to Austria.'

3
Wolfschanze

Franz's seat was comfortable, a high-back leather chair with bronze studs running along the armrests. On the desk was an assortment of photos. Mainly black and white pictures, they were of those who escaped Germany after the war, people James knew as a child: Adolf Eichmann, Josef Mengele, Franz Stangl and of course, there was Franz Wagener. Not smiling. Their eyes were lifeless.

The fire popped in the grate of Franz's study and the bottle was half finished. He drank straight from it. His first reaction had been anger. Why, he thought, had he not been told who his real father was? The anger gave way to a feeling of insignificance, as if he were not important enough to have been told. It was as if everyone had been conspiring against him.

He knew the likely reasons for keeping the secret from him, but as with anyone betrayed or badly hurt, he chose to ignore logic, to nurse his anger, and his pain. Finally, he felt intrigue.

'Hitler's son?'

The words hung in the air, unable to connect with any threads of sense. The name Hitler became alien. There was a man behind that word, that name, and he burned to know who he was. A man who had mobilised an entire nation, walked over Europe and led the world to the brink of collapse. Not a man who simply lived on the pages of cheap mass-market paperbacks or faded history books, but a man who had a direct influence on everything – who *he*, James was – and who all of his people that lived in Argentina were.

James turned the picture over in his fingers. In it, Hitler stood with his hands on a balcony, in front of a microphone. Below him, hundreds of thousands of troops were gathered in a square. It was a famous picture, the same that appeared on the paperback version of Ian Kershaw's biography of Hitler.

Hitler was addressing them. He – one man – addressing hundreds of thousands. With this kind of intrigue came pride. In spite of what he'd done, greatness was his. Although Hitler had counted on luck as well as a full set of enabling circumstances when coming to power, James thought, he'd literally turned the world on its head.

There was a letter on the desk, in a brown envelope that crinkled at the edges. In the middle was written, 'James Trevellian'. It had been sealed with wax, with his father's Death's Head ring, which James now weighed in his hand.

He hesitated. Then picked the envelope up, he slipped his finger along the edge, breaking the seal. His heart began to pound. A letter slipped out. It was written in his father's hand, or at least, James corrected himself, *Franz's* hand.

Dear James,

If you are reading this it means that I am dead. If all has gone to plan, I have told you in person what you need to know. All that is left to explain is why I didn't tell you sooner, and to impress on you what it means.

I wish things were different. I wish that you knew your real father from the day you were born. I wish that he could have held you in his own arms, as I did, and loved and cherished you and watched you grow up and become the man that you are.

I know that you would have changed him. Perhaps the world would have been a different place, although of course you were born after he had already taken his own life in the bunker in Berlin as the War was ending.

I want you to know that I have loved you as my own son. Not a day went by without me hoping and dreaming for you, as fathers do, to become the best person that you could, and you did. I am more proud of you than anything else, and I want you to know that I would have given everything up, in an instant, for you.

I have loved you like a father is meant to love a son, and perhaps even more than that. For in you, I saw him. I saw him staring back at me when I looked at you. I saw his artistic inclinations in your drawings. But in you, I saw more. I saw the fulfilment of his destiny. I saw, in you, a better man.

Of course, it was natural that we would look for a perfect replacement for our glorious leader. Your mother, my wife, was chosen as the host. Such were her athletic, intellectual and ideological attributes that there was no more perfect choice than her. I myself have never known a more superior being to your mother. Sadly, she died early on in your life, and you will never know her.

But your birth differs slightly from those of the soldiers or the generals we have cloned through mononuclear reproduction. In their case, a very scientific process is involved. In your case, it was artificial insemination, a more direct method. It took us a long time to set up the labs in Argentina. First, of course, we had to clear the space, dig out the tunnels and caves, and then to slowly but surely set up world-class laboratories and facilities. Hitler's semen was frozen, smuggled out of Germany via submarine after the war, and kept in special storage until the time was right.

The rest, as they say, is history.

As you read this, the twelve submarines that you have built are most probably near, or on their way, to Chile, where our NSS soldiers will board and be back to the Mediterranean Sea, ready to strike against our enemies. As you read this, you may already have in your possession that which Himmler tried so hard to get: *de Heilige Gral.* You will have the power to complete what he couldn't: the ceremony to unlock the power of the occult. As you read this, you may also soon have confirmation that the nuclear warheads you have built are armed and ready.

My son, if all of these things are true, it means that you have achieved more than all of us put together. More than Hitler, more than Himmler, and more than me, your surrogate father, who has slaved his whole life away for the cause, you have perfected our struggle.

You must never forget your roots. You must never forget who you are, James. You are Adolf Hitler's son, and one of the most powerful men on Earth. If you follow the path of your destiny, you will have untold power and glory.

Do not sway, son, as you go into the winds of battle. Carry your head high. Carry the standards of the Nazi people to the very top of the hill and, with everyone else vanquished, stake your claim to the palace and raise the flag of the Fourth Reich. Trample the enemy on the battlefield, never let up, and always remember, you are part of a family of exceptional beings: Aryans, the rightful race. You are a true, proud son of Germany; lead us to greater heights!

Heil, Adler Trevellian!

Chills ran up his spine. He closed his eyes and pictured himself leaning over the balcony that Hitler stood on addressing the masses. It would be his, in time.

As he opened his eyes, they danced over a file that had been prepared for him by Frieda. It related to the agent who had infiltrated more than their ranks. The agent who had called herself Liz Codwell. He opened the file. The first page contained a picture of her. They had used the picture and traced her. Now, he would finally know who she was.

As he looked into her eyes, he realised that he was probably nothing more to her than someone to be played. He read the name: 'Anna Leonova'. A Jewess.

He had been used, he meant nothing to her. His father had been right. He closed his eyes and cupped his face with a hand. The phone rang.

James picked up. 'Yes?'

'It's your man, in Prague …'

'Did they buy it?'

'Hook, line and sinker, *mein Führer.*'

'Excellent,' said James and rang off. He dialled a number.

'Move in.'

4
Wewelsburg Castle
Alme Valley

The curator paused on the top step of the ex SS guardhouse, a square building with a slate roof, and peered up at the circular south tower of *Schlöss* Wewelsburg. As a child, the three towers forming the points of a triangle, interlinked by curtain walls, never failed to inspire his imagination. Then, when he'd walked past the castle on his way to school, he'd imagined knights galloping forth to rescue damsels and defend the empire. But that was before the war. When Himmler signed a hundred-year lease for a hundred marks and the SS moved in, in 1934, the castle and its surrounds quickly changed.

The south tower was fading in the dim light. A curtain of snow was being rung down, the trees were like skeletons on the frosted embankments leading up to the castle. There were only a few days to go until Christmas. The parking lot in front of the old SS guardhouse, now the *Kreismuseum* that reminded why the holocaust should never be forgotten, was empty. The tourist rush had passed and almost all of the students had gone home for the holidays.

The curator turned the key in the lock of the museum's front door and tried the handle to make sure.

'Going home so soon?'

The voice startled him. He dropped the keys. How had he not heard or noticed the men? There were five of them, fanned out like a wall at the base of the steps. The curator regained his composure.

He tugged his sleeves over his dry knuckles and smiled. A yellow line of teeth jangled like Christmas chimes in their sockets as he answered.

'Home time now, I'm afraid. You'll have to come back tomorrow.'

'But its two minutes to five, and my friends and I have come a long way.'

The man speaking was bigger than the others. He stood in front of them, as if he were their leader. They wore black military uniforms, eerily familiar.

'*Traurig, mein herr*, but we are closed and everyone has gone home for the evening. There's no one to give you a tour.'

'A tour?' The leader stepped forward. His head was cocked to one side as he pushed back his coat to reveal a machine gun.

'A tour?' He was smiling now. The old man backed away against the door. The approaching man's hand went to the gun, his fingers slipped the safety catch off and, one-handed, he raised the gun to eye-level as he came closer.

'We are not tourists, *mein herr*.'

'Then, who … who are … you?'

'We?' the man looked at his colleagues. 'We are Nazis.'

The others laughed.

'And we've come to admire the handiwork of our forefathers.'

The man thought of the NDP, the right-wing party in Germany that had been attracting increased support from Germany's disenchanted youth.

'What do you want?'

The gun was now pressed to his temple and panicked fogs of breath escaped from the man's mouth.

'You will open the doors of this museum and go back inside.'

The man towered over the curator now. The sarcastic tone was replaced with anger.

'You will pick up the phone to everyone who works here – all staff – and you will tell them that, regretfully, *Schlöss* Wewelsburg has to close early for the holidays and that they will take paid leave until after New Year's Day. You will wish them a Merry Christmas, and then we will lock you into the office while we go about our business here. Do you understand?'

'Yes, ye-s, *mein herr*.'

Roger, the man pressing the barrel of the gun to the man's head, commanded one of the four Trevellian Enterprises men that stood with him to accompany the curator inside.

'See that he gets the job done properly and that he leaves no one out, and that he doesn't raise any alarm bells.'

'Zu befehl, Obergrüppenführer.'

The new Commandant of Wewelsburg Castle, the first in more than seventy years, stood on the top step and whistled. A few seconds later, three black minivans screeched into the parking lot. Their doors slid open, and Trevellian Enterprises mercenaries streamed out. They fanned into formation to await orders.

'Secure the grounds, leave no inch unmarked,' commanded Roger, as the distant sound of helicopters floated from above.

'Snipers to the rooftops. Crack team move in to secure the youth hostel. Tie anyone you find up. Question them about others who might be on their way. Lock this place down.'

The units dispersed, swarming all over the castle's grounds. Four attack helicopters hovered in and descended, one at each point of the castle, with the fourth landing in the courtyard.

5
Ben Gurion International Airport
Tel Aviv

Anna's foot tapped out a nervous beat. The departures terminal waiting seat was of the most uncomfortable type, a hard bucket that probed the contours of her back. Beside her, Ben sat and read a copy of *The Jerusalem Post*.

Although the discovery of the location of Trevellian's final ceremony was no small victory – quite the opposite, thought Anna, it was the single-biggest breakthrough of the case yet – she couldn't help but get the feeling that something was wrong. For the moment, she pushed the unease out of her mind and put it down to nerves.

As she watched the throng of passengers, Anna made a mental list of where they were. They'd intercepted some communication meant for a high-ranking Nazi at a dead letter box in Prague. Ever since the trail had gone cold after Nepal, Mossad agents had focused their efforts on intercepting communications to Lord Clive Codwell and other Nazis, to try and glean some clue as to where Trevellian was headed next.

They had received information that the next dead-letter box would be in Wenceslas Square, in Prague. Mossad agents had followed a man through the city to a newspaper dispenser, where they had successfully intercepted a fake 'advertisement' that pointed them in the direction of Bad Aussee in Austria, where the final ceremony was to take place. They also knew that a young Jewish girl had been kidnapped by the Nazis. She was somehow linked to the final ceremony, Ben had speculated.

Finally, Anna had handpicked a team of the best Mossad agents, strongmen and assassins, to fly ahead of her and Ben to Bad Aussee to set up shop and prepare for the final assault. Anna and Ben were now waiting to catch a flight to Salzburg via Vienna, under cover as journalists. They'd travel on to Bad Aussee from there. But somehow, it all didn't seem right. Why Bad Aussee?

Anna pulled out her phone to check her messages. There was only one – a roundup of all SIGNT (intelligence gleaned from the media). Anna, as usual, had requested more SIGNT from the country she was about to visit, Austria, but she'd also requested more from Germany.

Immediately, a piece caught her eye. It was a letter to the editor of *Der Spiegel* with the title: 'Commotion at *Schlöss* Wewelsburg'. Anna began to read with alarm.

Dear Editor,

I live on a farm in North-Rhine Westphalia near *Schlöss* Wewelsburg. I am eighty-nine years old and have seen and heard many strange things in my time.

But yesterday I saw some very strange things at *Schlöss* Wewelsburg as I was taking my evening walk. As I walked down an old country track, black minivans suddenly began to scream past in the road, and four helicopters materialised in the sky above the castle.

> I walked to the museum and was told by a guard dressed in a black uniform and brandishing a machine gun that the castle is closed for the rest of the holiday.
>
> My question is: did anyone else see this happening, and if the military are training here, why are they using Wewelsburg as a base? This is very strange.
>
> Maria Hasenjager

Anna dropped the phone in her lap and let the words tumble out.
'Oh ... my ... god ...'
'What is it?' Ben wore a brown tweed jacket, a checkered shirt and patchy jeans.
'We've been fooled.'
'What do you mean?'
'Here, read this.'
Ben read the letter.
'No!'
He handed the phone back to her. He stood up and began to pace. 'Why didn't I think of this? Wewelsburg ... it has a museum and ...'
'A youth hostel?'
'Right.'
'Let me try them.'
Anna dialled a number and hit speakerphone. It went immediately to voicemail in an old man's German accent: 'Thank you for contacting Wewelsburg Castle. We regret to inform you that we have had to close early for the holidays and will only be open again on 2 January 2013.' There was something strange about the voice. It sounded twitchy.
'They shouldn't be closed,' Anna said, scrolling down their website on her phone. 'It says here that they're only closed on 24 December and 1 January.'
Ben's look turned from sceptical to concerned. Then his phone rang.
'Hariri ... Yes ... What? ... No, that can't be right ... Are you sure? ... Send in backup immediately.' He rang down.
'What is it?'
'You won't believe this ... the team in Bad Aussee was ambushed.'

'No, are they okay?'

'Three dead.'

They were silent for a few moments. Anna decided against asking who the men were, as she knew it was likely to distract her.

'We need to get on the next available flight to Wewelsburg!'

'Call in our *katsa* in Berlin. Tell him to meet us with firepower and wheels at Frankfurt Airport ASAP.'

6
Frankfurt International Airport

Anna flicked her sleeve back to check the time: 21h58. Two hours and two minutes to go. It was a long way out of the terminal building into the car park but they couldn't run, couldn't draw attention to themselves. The *katsa* they were about to meet in the car park was smoking a cigarette beside a navy blue BMW M3. He was tall, thin, with blonde hair and sharp electric blue eyes. Heydrich had a quick tongue and wit, and was also known for his fast cars and preference for beautiful blonde German women.

'Bout bloody time,' he said, stubbing out his cigarette as Anna and Ben approached. He tried for Anna's bag but she dodged his hand and pushed her luggage into the open boot of the BMW.

They all got in – Anna in the back seat and Ben in front – and Heydrich eased the car out of the parking lot and onto the highway. They headed for the Autobahn, the A5 that snaked north towards Kassel.

Anna leaned forward from the back seat and spoke to Ben.

'What do you think they plan to do with the girl?'

Flashes of yellow beams shifted through the car as it passed under the lights.

'Legend has it,' began Ben, 'that the Thule society used to sacrifice children. They believed that children were powerful spiritual mediums that could channel dark energy.'

'Do you think they'll sacrifice the girl?'

'I hate to say it, but yes, Anna, I think it's a possibility.'

Silence settled in for a moment. Anna's heart raced ahead of the car.

Would James really sacrifice her?

'Anna, I'd highly recommend buckling up right now,' Heydrich said. 'We're getting on to the Autobahn and we're being followed.'

'What?'

'Black rider on a motorbike,' said Heydrich. 'Hold onto your g-strings, I'm about to open a can of serious heat.'

Anna strapped herself in. Heydrich dropped a few gears and flipped a switch on the dashboard. The car lurched forward into the night.

7
Autobahn 5

The rider's mechanical horse was black as the night, a 'vintage', dangerously fast, modified version of the 2000 Suzuki Hyabuso. The man riding it had been called by *Wolfschanze* HQ with an urgent assignment. Enemy agents were arriving at Frankfurt Airport. They'd had been followed there from Vienna and his brief was: 'Kill the men, take the woman alive.'

The BMW M3 straddling the road ahead was surprisingly fast. But his shock was replaced with confidence as he cranked up the throttle and marvelled at how quickly he caught the M3 as they reached Kessel and then veered left towards the countryside of North-Rhine Westphalia; the small dancing lights of the farmhouses bobbing like illusions at the dizzying speed.

'He's still on our tail.'

Anna was peering out of the back window and made out the figure in leather, glowing red in the tail lights of the car dangerously close behind them. She'd never been in a car as fast as this, and leaned sideways to look at the speedometer which clocked 295 kph.

Now, they were gambling, Anna thought. The other player at the table was a dark rider, while death played Bank, handing out an inevitable hand.

'Hold on, we're going to make a sharp turn. A short cut.'

Anna clutched the door handle and closed her eyes against the pull of the car as it veered onto an off ramp and Heydrich slammed on brakes. Anna felt as if she were about to be sick, but swallowed hard and forced her eyes open. She looked back to see the rider still dangerously close on their tail.

Heydrich swung the car through the apex of the turnoff perfectly and the road narrowed to a country track as he pushed the pedal down and the car roared through its lower gears. Anna breathed in short breaths of cold air that did nothing to loosen her chest. Now there would be increased hazards on the country roads – cows, tractors, dogs and people crossing and sharp kinks, potholes …

'Don't worry!' shouted Heydrich, seeming to read her thoughts. 'I know these roads well.'

Anna felt the car rise up onto a hill and knew what was coming. As the car crested the hill it took off and they were airborne for a few split seconds before the car touched down again with sparks flying out from beneath the chassis.

'He's still there!'

The red eyes of the back of a truck loomed up ahead on the road that twisted like a snake through the farmlands. Beside it and some distance away was a pair of glowing yellow lights – an oncoming car. The road seemed to veer off to the right and the approaching car was rounding the bend. As the BMW neared the truck, so too did the pair of yellow lights.

Heydrich slowed the car deliberately. Anna saw the biker catch up.

'I have a plan,' Heydrich shouted madly as he brought the BMW dangerously close up behind the truck and straddled both lanes. The approaching car's lights were too close for comfort. It flickered in warning. Heydrich seemed frozen. Suddenly they lurched forward and veered into the oncoming lane.

'Heydrich!' Anna screamed. He flicked a switch beside the steering wheel again and Anna felt the car kick up yet another gear as the nitro came into effect. Flames erupted as they pulled in front of the truck just in time as there was the terrifying 'pop' of the motorbike smashing into the car behind them.

They travelled the rest of the way in complete silence and ambled into the village of Wewelsburg like stricken dolls strapped into their seats.

Tree branches closed over the road like the fingers of a bony hand. It was winter and the bright stars of a country sky glittered through the branches. Heydrich drove off the road onto a gravel track, slowed up and pulled off into an open field.

The car beeped as the doors opened and they got out. They crowded over the open boot that glowed yellow in the surrounding gloom. A fine mist had rolled in over the plain and in the distance, Wewelsburg Castle was impressive. The north tower poked through the mist ominously. On top of the tower, the searching torch beams of Trevellian Enterprises guards scanned the surrounding countryside.

Heydrich took out Anna and Ben's bags, held down a latch and pushed the back seats forward to reveal a vault filled with every imaginable weapon Anna and Ben could want.

'Take your pick,' said Heydrich as Ben whistled softly.

'Impressive,' Anna commented, holding up an MP5 machine gun. She turned aside, pulled off her coat and jersey, put on a bulletproof vest and pulled her jersey and coat back on. She also pulled out some C4 packs made of a putty-like substance with small charges, and strapped them onto her waist beneath the bulletproof vest along with a detonator which she tucked into her belt. She also took an innocent-looking pair of gloves. Ben selected a sniper rifle with a silencer, a large knife and a Beretta. Heydrich opted for an AK-47 only.

They closed the car's boot and doors and slipped into the shadows of a forest on the western side of the castle leading up to an embankment. Ben led the way, followed by Anna and Heydrich. They crept north, carefully, and stopped in a wooded area above the north tower. Ben whispered quietly as they huddled together. Ben raised his rifle, switched the night-optics on and looked.

'Three men, patrolling in the moat, at the entrance to the crypt.'

Anna raised a pair of binoculars, flicked the night optics on and scanned the moat that ran along the eastern edge of the castle. The three guards outside the door to the crypt were tall, with semi-automatic machine guns held out in front of them, undoubtedly Trevellian Enterprises soldiers, Anna thought. One stood on either side of the door and another was directly in front of it, patrolling a short stretch that ran parallel to the castle's walls.

'If we get rid of them quickly enough,' said Ben, 'no one will notice.'

'But how?' Anna asked. 'The minute one falls, one of the others will shout and notify those guys on top of the tower.'

'Watch and learn.'

Ben raised the rifle again and paused, waiting for the perfect moment. The rifle stung with three quiet whips. Anna watched through her binoculars. The guard closest to them beside the door fell, and before he'd hit the ground the one on the opposite side of the door crumpled. A second later the third patrolling man fell to the ground. Anna turned to look at Ben in awe.

'What?' he said. 'I haven't been in an office my whole life, you know.'

They hurried, crouching, to the bodies and began to drag them towards the arched wall that ran over the dry moat that led to the castle's main entrance. In the middle, beneath the moat, was a hollow between the arches. They dragged the bodies into the darkness and rushed, in single file, along the eastern wall of the castle, pulling up short of the door that led to the crypt of the north tower. Ben motioned for Anna to move across to the other side of the doorway. Anna moved quickly and quietly. Then Ben motioned to her that he was going in. Anna nodded. Ben crouched and slipped inside, followed by Heydrich and Anna.

They descended some steps into the cavernous crypt, Himmler's hall of the dead. It was empty. Anna pressed into the middle of the chamber while Ben and Heydrich fanned out along the walls.

'There's no one here.' Anna's voice echoed around the chamber. She turned around.

Guns were pressed into Heydrich and Ben's heads and one was aimed at her.

'We've been expecting you,' said James Trevellian.

8
Wewelsburg Castle

'Now, drop your weapons.'

Guns clattered to the floor.

'Search them,' James commanded. Each one was frisked by a guard. It was a trap. It had always been a bloody trap. Right from Tel

Aviv, from before they got onto the plane, thought Anna.

'Tie them up.' James looked right through her. Something seemed different about him. It was as if he didn't know who she was. Did all that had happened in the last few weeks mean nothing to him?

Two guards came over and made quick work of tying their hands and feet together. One held their ankles together while the other strapped a plastic zip band around and pulled it tightly closed.

'James ... don't do this,' Anna pleaded.

'Bring the girl in.'

James ignored her, sweeping out of the room without another look in their direction. The guards carried the three prisoners into the middle of the crypt where a lowered central indent was. They were forced to sit upright, back to back in the middle of the dome-shaped room. The guards disappeared, leaving them in silence. Anna took the opportunity to look around for any possible escape routes.

There were four light windows that caught the dancing starlight; carved arches in the thick, rough sandstone walls. In the middle of the room, right at the crest of the dome, a swastika had been carved into the rock. It flashed golden in the amber light of the lamps above twelve pedestals around the chamber, which cast eerie shadows on the walls.

'Can anyone manage to check the time on their watches?' Anna asked.

'Can anyone manage to check *anything*?' Heydrich sneered. Ben shuffled and leaned forward.

'Here, try and see mine.'

Anna leaned to the side and turned her eyes as far as she could towards Ben, just barely managing to make out the time on his watch.

'Eleven-thirty. Half an hour.'

'Someone's coming.'

There were muffled footsteps, followed by the sound of something being dragged along the floor. Two men burst into the chamber, laughing as they dragged in a girl. Her hands and feet were tied and she was squealing in desperation.

'It's her, Ben!' Anna couldn't help the outburst, and one of the guards rounded on her and struck her across the face.

'Shut up, *Juden!*'

The Nazis left the room, the echo of their laughter following them up the stairs.

'Can anyone reach their phone?' Anna asked in desperation.

Anna remembered the gloves.

'Hold on, I've got a plan. Ben, do you think you can reach for my belt? There's a pair of gloves in there that I need you to get.'

Anna shuffled to her side and Ben leaned back, with his fingers groping at thin air.

'Move back a little more.' Anna shuffled backwards.

'There …' Ben pulled them out.

'Pass them to me.' Anna took the gloves in her hands and struggled to put them on.

'What use is that going to be?' Ben asked.

'No ordinary gloves.'

'The scissor gloves!'

'Right,' said Anna and moved two small blades out of position along her forefinger and thumb.

'They should have used handcuffs,' Anna said as she cut through the plastic bands on her wrists. She worked on her ankles and got up. There was a noise outside the crypt.

'They're coming, Anna! Sit down and pretend you're still tied up. There's no way you could make it out against so many of them, unarmed …'

Ben was right. Anna sat down, put her hands behind her back and placed her feet together out in front of her. Dark black-robed men with hoods over their heads entered. Each one carried a candle on top of an urn.

Each breath was a stolen moment inching towards zero.

The twelve dark knights of the Order huddled over their candles, chanting with blood-stained eyes. The urns, which Anna knew to contain the ashes of the dead Aryan warriors, were placed on the twelve pedestals in the chamber.

Anna couldn't swallow. She watched the twelve turn. She saw them face their leader, their dark faces shrouded above flickering candles. Their pagan chant built up from a softly murmured intonation to a crescendo that rattled the walls. Their messiah, James Trevellian, stood in the middle of the crypt and raised his hand in salute.

'*Sieg heil!*'

His warriors responded: '*Sieg heil*!'

The voices dimmed to a whisper.

'We are closer now than we've ever been.'

Chills ran up Anna's spine. This was a different man.

'The Order has not been here in nearly seventy years. The last time the Order met here, it was Himmler who stood and addressed our forefathers, the founding members of the Order. He gave us an instruction. It was a simple message. Honour the dead, he commanded, for they will come again.'

He held up both hands. 'We are finally home!'

The faces were hardened like stone statues.

'Things are different now, in the year 2012. In 1944 and 1945, Europe was in ruins. Our people were vanquished, stripped of their land and their dignity like vermin. They were robbed of their rightful purpose.'

His voice rose: 'Twice have we failed. But now, *kameraden*, now we set foot on the final climb to victory. We have the most powerful fleet of submarines ever assembled. We have an army, and soldiers, the likes of which the world has never seen. Even now, as I address you, we have in our possession the most powerful weapon known to man.'

James searched the faces of his knights. 'Tonight we unleash the dogs of hell. Our grandfathers, our great-grandfathers, and all those pure enough to join the Order of Blood will come back from the dead, a spiritual army that will return to take what is theirs from the living. *Herr* Patrick ...'

'*Mein Führer*!'

Patrick stepped forward.

'Bring me the case.'

Patrick leaned down and picked up a briefcase. He stepped down towards the circular indent. The black metal of the case bore an insignia in white: the Death's Head, set in front of a black sun with twelve lightning strikes that emanated from a central point like the spines of a swastika. James took the case and placed it down on the raised circular concrete of the inner ring of the crypt. He keyed a code into a keypad and the case clicked open. He stretched one side open to reveal a screen on the vertical side, and a keypad on the flat side.

'Behold, *kameraden*,' James's eyes seemed to light up with an opal glow. 'The Final Solution!'

On the screen, in green letters, was a request to key in the detonation codes.

'The time now is thirteen minutes to twelve.'

He punched in the access codes before Anna could react. She stifled a whimper. *There must be a way to stop it.* Tears welled in her eyes. *How could he do this?*

'At exactly twelve minutes to twelve, I will push the button to begin the countdown. *Herr* Patrick, if you will ... count down for me.'

Patrick rolled up his sleeve and looked at his watch. A deafening silence descended like cloud.

'Fifteen, fourteen ... seven, six ... three, two ...'

Now! Anna flung out her arms. Two pieces of C4 explosives shot from either hand and she reached down towards her belt and pressed the detonation button.

An explosion ripped through the chamber, mangled pieces of body parts, rocks and a thick cloud of dust flew up in the air.

Anna dived towards the entrance, where she'd noticed a guard with a machine gun. By the time she'd reached him, he was dead, and was slumped over his weapon. She heaved at his fleshy torso and slipped the gun out, her hands dripping with blood. She turned around with her teeth gritted and saw the carnage that had been caused. Most of the men were maimed or dead, lying like rag dolls with their stuffing coming out. Some whimpered. Anna flicked the safety catch off and unleashed a spurt of bullets wherever she saw movement, aside from the middle, her eyes flashing orange in the glow of the gun fire.

There was no more movement. Anna walked over to James. He'd been shot, in the stomach. She kept the gun solidly aimed at his head, leaned over the briefcase and flipped open the screen. The keyboard was covered in dust, blood and rubble, but a digital clock counted down to zero.

'How could you?'

Anna rounded on James. She felt rage like she had never felt before swelling inside her, and pressed her finger gently against the soft trigger, but darkness came and cloaked everything. She felt blood dribble down her head and the last thing she saw was Patrick standing over her.

Two blobs blurred her vision, humanoid forms without features that gradually sharpened into focus. James and Patrick kneeled. Patrick held the Jewish girl's forearm out. James was cutting at it with a knife. When blood spurted out, he removed a green object from a chain on his neck and held it beneath the arm to catch the dark red drops.

'With this blood,' he hissed, 'I summon you, god of all Norse gods, Odin, to invest in me, Hitler's son, the supreme knowledge and power to rule over all the dominions and restore the Aryan people to their glory. I call on our forefathers to return!'

There was no time to think. The screen of the nuclear detonation case read two minutes to go. Anna tried to get up, but her wrists and ankles were bound. A searing pain stabbed at her head. Blood tricked down like a small stream cascading over a fall from the girl's arm and the stone lit up. Strange green shapes – skulls and ancient runes – swirled on the walls of the room. James stumbled to his feet, holding the stone up. Patrick shielded his eyes and seemed to grow weak. Energy swirled around the room, sucked into the vortex that was James Trevellian and the grail stone.

Patrick passed out and Anna felt her power being sapped from her, slowly, melting away ...

This must be a dream, a Kafka hallucination. Anna closed her eyes. She felt herself lift off the ground. When she reopened her eyes she saw that everything else – rocks, body parts and objects – were levitating and swirling around James, faster and faster like a growing tornado. James's eyes glowed an electric green; light pulsed out of them and showed at the crack of his mouth and through his nostrils.

Anna struggled to find her voice. She tried to call out, but nothing more than a stifled whimper came. More and more strength was being sapped from her body. Finally, Anna managed to squeeze out a single word out.

'James ...'

His eyes narrowed on her. She felt herself being lifted up further and drawn towards him. She seemed to be moving faster around him, but the closer she got to him, the more energy seemed to drain from her.

'Who is James?'

The voice was not his.

He stared at her. The green light became so bright that Anna had to close her eyes again, blinded. She was barely managing to hold on. *This is it: one more effort.* She opened her eyes and saw that the walls were transparent. She heard a faint sound that grew louder and louder. What was it? The sound of boots trampling, like a marching army. Outside, legions of SS men – the fallen dead that had been re-awakened – returned to their homeland to serve the new *führer*. '*Sieg heil!*' their generals chanted as they neared the castle.

A green tornado swirled above the legions, emerald strips of lightning crackling from its epicentre directly above the castle. Everything seemed to be coming from James. He was standing at the centre of the Aryan universe, and he'd opened a portal to hell, thought Anna. With a last effort, she eked out her final attempt.

'James, if you're in there somewhere ...'

45 seconds.

His head crooked slightly towards her.

'You need to listen to me ...'

40 seconds.

'That night, when we made love ...'

30 seconds.

'It meant a lot to me. The thing is ...'

25 seconds.

'... I love you, James.'

Just as the lights faded from her eyes, Anna forced the final words out: 'I'm carrying your child ...'

9
Wewelsburg Castle

When Anna reopened her eyes the green glow was gone. The walls were back in place, no longer transparent. The strange green soldiers were gone. The sound and the chanting and the marching had stopped. She felt as though she had woken from a very long dream that she knew could only have lasted a few seconds. She was on her hands and knees, crawling towards the briefcase. James was beside her, looking alert once more.

'You're back!'

'From where?' asked James absent-mindedly. 'We need to de-activate the bombs!'

'Do you have de-activation codes?'

'No.'

'So how do we ...'

James stared blankly at the screen.

'James?' Anna screamed and shook him by his shoulders.

6 seconds.

'James!'

5 seconds.

His fingertips danced over the keypad.

4, 3, 2, 1 ...

Epilogue

Maldives
Two years later

His arms were wrapped tightly around her. The horizon was a burnt orange, and the water lapped around their ankles.

'He's asleep now.'

'Finally. Little terrorist. He takes ages to get to sleep. Is this normal?'

She turned around to face him and they paused. She looked into his eyes and found what she had been looking for.

'James, there's something that I've been meaning to ask you.'

'Anything, my love.'

Anna leaned her head against his chest. 'I suppose ...' she looked up into his eyes. 'I suppose ... oh, never mind, it's nothing.'

'No, what is it?'

He pressed her closer.

'That night ...'

They had never spoken about it. The bombs had been deactivated at the last second. James's final act as leader of the Fourth Reich had been to dissolve the war council and command his troops to stand down. He had made an offer to each citizen of the Fourth Reich to provide fake documentation with which they could quietly slip into any country of their choosing, aside from the clone soldiers who would remain at *Drachenfeld*, working in the huge bureaucracy departments and factories that would be set up to support the Enterprise's new business.

Trevellian Enterprises' assets had been sold off to set up companies and an aid fund with the focus of creating cross-cultural dialogue and interaction among the youth. It would take time, but a new generation could be groomed that didn't harbour the hatred of their fathers.

'Well,' Anna began, 'that night when you de-activated the bombs with the code. I said something like, "James, you're back!" You looked at me and said, "From where?"'

'I hardly recall anything about that night.'

'Just before that you'd poured the girl's blood onto the stone and before you had been transformed into this ... Well, this *monster* ... It was as if you were possessed. You were filled with green light and you spoke in this strange voice. There were legions of dead Nazi warriors descending on the Alme Valley, like an army of spiritual soldiers ...'

James held her at arm's length. 'What on Earth are you talking about, Anna?'

'Light was shining from your eyes and ...'

'Anna, I think you must have hurt your head in the explosions. I passed out. I had a bullet in my stomach. When I came around, all I knew was that I was on my hands and knees, crawling towards the briefcase. I knew I had to punch in the de-activation codes. I did, and then I passed out again.'

'But you told me you didn't know the codes?'

'I didn't. My engineers had not given them to me. They came to me in a dream.'

'You dreamt them?'

'I haven't told you this before but, while I was knocked out I dreamt I was in some mystical, beautiful land called Olmo Lungring.'

Anna gasped. 'Olmo Lungring?'

'Yes, why?'

'It's the Bön "heaven". Bön is the pre-Buddhist religion in Tibet and Nepal.'

'Well, I dreamt that I climbed to the top of a high mountain, made of nine swastikas stacked one on top of the other. At the top was an ancient-looking monk who smiled at me and pointed to a monastery.'

'Tönpa Shenrab.'

'Who?'

'The founder of Bön. He was probably the monk.'

He looked at her, puzzled. 'In any case, it looked like a Buddhist monastery of some kind. I went inside and sat down, as if to pray or meditate. When I closed my eyes I felt the most inner peace that I'd ever felt in my life. I was suddenly filled with conviction. I saw two paths. One led to a future of untold misery and destruction. The other, well ... I knew then what I needed to do. It felt like I went back into my body, and the next thing I knew we were crawling towards the briefcase. I let my hands drift over the keypad. It was like they were guided by some force. I didn't know the codes then, and to this day I can't tell you what they were.'

Silence pressed between them.

'Ever since that day,' James murmured, 'I've felt like a completely different person. Up until then, I had thought that you had simply used me for your operation. I thought I hadn't had any impact on you at all. When you took off, from the yacht, and I learned who you really were, it made me feel used. It spurred me on to complete my Aryan destiny. But I think when you told me that you were pregnant, and that you loved me, I suddenly realised that maybe you *did* feel something, the way I had.'

'One thing that really puzzles me …'

'Is what happened to the stone,' James completed.

'I have no idea. It just disappeared. Just before we had ensured the girl's safety and took off into the night, I searched the floor where we were, but there was nothing. It had gone. I personally think that it was nothing. It had no power … We hallucinated.'

'You spoke just now about Olmo Lungring …' Anna said.

'What about it?'

'Do you know what the last part of the Buddhist chant *om mane padme hum* means?'

'What?'

'The jewel in the middle of the lotus. And Olmo Lungring is meant to be a lotus-shaped paradise, in the middle of which is the jewel, the *point* of enlightenment. In your dream you climbed to the top of the mountain in the middle of Olmo Lungring, and there, you found enlightenment. I think that the stone must have helped you to do that.'

'Hmm,' James looked pensive.

'For my part,' Anna continued, 'I think it just helps you to see what you really want. There's no doubt that it *can* be used for great evil, but I think ultimately, it depends on who is wielding it.'

'So I'm not *such* a monster then?' James smiled.

'Not *all the time*.'

Then Anna's phone beeped in her pocket. She read the text and laughed.

'Who is it?'

'Ben.'

'What does he want?'

'He wants to know when I'm coming back to work.'

'And what are you going to reply?'

'"Never."'

There was a cry from the cottage near the beach. A little bundle of joy spilled out onto the steps, toddling towards his mother and father. Anna leaned down to scoop him up in her arms and twirled him around.

James swooped Anna and the child up in his arms. They fell into the water as the sun sank below the horizon and a deep purple glow spread out at the edges of a navy sky.

New York

The office was cool, spacious.

Through the window, the city stretched out all the way across Greenwich Village, Lower Manhattan and, finally, to the Statue of Liberty in the distance.

The man known as 'Heydrich' in Mossad circles stepped out of the shadows of an entranceway and stood in front of a desk. Behind it, there was a silhouette's outline. The person the outline belonged to was smoking. Heydrich couldn't make out a face. Heydrich's hands were clasped in front of him, sweaty and twitching.

'You have the stone?'

'Yes, right here.'

Heydrich opened his hands to reveal a pouch. From it a light spilled out of the top, green and faintly bright.

'Good. On the desk.'

Heydrich stepped forward.

'No, not too close.'

Heydrich stopped and leaned over. He put the pouch down and backed away.

'Good. That's *very* good.'

'Took it while they were still in a daze in the crypt of the castle.'

'You've done well. Israel is an important market, its protection is imperative.'

Heydrich was silent, rubbing his hands together although he didn't know it.

'If I may ask …' he said at last.

'Yes?'

'About the … About the payment, sir. Twenty million.'

'Ah yes, *that.*'

The figure seemed to slip forward.

'You won't be needing it.'

'The … the twenty million?' Heydrich stuttered, intermingling his words with laughter. 'I could really … use that money … right about now. You see, I … owe …'

'Not anymore.'

'Not anymore?'

The figure leaned forward and opened a desk drawer. Heydrich began to back away.

'No, you see …'

Heydrich backed into the wall and began to fumble at the lock.

'… the only thing you'll need in the place you're going …'

The door was locked, Heydrich began to panic.

'… is …'

The gun whipped. Heydrich fell to the floor.

Acknowledgements

This book is dedicated to my loving wife Francis, to whom I've been married for twenty-five years, and my adorable daughter, Angelique. They fill me with love, happiness and inspiration, a family that every man would be truly proud of. To my dearly departed parents, who will be smiling above from heaven, and to God, for strength and wisdom.

Publishing a book is like planting and growing a tree. It starts with a seed, a small (but incredibly powerful) distant dream that holds so much promise. With love, and with patience, the seed is planted and the sapling grows. Before you know it, the trunk and branches are reaching out, feeling for purpose, and the author, in the book's springtime, breathes life into the blossoming flowers. In full summer, the fruits of labour are sweet, and the book ripens. Then comes the autumn of editing. The author watches his wild ideas and eccentric language fall like leaves to the ground. A cold winter of uncertainty sets in before the book is published: how will it be received? And then, pregnant with hope, spring comes once more, and new seedlings are planted, feral children of the imagination.

As 'fanciful' fiction that borrows from some exceptionally interesting bits of history, my sincere hope is that *The Wewelsburg Covenant* will be entertaining, and if only a handful of people enjoy reading it, then I have succeeded in the purpose of its publication.

Thanks are due to those who helped transform this book from a distant dream into a polished product. Firstly, thanks to the author I have never met, Nigel Graddon, for writing the thoroughly entertaining book, *Otto Rahn and the Quest for the Grail: The Amazing Life of the Real 'Indiana Jones'*, which I read on Kindle in less than a few sittings. Thanks to my editor, Nicky, who did a fantastic job, and to Di, for her careful proofread.

Special thanks to Annalina, Herald and Warren.

And finally, to Tom West, my sincerest appreciation for his invaluable support and friendship in the journey undertaken in the writing of this novel, and for his incontrovertible strength of character.

Made in the USA
Middletown, DE
04 June 2021